I0785547

Icefall
Northpost
Winter Lake
Sedda
Shadowmire
Stormfire L
Torrdale
The Realm of
Erras
Safareen

Khan Khar
East Bay
East Watch
The Midnight Sea
Oyster Cove
thBrekka
Blackport Bay
Alta Prime
S

REY WICKS

LEGION OF FIRE

The Legend of Chaos

I

Curious Corvid
PUBLISHING

Prologue

A long time ago, the birth of Erras and the Far North came in the form of an icy continent along the Midnight Sea. An anomaly of weather and sea brought the land that spanned hundreds of miles to the surface. The lands to the north remained frozen but warmed to the south, where it met the ocean again. A tribe of people who wished to escape a life of starvation in their homeland arrived from an island to the west.

From a land far away and to the south were gods who escaped the persecution of kings. They sailed to the Far North, hoping to find a place they can freely practice their magic and begin a new civilization of gods that one day would overthrow greedy kings.

Upon landing on the snowy shore, the gods built a city inside the cliffs they called Sedda, to shelter from the endless winter. One day, the gods hunted in a forest south of their newfound city. In the woods lived the tribe of heathens who watched from the trees. The heathens were hungry, afraid, and curious. The gods invited them to Sedda in exchange for their knowledge. The heathens obliged.

Over time, the gods and heathens lived in harmony. Baze, the god of fire, became bored of his new life and took a wife of the heathen tribe. They birthed a child who held the same extraordinary gift as his Father. A new era began. The people called the child Dragon. Dragon gave the heathens their name; the Sinook. He trained them to fight and be fearless.

When Dragon decided he would leave the Far North to rule over all of Erras, the Sinook feared his strength and banished him to the mountains. Dragon hid in the caves until one day, he discovered a plentiful valley. He called it NorthBrekka. He took more wives, created a nation of people, and found that there were people who lived south of the mountains.

Dragon felt threatened. War erupted along the territory boundary as the people of Erras and the Far North learned of Dragon's intent to devastate all in order to rule. Not only the Sinook but all people fought bravely against the god, but they could not stand against his strength. The lives of many dwindled to a mere few. He chose to save those who would bow to his reign.

Over time, his power continued to rise dangerously until his children grew outraged by his sovereignty. They fought against him to protect Erras and the Far North. He relinquished his reign to his firstborn son and fled Erras to avoid an uprising from the Sinook. Dragon was named a demon warrior, and his family was burned, but one child survived after changing his cursed family name to Drake. The Drake name became sovereign among Erras and the Far North, and life became plentiful.

The Sinook divided the lands of the Far North from Erras. The remaining gods gifted their chosen with secrets and powers that were kept hidden for centuries. Until the day twins were born to a great king of NorthBrekka, and the lightning brought back a dark history that would change the world forever.

CHAPTER 1

Prince Sebastian

There was a darkness within him that the people of Erras feared, yet his Father, the king, refused to believe. He argued that his sons would not be made out to be monsters. The people claimed that only one would hold the power that would bring disaster to the world.

In a time where war and family grew heavy in the hearts of those who inhabited the lands, greed and dishonor plagued the minds of those who wished to rule. This is the story of brothers who tore the nations apart. Amid a family rivalry, another hid in the begotten land. And who only understood anger and vengeance and desperately strived for revenge against those who betrayed him.

Twins. Identical twin boys. It was a miracle for anyone, but for a king and queen to birth identical twins was a reason to celebrate. The twins were born on the summer solstice. In the North, the solstice meant the snow would melt, the fields would flourish, and the people would decorate, harvest, and come together in unity and joy. On this particular solstice, the day started beautifully. The sun shined bright, the feasts were plentiful, and NorthBrekka was picturesque. When the evening came, clouds gathered over the mountaintops while the king and queen took a stroll in the garden. The queen fell to the ground, grasping her stomach, and with that came Tomas and Sebastian.

An explosion of lightning that caused two babies to shriek to life surrounded the garden. All of NorthBrekka was silenced at that moment until a burst of energy filled the sky. A touch of two tiny hands connecting to form an everlasting bond could bring hope to a kingdom and panic to a country. A prophecy was written, and a king buried the miracle in a journal hidden beneath the floorboards in the castle. He knew it was the only way to keep his perfect twin sons alive so that they may one day rule over all. A secret that could only remain hidden for so long.

The story begins many years ago on a frigid winter day. The Drake twins were exact opposites in every way except their faces. Tomas was intelligent, vigilant, and obedient. Sebastian, on the other hand, was reckless, volatile, and wild. One morning, Sebastian noticed Tomas still in bed with a book covering his face and a page partially stuck to the drool on his cheek. As he tossed things about in the wardrobe, he heard Tomas groan.

"Sebastian, maybe you should stay home today and keep me company," he said as Sebastian tossed boots, pants, and a coat onto the floor, leaving a disaster of a mess in the corner.

"Why would I want to lie around and read books all day? Your life is so boring, Tomas. I need to breathe fresh air outside this damned castle, away from all of you."

"That was not insulting at all," Tomas said. "That is my coat. Are you going to clean that up?"

"My coat is torn. I need a new one. Why don't you come with me today? I won't be out long."

"You shouldn't be going out at all. It looks like a storm is coming."

Sebastian stopped and stared out of his bedroom window, noticing thick gray clouds building off in the east. This was not unusual in NorthBrekka. It was a cold and dreary land that snowed much of the winter season, about nine months out of the year. The summer season was warm only during the height of mid-afternoon, and the sun only shined a short time before the clouds would settle over the kingdom.

Castle Drake sat on the side of a vast snow-capped mountain range called The Break. From the edge of the castle court, one could view the glistening blue water of a wide-stretched lake and the bustle of a small village nestled within a grassy prairie filled with wildflowers. In the town by the lake, the sun shined more often, and the warmth came longer, which made farming ideal in the summer.

With only a few roads in or out, NorthBrekka was quite difficult for invading armies to reach. West led to the mountains on a narrow pass, to the township of Shadowmire. South of Shadowmire, a prairie that flourished to the west of the lake, edged the border of Torrdale. To the east was a treacherous mountain pass, often shrouded in ice and snow, that went high into jagged summits and led into the Far North and then the sea. One road led south and into NorthBrekka. It was heavily guarded from the ground to the bridge leading up the mountain and the landing outside the castle grounds.

"There is something that caught my eye the other day. A quick peek is all I am going to do. After that, I will ride home, I swear."

"Your adventures are never a quick peek. You will be gone until night, then I'll have to listen to Father start screaming again at dinner because you are not there, and I get stuck defending you. Please, brother, stay home today."

"Calm down, Tomas. I swear I will be home early, long before dinnertime. Besides, I promised Will I would help him make my new saddle today."

"Oh, so you are spending the day with Will," Tomas said with a smirk. "He likes you. Not surprising. It's how he looks at you that gives his intentions away."

"You are so annoying," Sebastian said, looking excited. "I am leaving now-goodbye, brother. See you at dinner. Stop smiling like that!"

Sebastian hurried away. His cheeks still burned from blushing as he rushed through the kitchen, grabbing a biscuit on his way through the door closest to the stables. It was early, so Will was not working at the forge. Will and Sebastian had been close friends since they were children. When Sebastian was not on his next adventure, he was usually with Will, riding horses, swimming in the lake, arguing over who was better at swordsmanship and archery.

He headed off into the high mountains. There was a cave he had found several days prior. He wanted to take a better look inside while he still had the light. But after one exciting find after another, he came to the surface to see the night had come. His heart was racing as he climbed upon his saddle and rode his black steed, Ossian, down the mountainside. There was no telling what was coming, but he knew it was dangerous and that his Father would be angrily waiting in his war room. To Sebastian, rushing home at dusk was nothing short of routine, but this time he felt different.

It was much colder than when he ascended the mountain, and the sky had become stormy and thick with clouds shrouded in a dark haze. He dreaded what his Father was going to say when he faced him.

CHAPTER 2

A Feat of Fury

King Ivan paced on the war room's terrace in Castle Drake, watching the skies grow angry and dark. Word arrived by a crow that flew from the most eastern part of NorthBrekka, where a band of knights managed the northern and southern border, as well as the sea.

The message brought the most disturbing news, which led to the king's worry for his third-eldest son's late return home. Most of the Drake siblings were already fed, washed, and preparing for bed. Barron sat in the corner, tapping his foot on the floor, watching his Father mumble about being irresponsible and careless. He would smirk every time his Father would say Sebastian's name and mention how he wanted to beat him.

"Father, would you like me to go in search of my brother? I am sure I know exactly where he has gone."

"Are you mad? Do you think I would send my oldest boy out with this storm coming? I sent men after him, but Sebastian better have a good reason for being out there."

"Doubtful. Sebastian never has a good excuse for his insolence. You are too easy on him, Father."

Ivan looked over at Barron with an annoyed expression. Queen Emelia entered the room and sat next to Barron.

"Barron is right, my dear. Sebastian is getting out of control. You must put your foot down before he does something that gets someone or himself hurt."

"You are right, but if I restrict his freedom, he will rebel a lot worse than he already does. The two of you do not understand why I give him so much regard. He needs to learn for himself."

"When he ends up in prison, you will regret having any regard for him. He is disloyal and embarrassing to our family name, Barron snapped.

King Ivan glared at Barron, then snatched him by the shirt collar. "How dare you question my decisions about what is best for my children! Off to bed before you make me angry."

Barron stared at his Father boldly before stomping out. Emelia paced with her head staring at the floor.

"You are always hard on him. He is just trying to prove himself as a worthy future king. He is not wrong. Sebastian is getting worse every year. If you do not constrain him, he will end up in grave danger."

"Barron has much to learn about being a king if he wishes to sit on the throne. He wants to control everyone, not lead them. Sebastian, on the other hand, has a good heart and is fearless."

"Are you saying you will crown Sebastian over Barron?" Emelia interrupted. "Do you think that is wise? Barron would lose himself. He has a lot to learn, but you cannot be serious about handing the kingdom to Sebastian. He is not ready."

"He will be. Barron cannot wear the crown. There is something not right in his mind. It is poisoned," King Ivan said, turning to the outside again.

"How could you say that about your son? He may be a bit brutal, but he feels threatened by his brother. You said yourself that your own brother was quite vicious, and he still grew up to be a good man and a good king."

"My brother was a good man. But he died because he was too militant. He had no common sense. Now leave me to my madness, woman." As the snow fell heavier, he caught a glimpse of a black horse in the white flurry. "There he is."

"You must be firm with him tonight, Ivan. Make sure he understands you mean what you say, even if he gets upset. You need to break his heart every once in a while." Emelia got up to go to bed.

Sebastian quietly snuck past the guards, hoping he would not be caught, and slinked off to his bedroom. Sneak he did, only a guard caught him out of the corner of his eye and snatched Sebastian by the collar of his shirt.

"Your Father wishes to speak to you, my prince."

The guard took Sebastian to the war room, pushed him inside, and closed the door behind him. King Ivan stood staring out with his back to his son.

"Do you understand how angry I am?" he asked.

"Father, I am sorry. I lost track of time. I thought it was still sunset, and I-"

"I do not care about your excuses! You do not understand how dangerous it is out there-tonight, of all nights-for your foolishness. I sent two of my best knights out to find you. How could you do this to your family, to me?"

"Father, what are you talking about?" Sebastian dug into his thoughts, wondering if he had forgotten something important that his Father announced. "Was there a guest I somehow forgot was arriving, or a feast, or special announcement I missed? I am deeply sorry. I did not mean to be late."

"Are you completely ignorant, boy? Is there no thought in your head as to what is happening? Have you not seen what comes from the east?"

Sebastian seemed confused. "What do you mean? Is war upon us?"

"No, stupid boy! I mean the sky. A winter storm is on the horizon. I received word from the east that this storm is the deadliest winter storm in this land in decades. It brings a cold with winds so extreme that anyone caught outside would certainly die, and my son was missing from the safety of the castle."

"Father, I did not see this storm. How could I know this would happen? I am home now, Father. Alive and well."

"You were to be home before the light of day was gone, but as usual, you were not. You caused me so much grief over the years, Sebastian, and this is the last straw. I will not tolerate your egregious lack of regard anymore. If it were not for the storm, I would banish you from this kingdom and this family. You are nothing but trouble, and you listen to no one. I've had it with you.

Go to your room. I do not wish to see you again until I ask for you. Do you understand me?"

Sebastian stared at his Father but said nothing. He was broken inside and had no words. His eyes welled up with tears, but he stood firm on the outside. On the inside, he was lying on the stone floor in pieces.

"Father, let me explain myself. I did not mean to be out so late, I swear. I was not trying to disrespect your wishes. I honestly lost the time!"

"I said go to your room!"

"Why will you not listen? You never listen to me! You always think that I am so bad. Well fine! If I am so horrible, I will go. You don't need to worry about me anymore. I am nothing but a disappointment to you, and nothing I ever do will be good enough in your eyes. I am sorry I will not be like Barron and be the perfect obedient son. I am sorry I am not like Tomas, who is smart and wholesome. I am never going to be the son you want. I should've never come back!"

Sebastian shivered with fear, hurried from his Father's war room, and headed quickly to his quarters. He was angry, with only the thought of his Father telling him he would banish him in his mind. He decided if his Father wished him to leave, he would go.

Sebastian slammed through his bedroom door and kicked it closed. Tomas stared at him wide-eyed.

"Do not say a word!" Sebastian snapped, then started gathering warm clothes, bow and quiver, sword, and rucksack.

Tomas observed him curiously. "What are you doing? Where are you going? You are not going out there."

"Are you going to stop me?" Sebastian said. "No, you will not. So sit there and shut up. I am leaving, and I am never coming back, ever!"

"You cannot! The storm."

"I do not care! I am going. Father wants me gone, so I am leaving."

"You are lying. Father would never send you away. He is angry, but he is more afraid of you being lost in the storm. If you go, you will die!"

"Good! I will not be a burden anymore. Father said it himself. He said he would banish me. I am saving him the effort by leaving tonight."

"Sebastian, stop. You are not going anywhere." Tomas jumped up and stood between Sebastian and the door.

"Move out of my way, Tomas. I am no longer a member of this family. I am no longer a Drake. I am not your brother anymore. I am nobody."

"That is not true. You are staying here!" Tomas said as he pushed Sebastian back toward his bed. "I do not want to hurt you, brother, but I will stop you by any means necessary."

Sebastian laughed, grabbed Tomas, spun around, and threw him down with ease. "Do not make me laugh. You cannot stop me."

Sebastian grabbed his bag, threw it over his shoulder, and took one last peek at Tomas, who was still on the floor with tears in his eyes. Sebastian felt terrible but stifled his feelings and said a quick goodbye before leaving.

His guilt hit hard as he made it down the stairs and to the castle doors. He started tearing up and wanted to hug Tomas but continued through the doors.

Two guards stood between him and the outside. One grabbed him by the collar and pushed him back inside. "Young Sebastian, you are not permitted to be outside this night. It is dangerous. Your Father will not permit it."

"My Father has banished me; therefore, I am trespassing on these lands. Let me leave."

"I cannot do that, my prince."

"I am not a prince. I am not a Drake. I am nothing, no one. Move aside, now!" Sebastian said, shoving his way past the guards and hurrying toward the stables.

Ivan sat at his desk with his face in his hands. "I should have not said that. If Sebastian runs away before he finds out about –"

He heard the clink of metal come fast to his door. It flew open to reveal two guards appearing distressed.

"Your Majesty, your son, Prince Sebastian, he has left the castle. He claims he has been banished. My king, he is leaving!"

King Ivan was sipping his tea, then dropped his cup at hearing the news. "The two of you let him leave? Well, do not stand there, after him!"

King Ivan shouted for his men, who were on duty around the castle. A group of knights and guards gathered in the great hall. Tomas hurried to chase Sebastian but was halted by King Ivan. Barron, the eldest brother, ran to meet his Father in the hall.

"The two of you can go back to bed. Let the men handle this."

"Father, I can help."

"My son has left the castle. The storm threatens to bring hell upon our keep. We must bring him home before the cold takes him. Gather your warmest clothing and prepare to ride," Ivan said, ignoring Tomas.

"Father, please. Let me help. He will listen to me."

"Out of the question, Tomas. I could lose one of my sons. I will not risk your life, nor yours, Barron. Off to bed, both of you. This is my fault. I have to bring your brother home."

"Father, at least allow me to assist. I am the fastest rider in the kingdom, and I am sure I know where to find him," Barron said.

"I said no!"

Ivan shoved his way past his sons and started toward the doors. His men were positioned in the stables. Ivan walked in and immediately looked to where Sebastian kept Ossian. The black steed was not in his stall, meaning Sebastian was long gone, riding rapidly away from the protection of NorthBrekka.

"My son is out there, somewhere. If he is wise, he rode west away from the storm. He rode through the mountains because he knows those roads best. He passed Shadowmire and went over The Break. Once he descends the mountains, he will pass into the outer realm of Torrdale. They are our allies but keep in mind, Sebastian is a stranger in those lands. They will take him prisoner. We must track him down before he reaches Torrdale and return to the castle before the storm is in full force."

Sebastian rode fast up into the mountain pass. He considered traveling east to spite his Father but headed north onto the road that would turn west once he passed the village of Shadowmire, then south toward Torrdale. There was no thought as to where he would go from there. He only knew he must outrun the storm or risk death.

Shadowmire was as loud and barbaric as ever, with soldiers of the North drunk and arguing in the streets, brothel women selling their bodies, and townsfolk keeping a wary eye. Sebastian did not stop to make small talk. He rode into the western pass until the mountains were behind him and the lands opened to hilly fields and open land.

There was a low wall ahead in sight, which separated NorthBrekka from Torrdale. He slowed Ossian and crept cautiously forward. It was quiet over the wall, which Sebastian found surprising. There were no guards or soldiers along the border on either side.

He found a place to stop and let Ossian rest, eat, and drink from a stream. His stomach knotted up, thinking of his family and the storm. He was worried that his brothers and sisters would suffer if the storm was as terrible as predicted, but his Father's harsh words reminded him of why he left.

As he reminisced, there were voices in the distance. Over the wall, a few men on horses rode forward. They were discussing the storm, estimating how long it would be before it reached Torrdale.

Sebastian listened closely as one of the men spoke directly to another man he addressed as Prince Cyrus. Sebastian checked cautiously over the wall to see who this Prince Cyrus was. His Father talked of his friend from Torrdale, a prince at the time, now King of Kings who resided in the South.

King Roman was a prince of Torrdale and brother of Prince Cyrus. When Roman was 17, the king of the capital city, Alta Prime, broke a long-standing agreement of an alliance between Torrdale and Alta Prime. Because Torrdale sits above the northern border, it is considered a part of the North. The South and North were previously at war over which king would be King of Kings.

When Roman marched to Alta Prime and faced the king, they fought until Roman beheaded the king. From then he was crowned King of Kings.

Roman reinstated the treaty and left his little brother, Prince Cyrus in charge of Torrdale. Cyrus's job was to keep NorthBrekka and Alta Prime from going to war again.

It was dark, but Sebastian could tell Prince Cyrus was young, his age at least. He made out the dark wavy hair of the prince, blowing softly in the cold breeze. He stared at him admiringly until he heard one of the men state that the storm was quickly gaining size and strength. Sebastian decided he needed to slip away and keep going.

Ossian was down the way, gulping water. Sebastian crouched down out of sight, crawled down the hill, and climbed onto his horse, and slipped away from the wall. He wandered to the east, unsure where he could go. The only place he would find refuge would be in Shadowmire, but it was far away now.

Sebastian accepted that he made a mistake in leaving as he gazed upon the storm growing nearby. He led Ossian to the lake the separated NorthBrekka and Torrdale at the mountains' base. He climbed down from his horse, patted Ossian on the nose and told him to run away west as quickly as he could muster, but Ossian refused to leave his master.

The storm began to crackle with thunder and lightning. Sebastian stood still, watching, knowing it would soon overtake his position, and he was prepared to perish under the bitter cold.

The fog began to fill the air, it started to snow, and the winds started to pick up. Sebastian turned to see Ossian stamping his foot at him.

"I told you to run away, but yet here you are waiting to die with me. I thought horses are supposed to be smart," he patted Ossian's neck. "I am sorry I led you to your end. We should've stayed home."

It started to get colder, and the snow fell even heavier. Sebastian was getting nervous as he paced back and forth. He thought he heard thunder coming from the mountains, but it appeared as an accompaniment of men on horses riding fast in his direction.

It was King Ivan and his men. A pang of guilt and fear washed over him when he could see his Father's angry face.

"Sebastian, what are you doing? Ride west, go!"

Sebastian stood looking first at his Father, then at the storm raging toward him as it began to cross the lake.

"Are you mad, boy? I said, get on your horse and ride."

Ivan halted just before he reached Sebastian and stared at his son with concern. Sebastian stared at the storm, not moving. Ivan leaped down and ran over to his son.

"Do you wish for death?"

"Perhaps I do, Father. There is no home, no family, nothing left for me. I am soon to be a ghost, forever cursed to roam these lands as no one, unnoticed and unloved."

"If it is what I said, I spoke out of anger. Believe I would never..."

"The storm is here. Go, Father. Run. I am fine here."

A familiar voice spoke. "Brother, please. Get on Ossian's back and ride west with us. Let us go to Torrdale and the safety of the Bolin Palace. Come on!"

Sebastian glanced at Tomas. "Why are you here? You could die. Leave all of you!"

Ivan jerked his head toward Tomas. "I told you not to come! You disobeyed me, Tomas. What is wrong with you? I could swear that you are more like your twin than you know. Both of you, ride west, right now!"

Sebastian turned away and stared into the storm again, focusing on it as if it had him in a trance. He closed his eyes and raised his hand like he wanted to touch the clouds. His Father stopped bickering with Tomas about how they would drag Sebastian out of there by his hair if he did not leave.

Sebastian mumbled to himself, "You cannot hurt me. I do not fear death. You are just a cloud, a storm, nothing but a simple deluge that will be dead as soon as you finish your little tantrum. I am stronger than you."

He was reaching for the storm. Sebastian, still mumbling, opened his eyes, which made Ivan gasp. Ivan stepped beside his son and peered at Sebastian with amazement.

"Your eyes have turned red," Ivan gasped.

Sebastian's hand was still outstretched. He saw Tomas from the corner of his eye slowly walk forward, his gaze locked on the storm as well. The knights and guards followed. Sebastian's fist emitted a soft glow.

The storm halted suddenly, lingering over the lake, swirling, causing the lake to freeze instantly. The ice spread fast and was nearing the place they stood on the shore. Sebastian was still mumbling with his focus locked. The snow came down fiercely, and the wind howled.

"What is happening?" Tomas said as the storm swelled and growled violently, causing the ground to shake. "Sebastian, please come away from there." He hurried over to his side.

Sebastian smirked and reached for Tomas's hand. The glow from his hand shined bright. Tomas looked at his hand, bewildered by the light. Sebastian let him go and reached back at the clouds, and shouted.

"Leave, now!"

With a rapid burst, Sebastian tore the storm in half. It stopped spinning, the snow dissipated, and the skies cleared to reveal the moon and stars.

Ivan stared at his son and laughed. "How did I not see this before?" He turned to Tomas. "That would mean, both of you...."

"What, Father? Both of us are what?"

"This is unique, my son. This is something not seen in these lands in a very long time."

"What do you mean, Father? What are you not telling me? What is happening to me?"

"Quiet, Sebastian. If outsiders learn of this, they will come after you and your brother. You were just babies when I first knew, but this, what you have done here tonight, will change everything."

"You are worrying me."

"We must ride back to NorthBrekka. I must protect you both. Come now!"

"But Father, you said you wanted me gone."

"I told you I did not mean that. Do not be silly, boy. You cannot be roaming the lands alone, not now. You do not understand what this means, and you are too young to explain it properly. When the time is right, you will know."

"What just happened?" Shouting came from behind the accompaniment. It was the men of Torrdale.

"Oh, Prince Cyrus, good evening. Well, I am unsure," Ivan said, glancing at Sebastian with a worried face. "The storm just fell apart. It is peculiar."

The young dark-haired adolescent boy with a charming demeanor approached King Ivan like they had known each other for years. The breeze tousled his wavy locks, making him appear angelic to Sebastian's eyes.

Sebastian was still frozen in place, staring over the lake at the clouds that were withering away. The voice of Prince Cyrus drew his attention.

"Well, thank the gods. We were worried when he crept away from our borders, then took his horse east. We charged after to stop him. King Ivan, can I assume this is one of your sons?" Cyrus said, sounding like an adult rather than a young man.

"Yes, this is my son, Sebastian, and his twin brother, Tomas. How are things in Torrdale these days, Cyrus? How is your brother? I have not seen him in ages."

"It is a pleasure to meet you both, Sebastian and Tomas," Cyrus said as he hopped down to come closer. "Torrdale is as boring as ever, and my brother is still a fat drunk."

Cyrus laughed as he got close to Sebastian but halted suddenly in place, staring at Sebastian with wonder.

"And is Roman planning to come to visit soon? He wrote to me a few weeks ago stating he would be in Torrdale to check in on matters, and on you."

Cyrus did not respond right away as he was still dreamily staring at Sebastian, and Sebastian stared back in a daze. Their eyes locked on one another. Ivan cleared his throat, which caused Cyrus to jump.

"Umm, yes, he is. He said he would meet with you here in Torrdale next month. Of course, you are welcome to bring your family as well. We would be happy to shelter you all."

"That will not be necessary, Cyrus. I will return in one month. For now, I need to ride home and check on my children. Good evening, Prince Cyrus. Sebastian, Tomas, let's go, now."

Sebastian glanced at his Father, snapped quickly back to Cyrus, smiled, and slowly walked away to climb onto Ossian. Cyrus grinned and gestured a goodbye, then watched them ride out east.

CHAPTER 3

The Prince of Torrdale

"Father, please let us come with you. We are dying to see Torrdale. You never let us go anywhere." Sebastian paced around his Father's office impatiently, knocking things over without thinking.

"Why the sudden interest in royal matters? You will be bored."

"I am bored here. Please, Father."

"Alright, but only if you stop this madness. You are making a mess. You and Tomas may come, but you need to promise that you will be on your best behavior, Sebastian. I cannot deal with you running off every second."

"I promise." Sebastian smiled wide as he tripped over the rug he kicked up during his rampage. Ivan rubbed his forehead with grief as Sebastian jumped up and ran up to his room to tell Tomas they would depart in the morning for Torrdale.

Early morning came, and Sebastian was dressed and at the breakfast table before his family awoke. Ivan came down, looking surprised to see his son already waiting.

"You seem excited," Ivan said.

"I just want to see something outside of NorthBrekka. That is all."

"Good morning." Tomas slipped in, yawning as he flopped down next to Sebastian.

"The two of you need to eat. We depart at first light."

They rode the long road that took much of the daylight to come upon the Bolin Palace that sat on the edge of a rocky cliff overlooking the western sea. Torrdale was a small kingdom, predominantly prairie with low mountains on the southern border and rocky landscape near the sea where the village and the palace sat.

As they rode through the gates, Prince Cyrus was already waiting to greet them. He smiled when he saw Sebastian had come and hurried forward to meet them.

"Good to see you again, Cyrus," Ivan said.

"Your Majesty, always a pleasure. My brother is waiting at the council table. He said to tell you he has wine waiting. Tomas and Sebastian, we are not permitted inside the council. Would you both like to come with me? I will show you around."

"Absolutely," Sebastian murmured, trying not to sound nervous.

They followed Cyrus inside, and Ivan hurried away to speak with the council. Cyrus turned to address the twins.

"Come on now. I will show you something you do not get to see in NorthBrekka."

Cyrus led the twins across the palace to the backside that opened to a room overlooking the sea. Tall as the castle stood, the room had large windows and comfortable couches lined next to a massive fireplace.

"So, tell me about the two of you."

Sebastian stumbled over his words, but Tomas interjected apparently noticing Sebastian was unusually quiet.

"Well, we are fifteen years old. I am the oldest by a minute or two. I like to read and write, and Sebastian is a chaotic mess that mostly gets into trouble."

Sebastian looked up quickly at Tomas at that last mention. "Tomas! That is rude."

"Well, it is true. You are like a cyclone everywhere you go. Once you're done, you run off all day on some wild adventure."

"What kind of explorations do you go on?" Cyrus asked, staring at Sebastian with interest.

Sebastian smiled at the idea that Cyrus was not focused on Tomas calling him a disaster. He loved talking about his explorations to anyone that would listen. "Mostly up in the high mountains, caves, and the small villages surrounding us."

"Shadowmire," Tomas said quickly, darting away as he laughed before Sebastian could slap him.

"Shadowmire! I've heard of it but never been there. I understand it is where all the dissidents go. Am I right?"

"Yes, and prostitutes," Tomas said, laughing even more after seeing the expression on Sebastian's face.

"That is not why I go there, Tomas," Sebastian said, sounding annoyed that his brother was making fun of him in front of Cyrus. "I like to gamble."

"And get drunk and pick fights," Tomas said.

"Sounds exciting," Cyrus said, looking right at Sebastian, fascinated by him more and more.

Tomas walked over to the window, seeming bored with talking about Sebastian. "May I go outside? I would like to look out at the western sea. I have never seen it."

"Sure. You are welcome to anywhere in Torrdale. Would you like to go too, Sebastian?"

"No, I am going to relax right here. It is cold out there. You may go if you like."

Tomas hurried to the door and went outside. Cyrus decided to stay behind too.

"I see it every day. Besides, I want to hear more about you. Does he always give you a hard time?"

Sebastian started looking less annoyed now that Tomas was gone. "All the time. He thinks he is funny."

"It is alright. My older brothers are mean to me. I would rather have one that just picks on me. So, do you have a girlfriend?"

"No. I am not interested in a girlfriend," Sebastian said but realized it sounded weird.

Cyrus hinted at a smile on the corner of his mouth. Sebastian could see Cyrus watching him and biting his lip. Sebastian saw Cyrus's hands tremble when he looked at him. He wandered if Cyrus was attracted to him but afraid of letting him find out. Shaking off his thoughts, he scrambled to find the right words.

"Me neither. My brother always introduces me to girls he thinks would be good for me. I would think by now he would give up."

Sebastian smiled, then laughed. They stared at each other in silence, studying each other's faces. Cyrus moved to sit next to Sebastian on the couch.

"I am intrigued by you. You do what you want, and you do not care what anyone thinks. You inspire me, Sebastian. I would like it if we could be friends."

Sebastian stopped staring at the floor and perked up. "I would like that too."

They both smiled and stared at each other again. Cyrus slowly moved his hand next to Sebastian's until they touched. He jerked away and apologized but set it back on the couch next to Sebastian's, as if checking for permission to keep it there. Sebastian couldn't take his eyes off of Cyrus's soft lips, strong jawline, and mysterious eyes.

Sebastian smiled and bit his lip. "So, what do you like to do for fun?"

"There is not much fun to be had here. I usually just go riding, and I like to swim in the sea in the warmer months. But unfortunately, since my brother is King of Kings, and my other brother is always away leading some ridiculous resistance group, I am responsible for everything that happens here. I do not particularly enjoy being in charge."

"I cannot imagine how daunting that must be."

"Trust me. It gets lonely. You never know who your friend is because they are following orders. It would be amazing to have someone to keep me company all the time."

Sebastian moved his hand until it rested against Cyrus's. He pushed his index finger until it looped around Cyrus's. The two of them glanced at their hands.

"What does this mean?" Sebastian whispered.

"I do not know, but I like it," Cyrus replied.

"I like it too."

"Boys! Time for supper." Ivan's loud voice scared both Cyrus and Sebastian. They jumped to their feet and waited for Ivan to join them.

"Time to eat, then get some rest. We ride home in the morning. Sebastian, call for your brother."

Cyrus smiled as Sebastian tousled his long hair across his face. When Ivan left the room. Cyrus reached over and pushed Sebastian's hair and tucked it behind his ear. Sebastian blushed and averted his eyes.

"You have a pretty face. You shouldn't cover it up."

"Please, do not call me pretty," Sebastian said.

"I did not mean to offend. I thought maybe you were–never mind. Sorry. We should call for Tomas, then head to dinner before my brother comes yelling."

Cyrus hurried over to the door and shouted for Tomas. Sebastian stood there dumbfounded. When Cyrus had tucked his hair back, an intense tingling sensation flushed through his loins, followed by a warmth that was so comforting, he never wanted it to end.

They sat down for supper. It was an awkward arrangement as Sebastian and Cyrus admired each other across the table while Ivan and Roman chattered about a treaty. Tomas's eyes shot back and forth in amusement.

Later, Cyrus showed them their sleeping arrangements, hesitating as he said goodnight to Sebastian. In the morning, they all gathered in the courtyard to say one last goodbye before departing.

"Will you come visit me?" Sebastian asked Cyrus.

"As soon as I am allowed. My brother does not let me leave the grounds, but I will ask until he gets annoyed and says yes."

Sebastian smiled, they hugged before Sebastian joined his brother and Father, along with the men of NorthBrekka, and they rode home.

CHAPTER 4

Barron's Secret Meeting

Two years later, on an island once a part of Erras, struck by an earth god many centuries before, stood a town of a particular tribe of people who had broken a peace treaty with the king of Kings many years back. The people were called Kuhar, and the land was called Khan Khar. And on Khan Khar sat a man who knew nothing but betrayal, who had vengeance in his heart.

"I am delighted to see you received my letter. I am glad you dared to come." His voice was silky and deep. His blond hair was unusual in these lands, but he was sitting upon a throne like he was in charge of everything.

"With those words, how could I resist? Now, you said there is proof of my little brother's gift. I do not have all day. Show me!"

"Easy, Barron Drake. Before I show you anything, I must know if we have an accord."

"Why would I agree to something if I do not know you speak the truth?"

"Does the promise of a crown and a country mean nothing? How do I know I can trust you? You are the one intrigued by turning on your kind."

"Is there something to show me or not, Sacha Khovell?"

Sacha walked over to a small door in the corner of the room in the Khasaliath Citadel, the palace of Khan Khar. He reached through the door, snatched someone by the hair, pulled him out, and threw him before Barron. Barron gawked at him.

"He is one of NorthBrekka's soldiers, am I right?" Sacha asked.

"Traki Modese. He is one of my Father's captains."

"Well, Mr. Modese, tell young Prince Barron what you witnessed."

"It was like the air was sucked out from around us. The storm was swirling over NorthBrekka, sheeting ice and snow down as no one had ever seen. It was terrifying and deathly if anyone was to be standing beneath it. Instant frozen death, they said. It was so cold."

"Yes, yes, the storm." Sacha sounded frustrated. "Get to the part about the young prince."

"He was standing at the brim of the lake outside of NorthBrekka. He fought with the king and ran away. The king gathered up a small number of us and had us follow. When we arrived, the prince was in a trance, it seemed. He was mumbling something strange I could not understand."

Traki paused, looking lost in his own story.

"Go on," Sacha mocked.

"The king tried talking to him, then Prince Tomas, but he did not snap from his gaze on the storm approaching the lake. As the water froze solid in moments, lightning crashed down all around, and the wind screamed through the air. The king shouted at his son. The prince opened his eyes, and his eyes shined bright like rubies. He reached his hand into the air, there was a rumble, the ground shook furiously, and there was a sudden loud crack! At last, the storm split in two, the clouds vanished, and the sky cleared. The king looked at the prince and said he knew he was special all along. He said he believes both of them, the twins, are unique. He turned to us and told us we could never speak a word to anyone about what we saw. I've kept this quiet for two years."

"Yet here you are, betraying my Father. Why?" Barron said as he twirled a dagger in his hand.

"A prophecy says the gods will return to save the world from evil. The prince may be the answer to our prayers."

Sacha laughed. "A savior. Or maybe he is evil. Now you know, Barron Drake, why I called for you to come. Do you understand what you must do?"

Barron was silent for a long moment, then nodded and turned to leave. He stopped before Traki and tightened his grip on the dagger.

"What are you going to do with him?" Barron said to Sacha.

"What would you do to a traitor? He betrayed your Father. It is obvious he cannot keep a secret. What makes you think he won't run to the prince and tell him of this meeting?"

Barron clenched his jaw, glowering at Traki who was begging for his life. He walked over and slowly dragged the dagger across Traki's throat, smiling as the blood poured down to the floor. "A traitor has no right to the life he was given. No one will cry for you. Your family will be shamed. Your body will be tossed into the sea. There will be no grave for anyone to grieve your death."

CHAPTER 5

The Art of Fire

In NorthBrekka, Sebastian explored a cave far into the heart of The Break, the ridge of the mountains that separated the north from the Far North.

"Sunset. Of course, it is sunset already," Sebastian said aloud as he climbed out of the mouth of a cave high above the kingdom of NorthBrekka. Groaning at the darkening sky, he hurried to brush the mud from his pants and boots.

"I wish I never had to go back there. We should just run away and live free in the woods beyond the mountains. At least there, we would finally have some peace. What do you think?" Sebastian asked. "Why am I talking to you about this? You are a horse. I think I might be losing my mind." He laughed as he patted Ossian on the neck. "Be home before dark, Sebastian. Do not let me catch you sneaking into the castle after dark, Sebastian. Do not make me ask where you are, Sebastian," He mouthed in his Father's tone of voice. "Do not be late for dinner. Do not walk into the hall filthy.

A prince is to behave properly. Stop acting like a heathen. Do this and do that and stop doing what you are doing. Quit being, well, you, Sebastian. Discipline, grace, kindness, and loyalty are the most important qualities of a prince, and right now, Sebastian, you lack all of them." He sighed deeply. "Come on, Ossian, we should hurry home."

"Sebastian!" King Ivan howled. "Where is that boy this time?"

"He has run off again. Off on another adventure, I am afraid, my dear," Queen Emelia said with a tired tone in her voice.

"It is nearly time for supper! Why is he always off running around? Why can't he be like his brothers and sisters for once?" King Ivan said while waving his hands in the air extravagantly. The queen slowly nodded her head and stared off into the distance while pursing her lips.

Sebastian's mother died shortly after giving birth to his younger brother Viktor. His Father married Queen Emelia only a few months after she became pregnant with his little sister Mary, and she gave birth to the remaining seven children after. She was a kind and caring stepmother and treated her stepchildren as her own. She was quiet and moved about the castle slowly and stealthily. Sebastian appreciated the fact that she never pried in his business, unlike his Father.

"Father, I have taken the liberty to make a list of training routines for my brothers while the summer approaches," Barron said as he swaggered into the office his Father would spend much of his time in. "I think that Tomas, Sebastian, Viktor, and Gentry should work on their swordsmanship, then archery to prepare them for their future with the guard, and they should..."

"I am not going to be a military man." Tomas walked in with an armful of parchment that he flopped down on the desk. "As requested, Father," Tomas said while opening a map that listed the kingdoms.

As Tomas and Barron looked over their Father's shoulder, Ivan pointed to Shadowmire.

"I received word that your brother was spotted in Shadowmire again. That makes the third time after I told him that village is off-limits. If he is there again today, I have no choice but to lock him in his room until he learns how to listen."

"He found a new cave system along The Break," Tomas said while pointing to a location on the map. "I know that is where he is spending most of his time as of late. He said it is the largest cave he's ever seen."

"When will he learn to grow up? He is going to get stuck down there one day, and I will be charged with fetching him out."

"As sure as you sound of yourself, Barron, Sebastian is strong and smart. He's been climbing through these caverns for years. I am sure he can handle it without your assistance," Tomas said with assurance.

It began to darken out, and all the children were in the dining hall when Ivan and Emelia entered the room. "Where is Sebastian? Is he not home?" King Ivan said while pinching the bridge of his nose, feeling frustrated.

"I am here, Father. Sorry I am late. I was talking to Mason about my new saddle when it got late," Sebastian said, hurrying to the dinner table as his family began to gather around.

"Your new saddle? Since when does *he* get a new saddle, Father?" Barron said, as he set a plate of food before his Father. Barron always insisted on preparing his Father's dish as he said he did not trust anyone else to do it.

"Tell the truth. You were in Shadowmire again, weren't you?"

"As a matter of fact, no, I was not, but thank you for your concern, brother. And yes, a new saddle because mine is too small now. It fits Gentry, and he is five years younger than me," Sebastian said with a smirk.

Ivan stood up and demanded the attention of his children. He announced that in the morning, after training, they would all be preparing for a ball.

"This ball will take place in two days' time. There will be music, dancing, and food. It is a celebration of a long-awaited peace treaty between the North and South."

"So, where were you today?" Tomas asked Sebastian when they were lying in their beds in their massive, shared bedroom. They were the only siblings who shared a room.

"Please tell me you weren't in Shadowmire. Father is not joking about locking you away this time. He is worried about you."

"I wasn't in Shadowmire. I grow tired of that place anyway. Women and booze are all it is."

"So, you don't enjoy the company of scantily clad women?"

"I am not particularly interested, thank you. There are not many women who I fancy. I am tired of Father trying to point me toward *fine young women I would be best suited to.* It's enough to make me never want to get married!"

"So, no women. Men perhaps?" Tomas said, prying. He turned to glance at Sebastian, who gazed at him with a surprised expression. "What? Do you think I don't notice how you look at men compared to women?"

"Just shut up and go to sleep," Sebastian said as he rolled over and pulled his blanket over his head. He fell asleep, but after only a few short hours, his mind snapped awake.

Sebastian tossed and turned which woke up Tomas.

"What are you doing awake so early, Sebastian? Go back to sleep; it is still dark outside," Tomas whined while turning over, facing away from Sebastian, and banging his head down onto his pillow.

"I can't sleep," Sebastian said.

"You never sleep! Now please, if you are going to be awake, be awake quietly!"

Sebastian was first at the table for breakfast when his brothers and sisters came in, yawning and rubbing their eyes. Sebastian sat there fidgeting, twirling his thumbs, and biting on his fingers. Usually, by now, he was already on the road heading out of town into the woods, but not today. Today was a training day for the older boys.

Sebastian was already a skilled swordsman and precise archer. He had been practicing since he was five with Will, the blacksmith's son, who was a few months older than him. Barron still thought he needed to train, under his watch, under his rules, so that he could pick apart everything he had already learned.

Gentry and Viktor sat down in front of Sebastian, looking at him, smirking but not speaking. "What?" Sebastian said, a little overly loud. His sister Mary jumped a little. "Sorry. What are you two smiling at?"

"Well, how does it feel to be confined?" Gentry handed a plate of bread across the table.

"Confined, strangled, tortured, annoyed. I am going to thrust my sword into Barron's face the first time he looks at me wrong."

"Sebastian!" Ivan thundered like he was not in the room yet.

"Father, I am sitting right here. You don't have to scream!" Sebastian explained but quickly fell silent upon seeing his Father's unamused expression. "What did I do this time, Father?"

"This evening, King of Kings, Roman Bolin of Alta Prime and his brother Cyrus will be arriving. I expect you to be here, present and accounted for. That goes for all of you. Also, there is to be an important meeting to discuss the future of our two kingdoms, and I need you all to be on your best behavior." He pointed at Sebastian. "Cyrus is your age. I expect you to be an ambassador for our kingdom. Show him around and keep him company for a few days until the ball."

Barron laughed so hard he nearly spit food onto the table. "Why would you put Sebastian in charge of such an important task? Cyrus is the King of Kings' little brother. Perhaps I should…"

"No! I asked my dear Sebastian to do this, and I expect him to do it well. He needs friends his age, and Cyrus is an ideal companion."

Sebastian perked up a little with excitement to see Cyrus again. He would get the chance to spend a few days with his new friend, who he had not seen in two years, while his Father and King Roman discuss the politics of the treaty between the north and south.

"Sebastian, you will meet with me privately after breakfast."

King Ivan left the room. Tomas leaned over.

"What did you do this time?"

"I do not know."

After breakfast, Sebastian went to find his Father waiting in a large open room in the castle's rear. There were no windows, only a single door.

"Come in, lock the door behind you."

King Ivan and one other man were inside waiting. Sebastian stared at the man.

"Come in, son. This is Aspen Hyle. He is from Sedda in the Far North. He is a trainer."

"A trainer for what?"

King Ivan nodded at Aspen, then sat down in the corner. Aspen walked over and inspected Sebastian. "Hold out your hands."

Sebastian put his hands out, still confused. Aspen studied them. "Show me what you did two years ago on the lake."

"I do not know what I did."

"Nonsense. Do you think I haven't been watching you over the years? I've seen you, up in the mountains, summoning puffs of fire and lightning from those hands. You try and try, then get irritated until you blow off in a fiery rage. If you are not careful, you will burn the world down. I am here to teach you to control that. Now, show me what you can do!"

Sebastian scowled at his Father. "You are having me followed?"

Ivan stood and smiled. "Look at what you can do. My son, the god of fire."

Sebastian looked down to see his clenched fists on fire with the flames whipping around him like a protective shield.

"Not just fire, Your Majesty. He is elemental. He is Chaos, the god of fire and lightning. The twin, Hydros. God of water and ice. These two are extraordinary, yes, but also dangerous. They must learn to summon their power without getting mad first."

"Teach them. That is why you are here. Do whatever it takes," Ivan said, then marched out of the room.

Aspen turned back to Sebastian, smiled, and got serious. He grabbed the fire poker from the corner. "Make a fire." He pointed at the fireplace.

Sebastian pointed his palm out and stared hard. Nothing happened. Aspen smacked him hard with the fire poker. Sebastian was ready to shout, but Aspen swatted him again.

"Try harder."

Sebastian gritted his teeth and shoved his fists forward. He concentrated until a vein until he felt sweat drip from his forehead. Still nothing.

Aspen smacked him again.

"Stop that!"

"Do what you are made to do!" He smacked Sebastian again, only harder.

Sebastian made a quick growl and threw his hands forward as flames surged from his fists, creating a tiny fire in the pit.

Aspen laughed. "Well, that might keep a cat warm."

"If you are so good at this, you do it!"

"Ahh young prince, you know I am not gifted like you. Smarter, yes, but not gifted."

Sebastian glanced at Aspen, focused again on the fireplace, then held his hands out until they shook. Not even a wisp of smoke escaped. He thought of Barron calling him pretty. Barron liked to anger him to the point of rage, then run to hide behind their

Father. Sebastian's face turned red, he screamed, yet no fire formed from his outstretched fists. He picked up a chair and threw it across the room.

Aspen had enough. "You need to cool down. Go away. Tell your twin to join me."

Sebastian stormed from the room. As he stomped down the hall, he pushed his hands out, spouting a bit of fire as he walked. He turned a corner and smashed hard into Barron.

"Brother, I am sorry. I did not know you were there."

"Why don't you pay attention to where you are walking? You are such a clumsy child. I often wonder how you are even a prince, let alone a Drake."

"What is your problem? I was just trying to apologize. You are always so vile toward me. What did I do to make you hate me?"

Barron ignored him.

"We are brothers. I do not understand why you are so angry with me all the time. Why do you despise me?"

"I don't despise you!" Barron roared. "I don't like you either. I am sick of your doe eyes and precious face every time you are in front of Father. He babies you. He lets you do whatever you want and makes up excuses for your behavior. He does not do that with anyone else." Barron growled before stomping away.

Sebastian hurried to his room and sat down on the window seat, staring out into the distance. He just kept hearing Barron's voice over and over in his head; "I don't like you." Sebastian never thought much of people's opinion of him, but this bothered him quite a bit.

After an hour or so, it started to rain. Sebastian sat with his forehead against the warm glass of the window, staring down at the people gathering up their goods and running undercover. He laughed while watching a plump woman chasing chickens, trying to shoo them into their pen.

Sebastian's face was pressed against the window when he heard someone come into his room. He looked to see Tomas with an angry expression. A tear rolled down Sebastian's cheek, then Tomas hurried over and wrapped his arms around him.

"We could gang up on Barron and beat him if that would make you happy."

Sebastian let out a weak chuckle, and a half-grin flashed across his face.

"What is wrong, brother?" Tomas asked, still holding him in his arms.

Sebastian just shook his head. "How was training?"

"Brutal." They sat in silence for what seemed like hours and watched it rain.

Nadya and Sara swung open the bedroom door, and Nadya excitedly said, "Wash up, boys. Father said King Roman is on the south side of the city. We are to greet him downstairs shortly!" She smiled at them both, then, her smile faded as the twins glanced at her, uninterested.

"Get off your ass and wash up now!" Sara said, and she slammed the door as she left.

Sebastian peered at Tomas, eyebrows raised, as they got up and started to disrobe. As the twins fussed over their outfits, they realized they were making a colossal mess, making them laugh. "You should wear red with gold embroidery, Sebastian. The color brings out your eyes," Tomas said, mimicking his stepmother's voice while swinging his hips back and forth.

"Oh, but this blue is so rich and bold. It screams, 'I am a prince, and I like to be fashionable.'" Sebastian joked back, his voice pitched high. Horns sounded as the outer gates lifted, meaning someone was coming into the castle grounds. The twins got solemn and started grabbing at the pile of clothing on the floor.

They wanted to be presentable and not like heathens, as their Father said. Sebastian donned the red with gold because his stepmother was right; the color was flattering on him. Tomas chose a deep-green cloak with a gold pin shaped like a crown to drape across his dark brown leather and linen.

Sebastian quickly brushed his hair back, trying to unknot the tangles in his thick chestnut locks. He washed the dirt from his face to enhance his high cheekbones, attractive, robust features, and dark-brown eyes. Tomas ruffled up his short, well-kept hair to make it fuller and checked his teeth before turning to open the door.

Lords and their wives and sons and daughters began filing into the great hall. Some struck up conversations with King Ivan as they passed, and some bowed quickly and kept walking. Some of the daughters would smile and wave at the twins as they passed by. Sebastian was bored, but he noticed Tomas was enjoying every moment of it.

CHAPTER 6

The King of Kings

"I don't care how many times I ride North; I despise the weather every time. It is always colder than all hell, snowing or raining. Of course, today, it just has to be rain," King Roman complained while riding north on his approach to NorthBrekka.

"Complain some more, why don't you. It is so much like home it hurts," Cyrus said. "You don't hear me complaining, though. I am happy to get out of the castle to visit another castle. The difference is this castle is full of kids running around being loud and breaking things."

"Be grateful, you little shit. You sit around all day with your hands down your pants, sleep late, eat, and drink wine. Ivan has boys your age. Maybe if you stop being such a snobby brat, you will have friends. Plus, he has daughters to look at," Roman said seriously.

Cyrus let out a snort and glanced over at his brother with one eyebrow raised. "I am sure it will be so much fun." However, Cyrus was secretly excited to see Sebastian again.

Like Sebastian, Cyrus was nothing like his brothers. Roman was loud and robust and liked to complain and crack jokes that were not funny, and Silas was a drunk womanizer. Cyrus enjoyed the finer things. His clothes were always the latest fashion, clean and well pressed, and he wore the most excellent boots money could buy.

They approached the city's inner villages, and people quickly ran out of their homes into the rain and the rapidly lowering temperatures to catch a glimpse of the king of Alta Prime and his army at his back.

The people of NorthBrekka were not kindhearted. Their lives were hard as they live and work in the cold, icy weather of the north. They did not like the people to the South because of the greed that caused a war between former allies. However, they were still excited to get the chance to see someone of such prominence grace their lands.

Most of the people had never met Prince Cyrus of Torrdale before. The girls would smile and wave at him as he passed by, and when he would wave back, some of them would squeal excitedly and blush. Roman straightened up his back and beamed at the crowd.

The horns from atop the castle's wall blasted loudly as the gate slowly rose to allow them entrance to the courtyard. The sounds of horse hooves thundered on the wet, muddy grounds.

"Hurry up now. I am tired of this wet, soggy air. I want a warm fire and a mug of ale and some dry boots," King Roman said, jumping down from his saddle. Cyrus rolled his eyes as he joined his brother and walked to the open doors of the keep.

They were met at the entry with warm blankets held by young handmaids who smiled and bowed nervously. Roman laughed loudly at the sight of Ivan. "Ah hah, look at you, you old bastard, it's good to see you, please tell me there is a good mead waiting for me?!" The kings embraced in a sincere hug and shook hands tightly, seeing who still had a firmer grip.

"Ahh, let us see you, old friend," Ivan said, laughing. "You're still ugly and fat and only came for my good mead as usual."

Cyrus stood wide-eyed, staring at the grown men poking fun at each other like it was a contest. Ivan's young children stood behind the older kids, watching nervously, while the older boys chuckled. The girls were appalled at the behavior.

Sebastian was quite amused, standing more forward than the rest, apparently enjoying the show of manly, testosterone-filled jabs. Cyrus caught sight of Sebastian first. He stared at him as if seeing a masterpiece for the first time. Sebastian had changed a bit in two years, becoming more attractive than he was before. Cyrus silently admired every feature, from his hair down to his boots.

As the kings stood there chatting, Ivan turned to his children. He began introducing them in order from oldest to youngest.

"My oldest boy, Barron, who will succeed me one of these days, and my lovely daughter, Nadya. Then there are my twins, who you briefly met before, Tomas and Sebastian. Ivan paused to allow the four of them to step forward and bow.

As Ivan introduced the rest of the children, Sebastian looked at Cyrus and smiled. Cyrus had yet to break his gaze; only his mouth had slightly opened. Sebastian tucked his hair behind his ear as he blushed and turned his head away toward King Roman.

"This is my brother, Cyrus, who is surprisingly quiet," Roman said as he jabbed at Cyrus's ribs, snapping him from his daydreams.

Cyrus mumbled, "What? Sorry? Oh, it is nice to meet you all." He gently bowed toward the Drake siblings. "I am very appreciative of your hospitality..."

"Isn't he adorable?" Roman said, laughing heartily. Cyrus glanced at his brother, sensing defeat as he realized this would turn into him getting picked on all evening.

"Come on, let me show you to your room so you can change into something warm and dry before you catch your death standing here freezing, listening to my Father's bad jokes," Sebastian said to Cyrus.

As they made it to the top landing where the bedrooms lined the hall, Sebastian stopped to think about which room he was supposed to give to Cyrus.

"Is it hard living with so many siblings?" Cyrus asked.

"Only if you hang around all day, which I do not for obvious reasons," he said, motioning Cyrus to continue following him.

Sebastian opened the door to a guest quarter and walked in first, then turned to invite Cyrus in behind him.

"So, what have you been up to over the last two years?"

"Mostly hiding," Sebastian said seriously, but Cyrus laughed. Sebastian laughed back, which lightened the mood. "Honestly.

You try being around twelve brothers and sisters all day. I look for a place to go and get some peace and quiet. Some days I walk around town or sit up on a ridge."

"That sounds nice."

"Well, if you would like, you can hang out with me while you are here. I can show you some of my favorite places to hide," Sebastian said, hoping Cyrus would want to come with him. "I will let you change clothes but think about it. It will be a lot of fun." Sebastian hesitated before stepping out of the room, and as he closed the door behind him, his heart began racing, and his face was hot and flushing. He did not know why Cyrus made him feel this way, but he liked it, and he liked him.

"He probably thinks you are a complete moron," Sebastian said to himself as he headed downstairs.

As he rounded the corner to the dining hall, he saw his Father and Roman sitting behind a pitcher of ale. He tried not to be seen.

"Come here, boy. Let me look at you."

Sebastian took a deep breath then walked in proudly with his head up and chest out, confidently striding toward the head of the table.

"He is a handsome lad," Roman said. "Tall and strong, defined body structure, thin but not gangly, an icy gaze in those dark, serious eyes."

"If I didn't know better, I would think you desire my son," Ivan said. Both men laughed loudly.

"Look at him! He is a goddamn angel. I bet the girls are begging for your hand in marriage, aren't they, boy?"

Sebastian did not know what to say, so he stood smiling while checking behind him, hoping that someone would come into the room to save him. There were around twenty families throughout the hall, but no one would step forward to interrupt the kings.

He began wondering if Cyrus was coming back downstairs tonight or if he had retired for the evening. He smelled venison and vegetable stew wafting through the air and realized how hungry he was.

"How long until supper?" he asked. Both kings laughed again. Ivan suggested he sit down.

"Is my brother still in his room?" Roman asked, which made Sebastian jump a little. "He's a bit of a princess when it comes to being clean and presentable."

"Umm, well, I guess so, at least that is where I left him," Sebastian said, trying not to sound too interested. He fidgeted with a spot on the table where the wood splintered a little. Just as servers began carrying food in, a few of his siblings finally arrived, and Cyrus walked in with his sister Sara. She had her arm cuffed around his. He was filled with pure jealousy. He tried to turn his head away and not notice, but he kept glancing in their direction as they sat next to each other.

Sara was barely fourteen She was not his blood sister. Sebastian's mother was out for a walk when she found a baby bundled up in the garden wrapped in blankets. No one ever came back to claim her, so they adopted her. She was growing to be incredibly beautiful. She was the only child in the house with fire-red hair and bright green eyes.

She was flirting with Cyrus. She giggled at almost everything he said, which Sebastian hoped Cyrus would find annoying, but he never showed any signs. Sebastian went back to picking at the table as Tomas sat down next to him, clumsily bumping him as he settled in his seat. Sebastian would not be distracted from his eager need to remove the splinter from the table.

"Training was rough today. Although, I think I am getting good at this. I wish Aspen would stop hitting me, though." Tomas laughed. "What's wrong with you?"

Sebastian stared at Tomas for a good few seconds without looking at anyone else and replied, "Whatever do you mean?" His voice sounded frustrated as he looked away, then let his head move to peer around the room. As his fell on Cyrus talking to Sara, he changed focus and accidentally caught King Roman's attention.

"Hey boy, why don't you fetch me another pitcher?" Roman gestured to Sebastian, waving an empty cup in the air. Sebastian got up and started walking over to another table where the ale sat.

"You don't have to do that," Cyrus said, coming up behind Sebastian, reaching around him so tightly that his hand brushed against Sebastian's arm. He walked the pitcher over, set it down quickly in front of Roman, and walked back over to Sebastian. "If you do it for him once, he will expect it every time."

Sebastian tried to think of what to say back, but he kept seeing his sister staring over at them like she was eagerly waiting for Cyrus to come back. Sebastian smiled a little. "So, I see you and my sister–"

"I thought about what you said earlier, about going on a hike with you. I think it sounds like a lot of fun. What were you saying about your sister?"

"Oh, umm, you two seem like you're hitting it off," Sebastian said, sinking a little. "I mean, she looks like she is enjoying your company." He was trying to find out if Cyrus was interested in his sister without sounding like he was panicking inside.

Cyrus stumbled over his answer, sounding confused. "I guess so. I mean, I don't know, she is nice, I guess. She seems to like to hear about what it was like to be raised by my brothers." He peeped at Sebastian like he was in pain. Sebastian was even more confused, standing there with one eyebrow arched, mouth slightly open.

"She is stunning," Cyrus said finally, choking on his words.

Sebastian laughed uncomfortably and gaped at his sister, hoping for words to come to him, but not a sound escaped him. His jaw dropped open further. Cyrus lightly put his hand on his chin to close his mouth for him. They stared closely at each other for several long seconds before someone yelled at them to sit down and eat.

There was a lot of loud chatter during supper as the Drake siblings were excited to host guests. Everyone wanted to talk to Prince Cyrus, even Sebastian, but he just listened. Cyrus looked flushed from the attention but was enjoying it nonetheless. Sara would lean toward Cyrus every few minutes. She seemed to find reasons to bump her hand against his or reach for the same food on the table, which Sebastian would shake his head about every time.

Tomas leaned in toward Sebastian. "You like him."

Sebastian did not react. He peeked at Tomas with his eyes squinted.

"You keep staring at him, and when sis acts like a desperate brothel girl, you groan noticeably. You're not fooling me, brother."

"You are reading way too far into it. Sara is a little too cute with him. It makes her look easy." Sebastian stabbed a little too hard on a potato and sent it flying across the table.

Tomas just laughed and squeezed Sebastian's leg under the table. "Don't be ashamed about liking a boy; it's alright. I don't care."

Sebastian put his fork down and leaned over to Tomas. "I can't like him. Could you imagine what would happen if he and I were ever together? How can I tell them?" he said, pointing over to the two drunken kings who were engrossed in their conversation.

"So, it's true," Tomas said. Sebastian nodded while picking his fork back up and began eating again.

Sebastian never put any thought into his sexuality. It was just something about Cyrus that made him swoon. All he knew was that Cyrus was the most beautiful man he has ever seen, and right now, Cyrus was interested in Sara.

As the servants cleared the tables, some of the smaller children broke away from the table to play. Sebastian was tired of watching the show that was unfolding before him. He asked his Father if he could see Aspen. Ivan smiled and nodded.

Cyrus walked over to Tomas and tapped him on the shoulder. "Why did Sebastian leave already? Is he alright?"

"I think he's tired. He gets cranky when he gets tired," Tomas said.

"I wanted to ask him something. Do you think he would be upset if I went after him?" Cyrus asked.

Tomas grinned a little. "I think Sebastian's had enough of hearing about Sara. You can ask me about her if you like."

Cyrus looked at Tomas and bit his lip. "I don't want to talk about your sister. She's great, but I think she is taking my politeness the wrong way." He noticed Tomas perk up a bit. "Please don't say anything to anyone, not even your brother, but..." He hesitated and then shook his head. "Never mind good night," he said and walked away quickly.

Sebastian worked hard in the training room that night. Aspen did not have to smack him as much as usual. He conjured fire and sent it freely around the room with his hands as guidance. When he waved in one direction, the fire followed.

"Excellent, young prince. Impressive. Now, the lightning."

Sebastian stiffened up and redirected his focus. He closed his eyes tight and unclenched his fists to let his fingers flow freely. A light cracked between them but quickly vanished. Aspen tightened his grip around the fire poker and pulled it back in position to smack Sebastian.

"No, I can do this." Sebastian held his hands in front of him defensively.

"Then do it already!"

"I am trying."

Aspen struck him across the wrists. "Now!"

Sebastian spread his fingers wide apart. Lightning intertwined between his fingertips. He moved his hands apart slowly as the lightning grew larger between his palms.

Aspen smiled in approval. "Now, make it storm. You can do it, my prince."

Sebastian waved his hands, then threw them with a flick. There was a thunderclap and a flash of lightning as a loud knock came on the door. Sebastian stopped suddenly.

Aspen went to the door where a man was waiting.

"That will be all for tonight, Your Highness. There is something I need to attend to. You did an excellent job. You and your brother are remarkable. Good night."

CHAPTER 7

The Blacksmith's Son

Sebastian went out into the courtyard and sat down by the archery range. He had his chin propped up on his knees when someone sat down beside him. He turned quickly to see Will.

"Rough night?"

Sebastian smiled at him. "I guess you could say that."

"How was the dinner party with the King of Kings?"

Sebastian sighed. "I am supposed to be keeping Prince Cyrus entertained, but he seems to be stuck on Sara. I don't know why it bothers me so much."

Will slumped down and moved closer to him. "Are you jealous?"

Sebastian ogled at him. "Why would I be jealous?"

Will laughed a little, then wrapped his arm around Sebastian. "You're cold. Where is your coat? I swear one day you are going to freeze to death out here."

Sebastian peered at Will, smiling softly, and stared at him, their faces close together. Will reached forward and touched his lips against Sebastian's. Sebastian met his lips and kissed him.

Will ran his fingers across Sebastian's cheek as their kissing became more intense. Will pulled back and smiled. "You know I will always have feelings for you, even if I can never be with you."

"Why can we not be together, Will? You know how good we are for each other," Sebastian said as he thought of Cyrus. His chances with Cyrus were gone, and he always had Will, who would die to be with him.

"Because you are too good for me. Because we are boys, and boys getting married to each other is not allowed. I just know one day I will lose you to some beautiful girl. You are a prince bound for greatness. I love you, Sebastian, but I know where I stand."

"You stand by my side, Will. I do not care what is right or what is allowed. I do not plan to stay in NorthBrekka much longer. I am going to start my path, and I want you to come with me."

"I'm sorry. We shouldn't be doing this. I do not want to hope for something that will never be, Sebastian." Will seemed disappointed. He stroked Sebastian's hand and moved in to kiss him once more. "I know we shouldn't, but I adore the softness of your lips. You are so perfect, my Sebastian."

Sebastian smiled, then kissed Will. He wrapped his arms around Will's back and pulled him close. Will excitedly climbed onto Sebastian's lap, put his hands on his chest, and untied his shirt, revealing Sebastian's chest as Will kissed his neck. Sebastian squeezed Will's hips, pulling him in closer as a sensation washed over him. He wanted Will in his bed.

"I've always wanted you, Sebastian."

"I want you too."

"You can have me any time you want."

"I want you now. Come to bed with me."

"What about Tomas?"

"We do not have to go to my room. Let's go to the stables."

They stood and walked together. Before they went inside, Sebastian pulled Will against him and kissed him again. He tore at Will's shirt, pulling it off, and kissed his neck and shoulder as his hands traveled down his abdomen. Sebastian untied Will's pants and fell to his knees as he gazed into Will's eyes as he asked for permission to finish undressing him. Will smiled and grasped a fistful of Sebastian's hair, then nodded his head. Sebastian grabbed Will's pants and pulled at them. There was a noise from behind the forge.

"Will, come on now! Inside," Mason, Will's Father, shouted. Sebastian fell back, startled, and Will pulled his clothes back on quickly.

"Will, stay with me."

"My Father is calling for me. He is going to come looking if I don't go."

"I can tell him you are helping me. He won't deny you from that."

"Time to go. Goodnight, my prince," Will said, looking lustfully at Sebastian.

"Goodnight, Will." He was panting as Will hurried to his Father, then disappeared.

Sebastian ran up to his room. Tomas was already snoring, so he snuck into his bed and fell fast asleep. It was the first night in a long while that he had slept through until morning.

He woke up with the sun hitting his face. Tomas was already up and gone. He climbed out of bed and dressed, washed his face and neck, then left his room. Sebastian passed where Cyrus stayed and wondered if he had slept alone or if his sister had been in his bed last night.

Only Nadya, Sara, Gentry, and a few younger siblings were there when he entered the dining hall. Some eggs and meat were still on the table, so Sebastian sat down, grabbing a plateful.

"Are you just now waking up?" Nadya asked.

"What time is it?" Sebastian said.

"Late," Sara said while glaring at Sebastian, which had him wondering what he had done this time.

"I was tired, I guess," Sebastian said, then began devouring his food. "Where is everyone?"

"Tomas is training, Barron is with Father..."

"Where is Cyrus?" he said without looking up from his plate. He heard Sara make a noticeably irritated hum noise but ignored it.

"He is waiting for you to get up so you two can go be stupid boys!" Sara said. She got up and stomped out of the hall.

"What did I do now?" Sebastian said.

"She likes him. She was hoping he would spend the day with her, but when she asked him, he said he had plans with you, and that pissed her off." Nadya had a hint of amusement in her voice.

"Well, if he'd rather spend the day with her, I won't stop him. I think he likes her too." He shook his head and grunted while looking down at the table.

Nadya stared at Sebastian, smiling, not saying anything until he looked at her. "He doesn't like her like that. I asked him because she would not stop raving about how handsome and kind he is. He said he thinks she is a nice girl, but she is not his type. However, she is obsessed with him, so I did not tell her what he said, and you can't either." Nadya pointed behind her, indicating that Cyrus was waiting in the garden.

"Not his type? What does that even mean?" Sebastian tried not to look happy, but he laughed a little too hard and finished his breakfast. "Well, I'm off then. Where is he waiting?"

"You two need to behave today. Do not take Cyrus anywhere dangerous. Make sure you come back before supper is set," Nadya warned as Sebastian walked away. He smiled back at her and nodded.

CHAPTER 8

A Ride into The Mountains

Sebastian stepped out into the sunshine and took a deep breath of the fresh, warming air. He noticed Cyrus standing by the pond, staring down at the water.

Sebastian quickly brushed at his hair with his fingers and picked at his teeth before walking over. He snuck up behind Cyrus, studying the way he stood so still and patient. Sebastian admired how Cyrus was so handsome with the sun's glow bouncing off his hair.

"You're not going to push me in the pond, are you?" Cyrus said, turning around with a smile on his face. Sebastian stopped and looked at him, confused, and laughed.

"I thought about it," he said with a note of sarcasm.

"So, where are we heading?" Cyrus asked, biting his lip and brushing his hair back. The sun showed the hint of red in his hair and outlined his body shape through his white tunic. Sebastian tried hard not to stare too long, but he had a hard time not looking up and down Cyrus's body while speaking to him. He did not often like to look at people in the eye, and he certainly preferred admiring Cyrus.

"I want to show you this place I like to go to when I just want some peace. It is where you can see the whole valley beyond the castle. It's quite lovely," Sebastian said and then rolled his eyes, thinking of how idiotic that sounded. Still, he quickly remembered what Nadya had said. "I am told we aren't allowed to go too far today, or else your brother and my Father would have our heads on a spike." This made Cyrus laugh.

They went over to the stables to find their horses. The blacksmith, Mason, and Will were fitting horseshoes. Will caught them walking around, immediately dropped his tools, and walked over to greet them.

"Your Grace, it's a beautiful morning for a ride," Will said, glancing over at his Father to make sure the blacksmith knew he was appropriately addressing the prince. He rolled his eyes and smiled at Sebastian slightly as he pinched his hand softly, wanting Sebastian to grab his hand. Sebastian only quickly pressed back and motioned Will to meet Cyrus.

"I'm Prince Cyrus of Torrdale," Cyrus said, asserting himself between Sebastian and Will.

Will quickly bowed, "Your Grace, of course, what an honor."

Sebastian laughed, "Well, isn't this awkward. You can stop pretending to be so formal any day now, Will."

Cyrus and Will stood close to Sebastian as they walked inside the stable and away from Mason. Sebastian was blushing inside from the attention.

"What trouble are you getting into today?" Will shoved Sebastian.

"We are just going for a ride," Sebastian said, shoving him back a little harder. Will quickly jumped back and grabbed at Sebastian's forearm, interlocking it in his own.

"We are saving the troublemaking for a day that the kings aren't drinking and arguing about who has more money, or who has a bigger militia, or who has a prettier wife," Cyrus said, trying to keep himself in the conversation.

Sebastian could not stop thinking about last night and how he almost made love to Will, and how all he could think about was Cyrus. This was not the first time Sebastian and Will had kissed, but it was the first time they become intimate. He cared a lot for Will, but he was unsure if it was his thoughts of Cyrus that had made him desperate for more.

Will held tightly onto Sebastian as the three of them chatted. Will made it evident that Sebastian was his. Cyrus stepped between them, gesturing to their horses. He mentioned the limited daylight they had for adventuring.

Cyrus and Sebastian mounted their horses and said their goodbyes. As Sebastian started to lead away, Will reached out and took Sebastian's hand into his. He leaned in to kiss the prince's hand and whispered, "Be safe, Your Highness, my beautiful prince," and stepped aside to let the men lead their horses to the trail.

As they took the road away from the castle, Cyrus grinned at Sebastian, intentionally bumped his leg, and asked, "What is the story with you and Will? It seems like you two are close."

"We kind of grew up together. My Father took in Will and his sister, Anna, for a few years. Will's Father was drafted to fight for your Father back during the Battle of Fire Mountain. After that, we just remained friends, kind of brothers."

"Brothers? I think he likes you a lot more than brothers should like each other," Cyrus said, laughing. Sebastian smiled and told Cyrus about the first time he and Will kissed and how they became close over the years. Then he told Cyrus that Will said he loved him, which made Cyrus frown with disappointment. Sebastian was unsure what that meant, so he quickly changed the subject.

"So, what do you think of my sister? Be honest."

"She is nice, but I think she is a bit..." Cyrus started saying, but Sebastian stepped in.

"Overwhelming, annoying, snobby... I am only joking. You two seem to like each other. I don't mind if you do, so you are aware." Sebastian nervously laughed but never made eye contact with Cyrus while saying that.

"Actually, you are right, she is a bit uptight. But she is also charming. She is just the kind of girl my brother would beg for me to marry," Cyrus replied, which shot a pang of emotions through Sebastian.

"Oh! Well, I'm sure she will be thrilled about that."

Cyrus looked over at Sebastian with a humorous confusion on his face. "Why would she want me to think she was annoying?"

Sebastian's head shot over in Cyrus's direction, and he replied, "I thought you were interested in being with her. I mean, you did just say she is lovely and would be a good match for you."

Cyrus changed to subject again but couldn't help stare at Sebastian in silence like they did when they were younger. Sebastian felt a breeze pass through his hair. Cyrus bit his lip and blushed.

They talked about the things they like doing in their time for a good long while. When Cyrus spoke about Torrdale, Sebastian watched him as if he were enchanted by him.

"Why do you stare at me like that?" Cyrus asked.

"I'm not staring," Sebastian said as he awoke from his daydream.

Cyrus smiled and let out a quiet laugh. "I don't mind. I am simply wondering what you're thinking about."

"It's nothing. Curiosity is all."

They rode off into the woods that lined the western border of NorthBrekka. Cyrus kept opening and closing his mouth like he wanted to say something witty. Sebastian started laughing.

"What is so funny?" Cyrus asked.

"You. Come on; I think we shall save the overlook for tomorrow. I thought of a better place to go," Sebastian said, taking the lead to a narrow, winding road that led up into the mountains.

"Where are you taking me?" Cyrus asked after they climbed up and over a smaller mountain.

"You will see, but you cannot tell anyone we were here, or else I will be in so much trouble. My Father thinks it is too dangerous."

Cyrus looked at Sebastian hesitantly but smiled. "I am excited to be a part of some of the mischief I heard about."

They rode through a small canyon and descended into what used to be a mining town many years ago.

"Here we are!" Sebastian said, smiling.

"What is here?" Cyrus said, looking amazed at the little town that was booming with business.

"This is Shadowmire- Sebastian started, but Cyrus interrupted.

"Shadowmire? I heard my men speaking of it, saying they go there to gamble, and it has the best brothels in Erras," Cyrus said.

"Yes, loose women are everywhere," Sebastian said with sadness at Cyrus's excitement over the brothels.

They rode into town side by side. Soldiers stepped aside and bowed as the princes passed. Sebastian stopped in front of a shabby pub. Cyrus gave him a look as they both hopped down from their horses.

"Are you afraid?"

"Definitely not!" Cyrus said, pushing Sebastian.

They walked inside to booming, shouting, and drinking soldiers playing cards. Women were running about half-clothed as soldiers grabbed at them.

Sebastian ordered a couple of pints, marched over to a card table, and dropped coins on the table, demanding a seat. Cyrus stood behind him, watching the game intensely.

"Does your girlfriend want to play too, Your Majesty?" a mean-looking man with a garbled voice said to Sebastian.

Sebastian raised an eyebrow in amusement, then turned to Cyrus. Cyrus whispered that he did not know this game as he tried not to embarrass himself.

"First of all, you don't speak of Prince Cyrus like that. Second, he can play if he wishes. He does not need your permission to sit. Last, I paid my bid, now shut your mouth and deal the damn cards," Sebastian said as he leaned in close to the man's face.

The man looked at Sebastian with certainty that he could crush Sebastian's bones with one strike. He glanced up at Cyrus, then gestured at the empty chair for Sebastian to sit.

Sebastian motioned for Cyrus to kneel next to him. "The idea of this game is to hold the most king cards by the end of the round.

Each player gets five cards to start. When it is your turn, you try to trick your opponents by throwing away cards, so they bet more coins. The more you throw away, the worst of a hand they will think you have. You can also dismiss your hand and wait until the next round, or you can lie and keep bad cards, pretending to have a lot of kings so they will dismiss. But you risk losing a lot of money. When you throw one away, you draw another."

Sebastian had one king in hand and four numbered cards. When it was his turn, he threw away two number cards and drew two new cards. One was a king; one was a picture card with a bird on it.

"What is that card?" Cyrus asked.

Sebastian shook his head and whispered, "I will explain after the hand." He dropped two more coins on the table. Another man dropped two coins, one dismissed. The dealer dropped his two coins, then stared at Sebastian intimidatingly and winked at Cyrus.

"She is pretty, Your Majesty."

"Insult him one more time. I dare you," Sebastian said.

"Now you know Grimmel, you would not dare strike the king's son. Shut your mouth and leave the Torrdale prince alone," A woman carrying beer said, approaching the table. She handed the pints to Sebastian and Cyrus, then kissed Grimmel on his cheek as he smiled and said, "Yes, dear."

Sebastian discarded another two cards and drew another. He pretended not to get anything good as he dropped one coin. The man across from him dropped five coins and smiled. Grimmel dropped five. Sebastian groaned and shot four more.

"Let me see them, gentlemen," Grimmel said.

The man across Sebastian revealed three kings. Grimmel laughed slowly and showed four kings. Sebastian rubbed his neck, then slowly started to turn his hand over, but he stood and slammed his hand down. It was two kings and the bird card. He laughed as Grimmel looked at him, unbelieving.

"The bird card means you automatically win the hand no matter what. There is only one in the whole deck," Sebastian explained. "It also means that the opponents at the table pay double what they bet. Now, pay up!"

"Here is your damn coin, now can I punch you in the face?" Grimmel said.

Sebastian laughed and looked at Cyrus. "Would you like to try?"

Cyrus shook his head. "We should get going."

Sebastian nodded in agreement. Grimmel waved them off. They walked out of the pub and were met with two pretty, young girls.

"Hello, my handsome prince. Fancy a go for you and your friend?" she said, pointing across the street at the brothel.

"You ask me this every time, and the answer is always the same, Kalina," Sebastian said.

"What about your gorgeous friend here?" she said, stroking Cyrus's cheek. "I would have fun with you."

Without even noticing, Sebastian grasped Cyrus's forearm tightly. Kalina and the other girl saw. "Oh, I see. You still fancy the boys, eh, don't ya, Sebastian? That is because you've never been with a woman. You do not know better. We could teach you. Come on now. Let me show you what I got between my legs. I promise you will love it."

Sebastian released Cyrus's arm, feeling the blood rush into his cheeks. "You may go with her if you want," he said with his voice trembling.

"Now, you embarrassed him, Kalina." the other girl said.

"No, thank you, but no," Cyrus stammered quickly.

The girls walked away laughing, whispering how Cyrus and Sebastian were lovers, making Sebastian even more embarrassed. "We should head back to NorthBrekka before it gets late."

On the road back, Cyrus talked about the card game and the tavern. "I thought that man was going to hit you."

"We got into a fight last year," Sebastian mentioned. "It was the day before my Sixteenth birthday, and I was drunk. I accidentally knocked his beer out of his hand, and he dropped his cards. He had the bird card, and the coin on the table was immense. He dragged me outside and punched me hard. Broke my nose. My Father went berserk. That is why I am not allowed to be here. That and I always end up in a quarrel or come home sloshed and upset Barron."

"You are not right in the head, are you?"

Sebastian looked at Cyrus quickly. "I don't like when people say that."

"I am sorry. I did not mean anything bad. You are just different than anyone I know."

"Everyone prides Tomas for his intelligence and poise. Me on the other hand, people think I am dense or something. I am starting to think they are right."

"Sebastian, I did not mean to offend you. I don't think you are dense. I mean, you are crazy, but in a good way. I like the way you are."

Sebastian grinned. "Thanks. It is nice to be complimented rather than being insulted or yelled at. You will start to notice that no one likes me much. That is why I run off so often. I don't fit in."

"Well, I like you. You are fascinating."

They got back to the stables early. Will was finishing up work for the day. "You can head inside," Sebastian told Cyrus. "I am going to speak to Will for a moment."

Cyrus stared at Will but spoke to Sebastian. "I'll see you at dinner."

Sebastian nodded and smiled. Cyrus started back to the castle as Will came over and grasped Sebastian's hand. This time, Sebastian held his too. Cyrus took a deep breath as his face turned red. He hurried inside the castle.

"How was your day in Shadowmire?" Will asked.

Sebastian swung around in surprise, then laughed. "Quiet! No one can know. How did you know?"

"You have beer on your breath," Will said.

"Are you sure about that?" Sebastian said playfully.

Will grabbed his face and kissed him. "Your lips taste like beer as well."

Sebastian laughed a little. "You always know."

"That is because I love you."

"Will-"

Will put his hand over Sebastian's mouth. "Shhh. Do not ruin my fantasies by rejecting me. I cannot stop thinking about last night."

Cyrus was watching from the window. He watched them standing inches apart, still holding hands, and sharing the kiss. His heart was broken and was hot with jealousy. As Sebastian walked away from Will toward the castle, he hurried to his room and met Nadya.

"Did you have fun?" she asked.

"A lot of fun. Your brother is crazy. I really like being around him."

"I think he likes you as well. He was really excited to spend the day with you. He was worried you wanted to be with Sara," Nadya said, then she stopped suddenly as if she had said too much.

"Why would he worry about Sara when he's with Will?" Cyrus said with a little too much resentment.

"Will?" Nadya said. "Let me explain the relationship between the two of them. Will is madly in love with Sebastian. Sebastian, I think he cares for him, but Sebastian has wandering thoughts. He enjoys kissing him; that is all. I've also seen Sebastian with his tongue down a few girls' throats around here. He is a pretty boy, and everyone wants to kiss him. Why does this bother you?"

"It doesn't!" Cyrus said defensively.

"You like my brother. Everyone does," Nadya said.

"He is under the impression that no one likes him."

"He is wrong. Sebastian feels inadequate, so he takes it out on himself. Hopefully, that will change soon. See you at dinner."

CHAPTER 9

The First Time

Later that evening, they sat down to eat. Sebastian and Tomas sat close and murmured to each other. Cyrus was chatting away with Viktor and Gentry. Sebastian glanced at Cyrus and realized Cyrus had been watching him. Both smiled before returning to their conversations.

Tomas and Sebastian were lying in the same bed that night. Tomas held his brother tightly and stroked his hair.

"You should come with us to the overlook tomorrow," Sebastian said.

"I would like to, but Father asked me to help him. Besides, you want to spend time alone with Cyrus, don't you?"

"I think I messed up," Sebastian said. "I was so embarrassed because those women in Shadowmire were teasing me again in front of him. When we got back, I stayed behind with Will. I mean, he does not like me like that anyway. He was drooling over the brothel girls. And Sara."

Tomas started laughing then stopped suddenly. "Shadowmire! Sebastian, seriously?"

Laughing, Sebastian climbed on top of Tomas playfully and put his hands over his mouth. "Don't shout it out!"

Tomas flipped him over onto the bed. "Cyrus likes you a lot. I see how he stares at you."

"You do not see anything. Besides, there could never be anything of it. He is a prince, and so am I. It would never work."

"Why? Or is it Will you are going to marry?"

"Will? Why would I marry Will?"

"Oh, come off it, brother. You damn near made love to him last night. You want him, but now maybe you love Cyrus. You poor thing."

"Shut up, Tomas. How do you know about Will and me?"

"Because Will tells me everything."

"Well at least I did not choose a woman who is already married."

"Just because Fiona is married to Barron does not mean she loves him. She wants to be with me. At least, that is what she tells me when we make love nearly every day when Barron is off being an annoying ass."

"Tomas, are you mad? You are going to get caught."

"What? She loves me, and I love her. We are going to run off together once I complete my training."

"Tomas, I had no idea you planned to leave."

"You can come with us-you, Will, Cyrus, whoever you want. We can start our own lives out there. Start a farm, live happily, just as you always wished."

Sebastian felt a jolt of excitement. They talked for a long while, then fell asleep. The following day, Sebastian was awake early as usual. He pounced on Tomas playfully to wake him. Tomas grumbled and kicked him, causing him to fall on the floor. They both laughed, then got up to get dressed.

"Behave today, please. No Shadowmire. Promise me," Tomas said.

"We are only going up the mountain, I swear it."

They went down to breakfast. Cyrus was already there talking to his brother and King Ivan. The twins walked in together, and Roman waved them over.

"I like seeing them together! Such pretty boys you have here," Roman said to Ivan.

Sebastian sat next to Cyrus. "Did you sleep well?"

"Yes, you?" Cyrus said.

"As well as I could, I guess. Are you ready to go up the mountain today?"

"I am! I want to see this view you talk about."

"I bet Sebastian wants to see *the view* as well," Viktor said under his breath.

Sebastian shot him a look that meant he would hurt him if he did not shut his mouth. He grabbed a biscuit, then gave Tomas a playful hug. Cyrus followed him out.

"We should get going. It takes a while to get up there."

They walked to the stables. Cyrus looked for Will but could not find him, yet he was happy about that. They hopped on their horses and began ascending the pass. Sebastian started prying again into Cyrus's interest in Sara.

"So, my sister was mad at me because you were not spending time with her. If you want to, I won't be upset. After supper, she attached herself to you again, and it seemed like you were having fun." Sebastian stared straight ahead while shifting in his saddle.

"Are you going on about this again? I think you understand the way I converse with her the wrong way," Cyrus said. "Tell me about you and Will. Be honest. He obviously likes you."

"There is nothing to tell there. I feel bad because the more time I spend with Will, the more affectionate he becomes. I am afraid to hurt his feelings, although I did almost make love to him."

"Is it true what the girls from the brothel said?" Cyrus asked.

The blood rushed to Sebastian's cheeks. "I am not sure about anything right now."

After a long slow walk up the mountainside, they arrived at the overlook. They dismounted their horses and let them graze while they sat down on the cliffside.

"I was trying to be nice, but I think she took my kindness the wrong way. After you left supper, she flung herself at me and would not let go. It was kind of embarrassing in a way as I don't like gi-" He stopped and did not finish what he was going to say, looking embarrassed. "Wow, you're right. It is lovely up here. Incredibly beautiful!"

"Don't change the subject now!" Sebastian said, smiling. "I think she is crazy about you, though. You will have to tell her before she tells my Father that she is interested, and the two of you end up engaged before you leave to go home."

"Oh, wow," Cyrus said, sounding worried. "I just don't see it working out between us. She isn't exactly my type."

Sebastian laughed heavily. "What were you about to say before you blurted out that ridiculous statement about the view? You do not like what? Girls?" he said as Cyrus blushed very noticeably.

Cyrus was looking out over the valley. He was breathing harder than usual and kept adjusting his jacket collar.

"I don't know how to tell her. She will want an explanation, and I cannot just blurt out things like that. My brother would kill me if he found out. How do you tell anyone something like that? Especially when I am constantly presented with suitable women, but they are not interesting to me," Cyrus said.

"I know how you feel," Sebastian said. Cyrus looked over at him, and Sebastian followed up. "My Father always tells me I should marry this one girl who is a lady of a well-off house in a nearby town. I do not love her. I am not interested. The good thing is, I do not think she is interested in me either."

"I'm sure she is, though. Any woman would be lucky to be with you. You are beautiful, magnificent. Don't be angry. I had to say it to your face at least once before you run off and marry some pretty girl, and I won't see you much after." Cyrus went on, sounding disappointed.

Sebastian wondered if Cyrus knew that he was fascinated by him. He tried to interject, but Cyrus interrupted, "I'm sorry. I do not mean to make you feel embarrassed. This got awkward fast. I hope that we can still be friends."

Sebastian started laughing. Cyrus's head cocked to the side. "What is so funny?" he asked, but Sebastian kept laughing. "Are you making fun of me?"

"Seriously? Do you think I want to get married and settle down and start a family? Me?" he poked himself in the chest. "Have you met me?" Sebastian said.

He calmed down, then moved closer to Cyrus. He put his hand on Cyrus's thigh and leaned over to get even closer. "I have a little secret too." Cyrus turned to face Sebastian, looking hopeful but unsure.

"Sebastian, I need to tell you something. I really li-" Cyrus started saying until Sebastian's lips silenced his. He flushed with delight as Cyrus kissed him back. They kissed passionately for only a moment before Sebastian pulled away.

"I'm sorry," he said, putting his hand over his mouth. "I've wanted to do that since last night. When I kissed Will, I was thinking about how I wanted it to be you." Sebastian was immensely proud of himself. Cyrus was flushed with excitement but seemed to be trying hard to contain it.

They stared at each other in silence and sat remarkably close, Cyrus's lips were inches from his and their fingers interlocked on the ground. Cyrus brushed Sebastian's cheek lightly, then tucked his long hair behind his ear to keep the breeze from waving it across his face. Sebastian felt the tingle of Cyrus's hot breath against his lips, which made him want to kiss him again, but instead, he froze.

He liked when Cyrus touched his face. He started to run his free hand across Cyrus's thigh. Cyrus adjusted his position to get his body closer to Sebastian. His hand ran across Sebastian's chest. He put his arm around Sebastian's waist and pulled him against his body. Sebastian squeezed his thigh and leaned in to kiss him again.

Sebastian pushed Cyrus down and straddled him. He began kissing his neck while Cyrus was trying to undress him. Sebastian ran his hands across Cyrus's body, then untied his pants. He removed his pants while he kissed his stomach gently. Cyrus ran his fingers through Sebastian's hair, enjoying how good it felt as Sebastian kissed his body.

"I struggle to describe how much I want you. Since the moment I laid my eyes on you, I knew you were the one for me," Cyrus whispered.

"I have been hiding the way I feel, but I cannot hold back. I do not know what it is about you, Cyrus, but I've lost all control over my actions being with you. You enchant me."

"Sebastian, I want you to lay with me. Today and every day forward. Tell me that you are mine!"

"I am yours, and you are mine, from this day until the end of our days. We will find a way to be together, no matter what I must do."

"Make love to me."

Sebastian started undressing. He stared into Cyrus's eyes, his heartbeat faster, and his stomach fluttered. He kissed him gently, adoring his pouty lips. When Cyrus kissed him back, Sebastian's body burned with lust. Cyrus kissed his neck and dug his nails into Sebastian's back as Sebastian was ready to take his body. Cyrus pushed him away.

"I have never been with anyone before."

"Neither have I. I want you to be my first."

"I want you to be the only person I ever lie with, Sebastian. I've never felt like this before."

"Are you sure you are ready? This is happening so fast."

"Yes. I do not care about courting and all that nonsense of waiting. I know what I want, and what I want is you."

Sebastian kissed Cyrus and bit his neck. Cyrus gasped when Sebastian took him. He closed his eyes and moaned softly to every thrust. Sebastian was in ecstasy. He flushed with pleasure and felt something he had never experienced. He was in love with Prince Cyrus.

They lay on the mountainside, undressed. Cyrus had his head on Sebastian's chest and was rushing his hair with his fingertips as they stared into each other's eyes.

"That was incredible," Cyrus said. "I dreamed that we were married and living far away from here. I thought it was a foolish dream to have, but now, it is all I hope for."

"Then we shall. Marry me, Cyrus."

"How can we? What is going to happen when your Father forces you to marry some girl?"

"I won't do it. If he tries, promise me you will take my hand and run with me."

"I will. I swear I am by your side no matter what."

"We should get going. I will not let you endure the pleasure of hearing my Father shout at me for being late."

CHAPTER 10

The Ball

They rode fast straight into the stables, jumped off their horses, and hurried into the servant entrance on the kitchen's side connected to the dining hall. Roman and Ivan were sitting with their ale. Sebastian's stepmother was seated close by, sipping her wine, and a few children were already there.

"Come here, boy!" Roman slurred. "My dear sweet brother, get your ass over here and sit down. You too, pretty boy." He motioned. "What did the two of you do all day?" Cyrus's face turned red, and his eyes grew wide. "What? Is it a secret?" Roman laughed and waved. "Stop standing there looking like you have done something stupid. Sit down and drink something before you run off to clean up before the ball."

Sebastian and Cyrus exchanged looks and sat down almost in unison. Sebastian reached for a drink and brushed his hand against Cyrus's. He grinned and pulled back. Roman was watching them closely and quietly. They shifted their seats away from each other, so they were not drawing suspicion anymore.

The tension choked the air out of the room. The rest of the Drake family had started filing into the dining hall. Some were happily finding their favorite seats at the table. They began reaching for food served, while others looked confused about why Sebastian and Cyrus were seated with the kings.

Barron was the quickest to react. His eyes shot wide open then he walked toward them. Sebastian sat up a little straighter and flicked his hair back intentionally to irritate his older brother.

"Father, what is going on right here?" Barron said, pointing lazily at Sebastian, who was acting intentionally pompous, now partially sticking his nose up. He acted like Barron would if he were sitting with the kings. Cyrus laughed a little.

"I asked them to come to sit," Roman said with a firm tone, staring Barron in the eyes.

Barron glanced over at his Father, wanting to argue, but knew it would make for a tense situation if he did talk back. Instead, he glanced at Sebastian, clasped his hand too tightly on his shoulder, and squeezed, making Sebastian scowl. "I think you should join your brothers and sisters and let the men speak," Barron said politely to Sebastian as he bent down. "What I mean to say is, get your ass up and sit with the rest of the children, or else."

"Or else what?" Sebastian pushed Barron's hand off his shoulder and stood to meet him face to face. This clearly surprised Barron, and he stumbled back a step. King Ivan stood up and walked around the table.

He grabbed both his sons by the upper arms, yanked them close to him, and spat out, "You both better behave tonight, or you will be locked away in the bell tower, together, alone in the dark. Do you understand me?"

Both boys answered, "Yes, Father." He waved for Barron to sit down next to Sebastian at the table. Barron smiled at Sebastian sarcastically. Sebastian stood there for an extra moment and looked at Cyrus in an annoyed fashion. Cyrus grabbed Sebastian by the forearm and pulled him down into his seat, looking at him earnestly, signaling with his eyes that Roman was watching him closely.

"I hope the meeting went well. I would like to know if there was a solution to all the problems. If there is anything you would like to ask me about it, I can share some of my ideas..." Barron was rambling on, trying to sound intelligent.

Still, Roman stopped staring at Sebastian and looked over to Barron to say, "What would you know about our problems?"

"Well," Barron said hesitantly. "I- I know that there is a long history of violence between our nations. The costs of war are completely detrimental to our families, and I, umm, I also know, umm..."

Sebastian was shocked that his brother, who was always so articulate, stumbled through an explanation. He looked up at his Father, who looked mortified by his oldest son's lack of knowledge. Roman waved off Barron to stop him from saying any more, and Sebastian could see the sweat roll down Barron's face. Sebastian saw Roman lean over to Ivan and quietly speak into his ear, something he could not make out.

Barron sat there, mumbling to himself. Sebastian could make out only a little of what he was saying, "That was stupid, why did I say that?" which made Sebastian smile.

"You should have paid attention better during lessons, and maybe you would know what the hell you are talking about." he said quietly to Barron. This made Barron's face fill with blood as the anger raged from within.

"Shut your damn mouth," he managed to say with gritted teeth.

"You two better go bathe and dress. The ball will start soon," King Ivan said, directing Sebastian and Cyrus to leave.

They both got up quickly as almost everyone else enjoyed their meals in their best clothing, even all the guests. Some of the daughters waved at Sebastian as he passed by. He nervously waved back.

They ran up the stairs to get away from everyone. "You can clean up there," Sebastian said, pointing toward a bath. "I will go to the one down the hall."

Cyrus stroked Sebastian's hair as he reached up and kissed him. Sebastian, for the first time in a long time, was happy.

Sebastian bathed and dressed in his most elegant dress coat. Sebastian kept brushing his hair differently, trying to think of how Cyrus would like it more.

They both stepped into the corridor, almost in unison. Sebastian walked up to Cyrus, slowly looking him up and down. Cyrus reached out to straighten up Sebastian's shirt buttons. "You look amazing. The ladies are going to fall in love with you at first sight."

Sebastian stopped him from fussing with his shirt. "I didn't dress up for anyone, but-"

"Would the two of you hurry up? Everyone is waiting." Nadya marched toward them. "Sebastian, your shirt is all crooked." She began unbuttoning it, revealing Sebastian's chest. Cyrus could not help but stare, admiring his body. Nadya laughed at how quiet they both had become.

"Are you ready, brother?" she asked.

"For what?" Sebastian answered while staring at Cyrus, who looked desperately sad all of a sudden.

"You and Tomas are being presented tonight. Be on your best behavior."

They walked downstairs together. Tomas awaited in the hall outside the ballroom dressed in a beautiful blue coat with silver embroidery glistening in the firelight. Nadya grabbed Cyrus by the arm, led him into the ballroom, and told the twins to wait until they were announced to enter.

When the announcement started, Tomas straightened up his jacket. Sebastian stared at the floor and sighed.

"Lords and Ladies of the lands, for your lovely daughters, I present you with the handsome Drake twins, Prince Tomas and Prince Sebastian!"

The doors opened.

"Smile. Everyone likes a smile," Tomas said.

Sebastian smiled evilly, until he saw everyone looking at them. They began walking in side by side, slowly as they had been told to so that everyone could get a good look at them. Ladies gasped in delight as they passed. The mothers commented on how handsome they were, which made Sebastian snort out laughter.

They approached the front tables where Sebastian's siblings sat. Cyrus stared at him, looking as if he wanted to lunge into his arms and express his desire for him. Sebastian almost hoped for it. They approached their seats in the front then turned to face the crowd before sitting.

"What is happening, Tomas?"

"It is the opening of the ball. Father said that he wants to show us off. Whatever that means."

King Ivan stood before the crowd. "Ladies and gentlemen of the north, for too long, we searched for answers. A prophecy said that the old gods' power would return to free the people from war and suffering. This power would come in the form of a new generation of gods, and these gods would represent the eternal balance. This is a time for celebration. Let me introduce the future of Erras." He turned and stepped away to present the twins. "My perfect sons, show the people who you are."

Sebastian and Tomas looked at each other, worried, but stood and faced the crowd of curious onlookers. Sebastian leaned to whisper in Tomas's ear.

"Tomas, I don't think we should do this. Aspen said it was dangerous for people to see what we could do."

"Father would never let anyone hurt us."

"My sons, show the people what you are."

Tomas stepped forward first. He touched his index fingers to his thumbs and pointed one hand up and the other down. A wisp of smoke formed from his fingers as he pulled water from the glasses on the table before him. Tomas formed the water into a ball, shot it into the air, then spread it around. He closed his eyes, and when he opened them, his eyes were bright blue. Tomas exhaled a stream of cold air, then repositioned his hands. The water turned to ice as he turned the water droplets into icicles.

Sebastian wore a slight grin. Tomas turned and looked at his twin. Sebastian stepped forward, pushed his fists out, and let flames escape his hands. Tomas stepped back. Sebastian swirled his arms around, causing the fire to expand around the room, melting the ice. He dropped his hands. The crowd stared at him, whispered to each other, and looked at Ivan.

Sebastian stretched his hands wide open, then closed his eyes. He threw his arms apart fast, creating a forceful lightning bolt that cracked all around. He opened his eyes and felt them burn for a moment. He remembered this sensation from when he was fifteen and fought the storm at Stormfire Lake. Then his Father said that his eyes had turned red.

Barron observed from his table. Nadya, Viktor, and Gentry all had their mouths dropped open in awe. Barron glowered at the twins. His upper lip twitched into a disapproving expression as the lightning surrounded Sebastian, creating blinding armor around him and Tomas.

Cyrus put his hands over his mouth. "Beautiful." he gasped. Sebastian stopped; the lightning disappeared. The ballroom was silent. Everyone started whispering as Tomas stood next to Sebastian. He could hear them muttering.

"The prophecy lives."

"One is good, and the other is evil."

"We can see who is the evil one with that violence in his power."

Cyrus stood up. "Stop that now. He is not evil. How dare you speak of your prince that way."

Ivan stepped toward the twins. Sebastian raised his hand, then clenched his fist. Every candle and fire in the room extinguished, and the room went dark. Sebastian stomped off the stage and bolted from the ballroom. He looked back to see Cyrus running after him.

Cyrus caught up to him outside. Sebastian stood there, trying to catch his breath. Cyrus rubbed his shoulder and brushed his hair back. "Are you alright? Can I do anything?"

Sebastian stood and faced Cyrus. "I am in love with you," He babbled out, which surprised him but also made him incredibly happy. Sebastian leaned up against the wall, feeling too embarrassed. He could not look at Cyrus.

"I love you too."

Sebastian straightened up his back and stood before Cyrus. He put his hand on his shoulder and spoke as he rubbed his neck. "I know it was too soon. I keep having these feelings that I don't understand, and when we had sex, it was like my whole world lit up."

Sebastian looked at Cyrus with his eyes wide open. Cyrus smiled and took Sebastian's hand and wrapped it around his back then lightly kissed him. "I was so amazed by you in there. It is incredible what you can do. I was so proud that I thought about yelling out to the whole room that you are mine. That way, no one would try to steal you from me."

"Runaway with me."

"Why would you want to leave?"

"Because bad things are going to happen to me if I stay."

"Where would we go?"

"Anywhere we could be together. I do not care. I only want you."

"The two of you better come back. Father is about to lose his mind. He has everyone calm. They apologized for calling you evil, but you have to come in and dance now, or Nadya said she would drag you both in by your hair."

Tomas's presence made them both jump. Tomas turned back to say, "Your secret is safe with me."

"We better go in and dance with someone. You do not want my sister to come out here. He is serious. She will drag us in there."

"Since we cannot dance together, will you meet me back out here after the ball ends? I want to speak with you before going to bed," Cyrus asked. Sebastian smiled and nodded excitedly.

They approached the entry to the ballroom and stood there looking in. The music played, and people danced. His Father and King Roman stood in the front looking cross.

"I will go in first. You come in after a minute, so it doesn't look obvious," Cyrus said, then he walked in.

Sebastian spied as Cyrus approached Ivan and Roman. They began questioning him. Roman patted his brother hard on the back. He decided it was time to show himself.

As he walked across the floor, people stopped dancing to stare at him, and others started whispering as he passed by. His eyes were focused directly on his Father, who was watching him approach. He stood next to Ivan, and neither of them spoke for several minutes.

"Father I..."

"Do not apologize. You did what you were told. You need to be careful, my son. I forced you to do this, and I am sorry. I did not realize what it meant. I made a mistake." Ivan started coughing badly. When he pulled his hand away, there was blood on his lip and chin. "Go on. Go and dance, enjoy yourself."

"Father, you are bleeding."

"Don't worry about me. Go on now."

Sebastian stepped away. He walked around the ballroom, seeing some watching him while the young ladies looked fixated as he passed by them. Before he could look away, he was surrounded by giggling girls.

"Will you dance with me, Prince Sebastian?"

"No, me! Dance with me."

They were blushing and giggling again. "Pick me. I promise I would be your best choice!"

Sebastian was overwhelmed. A hand reached out and touched his shoulder. "Dance with me."

The girls all stopped giggling. Sebastian turned to see Nadya. Sebastian smiled and took her hand, and they danced.

"Thank you."

"What? You wouldn't make up your mind."

"I would've chosen one once they stopped giggling."

"No, you would not. You would have run off as usual. You are too embarrassed to ask a girl to dance."

"I would have picked someone."

"What about Cyrus? Just announce it in front of everyone. What will anyone do?" Nadya said.

"Are you joking? What are you talking about anyway?"

"You're in love with him. He loves you. End of story," she said.

Sebastian stared at his sister, panicked. "How would you know any of that?"

"I can feel it," she said simply. The music stopped, and everyone turned to notice Ivan standing before them.

"Thank you all for a lovely evening. Tomorrow, we will continue to discuss the treaty. For now, goodnight." He turned and left.

"He isn't feeling well," Nadya said, then kissed Sebastian on the cheek and left. The room started emptying as people left to go to bed. Sebastian looked around the room and caught a glimpse of

Cyrus, staring at him before slipping out the side door. Sebastian followed.

Sebastian darted outside and looked around for Cyrus. For a moment, he was worried Cyrus had decided not to join him. He started walking around the courtyard and stared at the ground as he kicked at the rocks. He turned just in time for Cyrus to catch him and pull him close.

Cyrus smiled at Sebastian and pulled him in for a kiss, only this time it was much more passionate.

"Someone is going to see us," Sebastian said as he pulled back, but Cyrus held tightly onto him, pulled Sebastian's body against his and said, "I do not care anymore," very romantically. Sebastian smiled and took Cyrus by the hand and led him across the courtyard.

They went into the stables. Sebastian grabbed Cyrus and pushed him down to the fresh hay laid on the ground. He slowly climbed on top of Cyrus, and they shared a long, deep kiss. Sebastian started kissing Cyrus on the neck and working down his chest. Barron burst in, yelling. "You are an abomination, brother. You are evil, and now I see you with him. I will tell Father and King Roman about what I witnessed tonight!" He turned and walked fast toward the castle. Sebastian leaped up and chased after his brother.

He caught Barron right around the neck, pulled him to the ground with a swift move, and pinned him down. "You aren't going to say a damn word, you gutless bastard." Sebastian felt a mix of anger and desperation as Barron stared at him.

"Are you afraid that once everyone finds out that you are with a boy, that Father will think his precious, favorite child is nothing but a disgrace? He will disown you, and you will be nothing, a nobody, begging in the streets because Father will throw your ass to the dogs," Barron said, almost prideful, knowing how angry he was making his brother.

Sebastian tightened his grip on Barron's shoulders and lifted him just to shove him down hard against the cold ground. "Shut up! You can say whatever you want about me, but you will not ruin Cyrus's life because of your hatred for me. Do you have any idea what will happen to him if King Roman were to hear of this?"

Barron just laughed at the idea of it all. "What makes you think I care? If he is stupid enough to want you, he deserves to be wallowing in the mud with you."

Cyrus sprinted over to try and break up the argument, but Sebastian yelled at him to go inside and go straight to his room so it did not look like he was outside. But Cyrus would not leave Sebastian.

"I'm not going anywhere. I love you, Sebastian. We are in this together. Even if he is going to rat us out like the coward that he is."

Barron shoved Sebastian back, and he stood up fast and kicked Sebastian in the chest to knock him flat to the ground. "What did you call me?" Barron said, getting in Cyrus's face. He pushed Cyrus back. Sebastian jumped up, grabbed Barron from behind, and slammed him against the wall. Barron pushed back, then turned to face Sebastian and was met with a hard punch to his face. He held his nose in his hand and looked up at his brother, who was still clenching his fist, ready to throw another punch.

"I'm going to kill you. This is after I have your tongue removed and burn your pretty face, leaving you a disfigured mute that no one will ever recognize. I'll leave you to suffer so everyone will laugh at you, then I will proudly end you. You are evil. The people know it. You are right, Sebastian. I hate you. I always have, and I always will. I'll do everything in my power to hurt you from now until the day you die, and no one will even miss you or cry over you."

Sebastian was filled with rage and reached for Barron, threw him down hard, and pounced on top. He hit him over and over until he could feel how hot and sticky all the blood pouring from Barron's face was. He kept hitting him until Cyrus reached down to pull Sebastian back. Cyrus trembled as he held him. Sebastian could faintly hear Cyrus whispering, "It is okay" through his heavy breaths.

Sebastian sat there, staring at Barron lying on the ground holding his face. Barron started screaming for help, which made Sebastian leap onto his feet. He began to run, but he heard a truly angry and stern, "Stay where you are." It was his Father.

Ivan walked fast across the lawn and pulled Barron's hands away from his face to look at the damage. He looked up angrily at Sebastian and heeded the blood and scrapes on his knuckles. "Get over here, *now!*"

Sebastian walked over too aggressively and stopped once his Father stood and faced him. Ivan grabbed Sebastian's hands and studied them. "What is wrong with you, boy? What would possess you to do such a thing to your brother?" Sebastian just froze, staring his Father in the eyes.

Sebastian's heart pounded through the pulse in his wrists Ivan was still clinging to. Sebastian couldn't speak. Ivan's face turned red. He pulled Sebastian behind him into the castle without speaking, dragged him into his office, and slammed the door.

"What is the matter with you? I won't ask again."

"Did you not listen to what he said? Do you realize what he is going to do to me?" Sebastian said with shaking in his voice.

Ivan looked confused and scared. He had no idea what Sebastian was talking about this time.

"What is he going to do to you?" he said much calmer.

"He is going to kill me, Father. You cannot make him king. It will not stop with me; he will do this to anyone who opposes him. He will murder Tomas after me. He's mad, Father," Sebastian said, straining to hold back tears.

"Why would he do this? What made him say this to you?" Ivan asked in a worried tone.

Sebastian choked out tears and gasped, trying to breathe over his choking. "He caught me doing something." He was terrified to tell his Father about Cyrus, but he knew if he did not, Barron would. "I am in love, Father."

Ivan let go of Sebastian and backed up a step. "In love with whom?"

"I can't tell you, Father; you would hate me for what I would say," Sebastian said with tears streaming down his cheeks.

"I could never hate you, my son. You are different. You have always surprised me and scared me to death, but I will always love you, no matter what," Ivan said, wiping tears from Sebastian's wet face.

"For this, you will hate me. I swear you will." Sebastian stood there staring at his Father, hoping he would not make him say it, but Ivan insisted he finish telling him.

"Tell me who it is, boy."

Sebastian breathed with difficulty, which made more tears pour down his face. "I am madly in love with him. Barron caught us just before, kissing, and I wanted to be with him, Father. I wanted him so badly."

Ivan shook his head with his mouth gaped open. "Who? Wait, did you say to him?" Ivan said with shock in the tone of his voice. "You mean, with Cyrus?"

Sebastian looked up to meet his Father's expression, afraid to see how angry he would be but was met with curiosity. Sebastian nodded and swallowed hard. "Yes, Cyrus."

CHAPTER 11

Time Never Seemed to Pass

Ivan said nothing. He patted Sebastian lightly on the cheek as his son sobbed, embarrassed about what he confessed. Ivan hugged Sebastian tightly but began coughing again.

"Father, what is wrong? Are you ill?"

Ivan caught his breath. "Don't you worry about me, boy. Now, in the morning, King Roman, Cyrus, and I are leaving for Alta Prime. After you and Tomas displayed your power, there has been a lot of talk. I must go south to speak to the council. I need you to watch out for your brothers and sisters. Barron is in charge of the kingdom."

"Father, you can't leave! Please, not now. Why does Cyrus need to go too? If he needs to go to his home, I can take him..."

Ivan put his hand up, and Sebastian immediately stopped talking. "Since Cyrus rules in Torrdale, he is required at all council meetings. This gathering will discuss a treaty to open the borders between the North and the South for trade. He must be there."

Sebastian got angry and began yelling. "Did you not hear what I said? About what Barron will do. You leave, and I will be dead before you return." He started panting. "Fine. Go. Leave. Do not expect to see me again. I will disappear before Barron has the chance to end me. I don't care anymore."

Ivan reached out and put his hand on Sebastian's shoulder, and a tear ran down his face. He stared at his son sadly, then kissed him on the forehead.

"Once you calm down, go to bed. Come speak to me in the morning before I leave. I promise nothing bad will happen to you. I need to go speak with your brother now."

Ivan shut the door behind him. Sebastian stood against the wall, chest pounding, not believing he just told his Father about being in love with another man and that he did not care about his Father or anyone else.

Sebastian realized he had been sitting down with his back against the door for what seemed like hours. He had finally calmed down enough to stand up and reached out to twist the doorknob. The door whooshed open. Barron stood there sweating, looking vicious.

"You really do get away with whatever you want, don't you?"

"Barron, I am sorry for hitting you. I really should have-"

"Shut up, Sebastian! One of these days, you will get what is coming to you. Wait and see. You disgrace not just one royal crown, but two, and Father still acts like you are perfect and wonderful and that I am supposed to concede to you." Barron spit in anger. He grabbed Sebastian's shoulder, squeezed hard, then yanked him close. "I will never bow to you. Do you understand me?"

"I don't know why you would. You are next in line to be king."

"Don't ever forget that." Barron pushed him away and marched off with his typical pompous demeanor.

Sebastian rushed upstairs, knocked on Cyrus's door, and waited. Cyrus cracked open the door. Once he saw Sebastian, he opened it quickly, pulled him inside, then kissed him.

"I thought maybe it was your brother coming to scream in my face again."

"He did what?" Sebastian raised his voice.

"Shhh, it is alright. Come and lay with me tonight. If it is to be our last night together, I want it to be perfect."

Sebastian kissed Cyrus, then aggressively pushed him onto the bed. Sebastian held Cyrus against his chest and listened to him talk. Cyrus wanted a life free of a crown. He didn't want to return to Torrdale because he will be alone again.

"I worry I will never see you again," Sebastian said.

"Nothing will keep me from seeing you."

"I want to run away with you. We should leave and never come back."

"We will one day. But not today."

Sebastian's stared at the ceiling thinking that running away was only a fantasy. He felt that he was trapped in NorthBrekka forever. He wanted to learn to use his power but wondered at what cost. Cyrus mumbled, "love you" as he drifted off to sleep. Sebastian barely made out what he said, but knew he said love. It put a soft smile across his face as he closed his eyes.

Sebastian slithered out of bed in the early hours of the morning while Cyrus slept peacefully. He crept out the door, but before he took a step, he felt a sharp pull from behind. Barron held his hand over Sebastian's mouth and the other arm around his neck, dragging him down the stairs.

Before Sebastian could react, Barron dragged him to the dungeons, released him, then punched him hard in the face. With a manic look, Barron pounced on Sebastian, kicking him so hard several of Sebastian's ribs broke. He fell to his knees in pain, but Barron was not ready to stop. He repeated heavy blows to Sebastian's face and stomach. Then, Barron grabbed a tuft of hair and slammed Sebastian's head against the stone wall, which knocked him unconscious.

As the sun came up, everyone started arriving in the hall to eat and say goodbye. Cyrus looked around, wondering where Sebastian was. He went to Tomas for counsel.

"I haven't seen him since last night," Tomas said.

"He went to bed with me, but when I awoke, he was gone. I thought maybe he came to your room."

Barron walked by with a smirk as Tomas and Cyrus tried to guess where Sebastian wandered off. They assumed he went for a ride, but when Ivan and Roman came in, Ivan's frustrated expression let them know Sebastian was missing.

Cyrus saw Ivan lean over to Roman and say, "He may have run off. He does that when he is angry. Typically, one of the guards would have seen him go, but they have seen nothing."

"If we don't get riding to Alta Prime, we will get caught in the storm that is coming. We cannot wait all day for Sebastian to come home. He will get over his tantrum and be waiting when you get back."

He marched over. "We are not leaving until I have had a chance to say goodbye."

"That is not your choice. Now go and get your things. We leave before the morning ends."

"Brother."

"Why are you insisting on this, Cyrus?" Roman asked.

"Because I lo-. He is my friend. It is proper to say goodbye."

Ivan looked at Cyrus with wide eyes.

"It is only a short time, then when I return home, you may come with me. Sebastian will be waiting."

Cyrus looked appalled. "Do neither of you care at all about him?" He made haste out to the courtyard to look feverishly for Sebastian. He went to speak with Will, who already arrived at the stables.

"Will, have you seen Sebastian this morning?"

"No. Why? Is he missing as usual?"

"He slipped out of bed before I woke up. Now I cannot find him."

"You slept together last night?" Will sounded crushed.

"Of course. He is my intended. Never mind, it is clear no one is going to help me find him."

Will watched Cyrus walk away. He only hoped that maybe Sebastian slipped away on purpose, so he stopped working to go search for him.

The time came for the accompaniment to depart. Cyrus saw Ivan take one last look around then turned to his children.

"Take care of each other. Listen to Barron, and when Sebastian comes home, make sure he does not leave again." Ivan said while glaring at Barron. "I love you all."

Ivan began to ride away, followed by Roman and the southern army and some of NorthBrekka's knights. Cyrus lingered long enough to whisper to Tomas, "Tell Sebastian I love him."

Sebastian awoke to a rat crawling up his leg. He slapped it away and stood slowly from the pain. In the dungeon, he was alone except for one man who had been imprisoned for stealing a necklace from the queen several years ago.

"What could a prince have done to get himself locked away with me?"

"Shut up," Sebastian said. "Where is Barron?"

"Let me go check. Oh, wait. I cannot leave this damned cell, just like you, Your Highness." He laughed.

Sebastian shoved his hands against the cell door with intensity. A flash of fire escaped his hands.

"Ahh, so it is true. A prince born a god. A god that will end us all. Yada yada yada. You know the story."

Sebastian flashed an angry glare. "Who are you, and why are you mocking me?"

"Name's Angus. What else do I have to live for, Your Highness? What got you in this predicament? Is it because you are the descendant of the demon god?"

"Stop saying that. My stupid brother locked me in here because I beat him up."

"It looks more like he beat you up. You look terrible. You should have used your power on him."

"You should mind your business. I need to get out of here."

"Me too."

"Shut up, both of you, or I will run a sword through your stomachs and watch you both bleed to death slowly," Barron shouted as he came downstairs.

"Let me out, Barron." Sebastian seethed.

Barron laughed. "Not a chance. No one knows you are here. I am the only one with a key to the dungeon door, and I intend to keep you in here until you die, which will happen before Father makes it home, then I will have the chance to dispose of your body, and everyone will think you ran away for good."

"Why are you doing this?"

"Because it is what will make the world right again."

Barron walked over to Angus. "If you give him even a scrap of food, I will find your wife and kids and hang them in the gallows, then feed them to the pigs."

Barron laughed and left the dungeon, locking the door behind him.

A month passed, then another. Much to Barron's disappointment, Sebastian survived by eating bugs that crept into the dungeon as the warm weather made way for winter. Angus looked guilty when he took a bite of the stew he received at every evening supper that Barron hand-delivered. Barron seemed to purposefully bring Angus extra bread that smelled fresh, unlike what was typically given to prisoners.

In the third month, Barron came down looking hopeful. But Sebastian stood by his cell door smiling. Barron dropped the stew to the ground, unlocked the cell door, and grabbed Sebastian around the throat.

"Father will be home in a matter of a few days. You are supposed to be dead. Why are you alive?" he shouted. He began choking him.

"Let him go!" Angus threw a rock that hit Barron in the head.

Barron stood, went over to meet Angus face to face, and plunged his dagger into Angus's chest without a word, smiling as blood poured from Angus's throat as he choked obscene words. He looked at Sebastian. "Now, where was I?"

He took his dagger and held it to Sebastian's throat, piercing the skin. "Any last words, brother?"

"Go to hell." Sebastian's felt the burning sensation in his eyes when they turn from brown to red. He ignited his hands in flames, screamed, then, with a quick movement, he blasted Barron away from him, causing Barron to slam against the wall. His coat was on fire. He patted the flames out as Sebastian walked to him with the fire in his fists turning into lightning. Sebastian crouched down, reaching for Barron.

"What happened down here, Barron?" A voice came from the distance.

"Nadya?" Sebastian stopped and said.

Nadya came to a halt immediately upon seeing Sebastian for the first time in months. "Seb. I thought you ran away. I thought you were gone for good. But you have been here this whole time?" She turned to Barron. "He has been here this whole time, Barron! How dare you? How could you?"

Nadya lunged forward to attack Barron. She punched him square in the jaw. She went to hit him again, but Sebastian fell to the floor. The starvation had finally caught up to him, and the energy he had used to conjure his power was overwhelming. She shouted for Viktor and Tomas, then went to protect Sebastian while Barron scampered away.

CHAPTER 12

The South

Ivan sat at the table, waiting for the others to join him. He drummed his fingers softly, thinking about how long he was away from home. It was hot in the south. He could feel the humidity cutting his breath as he sat patiently waiting. He had been in the south three months now as part of the agreement to meet with the council. He was growing tired of being away from his family.

Six men filed into the room. King Roman was in the lead, followed by Cyrus, who was looking more depressed every day. The next two men who came to the table were Kavis of Safareen, Queen Lorna's cousin. Following him was the captain of the guard, an older gentleman who did not speak much. The last two men were Alta Prime's magistrate and his apprentice.

Everyone sat down and began ruffling through notes and sipping their wine. Ivan looked up at Cyrus, who was tapping his foot loudly on the floor. He had a blank stare on his face as he appeared to be reading something, although there was nothing in front of him. By the time everyone had become annoyed with the tapping, Roman had reached over and slapped his hand down on Cyrus's knee. It made him jump like he had just awoken.

"What in the hell is going on with you?"

"Can we begin?" Ivan said quickly and loudly. Everyone nodded. "If the heathens of the Far North fear an uprising of the demon god, they will come down from their lands. They do not want another war, but they will do what it takes to protect their own if they fear this prophecy."

"Do they even pose a threat?" King Roman asked.

"Yes, actually, they do," Michael said. "They own a vast territory, and the last time I checked, they have a militia that sits and watches from Blackthorn Forest."

Roman sat up a little straighter. "There will be talking across the nation. People will rise against Prince Sebastian if they believe he is the evil one. He will not have protection from either side if we cannot come together and create a plan if the prophecy is true."

"The armies of NorthBrekka cannot hold alone against a nation who will want my son's head. My son is not a demon. The prophecy is wrong."

"If that is true, we need to gain control of our people now. Gather our armies and prepare for war. If they come for him, we need to make sure our people are on our side. Ivan, I have a soft spot for Sebastian. I will do what is needed to protect him. What about Tomas?"

"They won't be after Tomas. They believe he is good."

"Do we know it is the Far North that is after the twins? Can we be sure?" The captain asked. "There are others out there that would be quick to turn."

"They called him evil," Ivan said softly. "I invited people from the Far North to the ball. I thought they, of all people, would appreciate the gods' power. I thought it would be safe, but they called my son evil. They will come to kill him. And if you are speaking of the Kuhar, they are a tribe small in numbers."

"Isn't the man who trained your boys one of the Sinook?" Roman asked.

"Yes, but Aspen believes in my son. He wanted to teach him to use his powers for good."

"Maybe it was unwise to leave him alone in the north." Cyrus spoke a little too loud. "He has no one to protect him if some heathen comes for him."

"He has an army and his brothers. Barron and Tomas would never allow anyone to take him."

Cyrus clenched his jaw. "I wouldn't be so sure."

As the meeting ended, Ivan stood and walked over to Cyrus as the other men were drinking their wine and chatting about war. He put his hand on Cyrus's shoulder and said, "Come speak to me in private later." Then he walked away and left the room.

That afternoon, Ivan waited in his private room. He heard a knock.

"Come in."

The door opened and Cyrus stood there fidgeting with his nails.

"You have the same nervous twitch that Sebastian has."

Ivan invited him to sit and offered him some wine, but Cyrus refused to drink. He sat down and stared at Ivan, waiting for him to start talking.

"Is there any word from him?" Cyrus asked.

Ivan shook his head and spoke softly. "Only messages I get from home are from Barron. Nothing more, nothing less. He assures me everyone is doing fine."

"How is it fine? He ran away before saying goodbye. Why would he do that? It doesn't make sense." Cyrus snarled. "Why would he suddenly turn his back on me?"

Ivan felt his stomach knot because the last words he shared with his son were Sebastian expressing his undying love for Cyrus. He knew since Sebastian broke down so hard that he would not suddenly change his heart overnight. "I agree, something isn't right there, but I know my son, and he loves you. When I get home, I will get to the bottom of it, but you must stop looking like you already died in the meantime. Everyone is concerned and confused by your behavior."

Cyrus had tears in his eyes. "If he loved me, he would send word to me. I sent letters, and nothing has come back. I just want him to know how I feel about that night and that I love him. I know I only knew him for a short time, but I want him back. I want him badly." Cyrus was trembling as he finished speaking. "Please, take me back north with you. I need to see for myself. What if something happened to him?"

Ivan waved for him to stop and wrapped his arms around Cyrus and held him tightly. "I will speak with your brother about bringing you back north, but he is going to have a suspicion. You are going to have to tell him eventually. How long do you think you can hide it from him?"

Cyrus's head shot up fast, and he looked horrified at the idea. "Have you met my brother?"

Ivan laughed at Cyrus's reaction. Cyrus just stared at Ivan with his mouth open. "I'm not making a joke! What do you think my brother is going to say when I tell him that I want to be with a man?"

Ivan did not know what to say. He stood there, rubbing his face. "I haven't put any thought into the way I feel about it either. I mean, I love my son. Although I always imagined him being a lord of his territory and having children one day and a wife that adores him. Not him having to hide from people that want him dead because he was born with a power that can destroy everything."

"But that is not what Sebastian wants," Cyrus protested. "If the world could see him for who he is, they would not fear him. They would love him as I love him. He wants to be free, and he doesn't want to marry someone because that is what is expected of him." His tone was getting angry, and he blurted out, "And Sebastian is mine! I want him to be happy, and I can make him happy. If he still loves me, I will be everything he will ever want. I will protect him with my life!"

Ivan's face his legs get weak. He shivered. He had never heard Cyrus speak so emotionally before. He stared at Cyrus for a few moments, then patted him on the shoulder. "Calm down, calm down. I will talk to your brother." Ivan dismissed Cyrus, who jumped up and walked fast out of the room.

The following day, Ivan went to speak to Roman in his office. Roman stood in front of Cyrus with his back to the door when he walked in. The look on Cyrus's face was fearful. He was sweating and red-faced. As he came in, he heard, "You are pathetic," and, "I should throw your bones to the dogs for this."

Ivan stood there, looking at Cyrus in silence. Roman had not noticed he had come in. "You are an embarrassment." Roman turned to Ivan standing by the door.

"When were you going to bother telling me that my brother and your boy were messing around?" He shook his head as he slumped down into his chair. "How could you be alright with this? Your boy. The future king of NorthBrekka lands is a lustful sinner who chases other boys. What the hell is wrong with these idiotic children?"

Ivan breathed in deep. He looked at Cyrus, who was looking back at him in shock until he coughed out, "King? What does he mean, king? Sebastian, king?"

Ivan ignored Cyrus and turned to Roman. "I am taking your brother north with me."

"Like hell, you are. If people think your son is evil, they will kill him and my brother. I will not allow this to go any further. Your son needs to stay away from my family," Roman scowled.

Ivan felt hot and stiffened up. He placed his hands on Roman's desk. "I thought my son had your loyalty."

"He does, but not when it puts my bloodline at risk. If I had known about this, I would have called off this meeting before it began."

"Cyrus chose to be with Sebastian. How dare you point fingers at my son. He did not know his power would turn the world against him. If Cyrus decides to stand by Sebastian's side, so be it. With a little training, no one will be able to stop my son from being the leader of the nations."

Roman stood slow to meet Ivan eye to eye. They stared at each other for a long while until Cyrus stood and loudly spoke up for himself. "I love him, brother. I loved him from the moment I first saw him. I do not care if you disown me or deny me as your brother."

Roman backhanded Cyrus hard across the face, which knocked him to the ground, then kicked him hard in the ribs. He stood over him and spat, "I will not allow you to go and get yourself killed for that boy. You disgust me for what became of you. I will make sure you never see that boy again, even if that means I have to get rid of him myself."

Cyrus was choking up blood on the floor. Ivan wrapped his arms around Roman's neck and pulled him back. "If you touch my son, it will be the last thing you will ever do. The pact is void. Keep your people away from the north, or we will direct our fight to you." He gestured for Cyrus to get up and follow him. They quickly shuffled out of the office and walked fast down the corridor.

"You just struck the king," Cyrus said in shock. "He will send men after us. We won't get far." Soldiers were waiting for them in the hall, and they reached out to stop them. Ivan unsheathed his sword as Queen Lorna stepped around the corner. She was smirking at them.

"Stop now," she said simply. Ivan stopped but still gripped his sword tight and pointed it at the queen.

Cyrus stepped between them and looked at his brother's wife. "Move. We are leaving. The treaty is void. My brother will regret threatening the future king of NorthBrekka."

The queen laughed slowly and reached in and kissed Cyrus softly on the lips. She laughed again and pointed at the two of them, indicating for them to come with her. She walked away, which left Ivan to follow her and address what her husband had just done. She just laughed at every word, then turned to sit down and looked at Ivan.

"I don't care about you or your lands. I do not care about my brother-in-law and your son with their adorable little infatuation for each other. War means power and money. It means my husband will march north to kill your worthless family, including your precious little boy, and come home a hero."

Ivan started to retort when Lorna put her hand up to silence him.

"I don't care," she said before he could get a word out. Guards entered the hall, followed by King Roman, who was red-faced and sweating. Ivan stood with his hand on the hilt of his sword. Roman looked at his brother and nodded to the guards.

Two men grabbed Ivan and pushed him down to his knees. Roman reached out and grabbed Cyrus around the throat. He was gasping for air as he tried to loosen the grip his brother had on his neck but could not.

Cyrus pulled at Roman's hands and managed to spit out, "Please stop," but Roman kept his grip tight.

Lorna cleared her throat, which caught Roman's attention. He let go and dropped his brother to the ground. Cyrus gasped for air with tears streaming down his cheeks. Ivan felt disgusted by his once best friend, shaking his head in disapproval. The queen smiled.

"My brother is dead to me. He will return to Torrdale and be held. He will not be allowed to leave the castle again. Ever! If he ever goes near your boy again, I will not let my grip weaken a second time. I will end him without guilt or sadness."

Roman walked away from his brother, who was lying in a fetal position on the floor, quietly sobbing and shaking. Ivan stared at him sadly. He thought to himself he would free Cyrus from his prison the moment he arrived home. Even if it meant war, he would allow him to live happily with Sebastian.

"As far as it goes for you, you are lucky that we share a long history of brotherhood. You will be escorted back to your home. I hope you know that war is coming to your keep." Roman stared down at Ivan, who was still on his knees, looking at him. "Our friendship is done; I will own the north no matter what I have to do."

Cyrus was carried from the room by three men who bound his hands and feet and gagged him. Ivan desperately wanted to assure him that he would help him, but he could not. Roman motioned for guards to take Ivan and escort him to his horse.

Ivan quickly gathered his belongings, shoved them into bags, and threw them onto his horse's back. His men were already outside the gate, waiting. He looked for the caravan leaving with Cyrus but could not spot them. He turned to his men and shouted, "We ride North!"

CHAPTER 13

The Vengeance of Barron Drake

Sebastian slept through most days and nights. He felt his strength returning. Nadya never left his side. She refused to let anyone near her brother, only Tomas and Will, were allowed in. Everyone was curious, but she would not let anyone stay long, especially not Barron.

Tomas insisted on delivering his meals every day so he could see him for just a little longer. Nadya would let him stay while Sebastian ate to tell them what he learned about their Father's return. Also, about how Barron was running the kingdom.

Most of the children stayed outside during the day. Nadya yelled at Barron to get away from Sebastian while he slept. Sebastian was angry and distraught, having no understanding of what was going on or if his Father knew what happened to him.

After a few days of eating regularly, bathing, and being pampered by Nadya and Will nonstop, his headaches and fever started going away. Will would come in and read to him or just talk, which made them both happy. He was able to keep down all his food, and he had energy again, although he was still depressed. Tomas came with the usual delivery of food and words for the day, but this time he looked excited.

"There was a fight in Alta Prime. King Roman tore up the treaty, and now Father is coming home early. That is all Barron would say."

Sebastian sat up quickly. He started to feel like himself again. He finally let Nadya trim his hair. She left it long, but it was off his shoulders and clean. He grabbed some bread off the plate and shoved a piece in his mouth. "Anything about Cyrus?"

Tomas just shook his head, looking disappointed. "Father will know." Will was smiling until Sebastian mentioned Cyrus.

Viktor poked his head in the door. Nadya waved for him to come in. Every time he visited before, Sebastian had been sleeping, so this was the first time they had seen each other in months.

"Wow, you grew up. How long was I gone?" Sebastian said, staring at his brother.

Viktor had grown several inches and let his blond hair grow out curly and hanging below his eyebrows. He hurried over and hugged Sebastian tightly. "I just heard Father will be home within a week. They said he has been riding with haste since he left the south."

"Good," Sebastian said, starting to climb out of bed with much of Nadya's disapproval. "I need to speak with him before Barron gets to him. He needs to know what happened here."

He quickly dressed in the clean clothing Nadya had brought for him. She kept attempting to get him to lie down, but he refused to comply. She threw her hands up and across the room. Sebastian was angry and on a dangerous mission to meet his Father head-on. Also, to find the love of his life no matter what anyone said.

"You need to lie down. He isn't going to be here today," She insisted, but Sebastian continued to push his way around the room.

He reached down and kissed her on the forehead and thanked her for taking care of him. "I have to speak to Barron."

He stormed out of the room and into the corridor. He realized that the room he had been in while healing was the same room Cyrus had slept in a while visiting. He stopped and leaned up against the wall and took a deep breath and could hear his sister say, "You go stop him."

Upon walking into the throne room, Sebastian saw that Barron was already waiting on his Father's throne. Barron looked up from reading a book. The smirk on his face disappeared as he noticed his brother. He stood up and walked toward Sebastian, who appeared ready to run a sword through his face. Barron slowly unsheathed his sword.

"Are you going to do something with that?" Sebastian said, nodding toward Barron's sword. Barron slipped it back into the sheath and instead gripped his fingers around Sebastian's throat and pulled him close to his face.

"How are you not dead?" Barron said, gritting his teeth. He shoved Sebastian back, waiting for him to jump at him.

"So that was your plan all along, to have me killed, for me to die in that cell. All because of our little fight in the courtyard where I bloodied your face. I knew you were pathetic, but not like that."

Barron laughed. "I see you're still upset about your little boyfriend. Do not worry. I am sure that sweet Cyrus is fine. When he and Father left for the south with King Roman and his men, the deal was to get the treaty signed among the nation's head of houses. Then, to have a celebratory wedding. This uniting Cyrus with Princess Violetta, who just happens to be Queen Lorna's baby sister. She is only thirteen, but she will be ready to make him some lovely babies soon enough."

Sebastian tried to hide his concern that quickly turned to anger. Barron smiled and continued.

"Matching her with the king's brother was the way they would show that the north and the south could unite in harmony. After the ridiculous display you and Tomas put on at the ball, the country is uneasy. It is a way to show both sides of the wall could get along. Of course, Cyrus was quick to say yes."

Sebastian stood there speechless with a tear rolling down his cheek. He was livid but could not get a word out, and Barron's smiling face only made him angrier. Barron wiped the tear from Sebastian's face.

"I hope you know that you and I are no longer brothers." Sebastian scowled. "We may share blood, but do not think that will stop me from ending your life."

Barron laughed. "You have always been so pretty, Sebastian. Bold, daring, and mostly fierce. But you stand no chance against me. I know all your weaknesses."

"I have no weaknesses."

"Oh, we will see about that, dear brother. When I take my rightful place on the throne, you will be the first to feel my wrath." He patted Sebastian's cheek spitefully and walked away laughing.

Sebastian lay in his bed, quietly staring up at the ceiling. He was repeatedly thinking about how Cyrus was married now, and it made him feel sick. He looked over at Tomas, who was sleeping soundly and lightly snoring. He got up and went to lie down next to his twin. He wrapped his arms around him and cradled his head against his back and fell asleep.

He slept uninterrupted all night. When he woke up, he was in the same position as when he fell asleep, and Tomas was awake but not moving.

"I didn't want to disturb you. You were sleeping so well." Tomas turned over to where they were face to face, the tips of their noses nearly touching.

He stroked Sebastian's hair back and tucked it behind his ear. This made him think of Cyrus and how he would do that to keep his hair out of his face.

"Where is our stepmother? I have not seen her since I came out of the dungeon."

Tomas just shrugged. "She hasn't been out of her room much. She has been seriously ill. She has been running a fever off and on for weeks now and coughs constantly. I am not sure how much longer she has."

"Do you not think that is odd? Father was ill before he left, now Emelia. Either way, I need to speak to Barron about what is happening."

"You mean how everyone in Erras is afraid of you? Because of the prophecy."

"That is not me. I can barely make fire and lightning. How would I tear the world apart? How do they assume that it is me?"

"Because there is only you and I born with these gifts. You have the power of fire, which is the same as the old god who destroyed all those people."

"That is ridiculous. How could you think I am the same as him? I have to clear my name."

Sebastian jumped out of bed and dressed. Tomas stared at him with concern. "Brother, what if it is you?"

"Do you honestly think I would destroy everything and everyone, Tomas?"

"No, but what if someone did something to provoke you."

"I cannot believe you of all people think I am what they are calling me." Sebastian shook his head and burst out of the bedroom with haste.

Sebastian found Will, hugged him, then pulled him away from the rest of the family.

"Would you like to go for a walk outside with me?" Will asked. Sebastian smiled at him and nodded.

They walked out into the cold air.

"I thought you left forever."

Sebastian looked at him curiously. "Why would I do that?"

"I don't know. Cyrus said that you were his intended. Is that true?"

"It was. He is married now, so it doesn't matter anymore. The only thing that matters is me finding out who I was born to be."

"You were born to be king of NorthBrekka. That is why Barron attacked you. He is jealous. If Cyrus is married, will you consider another as your husband?"

Sebastian smiled. "Perhaps one day." He stroked Will's cheek.

"Barron beat me too, Sebastian. I went looking for you. When Barron found out, he threatened my life and told me he would destroy everyone I care for if I did not stop. He knows how I feel about you."

Sebastian grabbed Will's hand and held it tight. "I'm sorry he hurt you. How do you feel, Will?"

"I have told you how much I love you, Sebastian."

Sebastian smiled and could feel himself blushing, but he still thought of Cyrus. Will moved as close as he could to Sebastian.

"I know how much it hurts to watch the person you love fall for another. Can I help get you past this?" Will said, then kissed Sebastian on the cheek.

Sebastian took a deep breath and looked at him with intensity. "Cyrus is gone. He chose his fate. I was imprisoned because I lusted for him. I was foolish. But you have always been there for me, Will." He pulled Will close to him. "Do you want to be with me?" he whispered.

Will smiled and nodded fast. "Yes, Your Grace. I want to be with you more than anything. I love you." He stopped speaking suddenly.

"Are you not afraid of what people say about me?"

"No. My Father said that people are afraid of what they don't understand, and if you are evil, we are all blind and ignorant. He likes you. He said you are the only one with any sense in your head."

"I am glad to hear it. I am sorry I pushed you away for Cyrus. I thought I was in love, but I was wrong. I thought he accepted my power, but he left me when he found it suitable. You are the one that has ever been loyal to me. I hope you will forgive me."

"Of course I forgive you. I never lost hope for us."

Sebastian kissed him, then pulled him against his chest. "Don't ever leave me."

"I never will."

A few days had passed, and Sebastian was frustrated with Barron's power over everyone in the kingdom. Barron berated handmaids for not being quick enough when he asked them to fetch things for him. He screamed at his siblings when they were too noisy when playing. He pushed Nadya around like she was a servant.

"Tomas, I need something to distract Barron. Can you ask Fiona to keep him away so I can look for answers? This is imperative. If the nations come for my head, I must know what I am so I have a chance to stand against them."

"Against them? Do you hear yourself? You could use your words and speak to the leaders."

"What good will that do? Please, Tomas. Ask her."

When Tomas left Sebastian in the throne room, Sebastian darted to his Father's office. He rummaged through scrolls, journals, and loose parchment. When he came up empty-handed, he burst his way out into the courtyard. He wandered around the archery range, talking to himself. Viktor and Gentry followed him, throwing out suggestions as he muttered under his breath.

A thundering sound came from the bridge. "Father," Sebastian whispered.

"Sebastian!" Viktor pointed behind Sebastian. Barron thrust his dagger into Sebastian's thigh before he could even react. Sebastian fell to the ground, clutching his leg. Viktor and Gentry rushed to their brother as Barron fled quickly.

Horns sounded in the distance. Sebastian lay on the ground screaming for someone to stop Barron, but the kingdom was scrambling to welcome the king home. They were not expecting him for a few more days.

Sebastian saw Will run into the courtyard looking flushed. He found Sebastian sitting on the ground with the knife still in his thigh with a distraught pair of brothers trying to help him to his feet. "Stop, careful, don't remove the knife!" His sudden presence scared Gentry and Viktor and they accidentally dropped Sebastian back onto the ground.

Will put his hand on Sebastian's thigh, putting pressure on his muscle, making Sebastian cry out in pain. "Hold still, my prince," he said calmly, looking Sebastian in the eyes. "Viktor, Gentry, please go get some rags to stop the bleeding until we can get him inside."

They sprinted toward the kitchens. Will kept his hand on Sebastian's thigh. "Don't look at it; just focus on this," he said, then reached in and kissed Sebastian. He gasped when Sebastian kissed him back. "I said I will stay by your side, and I meant every word. I will always be here for you. Always."

The gates opened. Men on horses filed into the courtyard. Sebastian caught a glimpse of his Father. He scanned the crowd hoping to see Cyrus but could not find him. King Ivan dismounted and looked around. His eyes met Sebastian's after Viktor and Gentry ran outside, followed by Sara and Nadya.

Ivan pushed his way through his men. Will held Sebastian tight as Ivan knelt and took Sebastian's face in his hands.

CHAPTER 14

Taking Command

Sebastian woke up lying in his bed with Will sitting next to him. He felt down to his thigh that was wrapped tightly and did not hurt much. He looked at Will closely with a smile. "Why are you still here?" he said softly. "Your Father is probably angry with you right now."

Will laughed and leaned in to kiss Sebastian on the lips quickly. "He knows where I am. He knows how I feel about you, so he let me stay. Will smiled, wrapped both his arms tightly around Sebastian, then put his head on his shoulder. "I love you," he whispered. "I always have. I always will, although I know when you see Cyrus again, you will want him and not me."

"We talked about this. Cyrus is married!" Sebastian said a little too angrily.

Will uncuffed his arms from Sebastian's waste. "I am sorry, Your Grace."

"You don't have to address me so formally. You can call me by my name," Sebastian said. Will smiled.

"I need to get up." Sebastian sat up and rechecked his thigh. He found his shirt and turned to Will again. "I have to speak to my Father."

Will jumped up to stop him, but Sebastian looked at him with a grim expression. As he walked down the corridor, Sebastian realized that his thigh hurt severely as he limped down the stairs. Once he reached the bottom landing, blood began seeping through his pants. He grimaced and kept walking to find his Father in the throne room discussing finding his oldest son with a group of knights.

Ivan waved his hand to quiet the chatter in the room. Everyone turned to watch the young prince approach the throne, clearly in pain as he winced with every step. The king sat on his throne very still, his eyes narrowed as Sebastian limped.

The knights began to file into lines along both sides of him and bowed as he passed by. He was used to being greeted formally but not like this; this was the way they greeted his Father.

"Father, I wish to take a group of fighters to track my brother down. I will bring him back so he can serve the justice he deserves."

Ivan smiled at his son, puffed his chest, and took Sebastian's hand. "You need to rest, my dear son. You are injured, your leg must heal or you will bleed out. I have already sent men in search of Barron. They have taken the dogs; they will find him."

"Father, you have no idea what he has done. You left a monster in charge of the kingdom." Sebastian started to say but was getting upset as Ivan stood to face his son. He wrapped his hands around both of his son's arms and squeezed them lightly.

"He was not to pretend to be king. I gave him strict orders that evening before bed. He wrote to me every week and informed me of what was going on in the kingdom. He was to ensure you and your brothers and sisters were training, studying, and eating. You were supposed to be the one sitting in my chair."

Sebastian's eyes grew wide. He was deeply confused. "He left me in the dungeons to die. I was locked away for three damn months. I sat in that cold, dark room. I got out only days ago, and... What do you mean I was supposed to sit there?"

Ivan's face was turning red as he listened to his son's voice get louder and angrier. Ivan held up his hand and said, "Nadya informed me briefly about what Barron had done but hearing it from you is different. It is unnerving." Ivan paused then shook his head. "You are my chosen heir, my son. Not Barron, you. I chose you before I left, and Barron knew this. He was upset, but I explained why he was unfit to be King of NorthBrekka. I only left him in charge because I had not told you. He said he understood." Ivan's voice trailed off, faintly mumbling. He sat back down on his throne and grasped his chest and began coughing again.

"Why me? I do not deserve this. I am a terrible child. I agree that Barron does not either, but Tomas should be next. Tomas is..." Sebastian froze in the middle of his sentence. "Where is Tomas? I haven't seen him since yesterday." Both Sebastian and the king jumped to their feet.

"Find my son!" Ivan shouted for his men to search the castle for Tomas. The knights hurried out of the throne room, spreading in all directions. Sebastian darted off after them, forgetting his leg was in pain.

He started up the stairs fast, screaming for Will. "Will, have you seen Tomas? Please tell me you have!" He gasped for air as he reached the top of the stairs.

Will ran to help him. "I have not seen your brother since yesterday."

Will helped him back down the stairs as knights were bursting through the bedroom quarters looking for Tomas. Viktor came running down the stairs behind them. "Yesterday, he went to see Fiona. I haven't seen him since."

"Fiona! Is she still here, or did she run with Barron?"

"It was only Barron fleeing," Will answered, and all three of the boys, Ivan, and several knights hurried toward Fiona's quarters.

Will opened the door to Fiona's room without knocking and held the door open for others to enter. The first person they saw was Tomas. He was lying on the floor, blood dry on his face and hair. Sebastian knelt and lightly slapped his cheek to wake him up. Tomas jerked awake and lunged up like he was ready to attack. Ivan reached down to help his son to his feet as others went to check Fiona, who was lying on the floor on her stomach.

"Where is that sick, demented bastard? I am going to kill him with my bare hands!" Tomas raised his voice, but Ivan quickly quieted him.

"He has gone, brother," Sebastian said, limping over to check Tomas's wounds. Sebastian started telling him what had happened when one of the men interrupted.

"Your Majesty, she is dead."

Sebastian felt all of Tomas's weight drop on him, but his injured leg could not support them, and they both fell to the floor. Tomas scrambled over to Fiona's body. The shrieking cries of a broken heart were horrifying. Will knelt to help Sebastian up, but he grabbed his hand to indicate for him to stop.

"Tomas, what happened?"

Tomas stared at the floor next to him. "I went to see Fiona like you asked. She never lets anyone except Barron and me in her room. I held her hand as she put her head on my shoulder. I asked her to tell Barron she wished to see him. She looked at me as if she wanted to hit me. I told her how important it was for her to do that. She told me that she hated him and begged me not to make her call for him. She told me she loved me. We kissed. I wanted her more than anyone in the world. I laid her on the bed and started undressing her. We made love until a knock came to the door. Fiona told me to hide. I slipped into the wardrobe and peeked through the cracks. The door opened and Barron came inside. At first, I thought he was just going to talk but he shoved her down and held her down by her throat as he used her body. Fiona pushed him away. Barron slapped her across the face. I was angry, but then she shrieked horribly. I burst through the door and kicked Barron in the ribs. He looked at me and laughed. I was still naked. Barron pulled Fiona by the hair and pushed her to the floor, then punched me in the nose. I tasted blood running into my mouth. I saw Barron's fist come at my face again, but this time I felt dizzy and sick. I fell and could hardly see, but I saw Barron stroke her hair and whisper, "You don't deserve me," into her ear. I heard Fiona scream. Then watched her fall limp as Barron left the room with a dagger in his hand."

The room was uncomfortably quiet as they all took a knee, mourning for Fiona. The only sound was Tomas's wails of pain and despair as he held her in his arms. They could see the spot on her chest where a dagger had driven through, and there was blood pooled on the floor.

The mood in the room was desperate. Desperate for justice and to comfort Tomas, take away his pain, and cry for Fiona. Ivan was the first to move. He dragged his troubled son from the room where Sara and Gentry were waiting in the hall. "Take him to his room. Fiona has been murdered."

Ivan went back into the room to find the men preparing to carry her away. He looked at Sebastian and Will as they were still there on the floor in each other's arms. "Son, I need to speak with you alone. Will, you should go and inform your Father what has happened. Ask if he can build her a coffin, something beautiful to send her home to her family in." Will nodded and hugged Sebastian, then stood to bow to the king before he left.

Sebastian climbed to his feet, and Ivan escorted him out of the room. They walked in silence around the castle for what seemed like forever. Sebastian noticed his father keep stealing glances of him. He pretended it did not bother him.

"What did you want to talk about, Father?"

Ivan drew a deep breath and explained why he chose him to be the next king. "You are a born leader. You are brave and strong. Most of all, when you enter a room, your appearance alone can command respect. You must realize how incredible you are, how powerful."

"Why is everyone afraid of me? They call me evil. I am not this man you think I am. I will be no more than an embarrassment..." Sebastian said in a frustrated tone, but Ivan waved his hand to silence him. He stood there, shaking his head, clearly irritated that his Father did not want to listen.

"You aren't listening. No one is going to follow me if they think I am going to kill them. No one will ever respect a man who would share his bed with another man over a woman. I do not want this. I don't want to be king."

Ivan stopped walking and stubbornly crossed his arms while staring at Sebastian. "You will do as I say, and I say you shall be king. This chatter spreading across the land will end. No one demands you to be normal or abide by some non-existent rule that you must be a certain way. You can marry whomever you desire, and you will rule as you wish, and the people will follow you no matter what. Now, tell me about Will and the sudden relationship that has developed there."

Sebastian started to protest again but figured it was useless. He gave his Father a worried expression upon his mentioning of Will but started to explain anyway. "He said he is in love with me. We have been friends for a long time, but I didn't know until a few months ago. He's handsome, no doubt, and he is a good man, but there is still something that is holding me back."

The only word Ivan had to say was *Cyrus.* Sebastian felt a stinging sensation in his eyes. He was angry that Cyrus had given up on him. Ivan put his hand on Sebastian's shoulder.

"I assume he has gone to his home in Torrdale. I do not know, though. The men dragged him out of the palace at his brother's command and were gone before I could find him again," Ivan said, not realizing that Sebastian did not know.

Sebastian was in shock and started to ask questions. Will dashed to them, breathing hard and trembling. He grabbed Sebastian's hand and gasped, "The kingdom is under attack!"

Ivan immediately darted to the balcony to look out over the town below. Sebastian rushed over and saw smokes billowing from homes in the distance. Much of the militia were already on their way to the fight. He shouted to muster the knights, then turned to his son. "Stay here and watch your brothers and sisters."

"Father, I can help. Let me fight."

"You are injured. I cannot allow my son to go into battle wounded. They will be after you and Tomas. I need you to find Tomas and hide."

"I am fine, Father. I will not sit here while enemies attack our city, my city. You cannot make me stay behind."

"If anything happens to you-"

"You said it yourself. They are after Tomas and me. This is my fight. Have Tomas stay behind."

"You are ready to take command. Go and speak to your siblings, then meet me in the war room."

Sebastian nodded and went to go find Tomas. He opened his bedroom door and Will sat on his bed.

"Where is Tomas? I need to speak with him."

"I haven't seen him. Is there anything I can do to help?"

"Will, I need you to make sure my brothers and sisters are safe. Take them down to the dungeons. When it is over, I'll send for you." Sebastian brushed Will's face with the tips of his fingers then pulled him close to where their foreheads were against each other's.

"I don't want you to go," Will said.

Sebastian sighed and looked at Will sadly. "I know, but this is my future. My people need me. It is time to grow up and be a man. Promise you will take care of them for me."

"What about your leg?"

"I promise I am alright. Don't fret over me."

"I love you, Sebastian."

Sebastian smiled. He wanted to say he loved him too but the words would not come to him. "Go find Tomas and tell him what is happening. I have to go address the men and prepare for war."

Will nodded, then kissed Sebastian. before rushing away. Sebastian rubbed his neck and thought hard about what he would say to the soldiers who waited for his leadership. He kept going back to his Father talking about him being the next king, and Cyrus, then felt guilty about taking Will's hand so easily, wondering if he should rush to Torrdale to get answers for himself. His heart belonged to Cyrus, but Will had always been there for him.

"How can I tell Will I can't choose him over Cyrus? I've already let it go too far." He spoke aloud to himself.

A voice came from the doorway that made Sebastian jump. "Your Grace, the men await."

CHAPTER 15

I Will Fight for You

Sebastian went to the war room where his Father and several men were strategizing. When he entered, they stopped and bowed to the prince. "Who are they?" Sebastian said, not considering the men that would follow the young prince into battle.

"We don't know."

They scoured the lands' maps to try and find any hint of something they did not know.

"Well, who cares who they are? The point is, those men are enemies who would dare attack our kingdom. Muster the troops and meet me on the courtyard," he said and marched out to prepare for battle.

He stood in the armory, dressing in thick leather and steel. Will came down to speak with him. He grabbed the bracers, slid them on Sebastian's forearms and tied them tight. They were in silence as he tied on pieces made to protect Sebastian's back. "I can help you on the battlefield. I have learned to wield iron. I've only been making swords and shields for this kingdom since I was a child..."

Sebastian interrupted him by grabbing his working hands. "I want you here protecting my brothers and sisters. They are safe having you guarding them."

Will began to protest, but Sebastian stopped him with a kiss. It quickly ignited into passion as Will started to take the armor off, followed by the leather. Sebastian picked Will up, laid him on the stone floor, and undressed him quickly. They were hesitant for only a moment. As they kissed, Sebastian held Will delicately, staring into his eyes. Suddenly there was a loud knock on the armory door. Sebastian stopped, turned his head, and laughed.

"Seriously?"

"Your Majesty, it is time," A man exclaimed.

Sebastian smirked and turned to see the desperate look on Will's face. "I have to go. I am to be king, and I must make sacrifices."

Will stood up to help him again with his armor. He was complete, holding his bow in his right hand with a sword on one hip and an ax on the other.

Ivan and his men waited in the courtyard with the militia, ready to march out of the castle walls. All men with armor, shields, and swords. Some on horseback, and some men on foot, carrying pikes.

Sebastian stepped over the threshold to a sea of steel and staring faces. All men were facing him now, and he immediately felt the pressure building in the cold air while the snow fell harder than before.

"I am not going to speak about victory or tragedy. I will say only this. I will fight for all of you. I will stand before you and face our enemies down alongside you. Tonight, we defend our home. Not all of us will return tonight. Some will return scarred and bleeding and broken, but we will return knowing we stood our ground bravely. If you fight for me, I will fight for you. Will you follow me?"

The men cried out and raised their weapons to the sky. Sebastian felt a surge of pride and adrenalin as he mounted his horse. Sebastian and Ivan marched to the front of the line and began their descent into the city.

The townsfolk were hustling to grab anything they could carry to save from disaster. Mothers took children and ran into the woods that lined the edge of the northern road before the mountains. The men marched in silence behind the king and the prince with their knights firmly at their backs. The sight of the mysterious enemies became more apparent as they increased pace to stop them where they stood. Sebastian strung an arrow in his bow and prepared to release it at the first man he could reach.

"I am proud of you, my son. I believe you are ready to be king."

Sebastian glanced over at his Father, then returned his eyes to the enemy's approach. "Archers, prepare to fire!"

Men rushed to the front of the line with their arrows drawn. The militia was at a halt as the enemy grew nearer. "Fire!" Ivan roared. A wall of arrows filled the snowy skies, blocking out the light of the sunset. Many found their targets, some missed, and Sebastian's arrow found the head of a large, muscular man with axes in both hands. The surge of men behind the archers sprinted past the men and horses, swords drawn, shields up, pikes out.

Ivan looked upon the enemies with his eyes narrowed and leaning forward. Sebastian watched his father, then loosened arrows on every man he could mark. Each arrow took down another enemy. Once his quiver was empty, he and his father unsheathed their swords and rode fast toward the mosh of fighting men before them.

A man charged King Ivan. Sebastian panicked as he tried to break his way free to protect his Father. He screamed and swung his sword at every man who stood in his way. The man reared back and swung his sword at the king's throat. An arrow sailed past Sebastian's head and into the skull of the man who dared charge the king. Sebastian turned to a knight standing atop a mound of bodies with his bow in hand. Just as Sebastian smiled, he watched a young enemy leap up behind the knight and sink his sword through his chest and slice down his torso.

Sebastian mounted his horse to chase down the killer. This man, about his age, came lunging toward him also on horseback. He swung a blade at Sebastian's head that barely missed and chinked against the steel armor on his left shoulder. He turned his horse after the man but was surprised when the enemy jumped from his horse, onto Sebastian's and pulled him to the ground.

He stared at Sebastian for a moment, shouted something he could not understand, and reached for his blade. As he unsheathed his sword, Sebastian pushed him away. The enemy warrior swung his sword again. Sebastian blocked it with his own. The crash of iron rang through his ears. They were caught in a game of power over chaos. The young warrior grasped Sebastian's blade in his bare fist and pushed it away from his chest. Blood streamed from his grip, yet his gaze never broke free of Sebastian's eyes.

His strength was intense. Sebastian's mouth dropped as his eyebrows moved together and his arms shook. Ivan shouted for his son, "You are the only one who has the power to defeat our enemies. Remember who you are!"

Sebastian looked at the warrior viciously. Without trying, he dropped his sword and threw his hands forward, blasting flames that set the man on fire. As the enemy shrieked, Sebastian took his ax from his belt and sunk it into his skull. The soldiers backed away, looking afraid of the prince's power. Sebastian looked around for his Father.

He panicked and began furiously cutting men down, sword in one hand, ax in the other. Two of his knights came, grabbed him, and pulled him away from the center of the battle. He did not understand why and struggled to be let free. The noise was deafening. The knight who was holding him was speaking, but he could not hear. He managed to break loose just as a bright green flash of light filled the skies.

The power of the blast threw every man standing onto their backs. The light was so bright they had to bury their faces in the snow to shield their eyes. As the light subsided, Sebastian sat up and looked around the field. Once again, he was searching for his Father but could not find him anywhere.

The men started climbing to their feet, searching for their king. Sebastian slowly wandered through the smoke, stepping over bodies. He turned over a few to check their faces as his men gathered weapons from the mud. He started to fear that his Father was buried in the heap of death that covered the ground.

He walked away from the battlefield and into the woods, wondering where the enemies had gone. He held his sword tightly in his fist and continued forward. As he approached the river, a man stood on the bank. It was dark, which made it challenging to find the man's face. He walked until he was close enough to hear the man's subtle shifting movements in the rocks under his feet. The man spoke, and it made Sebastian jump. "You did it. You are the reason for our victory." The man turned to face him as he spoke.

"Father!"

Ivan walked toward Sebastian. "Put your sword away, son." Sebastian realized he was still holding his sword out, ready to fight. He quickly sheathed it and walked to his Father. They embraced tightly. "I followed them as they fled but lost sight of them here."

"I thought the worst happened to you when I couldn't find you on the field. The men are searching relentlessly for your body."

Ivan gave out a loud laugh, followed by coughing. "We better go back before they panic and tell the queen I am dead."

They exited the forest to find the men still searching. They all abruptly stopped when the sight of the king came before them. "We ride to the castle. Gather the people into the keep. I have something I need to announce," Ivan said.

Sebastian was confused. "We won, "Father, why are you so worried?" Ivan mounted his horse, and before riding away, he looked at his son.

"This isn't over." He galloped away, followed by several knights. The men stood and stared at the prince, wondering what they needed to do.

Sebastian waved his arms. "Didn't you hear my Father? Move! Go, bring the people to the castle, now!" He hopped on his horse and rode fast after his Father.

Sebastian saw Nadya push her way to the front of the group as they approached the throne room. She lunged forward in a full run at her Father and Sebastian as they stood next to the throne. The others pushed their way to the front to wrap their arms around the Father and brother. Will stood back, watching the family embrace one another, looking hopeful for Sebastian's affection to come to him next.

Sebastian had finished greeting his family and was in a tight hug with Tomas as he noticed Will watching him. He stopped smiling and stepped slowly toward Will, who looked terrified from the sight of blood and mud covering his clothes.

As he got close to him, Will put his hand out on his chest to stop him. Sebastian moved to embrace him, but Will pulled away. "I was so worried..." he said, stuttering every word, then stopped when he couldn't catch his breath.

Sebastian reached out and placed his hand on his face. "I will never leave you. I promise." He pulled Will closer to him and wrapped his arms around his waist. "I promise I will always come back to you."

"I just didn't know what to expect to come of this night. Next time, you are taking me into battle with you. I will not sit by helpless and waiting. I am not a woman waiting for her husband to return from war while tending to the children. I am your man... What?" Will suddenly stopped when his eyes fell upon the smirk on Sebastian's face.

"What you did was noble. My family needed you more than I did. You are soon to be my husband. I chose you for a reason, not because I needed someone to stay home and wait for me, because you are the one I love, and you are strong."

Will rolled his eyes. "I was a coward tonight, my love."

They both went to hug one another, but King Ivan interrupted them by shouting loud enough for the whole hall to hear him. Most of the city folk had filled the room, as had soldiers and other members of the militia. Ivan motioned for Sebastian to join him in front of everyone.

"The men that attacked us are called the Kuhar. They are from the small island in the northeast called Khan Khar. They are hired men trained to kill on command. Someone sent them. I will investigate who, but the good news is they fled thanks to my son, Sebastian." Sebastian turned to look at his Father, confused.

Ivan continued, "Their commander was a young man named Khaliss. The commander is a role that the Kuhar only gives to the most ruthless and dangerous fighter. Khaliss confronted Sebastian and met his fate with the fire my son was born to conjure to protect us. The only reason some escaped with their lives is that they ignited a catalyst. It is a bomb that burns hotter than fire and blasts a blinding green light. They used this because they feared the power of the fire god."

The hall exploded into loud chatter while many were cheering for Sebastian's victory. He looked at Will, and Will was staring at him with a smile of pride. Sebastian stepped forward a few steps and put his hands up to speak; the room fell silent instantly.

"Tonight was no victory. We lost good men. Someone hired these men to destroy us. Did you forget that? This is not the end of it. This is not over. Someone will return to finish this. I did not know who that man was, nor did I care. He tried to kill me. I almost lost my life by his hand. If this taught me anything, it was that we were not prepared, nor was I. We must be ready for the next attack. I won't sit and cheer for this; I will be preparing for what's to come."

He was angry, and the mood in the room was no longer cheerful. People were whispering. Most were asking who would have sent the Kuhar, and others were questioning Sebastian's frustration. Ivan put his hand on Sebastian's shoulder and squeezed lightly. He pulled him back and stepped to speak next.

"My son has a right to be angry. We all should be angry. This attack was calculated by someone who knows our weaknesses, and they targeted us specifically. This was a vendetta. The time has come for me, your king, to decide. I will soon be stepping down from the throne. I have fallen ill and cannot overcome this ailment."

The room filled with gasps and sounds of shock. Even the Drake siblings did not know that their Father was dying. Some of them jumped to their feet and started to move toward him, but he motioned for them to sit back down. Sebastian stepped up to catch his Father's attention. He felt his stomach tense up. Ivan patted him on the shoulder and continued.

"As I become closer to my death, I will rely heavily on my children to keep this kingdom moving forward. Therefore, I want to announce..." He paused.

Sebastian stood there, shaking his head. He knew what his Father was about to say. He wanted to make it a visible protest, but Ivan looked at him without care and continued. "My son, the bravest of my children, Sebastian is now and until the end of his days, your king. Long live King Sebastian."

CHAPTER 16

King Sebastian

Sebastian felt pure frustration and fear. As the people cheered and chanted, he stood there, feeling a mix of sadness for his Father and anger. He shook his head and said to his Father, "I told you I did not want this." He turned and stormed away through the back of the room and away from everyone.

He stood in the next room, mulling it over, wondering if he should go back or just run away. He decided to run to the letter room to write to Cyrus. He had not spoken or heard a word from Cyrus since that night in the stables. He knew he had to tell him everything that happened and everything he felt.

The letter room was an ample, open space that housed crows. There was a desk in the middle with ink and parchment. Sebastian started to write before anyone could chase him down.

Cyrus, I am not sure if you are aware of the things that have unfolded. My brother, Barron, betrayed my Father. He locked me away in the dungeons for three months in hopes of my death. He tortured my brothers and sisters. When he got word of my father's hasty return, he ran a dagger through my thigh, then fled. The next day, my father and I looked for Tomas, but found Fiona dead. That evening, we were attacked by men I had never seen. We defeated them, but I fear things will only get worse for us. My Father is dying. He made me king. Imagine that.

I cannot fathom bearing that burden. I will for my family, and I will fight for them until it kills me. If this is to be my last words to send you, I must tell you, my heart is broken upon hearing of your marriage. I love you with all my heart. I always will love you. You have been the love of my life since the first moment I saw you. My love, I had to say it to you at least once more. I have chosen Will to rule by my side. He will never be you, but he will make me happy. You do not need to write back if you do not want to. I understand you have a new life with your new bride. I am pleased for you.

You will forever hold my heart, my love. Until we meet again.
- Sebastian Drake, King of NorthBrekka

He folded the letter neatly, stamped it closed, and sealed it into a leather pouch. He chose a crow to carry his message, strapped the leather to its back, and sent it flying to Torrdale. He stared out the window for a few moments when he heard footsteps coming up the stairs. Will came running at him, and they embraced each other tightly. "I'm sorry I ran away," Sebastian whispered.

Will stayed in his arms as long as he could, even after they finished hugging. He looked around the room, and his eyes darted toward the open window. "Who did you send a letter to?"

Sebastian hesitated at the question. He did not want to tell him he wrote Cyrus.

"It's nothing you need to concern yourself with."

Will's face turned red. "Cyrus. You wrote to him, didn't you? You want him to come back."

Sebastian gripped Will's arms and jerked him softly to make him stop talking. "He is not coming back. Cyrus is married and has his own life now. He does not want me, and I love you. I want to be with you. Why can't you understand that?" Sebastian squeezed Will's arms. Will looked even more upset at Sebastian's reaction, and he jerked away from his grip.

"You will never love me more than him. I should have known that you would be searching for him. You could have just let it go. I have been madly in love with you for a long time, and you never wanted me until you heard he was married. I was your second choice, and I resent that. I am good to you. I would do anything for you, but you still long for a man who left and never once wrote to you or came to see you."

Sebastian was shaking with anger. Will pushed his chest. "What are you going to do? Are you going to hit me? Or will you use your powers against me?" Will asked, stirring up more anger.

Sebastian slammed his hands down on the desk hard. "What in the hell is wrong with you? You say you love me, but you do not trust me. How will you ever be happy thinking things like that? You will be miserable and worried. I do love you. I wrote to Cyrus to tell him about us and that I am happy to have you by my side. If you cannot be happy, maybe you should leave."

Will clenched his teeth. He strolled up to Sebastian, then punched him hard in the jaw. He started to go but stopped when

Sebastian grabbed him and pulled him back. Will started to jerk his way free, but Sebastian tightened his hold.

"Stop fighting me!" He pulled him down to the floor and pinned him. "Do you want to be with me?"

Will was still fighting to free himself and did not answer.

"Do you want to be with me?" Sebastian said louder and more aggressively.

Will pushed him hard and stared at him for a moment. "You don't want to be with me."

Sebastian was furious. "How could you say that? If I did not want you, I would have let you leave. Instead, I allowed you to strike me without hitting you back. I am holding you here because I love you and do not want you to leave me. You said you would never leave my side."

Will stopped trying to wiggle his way out of his situation. He sighed deeply as he reached up and kissed Sebastian. "Of course, I want you. It is all I have wanted. No, I do not trust you. I feel like the moment you see him, you will forget me. You do not see how much that hurts."

He got up and left, leaving Sebastian sad and helpless. He sat on the floor, clutching his chest with tears building up in his eyes. He put his head on his knees and sat for a long time, thinking about how he would make Will trust him. Of course, Sebastian did love Cyrus, but Cyrus was gone. He moved on.

Will stormed to Sebastian's room. He met Nadya in the corridor. She was standing by the door, waiting. When she noticed Will, she was startled, "Where's my brother?"

"In the letter room, sending crows to Cyrus." He stormed past her. She had a screwed-up look on her face then followed him, catching the door Will threw shut.

"What happened between you two?"

Will swung around and sat down on the bed. "He won't let him go. I thought he could love me, but no." He started to choke up in tears.

Nadya looked suspiciously at him. "Did he say that?" Will shook his head no. "Why do you assume that?"

Will breathed heavily and repeated the entire conversation, including the fact that he punched Sebastian in the face.

"You hit him? Are you insane? He is our king! Do you have any idea what would happen to you if anyone else found out? If he did not love you, you would be locked away. He wrote Cyrus, so what! He was saying goodbye to him. He never got closure, never. He was ripped away from him, from us, and you. He spent months tortured in his thoughts. When he got out, who was there for him? You. You are the one he fell madly in love with. Sebastian would not be with you if he did not want you."

She walked out of the room and slammed the door behind her. Will started breathing hard and could not contain himself. His mind started assuming it was over between him and the man he loved, which caused him to go into a panic attack, crying out for Sebastian. Will always felt like Sebastian would never truly love him. He didn't believe Sebastian when he told him that he loved him. But hearing the words escape his lips was enough.

Will wanted to be with Sebastian so much that he accepted being the second choice. He sat in the bed staring at the door, hoping his lover would come be with him.

Sebastian stood against the open window when he heard someone coming up the stairs. Nadya walked toward him slowly. He did not react or speak. She put an arm around him. He put his arm around her. They stood there, staring out into the cold snow that was falling once more.

"Did it hurt when he struck you?" she said, checking his face.

Sebastian nodded and clutched his chest again.

"He loves you." she said, putting her hand on his.

"He hates me." he said with cracks in his voice. "He broke my heart. Every man I have loved has broken my heart. Maybe I'm not meant to be loved."

"You deserve to have whatever and whoever you want, brother. If you want Cyrus, ride to him. Leave! Get on your horse and ride fast. If you want Will, go to him. Hold him in your arms and tell him how much you love him, then tomorrow, marry him."

Sebastian started to speak but stopped and did not speak another word. Nadya began to move away from him, and before she left, she told him that their Father wanted to talk with him. She also threw in *Your Majesty* and a bow before leaving. That made Sebastian groan loudly, and he could hear her laughing.

He stood, working his mind over, trying to process everything that had happened. He mumbled out every thought in his brain. He realized he was discussing his next move with a crow on the desk in front of him. He shook his head and chuckled a bit, then remembered he had to see his Father.

Sebastian quietly entered the room and first saw his father sitting and watching out into the city. Ivan was next to a window in his chambers. He was smoking a pipe and sipping on wine. Tomas was sitting quietly across the room, writing something in the book. He only stopped and looked up when his Father would cough harshly. He was startled when he noticed Tomas, and immediately walked over to the desk where his brother was working.

"What are you writing about?"

Tomas barely smiled as he acknowledged his brother, stopped writing, and set his quill on the desk. He pointed to the header of the page he was finishing.

Sebastian turned fast to his father. "Why didn't you tell anyone you were so ill?" The heading of the book was written neatly and stated *The Life and Death of King Ivan Drake.* Sebastian stared at the words *and Death.*

"You are not dead yet."

Tomas stood up and reached out to his brother and grabbed his hand. Sebastian could feel his Tomas shaking. He was afraid, in the way that he knew something no one else knew. Ivan coughed again and motioned for his sons to come over and sit by him.

Sebastian cautiously approached his Father's chair. Ivan took both Tomas and Sebastian's hands, and they both knelt before their Father.

"My beautiful sons. My pride and joy. You both deserve the best lives I could ever provide to you. Therefore, on my deathbed, I ask you both to remain together forever. You were bound together at birth when the lightning struck Sebastian, and you touched Tomas's hand. From that moment on, the power of the gods made the two of you connected in a way our world cannot survive without. Always stay together. Promise me that."

Ivan stopped to catch his breath. Sebastian looked at Tomas, worried by the expression Tomas gave.

"Father, please do not overwhelm yourself."

Ivan waved his hand at Sebastian, then continued.

"The few people who saw what had happened said that the two of you were enchanted, and they called you Hydros and Chaos. Tomas, as powerful and remarkable as water, gives life to the world as we know it. Sebastian, as chaotic and uncontrollable as the fire that is both dangerous and magnificent. Chaos will constantly change the world. The two of you need each other. Without one, the other will certainly lose himself, maybe not in death, but in mind. Do you both understand what I am telling you?"

Sebastian saw his feelings on Tomas's face. They listened to the story their father told them. They were holding hands so tightly their knuckles were white. They both nodded in unison at their Father's request for them to stay together. Ivan leaned forward, kissed both of his sons on the forehead, stood, and stumbled over to his bed. The boys followed silently, and both sat on opposite sides of their Father. Each had one of Ivan's hands in theirs. There was not a sound in the room.

"My sons. You two are beyond special. The two of you are going to change the fate of the world. Never forget who you are." Ivan slipped into a rest that he would not wake from.

Sebastian and Tomas sat by their father with tears streaming down their cheeks. Their foreheads were touching, and they didn't speak. Sebastian looked up to see the others has gathered to look at their father, who looked peaceful in death, happily surrounded by his children. The queen walked over from her reading room and sat at Ivan's feet with her hand resting on his stomach. She was looking pale and withered.

She looked at Tomas and Sebastian and quietly said, "You both now understand who you are. Do not ever forget why your Father died. It was so the two of you could go on to do what you are born to do. I love all of you, my beautiful children. Always be there for each other." She gestured around the room to all the family. She lay down next to her husband and slipped away into the same peaceful sleep as Ivan.

Everyone gasped as Nadya reached over to check their stepmother. The queen had the same gray skin as their Father. "Why didn't she tell us she was ill?" she said, not expecting an answer, but Viktor always had to comment on something.

"How is it that they both pass on the same night, with the same illness? It does not make sense. Do you think they were poisoned?"

Sebastian turned his head slowly, feeling angry. He was about to speak up, but Tomas squeezed his hand tightly.

CHAPTER 17

Hydros and Chaos

The death of the king and queen spread across the five kingdoms. Messages came from every corner of the lands from those who wished to pay their respects. Sebastian lay in bed, wrapped in Will's arms, while Will read the letter aloud. "Oh, look, King Roman will be coming. Shall we throw a party?" Will said. Sebastian laughed and rolled his eyes.

"My Father dies, and every man and woman is gathering their best silk gowns and shiny armor to wear to my castle. They wish to pretend they give a shit about my family. How much fun will this be?"

Will looked concerned. "Is Cyrus coming?"

Sebastian didn't answer. There was not a letter from him yet. Nadya and Sara barged into Sebastian's chambers, looking stressed. "How can you still be in bed? Get up!" Sara whipped the blanket off the bed. "I don't care who you are. Get your ass up and get washed. We have guests." Will shot up fast, causing Sebastian to fall out of bed.

"Guests already?" he said, sounding surprised. "Who is here?"

Nadya opened the window to let the sun come in, then sat on the bed. "Are the two of you going to start fighting if you know who has arrived, or can you remain civil?"

Will's jaw clenched up, focusing on Sebastian, who was surprised, saying nothing with his mouth dropped open. "Cyrus." Sebastian gathered his clothes. Nadya grabbed Sara by the arm and left the room.

"Don't say it," Sebastian said without looking at Will. "I know what you're thinking."

"Wait! Sebastian, I love you. You mean everything to me. I refuse to lose you, don't forget me once you see him."

Sebastian stared at him for a moment. Will gathered up his clothing, looked back at Sebastian, then left the room.

He took a deep breath and turned to walk out into the corridor and down to greet his guests. Sebastian assumed it was Cyrus and his wife. He straightened up his clothing and combed his fingers through his hair, then checked his appearance in a mirror. He was a king. He had to look presentable, after all. He stopped in his Father's office and saw the crown waiting on the desk.

The crown was a beautiful silver with diamonds interlaced in the design to appear as snow glistening against steel. He held it in his hands and took a deep breath. He felt a hand reach around him and take it. He turned fast and faced down Tomas. Tomas was smiling at him, looking handsome as he placed the crown on Sebastian's head and adjusted his long hair. "It looks good on you. Are you ready to stand before the five kingdoms, brother?"

Sebastian sighed and shook his head and smiled, then nodded. Tomas laughed, "Just remember who we are. They will all fear us." He winked, leading the way out of the office, and Sebastian followed.

Loud, drunken laughter echoed as he approached the doorway to the dining hall. He stopped in his tracks, feeling disappointed. Tomas stopped and turned to look at him. "What's wrong? Come on. They're waiting to see you."

Sebastian rubbed his neck before he turned to walk into the hall. As soon as his presence was known, a loud laugh and slow clap came from one man he recognized by the drunken laughter. "King Roman, how good to see you again."

"Don't lie, boy. Come over here and let me look at your pretty face with that crown on your head. It is remarkable how such a beautiful piece of steel and perfectly cut gems can look ugly compared to you."

Sebastian scowled. He hated how Roman always commented on his looks.

"I am so sorry to hear of your Father's untimely death, as well as your stepmother. It was a serious loss. Your Father was my best friend."

"Are you sure about that? Last I heard, you wanted to go to war with my Father. He comes home, and we get attacked. Do you know anything about that?"

"Don't you dare accuse me of anything, boy!" Roman stood up so fast he knocked over a bottle of ale. "Your Father and I have always had different opinions on things. Our argument was nothing more than pitiful older men who were tired of seeing each other's faces. I would never harm my best friend. I wrote to your Father after he left, apologizing for my behavior. I did not send those men to your kingdom. That, my dear boy, was arranged by your older brother."

Sebastian suspected Barron over everyone. "How would you know that?"

"Because he tried to pay me to house his soldiers. He tried to bribe me to help him." It was not Roman speaking. The voice was coming up behind Sebastian. "He honestly thought I would help him after what he did to us."

Sebastian turned fast and saw him like it was the first time all over again. He reached out and took Sebastian's hand in his and smiled. His eyes glistened from the fire of the chandeliers hanging above their heads. "Sebastian, my love."

"Cyrus," Sebastian said but felt unhappy. Cyrus's smile quickly vanished, and he looked sad that Sebastian did not react in the way he was hoping.

Cyrus got closer and tried to take Sebastian's hands, but Sebastian pulled back. "No. You have a wife-"

Cyrus cut him off. "I got your letter. Whatever nonsense you were told about me was a lie constructed to hurt you. I have no wife. I never forgot you or left you." He started to stifle tears, "Once I returned home, I received a letter from Barron stating you were dead. I spent these last few weeks lost in my head, in pain, in sadness, until I got your letter."

Sebastian turned to Roman, but he was gone. Sebastian and Cyrus were alone. "Tell me what happened."

Cyrus sat down, motioning for Sebastian to sit next to him. "Letters from Barron came to Alta Prime each week. Your Father would read them aloud for me to listen because I was concerned when I never received a letter back from you. I sent at least a dozen."

Sebastian started to speak, but Cyrus put his hand over his mouth. "Let me finish." He stroked Sebastian's cheek.

"Your brother had your Father convinced that you were out of control, and that the people's fear of your power would grow if something did not stop you. Your Father insisted that Barron concede despite any warning. Ivan truly believed in you. Barron said that he understood and agreed and would step aside for you to take the throne. He was left in charge of the family while you were to take care of NorthBrekka while your Father went to meet with the council. I kept pleading with your Father that Barron had lied. He would not listen to me."

Sebastian pulled Cyrus's hand away. "How could my Father leave Barron at the head of this family after what I told him? Did he not believe me?"

"While in Alta Prime, I constantly chased your Father down to talk to him. After a few weeks, he started to listen as he was getting worried when you never responded to his letters. He feared that something was wrong, but he still stayed in Prime. It was not until the day we left that I begged for his ears to hear my words."

Cyrus paused and looked around. His eyes closed and he was silent. Sebastian wondered if he was thinking about the last night they shared together. Cyrus took a breath and looked back to Sebastian.

"I told him everything about us and about that night. He finally told me how you had told him that you loved me. He knew there was a problem, and Barron was up to something, so he devised a plan to leave before finishing counsel. Ivan feared your death, so he attacked Roman so he could get thrown out of Alta Prime despite my brother threatening war."

Cyrus held the letter Sebastian wrote to him like it was a treasure. "I told Roman about us. He was angry, sent me home, and kept me under watch. Barron wrote to me and told me you killed yourself. I was destroyed, depressed, and angry. I believed it was Barron's fault. All that time he was staging an army to march on NorthBrekka, then the Kuhar attacked. If I had known sooner, I would have sent an army. I would have come for you."

Sebastian was frozen with his eyes locked on Cyrus. "I cannot believe I was so foolish. Barron locked me in the dungeons, starved me, told my father I was home and well while telling my family I was gone. He tore us apart and brought an entire kingdom to its knees. He will pay, but first, I must bury my parents."

"I hear that you chose Will. I promise to be happy for you."

"Yes, I have chosen Will."

"Sebastian, I would give anything to have you back. I loved you from the moment I saw your face. When you and I were alone on that cliff, and we made love for the first time, it was the happiest moment in my life. My stomach tightened, and my heart skipped a beat. Every inch of my body was on fire, and everything I ever wanted or desired in life was nothing compared to how I felt about you. I still feel the same. I will do anything to win your heart again."

Sebastian stood frozen as Cyrus put his arms around him. Cyrus quickly reached forward and kissed him romantically. Sebastian pulled away, realizing it would crush Will if he continued but would destroy Cyrus if he stopped. They kissed again. As Sebastian stepped back, he heard a loud gasp behind him.

"How could you do this to me?" Will cried out with such pain and desperation in his voice that it cut through Sebastian like glass.

"Will!"

"I trusted you."

"You never trusted me!" Sebastian shouted. "You would lose your mind at the mention of his name. I told you he was married, and it was over between us."

"Clearly, it is not."

Cyrus stepped in. "I am not married, and I love Sebastian. If you wish to marry him, you will have to fight me for his hand."

Cyrus and Will stood glaring at each other. Both men were ready to strike at the other without hesitation. Will stood clenching his fists and gritting his teeth. "If you ever touch him, you will wish you never stepped foot in this kingdom again. He is mine."

Cyrus laughed and shook his head. "He was never yours."

Sebastian hurried away to the bench in the garden. It was placed in the exact place where their mother gave birth. He touched the ground, imagining what the scene looked like that day. He rubbed his forehead, feeling the weight of everything crashing down.

Tomas came walking toward him, looking like he wanted to say, "I told you this wouldn't be easy." After seeing the look on his brother's face, he didn't say anything. He sat down next to Sebastian, and they both stared at the ground.

"I don't know what to do," Sebastian finally said. "Cyrus and Will are both here. I cannot deal with this right now. I have five kingdoms of royals and lords and ladies coming here to mourn our losses. Now I have to deal with those two arguing with each other..." Sebastian got louder and more frustrated with every word until he just stopped suddenly and dropped his head in his hands.

Tomas wrapped his arms around him but could not help but laugh. "I can't believe I am hearing about my brother having boy problems." He started laughing even louder, which made Sebastian start laughing. "Maybe you should sleep in my room tonight, so they don't try killing you. Or let them fight, and whoever wins gets to marry you," Tomas said, laughing even harder. Sebastian could not help feeling better.

"Seriously, I have no idea what I am doing. Not about them, about the kingdom. I don't know how to be a king."

Tomas stood up and put his hand out for Sebastian to take it and come with him. They strolled back toward the castle arm in arm. Before entering, Sebastian pulled Tomas back. He stopped and was staring into the open doorway. "I can't go in there." He stood there, shaking his head, looking nervous.

Sebastian pulled away and Tomas walked back into the castle. He sat on the steps and thought about what he was going to say to Will and Cyrus. He didn't want to hurt either of them, but knew he had to choose. He was in love with Cyrus. Sebastian loved Will, but he didn't feel the same kind of energy and happiness like he felt with Cyrus. He made Will a promise that he would never leave him. The right thing to do was marry Will but his heart told him to be with Cyrus.

He stood up and began to pace. His mind became distracted as he kicked the same rock back and forth. He stopped when he heard arguing coming from the open castle doors. He walked inside to see Will, Cyrus, and Tomas standing in the hall. Will and Cyrus looked sweaty, and their clothes were crumpled. They did not acknowledge Sebastian standing there.

Tomas grabbed them both by their shirt collar and spoke. "The two of you need to figure out exactly what it is that you want from my brother. He is outside, upset, stressed out, and sick with everything. We just lost our father. How could the two of you be so selfish? If you cannot be men, leave, and stay away from my brother. He does not need this. He needs support. It does not seem like either of you can do that, not anymore. One of you is obsessed with him, which is not love, Will. The other barely knows him. It is called lust for a reason, Cyrus."

Cyrus turned and looked at Tomas fast. "Don't you dare insult my love for that man." He got up to storm away but was met by Sebastian.

All three of them stood and looked at Sebastian. He was exhausted, angry, and wanted it all to stop. "I never wanted any of this. I cannot justify an answer for either of you. My head is not clear and it is the worst time the two of you could have possibly decided to start fighting." He stared at Cyrus and never broke his gaze.

Cyrus pleaded with him. "My love, please listen to me. I am sorry, I never meant cause you stress. I was just so afraid of losing you again, I..."

Will walked over and stood behind Sebastian and held his arm. Sebastian looked back at Will, took his hand in his, and then turned around to Cyrus.

Cyrus reached out to take Sebastian's other hand. "My love, please. I cannot lose you again. I will die without you. Please do not do this. Don't leave me."

His pleading was heartbreaking; even Will seemed to feel terrible for him. Sebastian stood there, looking back and forth. He looked over at Tomas, who threw his hands up and walked away.

"I can't make this decision right now. I love both of you, but I cannot be caught between your arguing and your constant need to pull me apart from the other one. I have a kingdom to rule. We are on the brink of war, and my Father just died. I have a family to protect. I need the two of you as the strong men you are, and I need those strong men standing by my side." Sebastian pulled his hands away from both and left.

Cyrus and Will stared at each other.

"Should we follow him?" Cyrus asked Will.

"He said both of us can stand by his side."

"Could you handle that, Will? Would you share his love with me?"

"If it means I can be with him, I am willing to try."

"Then it is settled."

They both took off in a sprint after Sebastian, cornering him before he reached the stairs. They guarded him against moving in any direction.

"We promise we will be there for you. You are not going to struggle alone. Men and women from the other kingdoms will be arriving in a few days, and we will not let anyone overstep. They came for your Father, your stepmother, and you. Now, let us go upstairs. You need to relax," Cyrus said softly.

Will and Cyrus took Sebastian to the bed chambers and undressed him. Will messaged Sebastian's shoulders, releasing the tension in his neck, while Cyrus massaged his legs and feet. Will kissed Sebastian. Will was truly in love. Sebastian once told Will that he was the only boy he ever kissed. Then Cyrus came along.

Sebastian started untying Will's pants, then pulled Cyrus in for a kiss. He stopped for a moment. "Are you two going to be able to get along? I want you both. Everyone tells me that I can have anything I want. And this is what I choose but only if you can get along."

Cyrus and Will looked at each other. Cyrus kissed Will's hand, then pulled him over and kissed him. "I will do anything for you, Sebastian," Cyrus said as his eyes were locked on Will.

"Anything for you, my king," Will said. His heart beat fast. He had never given himself to anyone and wanted Sebastian to be his first. He kissed Cyrus, then moved to Sebastian and hoped his fantasies would come true. They finished tearing each other's clothes off.

Sebastian smiled and pushed Will down. He looked like an animal after its prey as he reached down to kiss Will once more until they heard a noise come from the door.

A handmaiden burst through the door to announce the bath was ready. When she saw three naked men in the bed, she hurried out of the room. All three of them laughed.

"I swear I will never get laid in this house," Sebastian said as he climbed out of bed

Will felt a bit strange and shy after all of what just happened. Will sat half-dressed at the edge of the bed while Cyrus was still lying there naked and partially under the blankets. He reached over and ran his fingers lightly down Will's back.

Cyrus asked, "How did you become so close, Sebastian?" He knew surprised Sebastian did not tell Cyrus about their past.

Will perked up a little and smiled. "I met Sebastian, before, when we were young, and my Father was in the war, but we never really thought of each other as more than friends. Maybe as brothers, but we were just boys. I was working on a new locking mechanism for the gates leading to the palace yard when we moved here. Sebastian was on his horse to do what he does best, disappear, and our eyes met. I nearly fell off the ladder when I saw him; he has always been so beautiful to me. I didn't understand it much, but when we kissed for the first time, I knew I loved him."

"Yes, he told me how the two of you grew up together. That you and your sister lived here," Cyrus said lazily.

"King Ivan was very fair to my family. My Father is taking his death very badly. He is worried Sebastian will not show him the same loyalty. I believe that is why he is happy for me to be with him, to ensure the pact between our families continues."

Cyrus stood and grabbed his clothes. "I had better go get washed."

That evening, the family gathered in the dining hall. This time the usual sounds of cheer and chatter were blackened by low mumbling. Cyrus and Will came into the gallery to see Sebastian sitting at the king's table with King Roman. They were speaking quietly and drinking ale.

Will sat down with the Drake siblings. He saw Cyrus approaching the kings cautiously. Roman spoke loud enough for everyone to hear as he offered his guidance on the future of the north. Sebastian appeared to be listening, but Will could see his eyes trail off. The room got quiet until Roman noticed Cyrus standing in front of him.

"What?" Roman snapped at Cyrus.

"I'm simply curious about this sight. It is unusual to see the two of you burrowed up speaking like best friends."

Sebastian laughed, then held out his hand for Cyrus to take. "Please sit with me, my love."

Roman stared at Cyrus. "I guess if you're going to be with a man, then it is a good thing you chose a king."

Will was jealous when he saw Cyrus sit next to Sebastian. Cyrus looked at Will and grinned. Will felt his stomach burn, then Sara caught his attention and asked, "Have you been working on anything new, Will?"

Viktor let out a snort. "Mostly, my brother," He piped up, which sent Gentry laughing loudly.

Sara's mouth dropped. "Grow up!"

This caught Sebastian's attention. "What is going on?"

Everyone silenced and looked at their king. He glared at Sara with intensity. "Sara, go now. You've caused enough trouble."

Will looked at Sebastian. "You don't need to..."

"Do you want to go with her?" Sebastian said with frustration in his voice. Sara turned and looked at Will, smiling. Will looked hurt but walked up to Sebastian and knelt before him. "Of course not. I wish to stay by your side."

Sebastian smiled and took Will's hand. Sara stormed away quickly. "Nadya, go with her. Make sure she doesn't do anything stupid." Nadya stood and nodded at her brother, then marched after Sara.

"What was that about?" Sebastian said crossly to Will.

"I know what the problem is. Sara couldn't have Cyrus; now she has a thing for Will," Gentry blurted out without thinking.

Will blushed as he gasped. "I wasn't trying to get her attention. I promise. My loyalty is to you alone."

"Everyone, go to bed. Tomorrow, guests will begin to arrive. Get some rest." Sebastian said to his family.

Roman took his leave. Sebastian sat with Cyrus on his left and Will on his right. They sat in silence as Sebastian mumbled everything he needed to do moving forward. thought over everything he was to do moving forward. He kept saying that he needed to find Barron. He shook his head, trying to focus on the men on his sides.

"After my Father and stepmother's ceremony, will you both take your place in my kingdom?"

"And just what place do you mean?" Will asked quietly.

Sebastian reached over and lifted Will's head by his chin. "That is for you two to decide. I need to know I can trust both of you," Sebastian emphasized.

Both Cyrus and Will nodded.

In the morning, Will bumped into Sara as he was heading down to breakfast. Sara was stuffing her things into a rucksack.

"Are you leaving?"

"I cannot stay here with Sebastian as king. He is dangerous. You should run too, Will."

"I could never. Where will you go?"

"East. I am going to find Barron. He is the only one who was ever nice to me."

"Your brother is a murderer. How could you go to him?"

"He is not my brother, Will. I am not a Drake. I hate Sebastian. I always have."

"The Drakes took you in when you were a baby. You can't seriously betray them now by running off to Barron."

"I can, and I will. He wrote to me asking me to come, showing me where to find him. You can come too."

"I love Sebastian."

"And Sebastian loves Cyrus. If you stay, he will cast you out you the moment he and Cyrus marry. You would be a fool to stay." Sara shoved past Will.

"You might be right, Sara. But I refuse to give up now. He is the only hope my Father and I have for living a good life. If I do not stay with him, we will be left to struggle with the rest of the peasants. I need him."

Will walked away toward the baths to find Sebastian. He peeked through a door to see Sebastian resting him head while soaking in the steaming water. Then he heard another voice. It was Cyrus.

Cyrus knelt behind Sebastian and reached to kiss him softly on the forehead. Sebastian looked up at Cyrus and smiled.

"What are you doing, my love?"

"My king, you cannot marry Will. He is using you. He told Sara his father wants the marriage, so Will is taken care of after his father passes. I am the one who loves you. I will never betray you, I promise. Please consider my hand over his."

Sebastian reached out to kiss Cyrus. "I asked you not to do this."

"I swear, I am telling you what I just saw. Please trust me."

"I will talk to Will, but for now, go and let me relax."

Cyrus walked toward the door. Will sprinted down the corridor, then down the stairs. He hid in a nook until he heard Sebastian yell "Where is Will?"

Will met him at the base of the stairs. He tried to catch his breath. He grabbed Sebastian at the shoulders and went in to hug him, but Sebastian pulled back with a jerk and looked at him furiously.

"Don't you touch me. I know what you did, what you said. You and my sister? After what we have been through together. I thought you loved me. Go home to your father, Will." He pushed his way past him.

Will spun around fast, grabbing Sebastian's arm. "No, it is not over. I love you with all my heart. You are mine, remember?"

"I really did love you," he said quietly, then pushed Will hard in the chest, which knocked him down. Sebastian walked fast down the stairs. "Do not follow me."

Will jumped up and began screaming. "Sebastian, wait! You were not told everything. Yes, I spoke to Sara, but I swear I told her I would not go with her. Sebastian! You said you would never leave my side! You lied."

Sebastian ignored him and kept walking away. Will walked down the corridor, screaming Cyrus's name. He began kicking open doors. Most rooms were empty, but he scared some of the little ones when he slammed through their bedchamber door screaming. Finally, he barged into Viktor's chamber, and Cyrus was standing there waiting.

Will's face was wet from sweat and tears. He lunged forward and jumped on Cyrus, knocking him to the floor. Will felt an arm loop around his waist. He jerked as he saw Viktor pulling him off of Cyrus. He swung and elbowed Gentry in the lip by mistake. Viktor was taller than the rest of them. He picked Will up and held him back with his arm wrapped around his neck tightly. Cyrus jumped up and punched him hard in the stomach, then in the face.

"Stay away from Sebastian! You are not a lord, a prince, or noble of any sort. You are not good enough for him. You were going to use him. How dare you play with his heart."

"I was never playing at anything. You were jealous. You did this on purpose," Will cried. "You ruined my life!"

Will took off in a sprint. The others ran down the stairs trying to catch him, but he was too fast. He ran straight into the throne room, where he found Sebastian sitting on his throne. His head was hanging, and the crown upon his head was glistening in the firelight. He looked up slightly, and the pupils of his eyes were red, which stopped Will in his tracks. He had never seen Sebastian's eyes change color. It was an intimidating sight.

"I told you to leave," Sebastian said.

He heard footsteps approaching. He saw Viktor, Gentry, Nadya, Cyrus, and Sara. They gasped.

"Sebastian... Your eyes. What is wrong with your eyes, my darling?" Cyrus said.

Will swung around, looking at Cyrus. "Stop calling him that. He is not yours!" He grabbed Cyrus around the neck and began choking him.

"Let him go," Sebastian said in a very calm voice. He walked forward slowly, and the fire of the candles began shining brighter and flickering intensely.

Will released Cyrus and turned to face Sebastian. Tomas walked into the room, hurried over to his twin, and put his hands on his chest.

"Brother, please, you have to calm down. You cannot control this yet. You are going to hurt someone," Tomas said, but Sebastian was ignoring him.

Sebastian pushed his way past Tomas and walked over to Cyrus, who was on the floor. He knelt to put his arm around him and lifted him, holding him up while Cyrus caught his breath. It was an obvious move of passion and love between the two as

Sebastian held him in his arms with Cyrus's head buried in his chest. Will felt defeated and started pleading with Sebastian again, reaching out to touch his shoulder.

"Please do not do this, my king. You are everything to me. I cannot live in this world without you."

"Leave." That was all Sebastian said, and he turned to take Cyrus to bed. Will fell to his knees, crying loudly, "Please do not leave me." Sara ran over to hold Will, and he cried into her arms.

Nadya stepped forward and looked at them both.

"You both need to leave! You know what you have done. He does not need this. Sara, how dare you? Why would you do this? You have always been a part of this family, but you want to throw it away for Barron. Why?"

"Because I love Barron. I always have." Sara said with an unusual, manic tone in her voice. "Will, one last offer to come with me."

Will choked back tears. "I love Sebastian, but I am afraid of him. He is so intimidating."

Tomas stepped forward and leaned down. "You should be afraid of him." Tomas's brown eyes were now blue.

"What are you? What are both of you?" Will said. "You two are not human. You can't be."

"No, we are better," Tomas said, then left the room.

Will jumped to his feet. "I don't understand what is going on here. I cannot stand by when my Sebastian promised me a life with him, then he turned his back on me just like that. Fine, I will leave if that is what Sebastian wants. He has torn my heart from my chest. If he will not have me, I will not stay. Sara, let's go." He reached his hand out to hers. She accepted it.

They both straightened up and walked away. Will hesitated with every step. He kept checking over his shoulder, hoping Sebastian would run after him, but he never did. They went to the stables, took horses, and left. He could see Tomas watching from his bedchamber window as they rode out of the kingdom. They were gone so quickly, giving up on their families and those they loved, distraught from hurt and heartbreak.

CHAPTER 18

The Funeral and a Message

Tomas entered the bedroom to find Sebastian stroking Cyrus's hair and kissing his cheek. Cyrus stared into his eyes as though he were looking into his soul. They both looked sad for each other. Tomas could hear Sebastian say several times, "I am so sorry, "and Cyrus replied, "Do *not be.*"

Tomas stepped in just enough to say, "they are gone. They have left the kingdom. I am sorry for both of you."

Sebastian turned and looked at his brother. He had a tear rolling down his cheek. He just nodded at Tomas in appreciation, then Tomas left and closed the door behind him.

"I really did love him," Sebastian said. Cyrus brushed his cheek with the tips of his fingers.

Cyrus asked, "What was with your eyes? Why were they red?" Sebastian shook his head, but Cyrus insisted.

"It came with my power. I didn't know I could do it until it happened. Do not worry, my love." They kissed and wrapped up in each other's arms and went to sleep.

Days had come and gone, and Sebastian was grateful for the silence in the castle as he lay in bed listening to Cyrus sleeping soundly. He was sad about Will leaving but still felt at peace. He smiled as the warm sun crept through the curtains and shined on his face, knowing it was brutally cold outside.

Cyrus started to stir as he awoke and stretched, then wrapped his arms tightly around Sebastian. He smiled and laughed lightly as he buried his face into his warm chest. Sebastian kissed him on the forehead and held him tight.

"I could stay right here for the rest of my life and be happy," Cyrus said.

Sebastian smiled, then made love to Cyrus before he was disturbed again. Horns began blaring, echoing through the castle. Sebastian rolled his eyes and stretched, yawning loudly. "Time to go. It is time to grieve my Father properly. Come now, Cyrus, get dressed. I need you on my arm today."

Sebastian and Cyrus washed their faces, combed their hair and began to dress in their finest. Tomas hurried in without knocking with a piece of parchment clutched in his hand.

"Don't you ever knock? I could have been naked," Sebastian said.

"Please, brother, we are twins. I know what it looks like."

Cyrus laughed while tightening his boots. Sebastian sat on his bed, half-dressed, staring at his brother, smiling while Cyrus kissed him on the cheek. Tomas sighed deeply, shook his head, and reached out to place the parchment in Sebastian's hand.

"What is this?" Sebastian said while unfolding the letter.

He started reading the letter to himself, and the smile quickly vanished from his face. Cyrus grabbed the letter and began reading it aloud.

"Dear brother,

I was saddened to hear of the death of our Father. I know it pains you to have such a heavy burden to bear alone. You were not meant to lead, let alone reign. Your grief will forever be my pleasure. I will be the first to inform you that I discovered an interesting little thing on the road late at night—your sweet Will traveling with my lovely Sara. I have intercepted him for your peace of mind, and he is safe here with me, for now. You will meet me on the East Bay Pass at the north and south crossing by the sea tonight if you want him back. You will come alone, or his safety will be heavily compromised. We will discuss matters of the utmost importance in these challenging times. If you choose not to come, I will send his head in a box, then I will come for Tomas's, and to my delight, yours. Think about your actions, brother, and I look forward to seeing you alone.

Barron."

Sebastian sat completely quiet and still.

"You cannot go, my love," Cyrus said.

"He has Will. He will kill him if I don't. He will come after you. I have no choice."

Tomas sat down next to Sebastian and put his hand on his chest. "Your heart is pounding out of your chest. Let me go with you, at least consider-"

"No! He said to come alone!"

"If you go alone, he will kill you," Tomas growled, his eyes turned blue, and his hands were freezing on Sebastian's chest.

Sebastian looked at him in surprise, then pushed his hand away. Tomas stared at his hands. His eyes turned brown again.

"We have guests," Sebastian said as he reached his hand out, indicating for Cyrus to take it and go with him. Tomas placed his crown on his head. They left the room together and walked confidently down to face the growing crowd.

The throne room was full of well-off lords and ladies as well as royal families. They all fell silent instantly upon Sebastian's presence. He walked toward the throne with a scowl on his face, with Tomas and Cyrus closely following. His brothers and sisters were all sitting in the front row along with King Roman and Queen Lorna. Sebastian turned and sat with elegance. He held his head high, letting his eyes gaze across the room full of people waiting for Sebastian to speak. Sebastian stretched his neck and looked out over the room discontentedly.

"Thank you all for coming so far from your warm homes to grace my halls concerning my late Father and stepmother. This is a time for great sadness. My Father was a strong man. He always had the best of intentions for his children and his kingdom. He did whatever it took to keep peace among our nations. He put a lot on us, his children, to be extraordinary. As we sit together, united, we must remember one thing. We are all different, but we are all the same."

Sebastian paused to take a deep breath. Roman kept a stoical expression, yet Sebastian could distinguish the sadness masked by the strength of a man used to loss. He looked at his brothers and sisters. Some, unable to contain their pain, while others wore a blank, broken face, unsure of what would come.

"We are living in this world for the same purpose. To build a world that is both beautiful and beneficial. To love and be merry.

To enjoy our freedoms and explore the unknown. We remember our lost loved ones. We think of the lessons they taught us and smile at their warmth. My Father and stepmother shrouded us in love and happiness. They were our parents, our friends, and our leaders. Never forget the lessons we learned. Never forget the great people they were. We will memorialize them in our hearts as we forever move forward. Now, let us pray."

The room was humbled with tears as everyone bowed their heads. Sebastian did not believe in praying so he kept his head up. He watched in silence as the room mumbled out their prayers, then looked again at him, waiting for what he would say next. He stood and stepped forward.

"I won't bore you all with heavy speeches today. I will end my speech with this. There is darkness in our lands-this burden to my own house, given by Barron, from the torment of his own mind. I do not ask any of you to stand behind me. I will face this myself to protect you all. We in the north are at war. I will stand with my head held high and my sword at my side-"

King Roman stood and interrupted. "You are not alone in this fight. Alta Prime will stand by your side."

This incited others to stand. Cyrus stepped forward. "Torrdale will stand by your side as well, Your Majesty."

Others knelt before Sebastian pledging their allegiance. This made him feel strangely uncomfortable. He sat back on his throne and rubbed his face. Cyrus patted his shoulder. Sebastian's muscles tensed and he straightened up his shoulders. Cyrus leaned down and whispered, "Calm down. They're trying to offer help."

"Is it possible, Your Majesty, that they attack you because of what you are? Your power has stirred unrest," another voice said.

"Who are you?"

"Jace Astra, of Oyster Cove and the city master's son."

"What standing does your word have?"

"The fear is that you will act unfavorably, especially after the loss of your Father, your newfound role, and of course, war. My Father's word, not mine."

Sebastian laughed. "You go tell the city master if he fears war, then to stay out of my way, and no harm will come to Oyster Cove."

"You need a teacher. One to educate you on how to use your power for good successfully. I have heard of a man who might be of service to you."

Sebastian ignored Jace's words. "Go home, Jace."

"Let me help you, Your Majesty."

"I said go! Now!" The room got quiet. "Now, continue discussing the war, gentlemen."

Sebastian listened as suggestions were made until he heard enough. By then, he was tired and frustrated, thinking of meeting Barron that evening and thinking about how he would face him and what he would say. He was also thinking of Will. He was not interested in seeing him but also did not want him to get hurt.

As he was going over his plan in his head, he realized the hall had gone silent, and Cyrus was squeezing his shoulder. He shook his head and looked to see the people whispering and staring, looking confused. He stood and motioned for everyone to stand.

"There is a feast awaiting this evening. Please join my family while we dine, drink, and remember." He turned to take Cyrus by the hand and pulled him away from staring faces. "I need to speak with you first."

Sebastian walked fast toward his Father's office, pulling Cyrus behind him. They went inside, and he quickly shut the door, then he spun around, feeling weak.

"I cannot entertain our guests this evening. I must meet Barron. I will need you to lie for me as no one can know I left."

Cyrus went to grab Sebastian's hands, but he pulled away. "You need to reconsider riding out there alone. You are a king. You should never leave the kingdom alone. At least let me go…"

"I said no. I will not risk anyone's life if Barron finds out you came with me."

"You mean you won't risk Will's life," Cyrus said with a hint of jealousy.

"Are you going to do this right now? Seriously, at my Father's funeral, you want to question me about Will? Have you gone insane?"

This seemed to stir up a lot of resentment from Cyrus as he cringed at Sebastian's reaction. He quickly straightened up angrily then pushed his way to the door while Sebastian tried to stop him by grabbing him around the waist. He pulled Cyrus close to him and stared into his eyes. "I love only you." He softly kissed him, but Cyrus pushed him back.

"If you love me, then marry me today before you go," Cyrus demanded.

"Cyrus, I want our wedding to be a happy moment. Not when my brother's demand burdens me. I promise we will be married soon."

Cyrus pulled open the door, and before leaving, he turned around to say one last thing. "If you are going to go, then leave. Do it now before anyone sees you. I will make something up, but when Viktor or Nadya search for you, do not expect me to chase them because I will not. When you return, if Barron does not cut you open, and Will is on your arm, don't expect me to stay this time."

Cyrus slammed the door shut and walked away fast. He was trying to control the tears running down his face before he had to face a room full of hungry people and tell them Sebastian would not be joining them. All Cyrus could think about was that he said he would leave Sebastian if Will came home with him. He wanted to turn around and go back to apologize, but his brother was waiting for him outside the hall entrance.

"You look like hell. Why is your face all wet? Are you crying?" King Roman said in the typical rude tone he used with his brothers.

"Leave it alone," Cyrus said as he started to push his way past his brother. Roman grabbed him tightly by the shirt collar and pushed him back against the wall.

"Let's go talk in private, right now," Roman said and began to drag Cyrus off without his answer.

"Where is lover boy? Did you have a fight? Well, get over it because something strange is going on here. I have a feeling the two of you are the ones behind it."

"Nothing is going on. Will and Sebastian fought, so Sebastian made him leave. He took Sara with him. Now he is in trouble, and Sebastian feels like he has to go and save him," Cyrus growled.

"Does this have to do with that idiot brother of theirs? That boy has always had something wrong with him. I warned Ivan of it, but he did not listen. Well, shall we go after them or not?"

"We can't. Barron ordered Sebastian to be alone, or else he will hurt or kill Will. He is sneaking off to go down the East Bay Pass. The ride will take him much of the day. He had to go now."

"He can't travel the pass alone. By the time he reaches the peak, it will be dark. He's going to get killed out there," Roman said as he started gathering supplies.

"Please, brother, just let him do this. He is strong; he will make it. Besides, if he comes back with Will, I am leaving. I'm not going to be a part of this..."

Roman's expression silenced Cyrus's tirade instantly. "Are you stupid? You love the boy, don't you? Would you walk away just like that? No, you would go home to your castle and cry like a little girl over it. If you want to prove your love, follow him. Who cares what Barron says? Get off your ass and go and take someone with you, so you don't get yourself killed too."

"You need to get everyone to leave after the feast. Yourself included. If Sebastian makes it home, there is no doubt he will be followed. You heard him; the north is at war. We are not prepared for this. Go home and gather an army," Cyrus said.

"If we leave, then we leave NorthBrekka helpless."

"If you leave and everyone else leaves, they won't have people to slaughter. Then you return and destroy Barron. Now leave it alone and do as I ask."

Roman grabbed his brother by the shirt collar and pushed him against the door. "Don't be giving me orders."

Cyrus tightened his jaw and shoved Roman's hand off his shirt. "I said, leave it alone. Sebastian will not be joining us today. We shouldn't keep everyone waiting."

Cyrus began to shove his way past Roman. His brother was much bigger than him, and all he had to do was step in his path again.

"I will make sure everyone is gone and safe. We will be back. Go after him."

He started to push his way back toward the entrance but stopped and leaned back against the wall as he began sobbing uncontrollably. Roman was not good at emotional things, but he reached out to hug his brother. He pulled Cyrus tightly into his embrace, trying to calm him before anyone noticed. He patted him on the back and tried reassuring him that he did not have to leave if he genuinely cared for Sebastian.

He expected more eyes on him as he entered the hall. The acknowledgment was on King Roman, and he heard faint whispering from those who wondered when the northern king would be entering.

"His Majesty cannot join us for this feast. He had a matter he needed to attend to right away and had to leave. He asked for everyone to enjoy the feast and apologized for his absence."

The whispers grew loud. Without explanation, some began badgering Cyrus for answers until Roman slammed his hands down on the table.

"King Sebastian's business is his own. Remember why we are here. Eat your food and shut up."

As the feast commenced, Nadya approached Cyrus and sat close to him, then she grabbed his knee and squeezed hard, causing Cyrus to gasp.

"Tell me where my brother is now!" she said fiercely.

"I can't. You have to understand."

Nadya was not satisfied with the answer as she got up and marched over to Tomas and badgered him for answers.

"Why are you asking me?" Tomas said.

"I can feel it within you that you are afraid of something. Tell me now or else…" she said with a tight grip on Tomas's hand.

"Or else what? Let me go."

His eyes began to change to blue, and Nadya jerked her hand away. "Stop that! You will worry our guests."

Cyrus was ready to sprint through the doors and go after Sebastian. Tomas grabbed Cyrus and demanded he sit down, but Cyrus pushed him back. "We have to follow him. He cannot do this alone. He is going to die."

"Would you get it under control? You know what will happen if Sebastian does not go alone. You read the letter." Tomas began until Nadya jumped up to face them.

"What letter? What are you talking about? What has happened?" She looked at them both as if she would drive a knife through their skulls if they did not start explaining.

"Not here," Tomas said, motioning for her to follow him.

They went up to Sebastian's chambers. Tomas handed Nadya the letter. She read it aloud quickly, and her voice grew louder as she concluded. Just then, Viktor and Gentry burst into the room. They had been listening behind the door.

"He can't take all of us. I am going to help my brother," Viktor shouted as he ran away.

Cyrus ran after him, then Nadya, Gentry, and Tomas. They caught him in the stables as he mounted his horse.

"Please, you can't." Cyrus fell to his knees. "He will kill Sebastian. Then he will kill Will and Tomas. Please, Viktor, do not follow him. I am going, but alone."

"I will not allow my brother to walk into a trap!" Viktor exclaimed as he kicked his horse and rode away fast.

CHAPTER 19

The Mad Prince

Sebastian took the trail through the mountains to meet the East Bay Pass. By this time, the sun was low, and the cold night was moving in. The pass was nearly impossible at night as the temperature dropped extremely low. The winds howled through the thin stretch of road between two tall mountains.

Legends say the pass was haunted by the men who built the road. They died of cold or starvation or from the animals living in the caves.

Sebastian did not fear tales or animals. He was not afraid of ghosts or the cold. He pushed his horse to run fast and not stop for anything. The ridge along the peak of the mountain was where the pass met the open road. There was no protection from the walls of the mountains, and the way dropped on one side. One mistake in footing meant death. He knew if darkness fell, he would not be able to see the ground, and his horse would fall, taking him down with it.

His hands were stinging from the cold as he tightened his grip on the reins. He struggled to keep his vision from getting blurry. It was so cold he could feel the moisture from his nose and mouth freezing on his skin. His bones ached with every movement, but nothing was going to slow him.

The sun was deep behind the mountains, and the dark began swallowing the path. As they made the final descent, the light vanished quickly. Sebastian felt his stomach churn as he strained to see the road below his horse's feet, hoping his horse could see better. He trusted his instincts and pushed forward, not slowing pace. His heart raced faster with every step as the hill descending the pass began to get steeper.

Sebastian began getting dizzy and could not hold his tight grip any longer. He started to tremble, and his legs shook hard as they tried to carry his weight. He could no longer hold himself up, and with one quick movement, he fell from his saddle and landed hard on the rocky ground.

He lay there, holding his shoulder as it throbbed in pain. There was faint light illuminating around him from the stars shining above. He finally caught a glimpse of the full moon coming from beyond the pass. It was warmer in the valley. There was no snow, and the winds were light. Sebastian stumbled to his feet, brushed the dirt off his coat, and then walked over to his horse, joining him for a drink of water. "We have to keep going. We still have far to go before midnight."

Meanwhile, Viktor rode fast as he approached the ascent to the pass between the mountains. It was blackened dark, so cold the air stung, and the wind cut through his lungs. His horse was hesitant to continue, but Viktor pushed forward. He heard shouting approaching him from behind and turned to see the others riding fast.

"No, don't follow me; it is too dangerous." He could not see their faces but felt he knew it was the others.

"I am not staying behind and waiting for the bad news," Cyrus said as he passed Viktor on the road. They could barely see each other's faces. Tomas then came upon them with a torch in hand, then Nadya with another.

"We will ride closely together, the torches in the back or the winds will put them out. I will lead with Viktor on my right side, and we will block the wind as much as possible. Easy we will go, but swiftly. Sebastian is surely already down the pass by now."

They ascended to the ridge. Cyrus halted, holding his hand in the air. "This is the most important part of the pass. We ride in a straight line, one before the other. One false move, and you die. Understand?"

Everyone quietly agreed, and Nadya passed her torch forward. Tomas moved to the rear of the group, and Cyrus took the lead on the descent. He leaned forward to hold his light close to the ground, watching for the edge of the cliff. No one spoke a word as they carefully made their way down. The brutal cold made it hard for all of them to sit still on their saddles.

"The air is so thin," Viktor shouted. "How much farther?"

"How would I know?" Cyrus answered. "I've never been here in the night."

Nadya was chattering her teeth and shaking. "I can't take this much more."

"Not much farther, just hang on. It is warmer below."

Cyrus was shaking badly. "I am going to have to walk the rest of the way." He jumped down from his horse, but Tomas yelled at him with terror in his voice.

"Get back on your horse!"

Everyone turned to look at him, wondering why his voice was so angry.

"We are being followed."

"Why are you just now telling us?" Viktor said. "What is following us?"

"Wolves," Tomas said. "They're waiting for one of us to falter. They are hungry."

Cyrus quickly jumped back on his horse. "Thanks."

"We couldn't tell Sebastian that we let his lover get eaten by wolves, can we?"

Everyone laughed wearily. Cyrus hurried forward on the path, which made the others nervous.

"What's with him?" Viktor asked.

"He and Sebastian started fighting before dinner. Cyrus told Sebastian he would leave him because Sebastian went to save Will. Now he is going because he feels guilty," Nadya said.

"Ah, a lover's quarrel. Why are we a part of this again?" Gentry said.

"Because our brother is stubborn and can't make up his mind about who he wants to sleep with more," Viktor continued.

"I can hear you all," Cyrus said. Everyone got quiet again.

As soon as the ground flattened and the air got warmer, everyone took a deep breath as they could see again. Tomas turned to see the wolves still following and started counting them.

"Eight. There are eight following us." Tomas jumped off his saddle and walked toward to pack.

"Tomas!" Nadya screamed. Cyrus jumped from his horse and ran to Tomas, but he pushed him back without speaking. He handed his torch to Cyrus and walked again toward the wolves.

The wolves growled and showed their teeth. Tomas's eyes turned blue. He growled back, then leaned forward, ready to lunge at the alpha. The gray wolf moved toward him alone, and they were soon nose to nose. She poked his chin with her nose then stared at his eyes. Tomas did not blink or move. Then, the alpha female pushed her head under his chin before turning to lead her pack back into the mountains.

"How the hell did you do that?" Cyrus asked.

"I wish I knew. I just had a feeling. Sebastian once told me a story about his encounter with wolves. He said he stared the alpha down, and she respected him. But let's go before the wolves change their minds."

Cyrus sighed and hung his head. "I do not understand what he sees in me. I have no miraculous stories of valor and bravery. I spend my days reading books and lying around in my castle when I could be learning about the world. I see why he loves Will. At least Will is not afraid to get his hands dirty."

"Don't say that Cyrus." Nadya patted him on the shoulder. "Sebastian loves you for who you are. He does not want someone like him."

"He doesn't even like himself," Tomas interrupted. "He likes Will because Will makes him feel good about himself. But you inspire him. He wants to be a better person for you. If you let his friendship with Will destroy what the two of you have together, you will break him. He needs you more than he knows."

"We should keep moving." Cyrus urged forward.

As midnight approached, Sebastian arrived at the crossing where the east road ended and only allowed north or south passage. In front of him was a ridge that dropped into the ocean, where the sea crashed angrily below.

He stared off into the blackness of the sea. There was no sign of Barron and his army. There was no noise other than the sea and a light wind. The full moon shimmered on dew of the grass in the field behind him as he looked around to find any sight of men. A faint hum crossed the wind. He paced back and forth on road leading from North to South.

The northbound road crept downward at a long slope toward the sea. It ended at the shore where tattered docks clapped against the rocky shore. No one used those docks anymore. He hopped on his horse and rode to the shore. A small boat sat tied to the end of the pier with the silhouette of a more massive ship out at sea. It was an odd sight as most large ships port in Oyster Cove to avoid the northern sea ice. This ship meant his brother came to the old harbor to remain undetected.

The shoreline was long but eventually cut off where the bluffs stacked to the crossing. There was no evidence of Barron or an army.

"Barron!" he screamed. "I came alone as you asked. Show yourself!"

He heard the humming sounds again, but this time they were louder. Sebastian was curious and began searching for the source of the noise.

"Hello? Barron, is that you, brother?" There was no answer. This infuriated Sebastian. "Barron! Where are you? I am here now, so face me!"

The humming sound became intense and started to sound more like crying. Sebastian realized it was coming from the boat resting against the dock. A torn old sail was all that he could see, but from beneath, it gave away the source of the hum.

Sebastian climbed down into the boat carefully and pulled the sail back. A beautiful blond-haired boy, bloody from being beaten, looked up at him with teary eyes. It was Will. He was tied up. His hands and legs were bound, and his mouth gagged. There were noticeable cuts on his neck where it looked as if someone had tried hanging him. Sebastian felt a hard pit hit him in the stomach, and he fell to his knees before Will and started cutting his bonds. Then he removed his gag.

"You shouldn't be here; it is a trap. Barron is not here, Sebastian; please go. Go home. He is there at the castle. He is going to kill everyone," Will said, choking out every word. Sebastian was so shocked by the sight of Will that he grabbed him and held him tightly in his arms.

"I am so sorry. This happened to you because I sent you away. I should have never..." Sebastian said quietly, but Will interrupted him with more aggressive tones.

"Did you hear what I said? He is going after the whole kingdom. He lured you away on purpose. He never meant to meet with you.

He will burn the kingdom to the ground, he said, and rebuild it for himself. Your people will be his slaves."

"Then why did he let you go?"

Will looked at him, "Because the boat is rigged to explode. Barron expected you to find me and try to rescue me, but it will explode if I get out of the boat. You have to go without me."

"I won't leave you."

Will pushed Sebastian off him hard, which made him fall back. Sebastian was frustrated, but then it hit him all at once.

"Wait. You said he was going to attack the castle. Do you know how many people are there for my Father's funeral? All the leaders of the five kingdoms are there. There is no way he will win that fight. There are hundreds of thousands of soldiers. He has no chance."

"Sebastian, you need to get back. Forget about me. Cyrus is there. He needs you, so let me die. I told you once; I do not want to live without you. I still love you."

Sebastian froze in place. "Cyrus. Oh hell, Cyrus. I am such a fool. I love you. I always will love you. It damn near destroyed me to send you away, but I thought you and my sister..." He stood in the boat and looked frightened. He rubbed his face and pushed his hair back.

"Your brothers. Your sisters. They need you," Will continued.

"I cannot let you die, Will. I just cannot, even after everything. I care about you. What can I do? What did he rig to this boat to make it explode?"

Will grabbed him and pulled him close, then kissed his lips. "There is nothing you can do. Just leave and save your family. I am good with this. I want this. Without you, I–"

Just then, loud noises came from the cliff. There were screaming voices shouting Sebastian's name. He jumped out of the boat and stared up, seeing the flickering of a fire. He recognized one voice, Tomas, because the sound was the same as his own. Sebastian started yelling back and waving his arms.

"Tomas, down here by the water. North on the road, I am here!"

The flickering firelight disappeared quickly, and it got quiet. Sebastian hoped Tomas had heard him, so he ran to the shore and watched for his brother to come. "Tomas!"

"Sebastian! Thank the gods we found you." This was not the voice of Tomas. Sebastian started toward the road in a sprint as he recognized the second voice as Cyrus's.

"My love, why are you here?" Sebastian said as he embraced Cyrus. "I thought you said you were leaving me. I am so happy to see your face."

"I was just angry and stupid. I would never leave you. I had to come after you. I couldn't let you die," Cyrus said, holding Sebastian tight. Then the others caught up.

"You're all here!" They looked confused as they thought Sebastian would be angry. Tomas ran over to him and embraced him tightly. Nadya pushed past Sebastian looking down at the docks.

"Where is our brother? I am going to cut his head off."

Sebastian grabbed her by the arm. "I am happy you're here, but you came for nothing. It was a trick. Barron lied; he is at the castle."

Nadya swung around and looked at Sebastian, confused. "How do you know that?"

Sebastian signaled for everyone to follow him.

They walked down to the dock where the little boat was tied to the end, seeing Will sitting in the middle. It was evident in the moonlight he had been beaten severely. He was bleeding from his head, which matted his blond hair. He had scrapes on his bare chest and arms, and the scratches on his neck were bleeding.

"Will, you're hurt," Tomas said painfully as he started to board the boat to look at him. "Come on. We have to get you out of here."

"No!" Will yelled. "You can't. I can't." He explained again the explosive Barron attached to the boat.

"If I try to leave, the boat will explode. I cannot let you all get hurt trying to save me. Just go, all of you. I will detonate it when you are all long gone."

Cyrus laughed, then grabbed Sebastian's arm, indicating for him to leave. Sebastian was shocked that Cyrus was so quickly willing to let Will die. He jerked his arm away, looking at Cyrus angrily. He grabbed Sebastian's arm again, only tighter this time.

Sebastian grabbed Cyrus by the throat and squeezed. "We are not leaving him, do you understand me? Leave if you want. I am staying."

Cyrus began breathing hard, shoved Sebastian off him, and mumbled, "I knew you would do this. I knew you would betray me the moment you saw him."

"Both of you shut up. We can figure this out," Viktor said, amused. "Maybe we can fill the boat with rocks to offset the weight for enough time to get him out." He started gathering rocks and tossing them into the boat.

Sebastian jumped back into the boat and knelt before Will. "We have to try. Take my hands. I am going to get you out of here."

Will looked up at Cyrus. "No, don't, please. He needs you. He loves you. I cannot hurt either of you anymore. Just go, all of you."

Cyrus looked at Will and started rubbing his neck. Then he grabbed a big rock next to his foot and tossed it in the boat. "Just shut up and let us try, for fuck's sake."

Sebastian held Will's hand tight, waiting for them to finish so he could save him as soon as he was clear to do so. Viktor stopped and calculated in his head that there should be enough. Sebastian tightened his grip and stepped back, ready to pull fast. Will stood, looking terrified.

"If this does not work, we all die. I am not worth your life, Your Majesty," Will said one last time.

Sebastian paused and winced. "Don't address me so formally. You know I hate that." Then he yanked Will, pulling him to the dock, and they stumbled back and fell hard onto the wooden planks. Sebastian held Will tightly against his chest with his eyes squeezed shut, waiting for an explosion. There was not one.

They sat up and looked at the boat, then each other. Will pulled Sebastian in for a kiss. Cyrus shook his head and walked away toward the road without saying a word. Sebastian pushed Will away and ran after him. Just as he reached Cyrus and grabbed him, there was the explosion they all expected. Cyrus looked mortified, but he grabbed Sebastian and held him, not letting him see what happened.

"No, you can't. Oh, my darling, no, don't look, please!" He was hysterically crying and holding Sebastian with all his strength as he struggled to break free.

Sebastian pushed Cyrus so hard he fell to the ground, then turned to look at the devastation. The boat had exploded and was burning so forcefully it lit up the sky. He looked at the place Will had been sitting, but there was only fire.

Sebastian was screaming horrendously. Nadya and Viktor ran over to pull him away. They had to struggle, but Viktor managed to pull him off the dock and to the shore. Sebastian fought to make Viktor release him but instantly stopped and froze.

"Gentry," he managed to pinch out of his mouth.

Gentry was lying on the sand, not moving, his eyes wide open, with a piece of wood from the boat pierced through his throat.

Sebastian opened his mouth to scream but nothing came out. He hurried over and held his little brother in his arms. Tomas was right by his side, then Viktor and Nadya rushed over to hold their deceased brother and cried together. Cyrus slowly walked over to the dock's edge and sat quietly, eyes streaming with tears as he stared at the place Will was seated before.

He reached his hand toward him, whispering, "I am so sorry."

Sebastian kissed Gentry's forehead and closed his eyes before laying him into Nadya's arms and walking away. He walked over to Cyrus and reached his hand out for his. Cyrus looked up at Sebastian and tried speaking but could not. He took his hand nervously, but Sebastian yanked him up and held him in a tight embrace. He whispered, "It isn't your fault. But I am going to kill the person who did this. We need to go back now."

Cyrus was locked in place, looking at the dock where Viktor was carrying Gentry. Cyrus did not say a word as Sebastian tried to get his attention. He started walking toward the pier again as he focused on the fire burning.

Viktor had Gentry wrapped in his coat and was stroking his hair. Nadya was still sitting in the same spot in the sand. She was staring at the ground, running her fingers through the sand and rocks. Cyrus stepped onto the dock and walked toward the fire. Sebastian got anxious and ran after him.

"What are you doing?" he asked. "I know how horrible we all feel, but we have to go now. Viktor, we must leave him. We will bury him here."

"Are you insane? He is going home to rest with our family and with our Father."

"How do you plan to carry him through the pass then? We can send people to him."

"We are taking him now!" Viktor demanded.

Sebastian stopped arguing and started focusing on Cyrus's odd behavior again. "Cyrus, we need to go now."

Cyrus knelt before the fire and poked at it, which annoyed Sebastian enormously. Sebastian began to yell, but Cyrus quickly interrupted. "This isn't Will."

Everyone instantly looked up at him. Sebastian ran over to him.

"It's the sail that is burning. We just couldn't tell because the flames were so bright."

"Then, where is Will?" Sebastian said, looking around. He walked straight across the flames and looked down into the boat, then jumped down into the water and reached down, trying to feel for a body but coming up empty-handed. He started looking around frantically.

"Sebastian," Nadya said, waving her arms at him, then she pointed as she got up and ran into the water.

He dove off the dock and swam in the direction Nadya pointed. Cyrus jumped down to the sand and began to follow, but Viktor grabbed him. Sebastian reached where something floated on the water's surface.

"Will?" Sebastian lifted him in his arms and swam to shore. Nadya hurried over and began checking to see if he was alive.

Sebastian slapped his face lightly while he stripped off his coat and wrapped it tightly around Will's cold body. Nadya pushed hard on his chest, which sent him into a panic as he choked out the water in his lungs. Sebastian held him upright and patted him on his back.

Cyrus came over and wrapped his arms around them both, trying to warm them. "We really need to go."

Viktor, devastated to leave Gentry behind, laid his brother on a grass patch near the road and promised him that he would send someone to bring him home. Nadya said her goodbyes to Gentry, then walked up the trail to the road. Sebastian handed Will off to Cyrus and sent them up the path as he fell on his knees next to Gentry.

"I am sorry, brother. I would never leave you, but we must go and help our family. I love you so much. I promise to bring you home and let you rest with Father. I promise."

He reached down and kissed Gentry's forehead, then took his horse and left to follow the others. As they met at the crossing, everyone stood looking toward the mountains.

"What are we going to do when we get there? We do not even know how many men he has. How are we alone going to fight an army?" Cyrus asked.

"There are soldiers from all over the nation there. Chances are, they have already defeated Barron," Sebastian said.

"No, they all left. I told my brother to make everyone go. I did not know this would happen," Cyrus said frantically.

Sebastian sighed deeply. "It's fine. We will fight them, no matter what. I will face my brother, and I will kill him."

Everyone mounted their horses, and Sebastian reached for Will's hand and pulled him onto his horse. Will wrapped his arms tightly around him and rested his head against his shoulder. Sebastian looked over at Cyrus, worried about hurting him, but Cyrus smiled and reached to hold Sebastian's hand. He whispered, "I understand." They started toward the mountains.

CHAPTER 20

Captured

Sebastian strained in the icy air atop the ridge. He was determined to focus ahead. He was cold and shaking. Will tried to help but being injured and soaking wet himself, was not helping at all. The journey back was tranquil. Cyrus moved forward to ride alongside Sebastian.

Sebastian noticed Viktor lingered in the back, looking angry. Nadya kept checking on him, but he would look away. They started into the descent through the windy trail. Daylight began poking over the mountain peak.

They came out to the overlook. Sebastian stared down at the kingdom, looking for signs of a fight. "It's quiet. Will, did you overhear any of his plans?" Will sat up and looked over Sebastian's shoulder.

"It isn't on fire like he said it would be. Maybe someone stopped them. All he said was they would burn it all down."

"Then this is a good sign," Sebastian said as he guided his horse back onto the trail and started moving down the mountainside faster.

"Sebastian, don't rush. It could be another trap!" Nadya called to him but followed quickly.

They approached the gates into the broad open castle grounds and slowed down as they knew the gates were never left open and unattended. There was no one inside or outside the wall. No one was working, cooking, speaking, or anywhere in sight.

They dismounted and walked around cautiously. Cyrus held on to Will as Sebastian walked toward the castle entry. The doors were open as well. He turned to face the others, looking confused. Everyone was looking lost about the situation, but there was a definite tension in the air.

"Barron!" His shouting echoed through the grounds. Everyone looked around nervously. Sebastian turned away from the castle and walked toward Will and Cyrus. He reached out to take their hands.

"Sebastian!" Cyrus shouted.

Sebastian felt a sharp pain as a rope looped around his throat and yanked him backward. Men scattered around the group with loaded crossbows pointed at their heads. The men kicked each of them down to their knees and began tying them up. Sebastian was being dragged away fast by the rope and was struggling to breathe.

"Tie him up over there," Barron said as he walked into sight. A stage stood with gallows set up for hanging.

"String him up, but don't hang him yet. Set him on his knees. Remove his shirt. Leave him there until I say. Put that one next to him," Barron said, pointing at Tomas. "We don't need him trying anything stupid. As for Sara, lock her in my chambers. She is now my personal slave. As for my brother, Viktor, put him with the others, and those two, kill them."

The men locked their crossbows on Will and Cyrus. They positioned themselves to fire, then Sebastian screamed, "No! Please stop. Do not hurt them. Kill me, torture me, do whatever you want to me but let them go."

Barron smiled as he motioned for his men to stop. "That is a fair offer. We will see how strong you really are. Lock them in the dungeon for now. This will be fun."

Sebastian was helpless as the men dragged Cyrus by his hair while he screamed out Sebastian's name, begging him to save him. Will was exhausted and frail as the men carried him by his arms. He stared at Sebastian, sobbing and muttering as they dragged them both inside and out of sight. Sebastian was breathing heavily to the point of getting ill. They brought Tomas over and strung him up next to him but not close enough for them to touch.

"They will be okay, brother," Tomas said quietly, but Sebastian locked on Barron and glared.

Barron approached Sebastian, bent down over him, grabbed his chin, and taunted him to the point of Sebastian raging. His eyes began to tingle and burn. "Are you mad, dear brother? Good. I hope you kissed them before you came down that mountain because it will be the last time you ever touch them." Barron laughed and pushed Sebastian. He walked away quickly and into the castle, then the doors slammed shut. They were left outside in the cold with two men watching them.

Meanwhile, Viktor, Will, and Cyrus went into the dungeons. The guard threw Viktor into a cell with a few of his siblings, who all ran over to hug him. Will and Cyrus could hear them asking about Sebastian and Tomas, then Nadya and Gentry. When Viktor told them of Gentry's death, they could hear crying.

Will and Cyrus were taken to a dark corner of the dungeon and chained to the opposite wall. They could reach each other but just barely. "What will they do to them?" Will asked.

"Barron is going to kill him. It is inevitable. Tomas too. He knows about their power. He won't risk keeping them alive for too long," Cyrus said painfully. "I'm sorry, Will. I have been a terrible friend to you and Sebastian. I was so afraid you would steal him from me that I couldn't see how happy he was with you."

"You had a right to be. I was hurt thinking Sebastian would choose you. He even said he would have us both, but I was too greedy to accept it even when it made him happy. I could be happy sharing his love with you if it meant we would all be together. I am sorry as well," Will said, squeezing Cyrus's hand tightly.

Cyrus looked at him and smiled. "We will need to be there for each other if anything happens to Sebastian. I can't imagine losing him, but I can't be alone if we do."

"Quiet! Both of you shut up, or you will regret it." A man came shouting at them. His accent was strange, but he was large and intimidating. Will and Cyrus stared at him curiously.

Nadya sat on the bed in Barron's chambers, fuming. She sat still and quiet with a knife in her hand, waiting for Barron to enter.

The door creaked open, and Nadya stood fast, blade out. It was not Barron. It was Sara. Nadya dropped the knife and ran over to hug her sister. Sara seemed cold to accept her, but Nadya kept rambling on about everything that had happened.

Sara was not very receptive to Nadya's explanation as she just lazily nodded. Nadya noticed and stopped. "What is your problem?"

"Nothing is wrong. Barron is my husband. He is good to me," she said in a monotone voice that was very unlike her.

"He is your brother!"

"Not by blood. Now draw me a bath. I would like to bathe now." Sara pointed to the room next to theirs. Nadya looked at her like she was mad. "Are you stupid? I said, draw me a bath now!" She pushed Nadya hard, which made her fall onto the bed. "Don't have me call my husband, the king, to make you do this."

"Sebastian is our king," Nadya spat.

"Sebastian will be dead soon." Sara laughed, then slapped Nadya hard across the cheek. "Now, do as I say, or you will be next in the gallows."

Sara started to walk out of the room. Nadya was seething. "How could you do this to your own family, you traitor!"

"I am doing whatever it takes to protect myself. None of you had any respect for Barron or me, so I am taking my chance now. Draw me a bath. I will not ask again." She walked through the door, slamming it behind her.

Outside, it was late afternoon, and the sun began to creep behind the mountains. Sebastian was nodding in and out of sleep. Tomas was sleeping, but when he woke, he complained he was hungry.

As it became dark, the men came out and lit fires all around the courts. Barron came out with Sara gripping his arm, and they sat down in chairs facing the gallows. He smiled at his brothers, then waved at one of his men, who ran inside and quickly returned with all siblings following, as well as Cyrus and Will.

All bound with their hands behind their backs. Men pushed them to their knees and lined up on the ground just before the gallows, so they had a good view. Each had a soldier with a crossbow pointed to the back of their heads. Cyrus stared at Sebastian as he felt this was when he would watch Sebastian die. Will begged as Barron stood before him. "Please don't do this. I will do anything you ask of me. Please don't kill him."

Barron looked at Will, surprised. "Who said I was killing him? Not today, anyway. Well, maybe. We will see how this goes."

Barron circled so he could address everyone. "My dearest family and friends. I am the oldest, and I have always been the head of this family. When our Father chose Sebastian to rule over me, I got my revenge, and then I did a little investigating. Father said they are descendants of the gods. Pfft. More like demons. Disgraceful abominations."

"Stop it, Barron. Shut your mouth now!" Nadya scorned. Sara walked over and slapped her again, making her lip bleed.

"Demons. They can't be allowed to be a part of this family anymore. They are dangerous and will only bring war and suffering to these lands." Barron finished.

"Why don't you fight me like a man?" Sebastian spat. "You are a disgrace and coward! You are a scar on this family. How dare you come back to our family's home and place a dark cloud over this kingdom? They do not deserve this. Fight me, and we will see who is fit to be king."

Barron smiled, then nodded to a man who stood behind Sebastian. The man pulled a whip from his side and swung it. It cracked hard against Sebastian's bare back.

"Again," Barron instructed, and the man swung and cracked a second lash on Sebastian's back.

"Keep going until I tell you to stop. My brother needs to learn his place."

The man struck Sebastian five more times. Sebastian was screaming in pain. Tomas was frantic, trying to rip his hands free so he could help his brother.

"Did I say stop?"

The whip slashed again and again. With each lash, Sebastian felt himself getting dizzy. Blood was streaming down his back. Three more times the whip struck him before Barron held up his hand. Sebastian had blood coming from his mouth, and he could barely see. The pain was unbearable. His flesh ripped open, blood pooling beneath him. Sebastian sat perfectly still with his eyes locked on Barron.

"I said I didn't want to kill him yet."

Cyrus's screamed, "Stop, please."

The man with the crossbow threatened to pull the trigger while another man held him down by his throat. Sebastian could see the terror on his face. Will refused to watch. He held his eyes closed tight, and his head turned, but one of the men forced him to look.

Sebastian was bleeding all over the ground. He was in horrible pain and fought to catch his breath. Will lunged back at the man with the crossbow and knocked him on his back. He jumped to his feet, then ran toward the gallows. Another man jumped out and kicked him hard in the face, and it knocked him unconscious.

Sebastian saw his younger siblings crying which made Barron angry enough to shout at his men to escort them back to the dungeons. The remaining siblings were Nadya, Viktor, and Mary. Will and Cyrus were kept behind as well.

"Where is our brother, Gentry?" Barron asked.

"You killed him," Viktor said with gritted teeth.

Barron laughed loud. "How could I have killed him? I've been here this whole time."

"The boat explosion you set up," Nadya said quietly as tears ran down her face.

"Oh, that," Barron acknowledged. "That wasn't designed to kill him. It was for Sebastian. But as you see, that didn't go as planned," he said as he glared at Will, who was still unconscious. Barron kicked him hard in the ribs, which caused him to jerk awake.

"You were supposed to die too," Barron said, bending down over Will.

"But it killed Gentry, so I am going to kill you," Viktor roared.

Barron hurried over to Viktor and grabbed him by the neck and punched him hard in the face until Viktor succumbed. Barron turned and stared at Tomas.

"Why do you think you are in the position you are in right now?"

Tomas did not answer but glared at Barron with a deadly expression. Barron raised an eyebrow. "Because you are ignorant.

You are one of my favorite brothers. I would have allowed you to be free if you had been loyal to me, but you chose to follow him. You could have been powerful and had respect. Still, you chose to follow that reckless and detestable, unworthy little bastard sitting next to you."

"That's enough," Sebastian forced out but just barely because every little movement hurt severely.

"You've made your point, Barron. Now let them go!" Nadya said.

"Nadya, quiet," Sebastian said. "It's me that he wants to hurt, not you."

Barron stood laughing. "No, brother, I want to kill you. I want you to die. So, if you could go ahead and do that, it would save us all a lot of trouble."

He turned and left after telling his men to take the others away. Cyrus proclaimed his undying love for Sebastian once more. He said that he would find a way to free him no matter what he had to do.

The next day, no one came outside except when the guards changed shifts. They would bring a small chunk of bread and throw it up to the twins. Tomas ate, but Sebastian refused. He was in so much pain he could not bear to move. "You have to eat," Tomas whispered.

Another day came, and it was the same routine. Tomas begged Sebastian to eat, but he again refused and pushed his food to his brother. It was snowing. Sebastian was shirtless and freezing, but the snow felt good on the gashes on his back that had finally stopped bleeding. He lay against the boards of the gallows with his face down, trying to stop thinking about the pain. Blood matted in his hair and stained his back. Tomas lay next to him. Sebastian shuddered and spoke.

"Tomas, when I die-"

"If you die," Tomas interrupted.

"If I die, take care of them. Protect our family from him. Don't let him win."

"You are not going to die. I will not allow it. I am going to kill Barron. The moment I break free of these bonds, I will wrap my hands around his throat and squeeze until I feel his life slip away. For what he has done to you, and to them, he will die by my hand."

Sebastian drifted to sleep.

As he woke up, Sebastian stared at the ground in front of him. He watched his tears melt the snow. "I am going to kill every last one of his men, and I will torture Barron until he begs for death. He will regret betraying our family." Sebastian whispered, "We have to figure out how to get out of these bonds."

Sebastian sat up a little straighter. He twisted at the ropes that bound his wrists. Tomas tried getting his attention to tell him to stop before he got caught. Sebastian ignored him and kept turning at the rope.

When he saw it loosen, Tomas immediately started to do the same. They worked at their bonds all day until they realized they could pull their hands out. "Wait, not yet!" Sebastian whispered as Tomas started freeing his hands.

The guards on duty made their usual visit, bringing bread to the twins. Sebastian held his bonds in his fist.

"Are you ready, Tomas?"

"Ready for what?" one of the guards asked.

Sebastian jumped to his feet, kicked the guard in front of him hard in the face, then leaped from the gallows. He took the rope, wrapped it around the guard's throat, and started strangling the man.

Tomas punched the other man in the throat, then conjured the water from a puddle. He waved his hands around and formed the water into a long spike of ice. He punched his fist out, sending the ice through the guard's chest.

Sebastian was enjoying strangling the soldier. The guard was clawing at his hands, hoping to break Sebastian's grip, but he could not. Soon, he fell, and Sebastian stared at his body and smiled. Just as he was enjoying his victory, men surrounded the twins, weapons drawn. Barron marched out, followed by men dragging Cyrus, Will, Viktor, and Nadya.

Barron noticed his men lying there in front of his brothers, and his expression turned into fury. He ordered his men to fire on his brothers. Just as the men cocked their crossbows, Sebastian saw Tomas's eyes turn blue, then felt the familiar tingle in his. The ground started shaking. Everyone looked around in confusion, but Barron's gaze locked on Sebastian, who appeared to be concentrating on something.

"Kill them now!" Barron screamed furiously. The men aimed their crossbows again, then Sebastian and Tomas grabbed hands as they looked at each other sadly yet angrily. Sebastian thought if they died, they would die together, hand in hand. They did not look away from each other but could feel the ground shake again, and a bright flash of fire and a freezing wind blasted the men on their backs.

There was silence. The guards on the ground all lay dead with burns and gashes across their bodies. Even the twins had no idea what they had done as they looked at each other oddly. Barron stared at Sebastian, then looked past him and nodded.

"Barron, your men are dead. Surrender to me or die."

"You underestimate me as usual." Barron waved his hand.

Before Sebastian could react, he felt the sharp sting of an arrow from a crossbow pierce his shoulder. He turned quickly, then shoved Tomas hard to make him fall to the ground as five more came at him at once. All hit him in the same shoulder and his chest.

Sebastian stood there, looking at the arrows that pierced into his body. His breathing was made short from the pain. Blood dripped from his mouth and nose. Barron grasped the arrow nearest to Sebastian's heart and twisted.

"I hope this hurts," he whispered as Sebastian shrieked in agony.

Will screamed and reached his hand toward Sebastian's. Barron stepped away. Sebastian stumbled to take Will's hand. The moment their hands met, Will fell into his arms. Barron ran his sword through Will's stomach, yanked it back, then thrust it through Will's chest.

Both Sebastian and Will fell to the ground. They lay face to face as Will slipped away to his death. Cyrus rushed to Sebastian, draping his body over him to protect his lover from Barron. Sebastian felt nothing and could hear nothing. He gazed into Will's hollow blue eyes until he felt Cyrus being ripped away from him.

"Cyrus, no!" Sebastian struggled to help him, but could not stand. He fell again to his knees. His head swam through the blurred image of Cyrus being beaten, kicked, and choked as he was dragged away.

Barron knelt before Sebastian and smiled. "Captain, take my brother. Put him in the coach. Take him as far north as you can bear to travel. When you get there, throw his body out on the icy ground and leave him there to rot."

"No, please, Barron. Let us bury him with our family. You robbed Gentry of this, please, not Sebastian too," Nadya begged, but Barron ignored her.

Sebastian drifted in and out of consciousness. He could not move, and Barron proclaimed him finally dead as he cheered for victory. Four men marched over and lifted Sebastian and carried him away. They dropped him to the floor of the coach and jumped inside and slammed the door behind them, then demanded the driver go north.

Cyrus screamed and began running after the coach, but two men dragged him away as he kicked and flailed violently. They pushed him into the tower and shut the door and locked him inside.

Barron turned to Nadya and Viktor, as they lay over Will, crying for him and Sebastian. Nadya cried, "I'm sorry" while stroking his hair. Barron lifted her by her arm and yanked her against his chest.

She cursed and slapped him hard. Barron stood still, watching her as she ranted at him. He almost seemed amused by her reaction.

Viktor was catatonic. A man came and picked him up, but Viktor collapsed back to the ground, so the man had to carry him over his shoulder. Viktor did not react and just stared in the direction the coach took his brother.

Tomas ran over and jumped on Barron's back and started striking him on his head. Barron shoved Nadya to the ground. He turned to thrust his sword toward Tomas, who had fallen back when Barron pushed his sister down. Tomas rolled out of the way of the blade and scampered to his feet. He reached out and grasped Barron around the neck, forming ice on his skin. Barron screamed and pulled on Tomas's hands, trying to break his grip.

"Maybe it is me who is the evil one after all. Perhaps you murdered the wrong twin, brother. I will make you suffer. I will make you beg for mercy." Tomas gripped Barron's throat tighter until water droplets suspended in mid-air around them. He twitched his head, then the water formed into shards of ice that pointed at Barron, waiting for Tomas's command. Barron managed to free his leg and kicked Tomas in the chest. He stumbled to his feet and took one step toward Tomas just as Nadya grabbed the sword Barron had dropped and pushed it through his leg.

Barron screamed and fell to the ground. Tomas reached down and pulled the sword out and was about to shove it through his chest. Men came charging at him, weapons drawn. He stopped, dropped the sword holding his hands in the air, and advised Nadya to do the same. Barron spat at his men to take them both and lock them up until he could decide what to do with them.

CHAPTER 21

The Far North

Sebastian stared through a small hole in the coach as it sped away into the dark of the mountains. His kingdom shrank from view, and he could no longer hear the commotion of his family screaming and fighting back from the hell that struck NorthBrekka that day. He tasted blood in his mouth and felt the scars on his back that had torn open again.

As everything went quiet and just the murmur of the enemy soldiers surrounded him, he felt weak. The coach sped as fast as the horses could run, going farther into the North. He could feel the blistering cold creep inside.

Sebastian was on the floor on his side. He bled from the arrows that were still in his chest. He was alive but barely able to move or breathe. His eyes were open, and he would sometimes see one of the men crouch down to look at him.

"How is he still alive?" a man said. He had a heavy accent that was gruff like he had something stuck in his throat.

"Who cares? He will not be once we get rid of him. He will freeze to death out there," Another man said.

"I'm about to freeze to death here. Maybe we should just throw him out now and turn back south."

"No! His Majesty said to take him to the ice. He will know if we didn't."

Sebastian started laughing. One of the men grabbed him by his hair. "What is funny?" he said in an aggressive tone.

"You called him Majesty. How is it that men like you, from a distant land, would accept my idiot brother as their king?" Sebastian said, laughing even harder.

One of the men kicked him hard in the ribs. Sebastian kept laughing until it sounded manic. "I think he is delirious," One of the men said.

The man reached down and grasped one of the arrows in Sebastian's chest and began twisting it. Sebastian screamed out in pain and contorted his body until the man let go. He started laughing again, infuriating one of the men, who grasped a chunk of Sebastian's hair on the side of his head and sliced it off with his knife. He began braiding it, then put it in his pocket.

"I will give this to the king as a gift after I tell him we had to cut your head off for acting like a madman."

They passed the forest that separated the northern kingdom from the far north, riding through the night. They continued at full pace for several days, riding in silence until evening fell and the coach began sliding on the ground beneath them. One of the men yelled at the driver to slow down as he peered out the window.

There were no more mountains this far north, just solid white as far as he could see. They slowed to a halt. One of the men opened the door and hopped out. He cautiously stepped around the ground.

"This will work. We are on top of a frozen lake. We will leave him here."

Sebastian felt hands grip around his ankles just before being pulled to the ground. He hit the ice hard. He stared at one of the men intensely.

"What are you staring at, boy?" the man asked. "This is where we leave you."

"Are you afraid of death?" Sebastian asked.

The man looked at him anxiously, then Sebastian kicked him hard in the knee. He could hear the bones in his leg snap with a loud crunch. Sebastian watched as the man fell hard, breaking the ice when he hit the ground and falling through into the lake below. Sebastian jumped back and laughed, then turned to look at the others. Blood was dripping from his body onto the ice. He began crawling toward the soldiers. They all hurried into the coach and screamed at the driver to go.

In only a moment, the coach was off in the distance. Sebastian stood there, staring at the hole in the ice. He realized he was freezing, so he began walking in the same direction the coach went as a stream of blood painted the ground around him.

He struggled against the cold and his hunger but forced himself to keep walking. The sun began to set. It was snowing so hard he lost the coach's tracks. He had no idea which direction he was supposed to walk.

As night came, Sebastian realized just how dark the Far North was. There was not much moonlight giving him any hope to see, but he kept going anyway. As the darkest of the night came, it began snowing harder. Sebastian was so painfully cold; his legs kept locking up. He started to crawl, but before long, he felt the same weakness in his arms. His body was freezing internally. He knew he would die soon.

He stopped and lay still, waiting for death to take him. He whispered goodbye to his brothers and sisters. Then, he told Cyrus he loved him and spoke to Will, Gentry, his Father and stepmother, telling them how hard he tried and how sorry he was.

He said nothing more as he lay in the snow, waiting for death. He tried to sleep, thinking it may be easier to pass away if he did, but the bitter cold prevented him from keeping his eyes closed.

The sun peeked over the horizon. He saw a blurry hint of its light, smiled at it, then closed his eyes, and kept them closed.

"Father, come quick! There is a man in the snow. He is hurt. I think he's alive."

Sebastian squinted and blinked fast, trying to clear his vision. He could start to make out the image of a girl kneeling over him. Then a man knelt next to her.

The smell of meat forced his mind to snap awake. He sat up startled when he realized he was inside a house and lying in a bed. As he stood to have a peek around, he felt his chest and realized the arrows were gone. The house was small, covered in fur rugs, and the walls hardened with mud and straw. Thin, hanging blankets separated a few beds. He poked his head through the blanket surrounding his bed and saw the man and two boys sitting at a table while the girl was cooking in a pot over a fire.

"Who is he?" one of the children asked.

The man whipped around fast and stared at Sebastian. He was very tall and broad, with a long beard. His hair was long, brown in color, and braided tight down his back. He stomped over until he was inches from Sebastian.

"Who are you, boy, and why were you in the snow? Don't you know you could have died? And why were there arrows in your chest?" he said with a mean and growling tone.

"Sebastian Drake," Sebastian replied. The entire room silenced and stared at him with wide eyes. "I was attacked and dumped out here by my brother's men.

"Wait. Did you say, Drake, as in the royal family?" the girl said, walking over fast.

"Amara, stay back," the man said.

Amara looked at her father angrily, then turned and went back to cooking. Sebastian ran his fingers through his hair and stopped when he felt the spot where the soldier cut a piece out. He stopped and shouted angrily. "I need to get home. My family is at war, and I—"

"You aren't going anywhere in your state. You are ill, so just lie down, and my daughter will bring you something to eat when it is ready. My name is Boris. That is my daughter Amara, my twin sons Hilos and Rigar. My wife, Flora, will join us soon."

"I appreciate everything you have done to help me, but I must get home. My brother is mad. He tried to kill me. My Father died and left the kingdom to me. I have to get home and save my family..." Sebastian started until he got dizzy and had to sit.

"You will stay. Rest," Boris said.

Sebastian lay down and fell fast asleep. Amara shook him awake that evening. She was holding a bowl of stew she offered to him as he sat up. "Thank you," he muttered. Amara smiled and brushed back the side of his hair that was still long.

"I can fix it if you'd like," Amara said. "So, you're a prince."

"King," Sebastian said while eating his stew.

"A king? So, your people attacked their king. What did you do to make them so angry?"

"They weren't my people," Sebastian said a little more angrily. He noticed Amara look at him nervously. "Sorry. My older brother is a traitor. He found the Kuhar and hired them to attack my kingdom. Then he became their king and brought them to NorthBrekka to kill me so he could rule."

Amara nodded. "I'm sorry to hear that."

Amara had long wavy brown hair that she let flow loosely. She had a pretty face and pale white skin, and green eyes. She seemed to take a liking to Sebastian. "I removed the arrows and patched you up. I also made a salve for your back. It seems to be healing nicely. You had an infection set in, but I have been treating it for a few days. I think you will be back to yourself before you know it."

"A few days?" Sebastian said quickly. "How long was I out?"

Amara laughed. "About ten nights. You woke a few times so I could feed you, but you weren't very coherent."

"Why are you helping me?"

"Most people say thank you," Amara said as she started walking away.

Sebastian groaned as he sat up. "I'm sorry, thank you. I just need to know when I can go."

"Oh, you can leave whenever you want, but since you're sick, you won't get far. It is winter, and it is frigid. There is a storm coming. So, if you wish to go, then go. Otherwise, lie down and rest." Amara said with a put off tone.

"I don't mean to be rude," Sebastian said.

"And I understand that you are a king, as you claim, but this is my family's home and our village. You will respect it. Do you understand me?"

Sebastian laughed loudly. "Okay, I get it. Well, if I must stay, can I go outside? Can I see the village?"

Amara jerked her head toward the door. Sebastian walked by and looked at the twin boys. "You know I have a twin brother too." The boys chuckled a little, and Amara smirked.

Sebastian walked outside the door. It was cold and windy. Amara followed him out and handed him a coat. "Take this. It is colder here than what you are used to."

"Thank you," Sebastian said, then smiled politely.

"You have a pretty smile," Amara said, then quickly hurried back inside.

Sebastian looked at her in surprise but then put his coat on as he walked. The village was small. There were several tiny houses like Amara's and a small forge close by where Boris worked. He wandered over, slowly watching Boris work at the basin, melting metals.

A woman came out from behind Boris quickly as she noticed Sebastian. She marched over and popped a knit hat on his head. "Your ears will freeze," she said, patting at his head.

Sebastian smiled in appreciation. Boris stopped working and looked at him, confused. "What are you doing out here? Go back inside before everyone sees you."

"That is no way to speak to a king," Flora snapped.

"He isn't our king," Boris snapped back.

Sebastian walked away. "Sorry, I'm just getting some air. I was wondering, where am I?"

Boris laughed. "Where do you think? This village is Northpost. It is as far north as any human lives."

"How far are we from NorthBrekka?" Sebastian asked.

"When the weather is fair, eight days' ride on horseback. Right now, in the winter, several weeks' ride, assuming you make it. You won't make it," Boris said, amused.

"I'm stronger than you think," Sebastian said.

"I'm not saying you're not strong. Those wounds would have killed most men. Who would be able to survive six arrows in the chest, let alone being stranded on the ice? I do not understand how you are alive. I know nothing about you, but I can see something in you, and it is intense. But if you go into that storm, you will not make it home."

Sebastian stood there, pridefully. "What am I supposed to do? Sit and wait for summer to come?"

"You can hunt and build and work," Boris said plainly as he went back to his forge.

Sebastian stared at the forge sadly as he thought about Will. Amara walked over with some torches as the sun was setting. "Why do you seem so grim?" she said, looking at Sebastian.

"My intended was a blacksmith," Sebastian said.

Boris jerked his head up fast. "A woman blacksmith?"

Sebastian smiled while looking down at the ground. "No. He was a man. His name was Will. My brother killed him. He died in my arms."

Everyone got noticeably quiet. Amara brushed his arm. "I'm really sorry."

Over the next few months, Sebastian started feeling like himself again. He would go ice fishing with Boris and bring home fish for the whole village. He got to know everyone. Many of the men of Northpost were harsh. The women were motherly, even the ones with no children. Some of the women, mostly the young stronger ones, were huntresses. Most adolescent girls would flirt with Sebastian often, but he acted like he did not notice.

Time passed by as winter turned to spring. Sebastian and Amara spent a lot of time together. They would often walk through the village talking, and he would help cook each night. They picked on each other, mostly, which made Sebastian forget about how angry he always was.

"You ready to let me fix that hair of yours now?"

Sebastian sat down and Amara began running her fingers through it. Sebastian closed his eyes and thought of Cyrus and how good it felt when he always played with his hair. As she ran a razor across his scalp, he lost the sensation of warmth. It was as if she was trimming away his fondest memories of Cyrus, but he let her work.

Amara pulled a section of hair across the crown of his head and lined it up, so it was even on both sides, tied it into a knot on top of his head, then cut the other side short with scissors. Once she had finished cutting around the side and back, she ran the razor across his scalp again. She untied his hair that she left long and brushed it back until she could tie it into a bun.

Sebastian felt across the back of his head and around the sides when she had finished. He went to the mirror and realized he did not appear as himself anymore. He looked older.

"That is how the warriors of Icefall wear their hair," she told him.

"Icefall?" Sebastian asked. "What warriors?"

Amara walked up behind him and wrapped her arms around him, looking at his reflection, and he looked at hers. "There is a village on the western coast called Icefall. It is named appropriately. The men there are all fighters that constantly train in the event war comes north again."

Sebastian did not say anything, just stared. Amara squeezed him tighter. "You are incredibly handsome," She whispered in his ear, then kissed it softly.

Sebastian pulled away from her. "I hate it when people tell me that."

"I didn't mean to offend you. I was just... I don't know, I thought maybe we..." She stumbled.

"I have someone back home that I wish to marry one day... if he still feels the same for me," Sebastian said, getting quieter toward the end.

"But I thought he was dead."

"I'm not talking about Will. His name is Cyrus. Prince Cyrus of Torrdale."

Amara looked confused. "So, there are two men you would have married? That's selfish of you."

Amara walked away fast and out of sight. Sebastian wanted to apologize to her but did not understand what he had done wrong.

"Amara, come back and talk to me. I didn't mean to say anything to upset you, but I thought you would understand that I prefer men..."

Amara poked her head from behind the curtain. "I understood that clearly. I just thought since we have so much fun together that you were... Nothing, never mind. It's stupid, so just forget I said anything."

Sebastian walked over and grabbed her hand, "You mean, you thought that I wanted to be with you? It is not a ridiculous thought, but you know I am trying to get back home. Why start something if I will be leaving?"

"I said to forget it. I just thought maybe you would stay..." she started.

"I am the king of NorthBrekka! Why would I stay here when I have my family, my kingdom, my lover waiting for me?" he said, a little more annoyed than he intended.

Amara stormed out from behind the curtain. "Then go home!" she said, then walked out the door, mumbling something about how she was stupid for falling for a foolish royal from south of the forest.

CHAPTER 22

The Darker Days

Cyrus sat by the door to the tower and spoke to Nadya any day she was allowed free time. She brought him extra food, parchment, ink, and even clean clothing when she could. They would talk about what was happening. Cyrus would always ask if there was a word from his brother.

Nadya spoke quietly through the hole in the door where Cyrus could hear.

"I stole a letter from Barron's chambers. It is from Alta Prime. King Roman took his army north after he returned from my Father's funeral. He gathered the Knights of Torrdale and rode to NorthBrekka. When they crossed the wall near Stormfire Lake, they stopped to rest. While they slept, the Kuhar ambushed them. They killed half of King Roman's men."

"What about my brother?" Cyrus interrupted.

"Roman took a mace to the chest. His armor didn't hold. It said it shattered his ribs. The battle went on for six more days."

"Did my brother make it home alive?"

Yes. He did. But with King Roman on his way back to Alta Prime, half the southern army destroyed, and the knights of Torrdale dwindling, all remaining soldiers were killed except for three young squires who were allowed to escape, along with a young knight I had never seen before. I don't know why they let them leave but if they wouldn't have, we would not know most of the story."

"You have to find a way to let me out," Cyrus said. "I need to get to my brother."

"How exactly do you plan to do that? I do not have a key, and the Kuhar are stationed all over the North. You will be captured and killed."

"How long have I been here, Nadya? I have to try."

Nadya thought for a moment. "It is almost Sebastian's and Tomas's birthday. That means it has been nine months. Summer is almost here. They will be nineteen, well Tomas will be."

"What if he is still alive?" Cyrus said.

"You and I both saw him die. He is gone," she said with an upset tone.

"Maybe, maybe not. If you let me go, I could go search for him," Cyrus suggested.

"Where would you go? The Far North is vast and brutal. Even if you did make it past the forest, how would you know where even to look? You would die before you found anything," she said with intensity. "I want to believe he is alive too, but we saw him fall."

"That doesn't mean he died," Cyrus said quickly.

Nadya saw Sara come into the courtyard looking for her. She whispered goodbye to Cyrus and dashed through another door into the castle. Sara walked around the square, yelling for Nadya. Cyrus got annoyed and told her that she was not there.

Sara was pregnant, and that meant she demanded constant pampering. She even started allowing her sister Mary to tend to her every want. Mary was quiet and did not argue much, which made Sara happy.

"How would you know where my sister is? You're locked in there where no one can see you, and you can't see out."

"I can hear still. I know if someone is outside in the courtyard."

"If you were not so stupid chasing after my idiot brother, then you could be in your cozy castle in front of a warm fire instead of in there," she said maliciously.

"I will never regret my choices in choosing Sebastian. Even if that means I will spend my life here for loving him. You are angry because I didn't choose you."

Sara laughed loudly. "You are a fool for choosing him. Sebastian was not fit to be king. I am grateful he is dead."

Cyrus burned with anger but decided to keep his mouth shut, which made Sara taunt him more. He sat on the floor with his back against the wall and put his head between his knees. He knew she would go back inside soon enough, once she realized she was bored and needed someone to rub her feet.

Tomas stayed in the highest part of the castle. A lookout that had one wall against the castle. The rest was a platform that spanned over the mountainside. If he fell over the edge, he would fall to the forest far below. Tomas was chained to the locked door that only opened from the inside. It was windy and cold most nights, but the days were getting warmer as summer approached.

The only time he saw anyone was when Viktor brought him food. He would try to talk, but Viktor quickly shook his head, shut the door, and locked it. Tomas did not understand why he would not speak to him. Barron came up some days and would sit just out of reach.

"Do you know why the heathens of the North killed the others like you?" Barron said. "It was because the gods became greedy. They were banished from their homeland for using their magic on the people. Then they came to Erras and did the same, only the heathens did not banish them, they slaughtered them and their families. You see, Tomas, I am protecting our family from being slaughtered. Sacrificing you and Sebastian is the only way the others can survive. Do you understand?"

"You do not care about the family. Times have changed. The people are not out for blood. They just need to see that we aren't going to harm them. You stand there claiming to do what is right, but you are exactly like the old gods. Vile, greedy, and dishonorable," Tomas said through gritted teeth. "How could you stand there, after what you have done? How could you sit in our Father's throne, in Sebastian's throne, after what you have done to our family and our people?"

"Our Father was a sick, old man who refused to see you both for what you are. Sebastian was nothing more than a reckless, disgraceful, moronic little boy..." Barron said until he stopped and stared at Tomas. He turned his head to the side and said, "You look nice with blue eyes.

"Father loved us all. Even you, Barron. What are you getting out of this? NorthBrekka will never bend the knee to you."

"They will when I break their legs. Sebastian is dead. What does that mean for you?"

"You are going to kill me."

"Maybe. I may not have to. Everyone know that Sebastian was the powerful one, the brave one, and bitterly angry. But you, Tomas, are not like your twin. You are smart, noble, and weak."

"Fight me and I will show you who is weak."

"I have obviously hurt your feelings. I don't need to fight you." Barron looked around the rooftop. "You will destroy yourself. Have a great evening, brother," Barron said as he hurried back through the door, locking it quickly behind him.

Weeks passed by of the same routine. Viktor watched Nadya follow pregnant Sara around all day, bringing her blankets, food, drawing her baths, rubbing her back and feet. Viktor had to do the same for Barron. Viktor was looking grim as ever. Most of his young and spunky energy was completely gone. He rarely said a few words in a day, and he never smiled. He started sleeping in Sebastian's bed with Gentry's blankets and would talk to Tomas like he was in bed next to him.

Every few nights, Viktor would wake up to Nadya laying down in Tomas's bed. They would stare at each other without speaking. Viktor was afraid that if the Kuhar heard them speak they would be locked in the dungeons again.

Kristoff was only ten years old. He didn't understand much of what was happening around him. He always looked up to Sebastian. He always said he couldn't wait until he was old enough to go on adventures with his older brother. His Father and Mother always said he looked exactly like Sebastian, except for the blond hair. He wanted to be an explorer when he was old enough to leave on his own.

As time passed, he and the youngest child, Pagan, starting roaming the castle, but they were followed by soldiers regularly. If they got too noisy, they went back to the dungeons. If they tried to go outside, they went back to the cells.

The summer solstice had come, and it was a warm morning. Mary was in a happy mood and was quietly singing while combing Sara's hair.

"Why are you so cheerful?" Sara said rudely. "Stop singing. It is annoying."

Mary sighed and rolled her eyes. "It's finally summer, and today is Sebastian and Tomas's birthday."

Sara just nodded slightly. "It's still annoying. Your singing, I mean."

"Can we do something nice for Tomas? Like, take him something for his birthday?" Mary asked in a worried tone. "It would be nice to take him at least a pastry."

"Barron will be upset if you do," Sara said. "I do adore birthdays, though. They were always fun before..." Sara stopped talking.

"Before all this," Nadya said as she took the brush from Mary. "Just let her take him a cake. Barron doesn't need to know that."

"Fine. Only this once." Sara agreed.

Mary smiled in excitement, then ran out of the room and quickly to the kitchen, where she snuck a pastry under Tomas's usual breakfast delivery. She told Viktor that she would deliver it today, snatched the key from his hand, and skipped quickly toward the stairway to the lookout.

Tomas was sitting in the sun, staring off into the horizon, when he heard the usual click of the key. He refused to turn around to see who it was because he expected no one to speak. He listened to a quiet "Psst" and turned around quickly. Mary was halfway through the door, waving at him. He looked at her questioningly.

"Happy birthday," She whispered and set down his food with the pastry showing. "Don't tell anyone I brought this for you."

Tomas hurried over. "Is it my birthday?" Mary nodded and smiled.

Tomas reached out to hug her as tears rolled down his cheeks.

"I miss him too."

Tomas cried a little more, thinking about Sebastian. "Thank you," he said, wiping his face. "This is very kind."

"I wish you could be with us," she said. "I have to go now before I get in trouble. I love you." She wiped the tears from her face while closing the door quickly.

Tomas smiled and held the cake in his hands. He looked up at the sky. "Happy birthday, brother," he said while choking back tears. Then he ate his cake happily, enjoying every bite.

Nadya went about her routine, then got a break as Sara was tired and wanted to sleep. Barron was out in the town, dragging Viktor alongside him. She went out to the courtyard and hurried over to the tower. She walked over to a soldier who fancied her. She had learned that when she was weary from waiting on Sara, he would rush over to carry the bedding or clothes that needed washing.

"May I have the keys to the tower? I am supposed to take Prince Cyrus his rations and clean clothing. Barron's orders."

"I will need to check with His Majesty first, my lady."

"He is in town today. He will be gone for some time. He needed new boots and armor. It could be a while. Anyway, he asked me to make sure Cyrus was tended to before Queen Sara awoke from her nap. I would hate to disappoint the king." Nadya stroked the soldier's hair while batting her eyelashes.

"Of course, my lady. But only if you will consider my hand in marriage. I have been watching you for some time. It would free you from this life of servitude if you did."

Nadya forced a smile. "I happily accept."

She took the key and hurried to the tower. Cyrus waited on the stairs, looking terrible. His skin was filthy, his hair was matted, and he appeared exhausted and ill.

Nadya gasped at the sight of him. "Cyrus, let me get you some warm water and soap. You need a bath, and then I will cut your hair."

"You will get caught."

"Not if I hurry. Barron is away in town, and Sara is resting. I will be back." She turned and rushed back out of the tower.

Cyrus tried to stop her, but she was gone. She was right. He was a mess. He felt his hair and sniffed himself, knowing he would never have let himself go like this, but what choice did he have?

Nadya returned, carrying two buckets and a bag on her back. She was struggling to carry the weight but was determined as she set the buckets down.

"Take off your clothes," she said, handing him a bag. It had clothes, soap, and a blanket inside.

"Are you going to watch me?"

"Now is not the time to be shy. Take your clothes off now! I'll help." She started washing his back and neck quickly, then moved to his hair as he washed his face and front. After he scrubbed down, Nadya made him sit down so she could cut his hair. She cut until it was free of the tangles and dirt and did the same to his face.

"There, at least now you won't have to worry about it for some time," she said, running her hands over his head. "I really should go."

"Nadya, please wait! You must help me escape. I beg you. I cannot stay here forever. I will return to my home."

Nadya shook her head in protest. "If he found out, he would hurt me, probably kill me. I am sorry, I cannot just let you go. Besides, they will catch you."

"I don't care if I die. Do you think I want to live like this? A prisoner? He took everything from me. He took away my life, his men may have murdered my brother, and he took the love of my life away from me. There is nothing left for me in this world. Please, Nadya."

Nadya cried with him, then took a rock and scraped her face until she bled. Cyrus looked at her bewildered. "Why would you do that?"

"So, it looks like you attacked me when I brought you breakfast. I will tell Barron you hit me with a rock, and it knocked me out. Go, Cyrus! Run. Go down the mountainside. It will give you time, and you will bypass the whole town. Once you reach the bottom, run into the forest. You will have to travel quite a long time to cross it, but keep going and you will find a trail that will lead you to the other side. You will know what I mean when you get there. Hurry."

Cyrus looked at her, astonished. "Thank you for everything. I am sorry if this puts you in danger. I always hoped you would be my sister when Sebastian and I were to be married..."

"Cyrus, go, please! You can make it home. I love you," Nadya said, hurrying him outside.

He snuck around to the back of the tower and began crawling down the cliff. Nadya looked for soldiers, gathered the buckets and dirty clothing, and hid them under an old cart in the courtyard. She had to pretend to be injured.

She waited for a couple of hours until men approached the gate. She lay down on the ground and made herself cry. The gates opened, and Barron and a few of his men came galloping on horseback inside. Barron immediately noticed her on the ground and walked over fast. He grabbed her by the arm and pulled her to her feet.

"What happened here?"

Nadya started shaking and said as dramatically as she could muster. "It's Cyrus. He attacked me! He escaped just a few moments ago."

She pointed in the opposite direction of where he climbed down. Barron looked at her disappointedly. "I told you not to go near him. You were to drop his food inside the door and leave. My beautiful sister, your face is ruined." He smiled, let her arm go, and walked away. He shouted at men to search the kingdom. He gave them orders to bring Cyrus back alive so he could kill him.

CHAPTER 23

Cyrus's Escape

Cyrus scaled down the cliffside as quickly as he could manage. He slipped a few times, which cut his hands open. As the reality of his escape set in, he realized he had to make a run across the open field to reach the forest. He stared around in every direction, checking for soldiers. It was clear, so he ran as fast as he could.

Cyrus turned and investigated the forest, unsure of which way to start. "She said I would know where to go. How would I know?" He started walking straight ahead, checking in each direction, looking for a path.

He continued walking, imagining he would stumble on the path somehow. The thick trees blocked out the sun, as it seemed like nighttime had fallen. The light coming through the treetops was dismal, but enough. As he trekked forward, he heard water in the distance. It was a stream that was runoff from a river flowing from the mountains.

Cyrus reached the stream and knelt to put his sore hands in the cold water. He sighed loudly, the feeling of the water soothing him. He then reached his face down to drink. It was so fresh and crisp; it made him feel happy for the first time in a long time.

He was concerned that he had yet to find the path. Each night he would find fish or rabbit to eat and light a small fire to cook, then sleep buried under leaves or branches in case the soldiers came through.

Late one morning, he noticed the stream was getting wider and moving faster and louder. A waterfall lay ahead of him. He froze in place and stared worriedly at his next choice, then rubbed his face nervously until a deer appeared across the way.

The deer stared at him, then bounded off. It became clear that the deer was standing on what appeared to be a pathway. It was grassy and narrow but clearly a path. He looked down at rapidly flowing water and then saw large boulders in a straight line barely peaking the river's surface.

Cyrus smiled and laughed happily, then jumped out to the first rock, realizing that he could stand there without the water pressuring him to move. He stepped to the next rock, then the next, until he reached the other side.

The path was right there in front of him, winding into the forest. He was excited to see it and took off in a dash. The sunlight began shining through the trees again. He knew he was getting close to the edge and kept running.

As he approached the tree line, he slowed down and stopped before the forest opened into a prairie. It was quiet and empty, apart from some small animals. He cautiously stepped out of the coverage of the trees, determined to continue forward even though his body was urging him to turn around. The grass was high and easy to get lost in. Cyrus kept moving forward until he had crossed the prairie and approached a small village.

He had never seen this village before and worried there would be Kuhar living there. Cyrus decided to stay within the cover of the tall grass and watch the town. He could see townspeople moving about with their day and saw no sign of Kuhar soldiers anywhere. He smelled cooking from a building at the edge of town closest to him. He realized how hungry he was and started feeling sick.

As he tried to decide whether to approach someone, he saw a man on a horse riding toward the place where the cooking was taking place. He observed, noticing the man was close to his age. He was handsome with blond curly hair that hung down to his chin. Cyrus did not realize that he stepped out of the prairie grass's protection until the man on the horse stopped and stared at him.

Cyrus jumped back nervously, and the man came riding over quickly. "Who are you, and where are you from?"

The man was more handsome up close, wearing thick leather and light armor and carrying a sword on his side.

"You are a knight."

"You have a good eye. I asked you a question," he said while drawing his sword.

Cyrus held up his hands. "I am Prince Cyrus of Torrdale. I was being held captive by Barron Drake. My brother is King Roman of Alta Prime. I can prove it." He held out his hand, showing the knight a ring that displayed the Bolin family crest with an emerald in the center, surrounded by a griffin.

The man jumped down from his horse and grabbed Cyrus by the shoulder. "Come with me, Your Highness. People have been searching for you for a year now."

"What are you talking about?" Cyrus asked. "Where am I? Who are you?"

The man pushed him toward the town. "You're safe. You are in Sun Shadow. It is the last outpost before the south crosses into the northern border. Your brother, the king, has had men searching for you. My name is Sacha Khovell, Sir Sacha Khovell."

Cyrus smiled and felt at peace finally. He knew he was safe under the protection of his brother. Cyrus sat down as Sacha brought him a big plate of food. He was so grateful for it he started stuffing everything in his mouth.

"Slow down before you choke," Sacha said, laughing. "I know you're hungry, but if you die now, the king will have my head."

Cyrus laughed. "Sorry, I am just so hungry."

"Tell me everything that has happened over the last year. After you eat," Sacha said.

Cyrus finished eating, chugged down a pitcher of water, then wiped his mouth on his sleeve. Sacha stared at him oddly, like he was watching a peasant eat for the first time. "Sorry," Cyrus said, laughing at his behavior. "A year as a prisoner, and one forgets he is still a prince."

Cyrus began from the very beginning, from when he first met Sebastian and the Drake family. He refused to leave out a single detail, even the love affair with Will and Sebastian. Sacha sat there staring, wide-eyed, absorbing every word. Once Cyrus reached the part about Sebastian getting whipped, he slowed down and started to choke up. Then he came to Sebastian's death, and he could not continue he was sobbing so heavily.

Sacha sat there and stared at him. He reached over and patted Cyrus's hand, then held it tightly in his own. "I'm sorry this happened. I cannot imagine losing the one I love. We received intelligence of the treachery happening in the north but not to this magnitude. King Roman will be devastated to hear of Sebastian. He had a soft spot in his heart for him. Please continue."

Cyrus cleared his throat and went on to talk about his time in the tower. He shared his conversations with Nadya. By the time Cyrus had finished, he realized he had his eyes closed. He opened them and looked around, seeing many men sitting around him, listening.

"So, do you know he is dead?" One of the men spoke.

"He is dead. Do not ask again."

"Why has no one tried to stop Barron?"

"At least five thousand Kuhar are living in NorthBrekka. One town cannot defeat them. The Drakes are his slaves. Sebastian is dead; please don't ask again," Cyrus said dreadfully. "When can I go to Prime? I need to see my brother."

Sacha let go of his hand. "When you are well. You need rest, and you require nourishment. I will take you myself once you are fit."

"I am fine. I traveled through half the north by myself with nothing. I can manage the ride south," Cyrus said forcefully.

"First sleep, then we ride in the morning," Sacha said, smiling.

Sacha escorted Cyrus to a tent with a large, soft bed inside. There was a place to wash and appropriate clothing for the prince to change into. He undressed and started to wash his face. Sacha walked in and stopped suddenly, staring at the prince's naked body.

"I apologize, Your Grace. Please excuse my rudeness," Sacha stumbled to say.

Cyrus turned and looked at Sacha, noticing he was still staring at his body. He walked over to the bed and sat down, still undressed, staring back at Sacha. "It is alright. It does not bother me," he said softly.

Sacha blushed a little, then tucked his hair behind his ear before backing out of the tent. Cyrus could not help but think of how Sebastian would have the same expression and tuck his hair when he was bashful. It hurt to think of it, but Sacha was stunning, and he thought of it as a compliment. He smiled then lay down, pulling the blankets over him. He was so happy to feel the softness and warmth that he instantly fell asleep.

Morning came fast. Cyrus was sleeping when he felt someone lightly shake him. He awoke to see Sacha sitting next to him with his hands on his chest. "Time to wake up, Your Grace. We eat, then we ride."

Cyrus watched as Sacha walked away, smiling at him before he left the tent. He felt guilty for feeling something for him. Cyrus got up and dressed, enjoying the soft clothing as it touched his skin. He stepped into the sun, took a deep breath, and then walked over to where breakfast awaited.

Once again, he ate quickly, which made Sacha laugh and shake his head. He liked Sacha's smile. He shook off his feelings, then finished eating so they could leave. They mounted their horses, joined by men of Alta Prime, and began their journey south to the kingdom. Cyrus was happy to see his brother again, but the pain of what he left in the north haunted him. Every time he felt relieved, his brain would remind him of what had happened and what was still happening. He wanted nothing more than to help the Drakes regain their home and end Barron's life for taking Sebastian away from him.

CHAPTER 24

The Summer Solstice

Back in the far north, Sebastian woke up early. He did not know the day, but he stepped outside and looked up at the bright sun. He was grateful for the warmth. Amara came out and put a coat around him.

"It may be the solstice, but it is still cold," she said, smiling.

Sebastian looked at her, surprised. "Today is the summer solstice?"

Amara happily nodded. "It is a big day here. We celebrate it every year as the day we get to travel to see our friends in the west. They have a festival because this means it is the fishing and mining season. The ice starts to melt, and the snow gets thinner."

Sebastian just laughed. "It is also my birthday."

Amara smiled and jumped up to hug him tightly. "Another reason to celebrate! Happy birthday. I will tell everyone."

"No, you don't need to. Today is your people's day. I don't want anyone to make a fuss over me," Sebastian said.

"Are you joking right now?" Amara responded. "We will celebrate summer and your birthday!" She skipped away quickly.

Sebastian groaned loudly and walked over to the forge, where Boris was gathering supplies. "My daughter likes you," Boris said, not looking at Sebastian.

"I don't know what you mean," Sebastian said, although he did know what Boris meant. He looked at Boris and noticed him staring. "I can't. I have someone at home. She knows this."

"It has nearly been a year since you came here to us. You have nothing back home anymore."

"Don't say that! My family is there. When I return, they will be surprised to learn I am alive, and I will cut my brother down for what he has done. I will destroy every one of the Kuhar with my bare hands. Then I will claim my place on the throne and marry the man I love." Sebastian sounded maniacal. Boris's slowly backed away from him.

"If you return home, you mean. You need to prepare to depart. We are leaving soon for Icefall," Boris said plainly, then pushed past Sebastian to his home.

"Boris, I apologize. I did not mean to yell."

Boris was inside already.

Later in the morning, everyone gathered along the road to leave for the west. Many had colorful clothing to celebrate the solstice. Amara stepped up next to Sebastian. She was wearing a long green dress and had her hair braided and pinned in a bun. She looked incredible, and Sebastian stared at her pleasantly.

Amara's family joined them. They were all fantastically decorated and lovely. Even the twins looked adorable in their matching outfits.

"Come here, sit down." Amara signaled for him to sit on the wagon. She knelt behind him and started braiding his hair. She then tied it up on the back of his head and wrapped his hair's long tail in colorful leather strands.

"This is how all the warriors wear their hair."

Sebastian felt the braids. "Thank you. You look lovely."

Amara beamed, then reached into a bag and pulled out an incredible, black woolen coat. It was intricate. "I made this for you," Amara said as she helped him put it on. "It fits you perfectly. You look fierce."

Sebastian liked the coat a lot. "You made this? For me? I don't know what to say."

Amara smiled. "Consider it a birthday gift."

The townspeople began their journey. Some were riding in the large wagon pulled by a set of long-haired horses. The rest walked. They arrived in Icefall in the evening. Upon approaching the city, Sebastian noticed Icefall was a fortress. Much more expansive than the small village they had left. There was a manor in the center of the city surrounded by houses and a cathedral.

The city sat at the edge of a cliff. It overlooked the sea that started to melt as waves broke over the ice onto the rocky shore below. As they entered, a crowd of city folk lined the streets to welcome them to the city. They were all dressed in colorful clothing and hats. They waved as the wagon passed.

They reached the entry to the manor. Sebastian followed Amara and her family inside. A man that Boris called Marquess Vigoras waited to greet them. Amara informed Sebastian that Vigoras was the leader of the far northern territory.

Vigoras had four sons. The oldest, Dom stood in front of him. He was tall like Sebastian, with silvery-white hair, but Sebastian could not help but stare at Dom's eyes. They were the brightest blue he had ever seen, next to Tomas's when he would turn. Dom had pale white skin and was muscular with tattoos on his chest and arms.

"Overwhelming?" Dom startled Sebastian.

"It's a bit much."

"I agree," Dom said. "I don't much like parties. Always too many people in one crowded place."

Sebastian was intrigued. His eyes were dazzling even in dim light, and he always had a soft smile. His face was sultry and incredibly dramatic, yet so beautiful it was hard to believe he was human.

"Come on, we should join everyone in the ballroom. My parents are excited to meet you."

"I thought the people of the Far North feared me. There was people from here at the ball in NorthBrekka. The things they said about me were—"

"They weren't people of Icefall. Trust me. You have allies here."

Sebastian noticed many of the men were dressed and wore their hair the same as Dom. These were the warriors that Amara had told Sebastian about. They were the Sinook.

Amara introduced Sebastian to anyone she thought he should know, which was nearly everyone. Sebastian was getting tired of being shoved around so much.

Finally, after a much-needed break, one of Dom's brothers came and asked Amara to dance with him, which she happily accepted. Sebastian snuck off to a less crowded corner and leaned against the wall and rested his eyes.

"I am just grateful your brother asked Amara to dance. She drags me around like I am her pet," Sebastian said.

Dom did not speak but just smiled, then licked his lips and turned to look at the crowd dancing.

"So, you are one of the warriors, am I correct?" Sebastian asked.

"Yes, I am Sinook. My name is Dominic, but you may call me Dom if you would like. And you are Sebastian Drake, king of NorthBrekka, am I right?"

"I was king until my brother ruined my life and everything else." Sebastian paused. "Sorry, I am still pissed off about it."

Dom looked at him with that sultry look again. "You are still king of NorthBrekka. No one can just take that away. You are our king as well."

This took Sebastian by surprise. "I thought there was no king this far north."

"No, you are the king of all the North. Everything above the southern border is your kingdom from NorthBrekka, Torrdale, all the way to the top of the world. If you do not believe me, ask my Father. He will explain it to you better. He taught us about your family and your family history. My Father respected your Father," Dom said seriously.

"I always thought..." Sebastian started but was interrupted by a horn blowing.

"My Father is going to speak. You should go to the front of the room. He will be excited to meet you finally," Dom said and gestured for Sebastian to walk with him.

Sebastian approached the stage where the marquess was standing and waiting patiently. He was striking like his sons, only much older and taller. A woman stood by his side. She was darker-skinned, quite beautiful, with long black hair braided down to the small of her back. It was Marchioness Vinita Sage. She was Dom's mother.

Sebastian remembers his father once telling him about the enchanters who lived in a town in the Far North called, Sedda. Enchanters had tattoos with symbols of the sun on one forearm and the moon on the other. They all also wore a crescent tattoo on their forehead. Sebastian was fascinated with Vinita as she stood so perfectly still with grace and poise beyond any he had seen. She had the tattoos.

As the marquess began to speak, Sebastian felt the touch of Amara coming up behind him with her Father and mother and the twin boys behind their mother's legs. He noticed Dom was staring at him again and could not help but stare back. Dom licked his lips again and nodded for Sebastian to listen to his Father.

"We have gathered on a historic night on the day we leave winter behind and welcome the warmth of the short summer. This is no ordinary solstice that we celebrate this day. The gods have blessed us with a gift. This gift is standing before me now. A child was born this day, years' ago. He was born to a storm the gods evoked upon the north to blessed with power to be an ambassador to our world. This young man was brought to us in a time of great need. There is a dark force lingering over the lands below ours. Our king of all the North, our fire, our fury, and our greatest gift, King Sebastian Drake." The marquess reached his hands out for Sebastian to join him.

Sebastian looked at him with horror until Dom bumped him. He hesitated and stepped on the stage and rested his hands in the marquess's. He kissed both of Sebastian's hands, then Vinita curtsied at him. There were apparent whispers about him as everyone thought him to be dead.

Vigoras pulled Sebastian's coat and shirt to the side and looked at the scars on his chest. Dom craned his neck to get a good look as well, and his brothers were trying to look over his shoulder to see. Vinita placed her hand on his chest and let out a quiet gasp as she pulled her hand back fast and stared at Sebastian sadly.

"I want to thank Boris and his lovely family for taking His Majesty into their home and healing his wounds. They are truly blessed to have the opportunity to save our most important savior," Vigoras said.

Sebastian looked at him in complete confusion. Vigoras clapped his hand on Sebastian's shoulder then waved his other hand in the air. "Tonight is also our great king's birthday. Let us commence the celebration."

As the people dispersed back to dancing and eating, Sebastian stared at Vigoras questioningly. "What do you mean by savior?"

"You don't know who you are, do you? I told your Father he should have told you and your twin sooner."

"He told us about our powers and the lightning, and we had a bit of training from one of your people, but there is much I do not know," Sebastian started, but Vigoras interrupted.

"Not tonight. Tonight is for festivities and celebrations. Come and speak to me in the morning. Now go have fun, Your Majesty."

Amara forced Sebastian to dance with her, much to his despair. "Can you just have fun? I am not trying to flirt with you. I know you like boys. I just want to dance with you. That is all, I swear."

Sebastian laughed and decided to try to have a good time. Later that evening, as people started to go to their homes and Amara put her brothers to bed, Sebastian decided to walk.

He wandered out to the edge of the city and peered out into the sea. The air coming off the water was cold, and it made Sebastian shiver. When he was considering going back to the manor, Dom came and stood next to him. He did not say anything but seemed to notice Sebastian shaking and looked at him curiously.

"Why are you so mysterious?" Sebastian asked.

"Why are you?" Dom retorted.

"I'm not mysterious. I'm angry."

"You are mysterious and angry. You have a lot of rage built up inside that body of yours. That could be extremely dangerous for someone like you. You are cold. Would you like to come back to the manor with me?" Dom said in a tone Sebastian thought might be romantic, but maybe that was just how Dom spoke.

"Yes, but not yet. I can't handle any more attention right now."

Dom nodded and looked at Sebastian longingly. "Are you married? Have children?"

Sebastian shook his head. "No, to both questions. I was in love and wanted to marry, but I am unsure if he even knows I am alive."

Dom did not speak but stared at Sebastian with widened eyes, making his crystal blue eyes shine brighter than usual. Sebastian knew what that expression meant. "Yes, I said *he.* People always look at me like that when I mention my preference for a suitor."

"I don't think badly of you for it. I like that about you. You follow your heart and do as you wish no matter what others think of you," Dom said but stopped and bit his lip.

"What about you?" Sebastian asked.

Dom's face dropped. "I have a wife and a daughter."

Sebastian felt a knot in his stomach. "That's great! How old is your daughter?"

"It was an arranged marriage. My wife and daughter live in Sedda, my mother's birthplace. We have been married for just over three years. Neither of us is happy, but my daughter is my pride. She is perfect, so we make it work for her. She is three," Dom said, looking happier when mentioning his daughter. "Come inside. You look like you could use a good night's rest."

In the morning, Sebastian went down to meet Vigoras and Vinita. They were sitting in the conservatory built inside the manor. He walked in and looked around at all the beautiful plants.

"I love flowers. But they did not grow outside that far north," Vinita said. It was surprisingly warm as Sebastian entered.

Servants bowed quickly as he passed by. Vinita hopped to her feet, took Sebastian's hand, and sat him next to her on a soft couch.

Vigoras sat in an oversized chair across from them. Vinita had her eyes closed and was mouthing words to herself, although no noise escaped her lips. When she finished, she looked up at him sadly.

"You are incredibly special. You have love and family who miss you dearly. They mourn you every day. The connection between you and your twin is undeniable. It is so unique and beautiful. He is in pain and is straining to stay alive. He needs you more now than ever before. Without you, his life will surely be lost. You have the power to defeat him, the traitor, your brother. It burns inside you as you are a born leader. You are holding the power of the gods inside you. Nothing can defeat you; do you understand?"

"I don't understand my power. I have only learned a little. What is this power?"

"It is pure and uncontrollable chaos. With the right teacher, you will be able to harness your power and become who you were born to be," Vinita said smoothly.

"How do I train for this? What about Tomas, my twin? What about his power? How do I save them?" Sebastian had so many questions, but Vinita just put her hands up.

"All in time, Your Majesty. You will learn everything in time. You both will. Your brother is the key to unlocking your power, and you are the key to his. You must return to NorthBrekka."

Sebastian got excited. "I have been trying to go home for a year! It is all I want, but my brother has an army. I do not know what has happened to the militia of the north. I have no one."

Vigoras stood and spoke for the first time. "You have the Sinook. War is what they have trained for their whole lives. To follow you is their purpose. There are ten thousand Sinook all over the north, awaiting your command."

Sebastian felt a fire burn inside him. He left, feeling lit with excitement and searched for Dom, who was one of the captains of the Sinook. He found him and some of his men out in an open field practicing their archery.

He hurried over and stood next to Dom, who acknowledged him but did not speak. "I need to discuss the battle. If we are to go to war with the Kuhar, I think we need to talk. Can you ask for a meeting with your people?"

Dom smiled slightly and nodded. "Of course, but we need to get to know what kind of fighter you are as well."

Sebastian looked at him questioningly as Dom gestured for Sebastian to show them that he knew how to use a bow. "They need to know you can fight for yourself. They will not follow a weak leader. Hit that target," Dom said, pointing at a target set across the field.

Sebastian laughed as he knew he was a skilled archer. As he back an arrow, his hands began shaking. Dom stood close to him, making him feel his cheeks blush. He released the arrow. The men laughed loudly, and Sebastian stared at the target in disbelief. He missed the mark altogether. He was embarrassed as he noticed Dom was laughing as well.

He grabbed a handful of arrows and stuck them in a line in the ground in front of him. One of the men shouted, "Don't hurt yourself, Your Highness. It's admirable to admit you can't shoot."

Sebastian felt himself get hot inside. He closed his eyes and took a deep breath. His hands got extremely hot, and a glint of fire flashed from his fingertips. Dom stopped laughing and looked at Sebastian with a worried look on his face. He put his hand on his arm, and Sebastian opened his eyes and looked at Dom. Dom's mouth dropped open. "Your eyes turned red. You don't have to be angry. Just focus. Try again," Dom said.

Sebastian put another in the bowstring. He pulled back and exhaled, then released. This time, it hit the dead center of the target. The men nodded, looking unimpressed. Sebastian grabbed another arrow and quickly released it, hitting exactly where the first arrow was centered, cracking it in half. He continued without slowing to look, firing one after the next, each hitting the one before it. Once he ran out of arrows, he looked and saw each arrow had destroyed the prior, and there was a mess of broken arrows pierced into the target.

The men were awestruck. Dom smiled and looked at him. "That was impressive. How did you do that?"

"I've been training since I was able to walk," Sebastian said as he handed the bow to the man who mocked him before.

Over the next several months, Sebastian trained alongside the Sinook. He learned their fighting style, and they knew his. He and Dom spent much of their days side by side. They started learning everything about one another. Sebastian was highly attracted to him, but he knew Dom had a wife, and he had Cyrus.

One day, Aspen arrived in Icefall. Sebastian was excited to see someone from home. "Aspen, please tell me you have news of my kin, of Cyrus. Anything."

"Your Majesty, I was not in NorthBrekka when Barron took over. When I excused myself from your training the last time we met, I was called on an urgent mission to East Watch. My sister passed away."

"Oh. I am sorry to hear of your sister's passing. But I am glad you were not there to see Barron's siege. He probably would have killed you too."

"Yes, for training you and Tomas. I had been made aware of the situation in NorthBrekka. I was told you were dead. My heart ached for you until I got word you were here. I immediately came so I can continue your training. It is more imperative now than ever."

Sebastian spent evenings inside the atrium of the manor training with Aspen. He learned that Aspen was a distant descendant of Baze. The original god of fire. When Sebastian claimed that he and Aspen must be related, Aspen lit up happily. He started calling himself Uncle Aspen as a joke so he could continue passing insults and cursing at the king without repercussions.

"I swear if you don't learn to focus, boy, I will drop you off the cliff and save your brother the effort of beating your ass himself. Pay attention!"

Sebastian looked at him with disbelief. "That was cruel. How about I set your ass on fire. Then you will run yourself off the cliff and save me the effort of listening to your annoying voice."

"Did I hurt your feelings? Tell me, this new look you are wearing. The braided hair, the neatly trimmed beard, the fresh-stitched leather, it is all lovely, but you look like a girl."

"Girls have beards now?" Sebastian interrupted. "Or was that just your mother that had a beard?" He snapped a flash of lightning at Aspen, who deflected it with his shield. "And thank you for calling my look lovely. Do you fancy me now too?"

"Only in your most vivid fantasies, Your Majesty."

Sebastian sent a roaring fireball at Aspen that he barely dodged. "You wish you were the man that fills my fantasies. My dreams would make you blush."

Aspen paused after rolling to avoid getting burned. He breathed hard, then laughed. "Very good. You are getting stronger and more spiteful. I like that."

When Sebastian finished, he found Dom on the other side of the door. "Were you spying on me?"

"You really are amazing. I couldn't take my eyes off of you." Dom blushed and walked away.

On one late spring morning, Sebastian woke up to Dom sitting on his bed, watching him sleep. Sebastian sat up, startled. "What are you doing?"

Dom smiled while looking at Sebastian's bare chest, glistening in the sunlight that crept through the curtains. "We are taking a trip today. You should dress then eat. You will want to eat your fill. We are traveling to the fishing village, Sedda. You will meet my daughter." Dom patted Sebastian on the hand, then got up to leave. He stared at him, looking Sebastian up and down as he got out of bed undressed.

Sebastian hurried down to join the others for breakfast. As he approached the dining hall, he could hear a lot of loud chatter. He stopped to listen before entering. One man was complaining to Dom and another captain. Sebastian peered around the corner and noticed the man first as he was tall, muscular, with short black hair and a long-braided beard.

"Why are we following him? He is too young to lead an army into battle. What does he know about war?" The man who was complaining was shouting. The captain walked over and pushed the man back into his seat.

"He is our king. That is reason enough to follow him," the captain said simply.

"What do we care about, NorthBrekka? What have they done for us?" The man said.

Dom stepped over and slapped his hand on the table. He bent over to come face to face with the man. "They have done more than you know. If it were not for the Drake kings, the north would have suffered from the wrath of southern soldiers armed with iron and steel. They would have taken everything we have, including our women and children, forcing them into their beds. They would have slaughtered our elders and destroyed our homes. NorthBrekka is all that stands between them and us."

The man fell silent and looked around. Sebastian realized he had stepped into the hall and the captain was the first to notice him. He walked over and bowed to Sebastian. "Your Grace. I am Jon, captain of the Pike Sinook. I am at your service."

"Pike?" Sebastian asked.

"We are on the southeastern border. We are familiar with the Kuhar as they often use our ports to dock when they come to our lands to trade with the merchants in Oyster Cove."

Sebastian nodded in understanding. "Wait, trading with Oyster Cove? For what?" he said a little harshly. "The Kuhar aided my traitor brother in murdering my people and my family. If there is anything that you know."

"Your Majesty, I am here to help you learn their ways to defeat them," Jon added.

"Thank you," Sebastian said. Dom walked over and invited Sebastian to sit with him. Dom took Sebastian by the hand, which surprised him, but he accepted it as he interlocked his fingers around Dom's. Dom looked down at their hands, then up at Sebastian, and smiled. Sebastian noticed him blush a little.

"After we eat, I would like to show you something before we depart, Your Majesty."

"Sure. As I have said a dozen times, you do not need to call me that."

Dom looked surprised but smiled again, then began eating. Sebastian ate his fill, but Dom told him to eat more. He said the journey was long, and there would be nothing to eat until they arrived.

Once he had eaten enough for Dom's approval, he got up to walk away, following Dom out of the hall and down a dark corridor.

"Where are you taking me?"

Dom laughed a little but did not answer.

"If you plan to kill me and hide my body, I will assure you that I don't die easily," Sebastian said jokingly.

Dom laughed louder. "I would never hurt you, Sebastian."

"Then tell me where we are going?"

"We are here," Dom said.

There was nothing there. No windows, only a door. Dom grabbed Sebastian's hand and led him through the door. The room was a sanctuary. It was warm and decorated with beautiful silk and tapestries and carving on the walls with names. Sebastian looked confused. Dom turned to Sebastian, grabbing his face and pulling him in for a kiss. Sebastian stumbled back into the wall, then pushed Dom back.

"What are you doing? You have a wife, a child. I have Cyrus."

Dom pulled himself against Sebastian and pinned him against the wall. The tone in his voice was proud and demanding.

"Is this not what you want? Do not lie. I can see it in your eyes. I am yours. I will be loyal to you forever."

Sebastian felt a tingling in his stomach. He was attracted to Dom in the way he loved Cyrus, but the guilt hurt more. "I love Cyrus."

"And if your Cyrus is dead, then what?" Dom said softly with his lips remarkably close to his.

Sebastian was surprised by what he was hearing. "You have a wife."

"She does not want me," Dom said seriously. "And I want you." Dom's assertiveness excited Sebastian.

He ran his hand across Dom's chest. "I do want you. It seems to be all I can think about when we are together." Dom smiled happily, then reached in for another kiss.

Sebastian pulled away again. "No! I am in love with Cyrus. I will not hurt him again."

"Again? It has been a long time since you have seen him. If Cyrus is still alive, he has surely moved on with his life. You came to the North wounded terribly. Your people think you are dead. Your Cyrus thinks you are dead. He is not waiting for you."

Sebastian felt his stomach burn, then realized Dom was right. "This feels wrong."

"And it also feels right. It is our destiny to be together. Do you think I was sure about it at first? I had never imagined being with a man, but the gods demand our unity. You and I are bound together."

"And what if Cyrus is alive and waiting? What makes you think I will not run to him?"

"I know you will. I will not stop you but know that it was always meant to be between us. There are reasons our paths crossed. Not because you need an army, because you need someone who will understand and accept you for who you are."

"I don't understand anything you are talking about. How can you know this is the way?"

"Because I am linked to the gods, and you are a god. You are mine, and I am bound to you."

Sebastian leaned in and kissed Dom, then pulled back. "I cannot do this. I want to, but I can only think about Cyrus. If he is alive and waiting, I would feel awful."

"I understand but know that I will keep trying until I have convinced you to take me on your arm instead," Dom said with a smile.

Sebastian grinned and blushed. "You are mental. Trust me, you don't want me. I don't even want me."

"You are the mental one. But fine, if you insist, I will yield to your Cyrus, for now."

"We should go. We have a long journey ahead."

"As you command, my king."

CHAPTER 25

A Ceremony and a Tattoo

Dom and Sebastian walked back to the hall, where the men were quietly waiting for the command. As they entered, Jon stood up fast and bowed to Sebastian again. Vigoras and Vinita stepped forward. Vinita reached for Sebastian's hand.

She nodded at Sebastian. "Hello, Your Majesty. Are you prepared for the answers to your questions?"

"Yes, I have been waiting for a long time."

"Then go. March to Sedda. Learn from the storyteller. He will tell you everything you wish to know."

The room, filled with soldiers of the north, was as silent as the dead of night. They bowed as their king turned to face them. "We march to Sedda now."

The silence was broken by loud chattering as the men filed out the doors to the grounds. The day was warm but had a chill in the wind.

The onset of winter approached fast. Sebastian marched to lead the group with Dom and Jon on his sides and Dom's brothers at their backs.

They descended to the city and walked on a long, arduous journey along the coast to the small village to the south. They marched fast as the day hurried by them. The men were tireless and kept pace without wear. Sebastian did not understand the importance of this march to Sedda but pushed forward without question.

It was a long march, and the men were weary as they found themselves approaching torches on the border of Sedda. At first, Sebastian did not see anything but empty land ahead. He was confused and looked to Dom for answers. They navigated a steep decline toward the sands below.

The village was nothing Sebastian had imagined. It was intricate, with homes built into the bluffs that sat above the sea. They had to descend stairs that led down into the village.

Sebastian could see ships anchored into ports that spanned the coastline. The fishermen had already come in for the evening and cleaned the fish they would make for a feast. They entered a passage into the bluffs and saw a whole city was inside the cliff. Not just houses, but banks, shops, storage for food, as well as a cathedral that was like nothing he had seen before.

"All in good time. I will show you everything tomorrow. Tonight, we feast, and I will introduce you to everyone, including my little girl," Dom said as he noticed the wonder on Sebastian's face.

"This is incredible. How?"

Dom wrapped his arms around him tight. "I will let the storyteller answer all your questions. Come now, let us join the people. They have been waiting to meet you."

They walked through the village streets lit by torches. Sebastian tried to take it all in but was drawn away by the music. He looked ahead at fires burning high and people dancing around them. Men and women were singing and playing drums making the most rhythmic sounds he had heard. Women were coming toward them with platters in their hands. They offered food and drink to first Sebastian, then Dom and Jon, then to the others.

Dom led Sebastian into the festival and straight to a man and woman sitting in the center of everything. They were both wearing the same jewelry as Dom's mother. They had on silk robes, and their hair was painted in bright colors.

When he approached them, they both bowed and took each of his hands and kissed them. The woman stood before Sebastian and did not speak as she inspected him. She then spoke in a language he did not know.

"She said to take your shirt off," Dom translated.

"Why would I do that?"

"She wants to see your scars."

Sebastian was hesitant but removed his shirt. The woman put her hand on the arrow scars on his chest, paused for a moment, and then walked around behind him. He felt her touch his back in different places. He suddenly felt Dom's hand run across the scars on his back.

Sebastian frowned. "I know they are hideous. I wish you wouldn't look at them so closely."

"These scars are your story. They tell the tales of your life and what you have been through. It shows that you are a strong and worthy god."

"I am not a god."

The woman laughed and began speaking again in her native tongue as she looked at Dom to translate back. "She said that you have suffered, and you have lost dearly. Your body carries the sacrifice you made, and your survival is proof of your place among the gods."

"My sacrifice nearly killed me and left me broken with nothing but these scars that I have to look at for the rest of my life. I am not worthy of the gods, and I am not worthy of love. I am a monster."

The woman stepped away quickly and watched him fearfully as she bowed. "Calm down, my king. You are worrying the sorceress. She knows your power and what you can do. There is nothing for you to be ashamed of. I think you are magnificent, scars or no scars. I am the one who should be ashamed to be in your presence," Dom said.

"You have to be joking. You are one of the most perfect men I have ever laid my eyes on. I am nothing compared to you."

Dom stood and stared at him with his mouth open. "Then we are both mad. You have no idea how incredible you are to me and all of us. Your beauty is like staring into a perfectly cut diamond glistening in the firelight under the stars on the clearest of nights. How can you not see this?"

Sebastian did not speak a word as he suddenly felt overwhelmed with emotions. He was enchanted by Dom and falling in love. As he snapped back into the reality he was standing in, he saw the sorceress standing with her hands out, palms facing him. He slipped his shirt back on and peered at her ruminatively. She smiled and spoke only a few words that he understood. "You are a god."

Dom nodded at the sorceress and led Sebastian away. They sat down in a circle where a man was standing in the middle. "He is the storyteller. This is where you will learn the answers to your questions," Dom told him.

The man turned and stared directly at Sebastian. He was elated that the king was sitting and waiting for his story. It was not long before everyone gathered in the circle. The storyteller held his hands together as if in prayer. He silenced the crowd, and the town was deathly quiet.

"Sedda was founded when the gods Matra, god of water, Baze, god of fire, Litha, goddess of air, and Vidki, god of the earth, came from afar, floating on land. Standing on the sand below, they focused on this mighty rock wall. Vidki stepped forward and began to move the rock into shapes that defined our surroundings. Litha used her power to move the air to discard the rock into the sea. Matra used the water of the sea to wash away the dirt and grime from inside. Then Baze conjured up a roaring flame with which he forged the dwellings inside."

The storyteller stopped to ensure everyone still listened, especially Sebastian.

"We know the stories. We are living proof of the gods' selection of a race of humans to claim as their own. Each god took on lovers. They wanted to seed the world with their offspring to lead the world after the gods returned to the stars. All the children born to the gods were exceptional and powerful and passed their powers to their offspring. Over time, the gods' powers in their children became detrimental as they were using their powers to gain profit and control the lands. The children of Baze were the most dangerous of all. They would use fire's power to burn down their enemies and their villages. The first child of Baze was named Dragon."

Sebastian's head shot up.

"Let me finish, Your Highness. Dragon was a violent man who used his power to strike at anyone who spoke against him. His power became so mighty that everyone in the lands feared him. He gathered the other god-born children to lead beside him. He demanded Litha and Vasha, who was the daughter of Matra, take up as his wives. He wanted to see what would happen if he made children and mixed their powers. These children were born with considerable powers and were declared elementals by the gods. The elementals rose and exiled their Father as his power had become uncontrollable. The elementals were all destroyed by the Sinook except one. This child abolished the name Dragon to take on a name that meant Dragon in the old tongue. The Drake name was written into a prophecy that declared the power of good and evil would be rebirthed in the one who would be king."

Sebastian sat and stared at the storyteller like he was expecting more. The storyteller walked over and painted a symbol on his forehead. "Drake is fire; you are a Drake. Fire is chaos, and you are chaos. Drake means Dragon, and you are the Dragon."

"That is the elemental symbol of fire, a red triangle pointed toward the sky," Dom said.

"Are they going to kill me?" Sebastian asked Dom. "My distant relative was this demon god. That is why everyone wants me dead. They think I am like him."

"As long as you learn to control your powers and not use them as he did, you will be fine," Dom said, smiling with a hint of laughter. "Come on. The artist wishes to see you now," Dom said.

"Who is the artist?" Sebastian said without thinking much about anything.

"They give all the warriors these," Dom said, pointing to his tattoos. "The markings are sacred. They are for warriors only. You are a warrior now, which means you are one of us and we protect our kind. We believe in you, my king."

They walked into the artist's home. A woman was waiting at the table for them. She signaled for Sebastian to sit across from her and reached out for his arm. She took a sharp, flat tool and began carving on Sebastian's left forearm. Sebastian winced. Dom sat close by his side with his hand on his leg and arm around his back. It somehow comforted him.

When she finished carving, she smeared a black liquid she had made all over her work. She then cleaned it diligently until it revealed a tattoo that covered from his wrist to his elbow. It was simple but elegant. Sebastian could not help but stare at it.

"Thank you. It's beautiful," he said to the artist. She nodded and bowed, then Dom indicated it was time for them to leave.

"Now what?" Sebastian said.

Dom smiled and wrapped his arms around Sebastian. "It's time to rest. Tomorrow is a big day."

"What happens tomorrow?"

Dom stopped walking and turned to look at Sebastian. "Tomorrow, you meet your army."

Dom led the way down a long road that went deep into the caves inside the cliffs. As they rounded a bend, they heard a little voice shouting, and running toward them. The child stumbled as she ran. Then Sebastian heard what she was shouting.

"Daddy!"

The girl leaped into Dom's arms and hugged him tightly. Dom turned and looked at Sebastian. "This is my daughter, Torra."

Sebastian smiled at the little girl. Torra buried her face into Dom's shoulder. "No need to be shy, my sweet girl. This is Sebastian, our king."

Torra looked up at Sebastian again and smiled. They walked into the home and met Dom's wife, Ketya. Ketya was young and pretty with long black hair and dark skin. She walked over fast, bowed to him, began speaking with a heavy accent. "I am pleased to have you here, Your Majesty. Your presence here is a gift."

Dom walked away to sit with his daughter. They played in the next room as Ketya spoke to him some more. "You will promise me that you will keep him safe for her. She needs him in her life to teach her the way of the listeners."

"I promise to keep him safe," Sebastian said quickly, then paused. "What do you mean, listeners? You mean..."

Ketya nodded. "Dominic is from a long line of listeners. He is one himself as his mother is and his Grandfather was. Torra is a listener as well. You did not know this?"

Sebastian shook his head. Ketya patted him on the shoulder then went to join Torra and Dom. The interaction between Dom and Ketya was minimal. They barely looked at each other or spoke. The only thing he heard Ketya say to Dom was, "You better return for her when this is over." Then she got up and went to bed.

Dom stood and picked up Torra. "I am going to get her to bed; then, I will be back for you."

Sebastian sat at the table, looking at his tattoo. He ran his fingers along with it and felt the bumps in the skin where the blade had carved. It seemed like hours passed before Dom joined him again. Dom stroked his hair with both hands. Sebastian missed having all his hair. He loved it when Cyrus would tuck his hair behind his ear when it would fall into his face. Now all he had was the ponytail on the crown of his head.

Dom held his face in his hands. "I want you," He said in a whisper. "I am sorry. I cannot help myself."

Sebastian smiled and stood to meet Dom face to face. "We need to get some rest."

Morning came. Torra was running through the house, laughing, and shouting excitedly, which woke Dom and Sebastian from a deep sleep. Dom jumped out of bed first and quickly dressed. "Today is your day," he said before leaving the room.

Sebastian climbed out of bed and dressed. He could hear Dom playing with his daughter. He listened to the little girl's laughter as Dom chased her through the house. He could not help but feel guilt for taking her Father to war. He slowly made his way into the kitchen. Ketya signaled for him to sit and eat, then called for Dom and Torra.

They ate together quietly. After finishing, Ketya started cleaning up. Dom told Sebastian they had to meet on the beach with the others. He picked up Torra and gave her a big hug and a kiss. He was speaking to her quietly, so Sebastian offered his appreciation to Ketya for sharing her home. She kissed him on the cheek, then bowed before she continued cleaning.

Torra ran over and hugged Sebastian's leg. He bent down to hug her back, then she smiled and ran off to play. Dom gave a quick hug to Ketya, and then they left. They descended toward the beach, where Sebastian could see men lined down the shoreline.

As he walked out on the sand before them, they all stood at attention. Sebastian mounted a horse that was waiting for him while Dom joined the men from his city. He rode the length of the troops and stopped to inform them of what they were fighting. He spoke about his brother and his army and what they would face.

The men remained quiet and took in every word as he described the Kuhar tactics. They did not seem afraid or concerned. When he finished speaking, the men chanted and took a stance in the heathen army style. Sebastian looked among the crowd and felt confident in winning the war for the first time.

"Tomorrow, we will ride south with haste. We have the benefit of a surprise attack. My brother will not know we are coming. Barron believes I am dead. I know the land well. I know how to enter NorthBrekka through the mountains where the Kuhar will not post as the cold is too harsh and the air too thin. You benefit from being accustomed to the cold; therefore, I do not doubt your capability to survive the journey. We will descend into the city at night. We will be as silent as the dead and as invisible as ghosts. We will sink our arrows in their hearts before they know we are there. I know you all do not know me, but I promise to lead with fury. I promise to defend you with pride. All I ask is you leave my brother alive. I want the pleasure of his blood on my hands as I cut him down. I want to see the fear in his eyes as he falls before me. I want to feel the glory of his death at my hand!"

The men chanted loud with pride. Dom stared at him, looking worried but let off a smile as Sebastian met his gaze. Sebastian dismounted his horse and walked toward Dom, who stepped forward to take his hand.

"You have won their hearts as you have won mine. I worry about you taking on your brother. I fear that killing him will have horrible effects on you."

"After what he has done to my family, my lover, and me, he deserves the worst death. He deserves for me to destroy him once and for all," Sebastian responded.

"Your Majesty. Please come with me." A man walked over and bowed to him.

"Who are you?"

"I am Renault. I am the commander of the guard from East Watch. Vigoras asked me to collect you."

Sebastian nodded and turned to look at Dom, who was being led away by Boris. He questioned why such urgency, but Renault insisted he not ask questions and just hurry along. He looked back to see Dom walking away with Boris, talking casually.

As he approached the entry to the village, Vigoras and Vinita stood waiting. They reached out to take his hands as Renault bowed then left. He saw Dom go into a domicile across the village. Sebastian was still confused.

"This way, Your Majesty. Amara is waiting to clean you up," Vinita said.

"Amara is here?" Sebastian said happily.

"Of course, she insisted she prepare you."

Sebastian still looked confused but headed into a dimly lit dwelling with peaceful music played by a young woman sitting in the corner. It was warm and smelled like lilac. Amara came from the back room and ran to hug Sebastian tightly.

"I am so excited to see you again. You need a bath; you smell awful. Go!" she said, laughing while pointing to the back room.

Without hesitation, he walked into the small room to a tub of steaming water. He stripped off his clothes and climbed into the hot, soothing water. It felt good on his scars but even better on his achy muscles. He lay there for a while before Amara snuck in.

She began washing his back and hair. Then she started rubbing the knots out of the muscles in his shoulders. "You are tense. You should be happy. Soon, you will be going home."

Sebastian let out a small laugh as he enjoyed the massage. "I am happy, although I still feel guilty for being gone so long."

"Tell me about you and Dom. You two have grown close."

"He is incredible," Sebastian said as he blushed. "But I cannot have feelings for him."

"Because of your Cyrus?" Amara asked. "The gods chose Dominic for you because he is your perfect match. Consider my words, Sebastian."

"I always do. Your words are difficult to ignore. You will hit me if I try." Sebastian laughed. Amara splashed water in his face.

"He loves you. Do you know that?"

"I can't think about that, Amara. I have to think about what I might find when I get home. I have no idea what is awaiting over those mountains."

Sebastian finished bathing. He climbed out of the bath to find a beautiful outfit laid out for him to wear. The top was a thick black woolen coat with silver embroidery on the collar and sleeves and a white silk shirt to wear under, followed by black leather pants that seemed to fit perfectly.

When he walked out of the backroom, Amara had him sit in front of her as she began braiding his hair back. She pulled tight while weaving a thin red leather ribbon in the braids. She pulled the ponytail into a twisted bun at the back of his head. She laced his boots and tucked a red scarf around his neck and into his coat. As she looked him over, she asked what was missing. Just then, Vigoras came hurrying into the room with a box.

"Come now, follow me outside."

They walked into the courtyard decorated in silk and roses. Sebastian wondered where the roses came from. Then upon looking closely at one, he realized they were not real but made by magic. They glimmered in shimmering red light and floated along with the silk. He was entranced by how this was even possible. Then he saw Dom exit the dwelling he entered earlier.

"Wow." Sebastian breathed out. Vigoras glanced at Sebastian, beamed, then watched his son walk over to join them. He looked incredible, dressed in silvery silk draped in diamonds with diamond powder glistening on his skin. It was as if Dom were inhuman, like a fantasy. His white-blond hair was pulled back straight, he had silver symbols painted on the corner of one of his eyes. Dom looked at Sebastian as if they had fallen in love all over again.

Dom approached Sebastian and held his hands in his. They did not speak, only stared at each other with lust and desire. "One last thing," Vigoras said as he approached them with the box. He opened it to reveal a crown. The crown was black steel encrusted with ruby gems, and the prongs were sharp spikes with twisted steel. It looked as fierce as Sebastian was. Vigoras placed it on his head proudly and bowed while backing away.

"Please, let us celebrate this lovely evening as I present our king. Our God of Chaos. His Royal Majesty, Sebastian Drake."

The people of Sedda knelt and bowed their heads. Dom was the last to kneel and he did with grace and pride, never letting a smile leave his lips. He stood and stepped over to Sebastian, then turned to the people.

"Our king is feared among all. The great prophecy of the ancient power of Baze that passed down through generations until it struck our sovereign leader that stands before you now. Chaos was born to be violent, yet without chaos there would be no balance. Our king is the balance that will unify the whole world. Without him, we will all succumb to the real darkness that haunts these lands. Tonight is for him. Tonight, we remember our history. Dance, drink, and be merry."

Music began playing, and people started dancing. Dom held his hand out to Sebastian.

"Dance with me."

Sebastian took his hand and danced along with the people of Icefall and Sedda. The night was filled with stories, food, and jubilation. Sebastian enjoyed every moment in the arms of Dom. As the night grew to a close, Dom invited Sebastian to follow him.

They entered the room that was specially prepared for them. It was warm from the fire burning in the pit in the corner. There were candles lit all around the room. There was a bed with furs spread across it along with soft linens.

"What is this?" Sebastian asked.

"I told you. The gods brought us together to be together. I know you feel it as well."

"Dom, I do. I want you, trust me, but-"

"Cyrus." Dom again looked sad. He turned to set his coat down. He looked at the bed and the candles, then felt a hand stroke his hair, then cup his cheek. Sebastian looked at him like he wanted to comfort his broken heart. He kissed Dom's lips softly.

"You don't have to do this. I told you that I understand," Dom said.

"I know what you said. I want this as much as you."

He pulled Dom in for a much more romantic kiss. Dom pushed Sebastian on the bed and climbed onto him.

"I promise you will not lose your integrity with Cyrus."

"Let us not speak about him. Tonight is about you and me and this moment. Tonight is for us."

They made love until the night became silent, and the fires went out. The neatly decorated room was a disaster once they finished. Their moans filled the air which alerted the city dwellers to give them privacy. Dom was in ecstasy, and Sebastian had felt something he had been missing for nearly two years. Love.

CHAPTER 26

The Journey Home

Morning came fast Sebastian was awoken by the cold. He started to stir, which woke up Dom. Dom reached out, grabbed Sebastian around the chest, pulled him back down, and held him tight. "Not yet."

"We should probably start getting ready to go," Sebastian said as he tried to get up again, which was also Dom also denied. They both laughed and stared at each other.

"You are so incredible," Dom said. "I have never felt this way before."

"Neither have I." Sebastian agreed.

"Not even with your other love?"

"He is different. He would have been astounded if I had done the things to him that I did with you last night."

"So, he isn't fun, or he can't handle a little pain," Dom said with a laugh.

Sebastian shrugged. "He's simply different. I do not know how to explain it. He spent a lot of his life living alone. We really should go."

Dom stared at him but seemed to understand that Sebastian did not want to discuss Cyrus or their love life with him. He just nodded and released the grip he had on his chest. They both got up and dressed, then began to prepare for the long march south.

Sebastian looked at his battle gear. It was not metal armor like he was used to, but black leather pants with a black leather hooded coat with a thin mask to cover his nose and mouth against the cold and wind. Also, there was a leather chest plate and thick brown leather to protect his thighs, tall boots, and bracers for his arms.

After he dressed, Dom handed him the most beautiful bow and quiver he had ever seen. It was intricate with leaves engraved in the shaft and quiver. The quiver held arrows but also held a long knife as well as a smaller one. Dom told him it was a gift from his parents as he donned his own.

They walked outside to see only a few of the townspeople stirring. They walked over to where Vigoras would be staying for their time there. Dom's family greeted them, as well as Boris and Amara. Everyone smiled at them happily.

"Could you not stare?" Dom said as he was trying not to laugh. Dom's brothers broke out into heavy laughter.

"Come and eat. You need your strength before you go," Vinita said, inviting them to the table.

They ate and talked cheerfully, but Sebastian could not help but feel a pit in his stomach. His worry was apparent to Dom, who kept looking over at him as he rubbed his hand on Sebastian's back.

"You said it yourself; we will defeat them," Dom said.

Jon sat down next to Sebastian. "You have the best army the north could provide at your back. I sent word days ago to the king in the South of our plan. The south will be waiting if we require aid."

"You did what?" Sebastian choked on his tea. "What if it gets intercepted by a Kuhar soldier? They will know we are coming!" Sebastian said fiercely.

"My men will not have been caught. They are stealthy and quick, besides if they were caught, they would die before they spoke a word to the enemy."

"No need to fret now, my king. This battle will be your mark in history. You are the youngest king to go to war. Future generations will speak your name when they remember the great kings of old," Vigoras said.

As they finished eating, Boris sat down next to Sebastian. "Now, I expect you to take care of my daughter. If anything happens to her..."

"Amara is coming?" Sebastian interrupted.

"She will accompany you, yes. She is a great healer. You will need someone to help the men if they are injured."

Sebastian started to refuse, but Amara looked at him like she was about to scold him. Sebastian glared at her then said, "You can come, but you have to stay back. I cannot have you running around and getting in the way. That's how you will get hurt."

Amara looked at him in disbelief and shook her head. "Do you honestly think I am just going to go out and run in front of horses and charging men with swords and axes in their hands?"

"I was just making sure-"

"And another thing! You do not need to treat me like a child. I can handle myself out there!" Amara said sternly.

"Okay, I'm sorry, but-"

"I'm not finished. I am not a weak little girl. I do not need you to watch out for me. So, stay focused on the war and let me do my job, understand?"

Sebastian nodded while Dom and his brothers tried stifling their laughter. Boris never looked prouder as he got up to hug his daughter and wish her well. He then went over and gave Sebastian a big bear hug.

"Thank you for everything you and your family have done for me. It will not go forgotten. I promise," Sebastian said.

Boris nodded and began saying his goodbyes to the others. Vigoras and Vinita came and offered their last bit of wisdom, then bowed to their king before they went to say goodbye to Dom, who locked into a loving embrace with his brothers. Sebastian smiled, seeing the families showing their affection for one another, which made him more than ready to get home so he could do the same to his own.

Jon walked over and clapped his large hand on Sebastian's shoulder. "It is time, Your Majesty. The men are waiting on the road above. We need to march now. I want to get as far south as we can before dark."

Sebastian agreed, and they set off to join the soldiers waiting anxiously for their arrival. The townspeople were lined along the streets to offer their wishes as Sebastian, Jon, Dom, and Amara walked toward the open face of the rock.

They ascended their way to the top, and as they came to step foot on the surface, Sebastian stopped in awe.

Warriors from every northern town and village were waiting, standing perfectly still. They were armored in leather and steel with shields, bows, swords, and axes. Some were on horseback and some on foot. Amara went to join the line of wagons. She gave one last menacing look at Sebastian, then smiled.

Sebastian, Jon, and Dom walked to the front of the line, where three horses waited for their riders. One of the captains stepped forward and handed Sebastian an ax to hang from his belt, then Aspen approached with a beautiful sword. "This was made for you. It was forged by halo steel. It is the finest and strongest steel known. They called it halo because they say it was a gift from angels. Not many have a sword of this quality."

Sebastian looked over the sword with a smile. It was intricate with a beautiful hilt carved with dragons and wrapped in elegant black and red leather. He sheathed it. "Thank you. This is the best gift I have ever received." The captain bowed to him

"Drake is derived from the word dragon, and you have the god power of fire. You are our dragon. Now lead us into battle with pride and honor, Your Majesty."

"Are you coming with us, Aspen?"

"I am getting too old for battle, my king. You have much to learn still, so make sure I have a castle to return to so that we may continue our insults while you puff your pathetic fireballs at my face."

"I cannot wait until that day comes."

Sebastian mounted his horse and started marching forward with Dom on one side, Jon on the other, and a vast army of heathen warriors at his back. He felt ignited by the sounds of many horses' feet crashing into the snowy ground and the thunderous footsteps of men with the chink of steel from their armor crashing against itself. Their journey was beginning.

The first night was noisy. The men chatted and drank. When hunters returned with deer, they ate. It was cold and snowing.

Sebastian sat by the fire, quietly listening to battle strategy ideas, but he was too tired to add his opinion. He lay down and enjoyed the heat on his face as he drifted off into a deep sleep, but it did not last as long as he wanted.

As daylight broke, Dom was still asleep while many of the men were gathering themselves to depart. Sebastian returned from a walk he took in the early hours of the morning.

The next evening was the same. Singing, chatter, eating and drinking.

The following day, they came to a river, and the entire army stopped. Jon dismounted, walked over to the water's edge, and began poking at the ice with his sword.

"The ice is thinning, but I believe we can still cross. We should go in groups, not all together," Jon mentioned.

Sebastian turned and looked behind him. "Are you sure? Do you think the wagons will make it? They're much heavier."

Jon nodded and signaled for the first group to start crossing. "Front line only."

The first line walked and rode to the bank. Sebastian and Dom were the first to step their horses down to the ice, followed by the front line. As they crossed the river, Sebastian kept looking down to check the ice.

"It's fine, Your Majesty. Don't worry now," Jon said.

They crossed, then waited for the rest of the accompaniment to catch up. Sebastian went to sit by the bank to watch. Dom wandered off into the woods behind him. He watched as Jon shouted commands to the following line. He took out his sword and began studying it some more while trying not to think about Dom.

As several more lines had crossed, Dom still had not reappeared, and Sebastian was getting worried. He stood and sheathed his sword, then started walking toward the woods. He followed his footprints in the snow, which ended at the trunk of a large tree. He looked up to see Dom sitting on a branch.

"What are you doing up there?"

"Clearing my head," Dom said.

"You're angry with me. Why?" Sebastian asked.

"What makes you think that?" Dom said with a bored expression. Sebastian stared at him with disbelief.

"You haven't spoken to me all day, or looked at me, or acknowledged my existence."

"What are you going to tell him when you see him? About us? Or when I go back to Sedda to visit my daughter, will you forget me?"

"What do you mean? Why would I ever forget you?" Sebastian said sadly.

"Because you will have him again, and I will be nothing."

Sebastian shook his head angrily. "What happened between us in Sedda meant something. I love Cyrus, I will not deny that, but you are right. It has been two years. Maybe it is time I move on. Maybe I will see him and run into his arms. I do not know. But, if you are set on being mad at me, then so be it. Just come down from there, please."

Dom leaped down. They started back toward the encampment but were stopped by several men with swords drawn.

"You will go no further. Take your men and go back to Icefall before we have trouble."

"You are on the wrong side of the border, Safar," Dom said, stepping forward.

"What business does a soldier of Safareen have this far north?" Sebastian asked.

"Our business is keeping the evil from crossing into Erras. You have no place there anymore, heathen."

"NorthBrekka is my home and my kingdom. My family is in danger."

"Yes, in danger of you. You know what you are. My name is Getsu Gemsum, leader of the Safar elite militia. We have come to stop the evil one before he has a chance to embody his dark power. You will bring death to us all. Take your heathens back to Icefall. I will not tell you again."

"You dare come into my territory and threaten my king! There are ten thousand northern soldiers just outside the woods. You have no place to tell us where we cannot go." Dom came face to face with the Safareen soldier.

"If we kill both of you right now, then we will be gone before your people finish crossing the river. There are twenty of us and two of you. We are highly skilled combat fighters who have trained since we could walk. The two of you are a savage child who has never seen a real fight and a spoiled royal who pretends he is something powerful."

Sebastian formed a fireball in his fist and sent it flying at the Safar. Getsu screamed out for his men to charge at the king. Dom pulled two knives from his belt and met Getsu in combat. He was much faster and more agile than any Safar. Sebastian unsheathed his sword and went into battle with two Safar. He quickly took them both down.

Dom was still locked into the fight with Getsu. Sebastian went to help and was grabbed from behind by a woman. She was on his back with her arms tight around his throat. Sebastian tried to reach back to catch her. He grasped her wrist with his hand ablaze and held it until she jumped down.

She was holding her arm tight. Sebastian could see that she was young. She looked up at him, scared.

"Get out of here. You do not belong in this fight!"

She snarled and lunged at him again at the same time another Safar rushed toward him. The force of the other man threw Sebastian, himself, and the girl tumbling down a snowy hillside. They rolled from the forest. Sebastian saw the frozen river and tried to halt himself, but it was too late. The three of them crashed hard on the ice, busting it open. The three of them fell into the river.

Sebastian heard Jon shout for him. The rest of the Safar poured from the forest, followed by Dom and Getsu, who were fist fighting. Dom kicked him hard in the face, throwing him back down the hill where Renault captured him. Dom saw Sebastian in the water and took off in a sprint to rescue him.

The girl was holding Sebastian down by his head while trying to keep herself afloat. He tried to summon his power, but every time he would make a wisp of a flame, she would push him under again. Jon reached the edge of the broken ice, dropped down, and reached for Sebastian's hand. The other man in the water already succumbed to the cold. He did not resurface when he went under the water and was swept away under the ice through the current.

The Safar soldiers were no match for the northern army. All but Getsu and the girl were dead. Dom reached the shoreline, then dove into the river to help Sebastian. He elbowed the girl in the face, knocking her out. He pushed her toward Jon, then pulled Sebastian to shore.

"My love, are you alright?"

"I am freezing," Sebastian said through chattering teeth. "I am alright. Thank you for saving me."

"I will never let anyone take you from me."

"Jon, take the girl over to the other one. They are our prisoners now."

Jon carried the girl over his shoulder, then set her down next to Getsu. "What is your name, little girl?"

"Avina Turk. I am the princess of Safareen, so I suggest you let me live!"

"We have no intention of killing you, Princess," Sebastian replied.

"She tried to kill you, Your Majesty."

"A lot of people want to kill me, Jon."

"Why is Safareen interfering in the business of the north? You have no right to be here. This is a blood war."

"We have been tasked with taking your head."

"By who?"

"I will not say. That is the business of Safar and no other. We are trying to save the world from the likes of you, demon."

"I am no demon. I have no desire to kill the people of Erras. I only want to take back my kingdom from my brother. He is evil, not me."

"How do you people live here? I am about to lose my toes. Can we get a fire started if we are going to sit and chat?"

Sebastian smiled, knowing he was freezing but did not want to show any weakness. "Fine, we camp here for tonight."

Sebastian stomped away toward one of the wagons. Amara was taking out a blanket, then pulled it tight around Sebastian. "You are so cold. You are going to have to get out of those wet clothes," she said as she dug for dry clothes for him. "What about her?"

"Who cares?"

"She is a princess. I suggest you be careful."

"Safareen needs to be careful."

"Sebastian, I love you like my own brother, but you have to learn there are people out there that are not going to like you, but you are a king, and as a king, you have to have strength and kindness."

Sebastian smiled at Amara, then laughed. "Alright, take her some dry clothes and a blanket."

Amara smiled and kissed his cheek, then went to take Avina warm clothes. Sebastian went to find Dom, who was finishing setting up a tent for them to sleep in.

"Let me do that." Sebastian stepped inside, took fire logs from Dom, set them, conjured fire in his hand, and ignited the wood.

"You are so cold. You are shaking. Your lips are blue."

Dom pulled Sebastian's coat off, then his own, and pulled him against his chest in front of the fire. They held each other tight with their faces close together. Dom stroked his face, then continued to take off Sebastian's wet clothes. He held him against his bare chest. They were both cold, but soon Sebastian warmed, then lay down under a thick fur blanket. Dom kissed Sebastian and stared into his eyes.

"I am sorry about today. I was jealous, and it got us into trouble. This was my fault."

"It is not your fault. They were waiting to attack us. We are alive, warm, and together. All that matters in this moment is that I want to make love to you right now."

Dom smiled, then climbed on top of Sebastian. They could hear the men's chatter and smell food cooking, but nothing could take them away from that moment.

Morning came and went. They marched on into the fourth day. The mountains before NorthBrekka became truly clear in the near distance. They would arrive at the base of the hills at night. They set up camp and started fires, and everyone gathered in a large circle. Sebastian stood in the middle.

"Tomorrow, we will take the pass that will come over the top of the summit and down into Shadowmire. It is a treacherous road. Rest well tonight. Tomorrow will be difficult."

"Shadowmire? When we arrive in Shadowmire, Your Majesty, I must insist that we rest there before the battle. There is plenty of food, drink, and weapons," Jon said.

"There are also women." Another Sinook soldier said, then the other soldiers chuckled excitedly.

"Yes, of course. Shadowmire will provide. We will stay for a night, but only a night. Remember why we are on this quest," Sebastian said before he went to speak to Getsu and Avina.

"If you ever wish to see Safareen again, you will tell me what I need to know. What is happening in Erras? I have been gone for two years. Certainly Barron's reign opposes a threat to the southern kingdoms."

"The people believe you are dead. The new king is planning a truce with the other nations. The only kingdom that has not signed the treaty is King Roman. Barron will rule, and NorthBrekka will be the new capital of Erras. Those who sign will have plenty for their kingdoms. The people will have food and warmth in the winter months, and there will be no retaliation for those who followed you. All who refuse to comply will die."

"If my brother takes reign of Erras, he will not give you anything he promises. My brother is manipulative and traitorous.

He cannot be trusted. What about Torrdale? Has Prince Cyrus followed Barron?"

"Prince Cyrus has not been in Torrdale in years. Not many have heard from him. They say he lives in Alta Prime with his intended," Getsu said.

Sebastian felt a sharp pain in his stomach. "His intended?"

"Yes, a young knight of Alta Prime. He rescued Prince Cyrus from the north a year ago."

Sebastian looked off into the distance at the mountains leading to NorthBrekka, feeling depression set in.

"What are you going to do with us?" Avina asked.

"When we arrive in Shadowmire, I will release you both on your word you will not stop until you reach your home. I will send men to escort you. I cannot have you interfere in my war. Remember this kindness when I defeat my brother and seek loyalty among the nations."

In the morning, they stretched across the narrow road climbing the mountain. By late day, they came down into the familiar road into Shadowmire. The townspeople stopped suddenly at the sight of the Sinook. With Sebastian leading, the people came out from their homes and shops in curiosity.

"I do not expect loyalty here, but my men are hungry, and we need rest," Sebastian said.

"Do not forget we want women," a soldier said loudly as he noticed the brothel nearby.

"Go on, men. Have your fill of ale and whores. Rest well. We travel again at first light," Sebastian said, then turned to Dom. "Feel free to enjoy yourself too. I will not stop you from pleasure."

Dom looked at Sebastian with surprise, but Sebastian hopped down from his horse and marched into the pub. Dom started to follow but was stopped by a whore running fast in his direction.

"You are one of the most beautiful men I have ever seen. Come, lie with me, my lord. Any man who follows the true king deserves the best women we have."

Dom stared at her strangely but walked quickly away from her without a word, following Sebastian once more. He walked into the pub to find Sebastian sitting in the corner alone.

"Why would you send me away with those kinds of women? Do you wish for me to not be with you?"

"Of course I want you with me, Dom. I just need a moment. I am about to go to war against my brother. I have not seen my family in years. I know not what I will see or find. My whole family could be dead."

"Or they may be well alive, and when they see you, they will find their hope again. Sebastian, I am here for you, by your side, always. Do not forget that. The gods sent you to us, and me for a reason. We will stand strong with you. We will go to war to save the north in two days, and you will reclaim your throne and rule. I will be on your arm through it all."

"Cyrus is getting married. Getsu informed me of this last night. You were right, Dom. He has forgotten me."

"I am sorry to hear of this news. I promise I will always be yours, no matter what, if you accept me."

Sebastian took Dom's hand and lead him away to a place to rest. That night, as the town grew quiet, Dom held Sebastian tight in the warm bed they were given by Grimmel and his wife. They made love until morning broke, like it would be the last night they would get to be together in this way, and they departed for their final approach to NorthBrekka. As they climbed the tallest mountain, the air became thinner and colder. The winds were howling through the walls between the two peaks the pass divided. By night they were at the summit. It was blindingly cold.

Sebastian led them to the place where he first discovered an extensive cave system. It was large enough for the wagons to enter. The cavern was enormous but could not house the large army completely.

Dom sat next to Sebastian where he stared down into a steep descent to another level in the cave.

"When I was fifteen, I came here for the first time. I did not have a torch, but I wanted to go down anyway. I lay on my belly and slid my way down. I was so afraid because I could not see a thing. As I slid down, I wondered how long it would be before I found the bottom. When I finally touched it, I felt around, trying to figure out how much room I had. I kept swatting at the air, then I stood up fast and smashed my head into the top of the cavern. It hurt so bad," Sebastian said, laughing. "When I decided I had better go back. I crawled here, but there was a pack of wolves sleeping on the ground. I was afraid to move or breathe. I sat there and stared at them, hoping they would not see me. I waited for so long. The day had started growing dark. All I could think of was how angry my Father would be at me for not coming home before nightfall. The next thing I knew, I was waking up to the sun shining into the cave, and the wolves had gone. It was morning. I ran out of there so fast and down the pass. It took me half the day before I reached the overlook of my city. I rushed down to the castle and decided to tell my Father that wolves trapped me. When I did, he scolded me first for not coming home that night, then again for lying. He then made me spend the entire day polishing silver with the servants. I was not allowed off the castle grounds for days. I was so angry I decided to start a fire in the kitchen. I got my ass beat so hard for that."

Dom laughed hard. This was the first time Sebastian had shared anything personal that made him smile. Most of what he knew of Sebastian was dark and painful.

"So, what is down there?" Dom asked.

"A lake," Sebastian said happily. "Full of blind fish. It's so deep that I have never been able to reach the bottom."

"Blind fish?" Dom said.

"Yes, there is no light down there, so the fish go blind. It's kind of frightening."

Dom nodded and smiled back. "Maybe you can show me one day."

"I will. I promise," Sebastian said.

"Did you ever see the wolves again?"

"Yes. I used to come here a lot. One day, I came up, and they were there again. Only they were not sleeping. They saw me instantly. I slipped and fell to the bottom. I climbed back up, and they were waiting for me. I stared at the alpha wolf in her eyes. She came over, and it was the strangest thing. She rested her head on mine for a moment, then they left. I nearly passed out!"

They laughed again. Dom pulled Sebastian away from the hole, telling him he did not want him to fall in while they were asleep.

"When I got out of here, I rushed home to find my Father angrier with me than ever. He threatened to banish me. I was so angry I ran away when a storm was approaching. That is when I discovered my powers. I stopped that storm from killing my family. That was when everything changed."

"I imagine it was glorious."

"Not for me. For me, it was the worst day of my life. I just wanted to be a normal boy. I hate that everyone praises me or hates me for what I am. I don't want it." Sebastian got up to address the army.

"Tomorrow, we make our last journey. Once we leave this cave, we have entered NorthBrekka. Much of the day will be gone by the time we come to the end of the pass. We will stop and wait for the night. Chances are, we find Kuhar soldiers at the end of the pass. Kill on sight. When night falls, we will come to the overlook where we will make our first stand. Once the soldiers and my brother realize what is happening, then we will wage war. Take caution not to harm my people or my family. I will guess Barron will use them as shields. Get rest. Tomorrow, we fight."

CHAPTER 27

The Battle of NorthBrekka

The morning was cold and snowy. The men filed through the pass. Sebastian and his trusted companions mounted their horses and led the way down. They approached the last stretch before coming to the end of the pass and halting. listening ahead for sounds of movement. Sebastian and Dom readied their bows. Jon had his hand on his sword hilt.

They prepared to move forward, but a sound came from above them. It was not human, but growling. Sebastian looked up and saw the fierce faces of a wolf pack watching them. Dom strung an arrow and prepared it to fly. Sebastian waved him off as he stared into the alpha's eyes. The wolves leaped down before the men. Sebastian cocked his head to the side, then the alpha walked over and stood by his side. The rest of the pack joined their leader. The men looked amazed at Sebastian's power as he not only led men but wolves as well.

They slowly moved forward as they descended to reach the overlook. The wolves took a slight lead as the sunlight crept behind the mountains. They approached the lookout where six Kuhar men were posted. Dom and Sebastian fired arrows straight into the hearts of two men. The wolves took the other four down with ease, tearing at their throats, arms, and legs.

As the men sat and waited for the dark of night, Sebastian watched his castle from the overlook. He noticed the banners had changed from his family crest to a serpent twisted around a horse and had words written in the Kuhar language.

He could count the patrolmen on watch for the night in the castle grounds and outside the gate. He relayed the information to Jon, who spread the message to the rest. The wolves were chewing on the remains of their victims. Sebastian could not help but enjoy the sight of it. He looked over to see Dom leaning against a rock, patting a young wolf on the head.

Dark had fully taken over the kingdom. Sebastian signaled for several archers, including Dom, to join him on the edge. As they sat and waited, Jon placed his hand on Sebastian's shoulder.

"Before you lead us into battle, I wanted to say something. My king, you are an inspiration to us all. I know you don't like to be praised, but I admire you. You are stronger than all of us together. From this day forward, you will be known for more than your powers. You are legendary, invincible, and mighty beyond anything the world will know. You truly are the dragon, and we are your wings. Let us carry you into battle as your fire lights our path to victory. We are forever, until the end, side by side with the God of Fire. Chaos. Sebastian, lead us. We are at your command."

Sebastian nodded at Jon then signaled for the archers to prepare. Each of them drew back an arrow and aimed at their intended kill.

"Steady. Fire on my command," Sebastian said calmly.

The men waited patiently for the word to release. Their hands were steady and their aim true. Sebastian adjusted his aim for the man standing on the gallows.

"Ready men. Steady. Make your arrow find a heart to pierce. Fire!"

Arrows screamed across the sky. Each man immediately strung another arrow while waiting for results. The men on the grounds below dropped. The man on the gallows took an arrow through his neck. He stumbled backward and fell from the stage. Only a few men survived.

A horn sounded from the gate as men ran from the housing units built along the wall. The Sinook loosed more arrows, killing more Kuhar. Sebastian signaled for his men to stop and to fall silent as the castle doors opened. They crept down to a lower point on the mountain to see more clearly. Kuhar soldiers marched out of the castle in groups. The courtyard filled, and the gates opened with soldiers lining the wall and outer grounds. The city, too, was filled with soldiers as far as Sebastian could see.

They reached the lower point and stopped on edge, looking closely upon the soldiers who still could not quite see them. Sebastian, Dom, and Jon mounted their horses and waited. The Kuhar escorted the Drake siblings out of the castle, one by one. First, his sister Nadya. The soldier dragged her by her hair as she screamed and cursed. Next came Viktor, escorted by two men, each with a sharp prod in hand burrowing in his neck. Then came Mary, followed by the smaller children who tiptoed, looking scared. Sebastian noticed Kristoff looking much older than he remembered.

He counted off his siblings to see how many remained. He counted six. Then Sara came next, carrying a child on her hip. Barron followed outside with a chain in hand. He pulled on it tight, and Sebastian's head popped up fast, and his eyes widened as Tomas came stumbling through the doors.

Tomas looked like death was begging for him. He was skinny, his hair was matted, and his skin was filthy. He struggled to walk and keep pace. Barron kicked him in the hip to make him fall in place next to the others. He realized that three of his siblings were gone. Gentry, he knew had died, but the youngest children were gone. He assumed they were dead as well.

Barron shouted, "Reveal yourself. The royal family of the North is on their knees. Their fate is in your hands. If you loved your kings of the past, you would do anything to save his family from death. All you have to do is come stand before me."

Sebastian signaled for his men to remain silent. Barron looked around into the dark of the mountains. Sebastian saw Barron signal for one of his men. The large, tall man stomped over. Barron yanked the chain that was binding Tomas until Tomas was on his feet. The man struck Tomas in the stomach, then he pulled a knife from his belt, gripped Tomas's hair in one hand, and craned his neck back as he prepared to slice his throat.

Barron waved for the man to pause. "Reveal yourself, or you will watch all of them bleed."

Sebastian's family were lifted to their feet and a knife held to each one of their throats. Sebastian drew an arrow fast and released it. The arrow flew directly into the eye of the man who was threatening Tomas's life.

The giant Kuhar soldier fell dead at Barron's feet. Barron looked around angrily. "Show yourself now!"

Sebastian's men lined up loosed arrows. Each hit one of the men holding a blade to the throats of one of his brothers and sisters. Each fell dead behind the frightened Drake siblings. Barron screamed out in anger and then stopped immediately as he turned his head directly to where Sebastian and the heathen army waited.

Sebastian smiled down at him as he held a fire he had just lit in his hand. "Forward, march!" They descended the hillside. They did not take the path but the rocky slope down to the grounds. Barron glared at the army pouring down the mountain. As Sebastian turned to see his army at his back, an extraordinary sight lit the stormy sky.

The Sinook, descendants of the old gods, gifted with abilities passed from one bloodline to the next, evolving over centuries, combined as one unified legion. It was if each thunderous stamp of a horse's hoof caused the grounds below to quake. The air seemed lighter, but that was not magic. The real magic of the Sinook came in the form of earth. The one element neither Sebastian nor Tomas had been given control over.

Rocks, sand, and boulders lifted from the ground, and with an elegant gust of a gale force, the earth surged down onto the confused Kuhar soldiers. The front line diminished, leaving King Barron standing in the courtyard, trembling. Sebastian lit the widest smile, staring into the confused faces of the enemies ahead. He ignited his fists into fire and sent his power raging forth into battle.

The Kuhar soldiers lunged forward to stop them. Sebastian drew his sword, which prompted his men to ready their weapons in hand as they approached the ground. The men guarding the entrance to the castle courtyard prepared to loose arrows, but before they could release them, the wolfpack dove from the path directly above them and began tearing them apart before loosing a single arrow.

Barron watched the wolves with pure terror in his eyes. The wolves moved quickly from man to man, and they ripped and chewed at the enemy soldiers' necks. Sebastian reached the ground first, along with Dom, Jon, and the first line. Sebastian pushed his horse through the large crowd of Kuhar coming toward them as he swung his sword back and forth, cutting down anyone who dared come near him.

The Sinook army was strong, but bodies of both sides littered the ground, the piles growing larger by the minute. Sebastian sheathed his sword and dismounted his horse. He saw Jon ahead of him, who had lost his sword in hand-to-hand combat with a Kuhar soldier. He grinned as Jon picked the man up and broke his back over his knee.

The battle lasted long through the night. Sebastian looked around, seeing his army viciously fighting the Kuhar. Blood flowing, painting the snow red from swords cutting open both Sinook and Kuhar. Bodies lay still on the ground with arrows through their faces and chests. The Kuhar ran toward him with fury but were met with Sinook, who risked their lives to defend their king, using their strength, weapons, and magic to fight courageously.

Sebastian had reached the gate where the heathen army was ready to take a last stand. The wagons that were holding the weapons lined the road. Horns blew in the distance. He turned and looked across the city, seeing men on horseback coming fast. It was more Kuhar, many more. Sebastian's eyes widened, and he screamed for his people to fall back and reform together and prepare for the next wave.

The northern army was weakened as the numbers cut by half. The Kuhar approached with large swords drawn. Sebastian glanced over at Dom, who was looking tired but ready. Sebastian could not make out where the end of the line of the approaching enemy was. He turned and looked through the gates at his family, who were being held back once again by soldiers.

Sebastian noticed Barron and began walking toward him. His eyes burned with the tingling sensation much stronger than normal. He felt the heat intensify inside his body as the enemy grew near. He caught the attention of Barron. Barron turned slowly and looked into the red eyes of his brother.

"Sebastian?" Barron said with a loud, angry tone. "How could this be?"

The Drakes all snapped their attention to the man standing in the gate entry. Tomas shuddered in laughter. Nadya and Viktor cheered happily. Sebastian started walking toward his brother until he heard Dom shout.

"Sebastian! Stop."

Sebastian turned to see the Kuhar nearly upon them. Sebastian felt an intense sensation tingle across his chest and down his arms. He held his hands up to stop the men from riding, fast. As they were only a few feet from him, his hand ignited in a fire. A loud blast and flames burst forward toward the Kuhar.

Sebastian stood calmly with his hands out, fire flowing freely from his fingers. The Kuhar were frantically trying to escape the flames. He turned and looked at his men as his powers extinguished. The heathen army lunged forward with their weapons drawn. Sebastian screamed and pulled his sword, and the battle resumed.

Satisfaction burned on Barron's face. He seemed confident the heathen army could not hold on much longer. Sebastian began yelling at his men to pull back. Dom grasped Sebastian's hand tight and stared at him with dread as they backed themselves toward the castle gate again.

"We will follow you until the last man stands before them. I will not leave your side. I love you now and even in death," Dom said.

Sebastian brushed his cheek then heard a loud noise coming from the south of the city. He turned to see the banners of Alta Prime rushing into view. The southern army fiercely rushed the Kuhar and began cutting down Barron's men. Sebastian shouted for his men to fight, and the heathen army screamed and ran back into battle. Dom climbed to the wall and looked at the scene from above. Barron stepped forward and signaled for his men to fire. Dom shouted down to the men fighting on the ground below.

"Take cover!"

The heathen army dove toward the protection of the wall as globes went sailing over their heads. On impact, the bright green explosion reminded Sebastian that the Kuhar could make catalysts. The bombs hit two of their wagons. Sebastian jumped up and ran toward the fires burning. He was shouting for Amara.

He saw his men at the wagons burning on the ground in the rubble. He looked for Amara desperately. He stood in the fire, yet he was not burning. The Kuhar saw that Sebastian could resist fire and shouted for their men to rerelease the trebuchets.

"Sebastian, look out!" Dom screamed from the top of the wall.

Barron twisted around fast and looked directly up at Dom. Dom fell to take cover as bombs flew over his head. The bombs exploded around Sebastian, and a bright-green light blocked his view from his family. Sebastian heard Barron shout at his men to stop. The light went away. He was surrounded by smoke and fire. He heard Barron speak again so he crept toward his voice.

"Where is your king?" Barron said to Dom. Dom did not answer and again turned to look for Sebastian.

Barron turned fast, walked over to pick Tomas from the group, and dragged him to the open grounds. He threw Tomas down on the snow. "Tell my brother to come forth, or I will end this one's life!"

Dom looked at Barron, then leaped down from the wall. He held his ax in his hand and slowly walked toward Barron. "How dare you command my king?"

The Sinook captains gathered in the courtyard behind Dom. Jon was in the back of the group with an injured Amara at his side. Amara looked down at a man lying face down on the ground.

"Tomas?"

Tomas's head jerked up. She immediately recognized his face as being identical to Sebastian's despite his health. Barron looked at her with disgust.

"How do you know my brother?"

Amara gave Barron a hateful glare. "Because his face is the same as our king's. Your brother, his twin, Sebastian. The one you only thought you murdered is the true king of all the North, and we have come to destroy you," Amara said.

The Sinook captains tried to make her quiet, but she refused. Barron started to laugh, then looked directly at Dom. "And who are you, letting a woman speak for you?"

Dom stepped forward. "I am Dominic Sage Alcala. Lord of the North, leader of the Sinook. As she said, we are here to take back what belongs to our king."

Tomas looked at Dom like he was relieved for the first time in two years. Nadya gasped, and the other siblings stared in awe. Barron looked angry but then started laughing.

"My brother, Sebastian, is dead. No one can survive the power of my people's weapons. They are made to melt the flesh from your bones on impact. My stupid little brother may have survived being maimed and impaled in the past, but he will not have lived through the blast, and now I will end his twin and destroy the line of the demon gods forever. No human deserves such power."

He pulled Tomas's hair back with a sharp jerk and held his knife out. As he moved to slice his blade across Tomas's neck, an arrow shot through his hand. He dropped the knife and Tomas, then looked toward the gate. He walked toward them from the smoke, holding his bow in hand.

Tomas looked up with his blue, glowing eyes. "Sebastian?" he muttered.

Sebastian emerged from smoke and fire unscathed. He smiled proudly, then pounded his fist on his chest. The Sinook followed suit, pounding on their chests and stomping. Inside the castle walls, on the grounds of the kingdom, and along the wall stood the Sinook, proud and brave. The ground thundered under the cadence of an army designed to follow the true king of all the lands. Their marched halted as their king approached. The Sinook walked behind him, and as many that could fit entered the courtyard, joining their captain.

As Sebastian walked, the alpha wolf ran to walk by his side. She stood close and protectively as she snarled at Barron. Sebastian wore a slight smirk as he knelt and held Tomas's face in his hands. "My brother," he said as he pressed his forehead to his twin's.

"Well, well, well. Look at you, brother," Barron taunted. "You really are a heathen, aren't you?"

Sebastian glared at Barron but turned back to Tomas. Tomas started laughing and crying as he climbed to his knees to wrap his arms around Sebastian in a tight hug. Barron stood behind Tomas, looking manic. He pulled his sword from his sheath and went to plunge it into Tomas's back. Sebastian fell back as he threw Tomas to the side, then kicked Barron hard in the gut. Barron folded in pain, then Sebastian leaped forward and pulled him to the ground. Sebastian began striking Barron repeatedly in the face.

Barron was bleeding heavily. Tomas reached up to grab Sebastian's arm but was not strong enough. Dom ran over and grabbed at him, trying to force him to stop hitting his brother.

Sebastian pushed Dom away from him, then went back to punching Barron in the chest and ribs. "I'm going to break every bone in your damned body. I will cut your face, rip out your tongue, burn your body until you are so disgusting to look at that even the whores would not beg you to lie with them. I will throw you into the street for soldiers to piss and spit on you," Sebastian screamed so loud he shook, and the skies clouded over, hinting at lightning and thunder. "Remember that? Isn't that what you said you would do to me? You tortured me, whipped me, had your men put arrows through my chest. You left me to die in the cold. You murdered Gentry and Will."

Nadya chimed in, "He murdered the little ones. They would not stop crying because they were hungry. He let his men bury them alive. They were just children! They were our brother and sister. He deserves to suffer."

Sebastian had stopped hitting Barron and stared at Nadya. His head was cocked to the side. Dom wrapped his arms around him from behind him and pulled him away from Barron. Tomas held on to him. He gripped his hand and stared into his brother's eyes.

"Dominic, get back," Sebastian said.

Dom slowly moved away, watching the twins in wonder. Their interlaced hands began to glow. Sebastian could feel a strong power coursing through his veins. The others, including Barron, stared at their hands nervously.

"He deserves nothing. He does not deserve life. Not even suffering is bad enough. He deserves nothing more than a painful death."

"Stop, no, please!" Sara shrieked.

He heard footsteps behind him. Sebastian looked up and saw the southern army approaching. Sara stood before him with a child in her arms. The little boy resembled Barron in every feature. Sebastian looked at her with disgust.

"This is Corbyn. He is your nephew. Please, we will go far away. You will never see or hear from us again. Don't take away my son's Father."

"How could you betray your family? You deserve to be punished, but he will not leave here alive," Sebastian said.

Sebastian's fury ignited as a glowing electric light cracked from his fingertips. The air became silent and still as his family and his people watched in fear. Tomas held his other hand tight with his eyes focused on Barron.

Barron mumbled, "It's the lightning. Your powers came from lightning." He was in shock.

"Sebastian, please, I beg you, don't do this!" Sara cried. Corbyn began screaming. Nadya ran over and pulled them to the ground and hid their faces just before Sebastian reached out to strike Barron. He grazed Barron's face with the lightning bolting from his fingertips, teasing his death. He pulled his arm back again and let out a scream as he went to fatally strike Barron. Tomas pulled Sebastian against him. Sebastian felt suddenly cold as his muscles locked up, breaking the lightning.

"Stop, Sebastian, please stop. If you do this, you will regret it for the rest of your life."

"He deserves to die."

"He deserves to suffer, as he made us suffer. Brother, do not take his life, not now."

Sebastian stared at Tomas, then looked at Barron, who gazed up at him fearfully. "Tomas, you know he deserves this. Why are you stopping me?"

"Please, Seb. Send him to the dungeons. Calm down, then you can decide his fate. I beg of you."

The remaining Kuhar fled from NorthBrekka. Nadya scooped up Corbyn and held him in her arms. Amara checked over Tomas, who had collapsed after using his power. Dom tried to snap Sebastian's attention away but could not.

Viktor approached Sebastian with caution. "Brother? We thought you were dead. How?"

Sebastian looked at Viktor then pulled him in for a hug. Nadya set Corbyn down next to Sara, who was in shock. She ran over and grabbed Sebastian, knocking him over.

"You look so different," she said, feeling his hair and face. "I can't believe you're alive. We had given up hope." She started crying and hugged him again.

Sebastian looked at his men, who were watching closely. Dom was close by as if he were still there to protect him, just in case.

"What happened to NorthBrekka militia? Where are the people? What happened here?" Sebastian asked.

"The townspeople were sent to Torrdale. Anyone who refused was killed on sight. The militia was forced to join the Kuhar or get beheaded. We lost half the militia," Nadya said, then she informed him of everything else that had happened in the last two years. She told him how Tomas was tied to the lookout and how he starved and suffered without protection from the elements.

Sebastian held Tomas in his arms. "Now, you will help him as you did me all those years ago," he said seriously to Nadya. He signaled for his men to help carry Tomas inside the castle and asked Amara to check over his brothers and sisters.

Nadya looked at him and said, "I barely recognize you. You have changed. You look, troubled." She followed Tomas inside, she watched as Dom came over and took Sebastian's hand.

"Sebastian, look," Nadya said, pointing past the men toward the castle gate.

The Prime army gathered outside of NorthBrekka and a rustle of movement came from the soldiers' center. Sebastian put his hand on the hilt of his sword. The alpha wolf stood between him and the Prime soldiers, growling.

As the rustling came closer, the face of a man came clear. A beautiful brown-haired man pushed his way to the front of the line and stopped in place when his eyes locked on Sebastian.

"Cyrus!" Sebastian said, almost choking from excitement.

Sebastian's smile vanished quickly as he noticed Cyrus was not as excited to see him. He walked forward and stood next to the wolf. He knelt and patted the wolf on her neck. He looked into her eyes and smiled and nodded his head toward Dom. She immediately went to lay on the ground next to where Dom was standing. He stood and looked at Cyrus again.

"You don't seem happy to see me."

Cyrus forced a smile. "I am sorry, but I have no idea who you are."

CHAPTER 28

Memories

Sebastian noticed Cyrus standing hand-in-hand with what appeared to be a young knight. He felt something was familiar about the knight, but he had never met him.

"What do you mean, Cyrus? We were—I mean, how do you not know me?"

"I am not sure. Should I?" Cyrus looked confused at the knight.

Sebastian's heart dropped. He realized that he must be the knight Cyrus intended to marry.

The knight smirked at Sebastian. "My name is Sacha Kovell. I lead the encampment of southern soldiers in Sun Shadow. We have been watching NorthBrekka for a long time." Sacha whispered something in Cyrus's ear. Dom hurried over and took Sebastian's arm.

"Come inside. Your family needs you."

He stared at Cyrus as he backed toward the castle. Cyrus laughed at what Sacha whispered, then kissed him. Sebastian turned and took off in a sprint across the grounds, disappearing into the city with Dom following him closely.

As the morning grew late, Sebastian and Dom returned to the castle. Viktor met them at the gate. He hurried downstairs to meet them at the doors. Sebastian paused before entering the castle. Dom took his hand. Sebastian was shaking.

"I am excited to meet your family and learn about the world you grew up within. Don't be nervous now."

Sebastian drew a deep breath and turned to take the lead into the castle. As soon as he stepped foot over the threshold, Viktor met him with a big hug. Sebastian laughed and happily embraced his little brother.

"Viktor, this is Dominic. He is the leader of the Sinook." Sebastian wrapped his arm around Dom's back.

Viktor looked at Dom, then reached out to shake his hand. "Wow, I would have guessed you only would have been with Cyrus." He stopped immediately. "Sorry."

Dom smiled and looked uncomfortable. Sebastian sighed but then smiled. "Where is Tomas. Is he alright?"

"He is resting but doing better. Nadya is taking good care of him. Come on. I will take you to him," Viktor said as he led the way to Tomas.

They entered the bedroom, which Tomas and Sebastian had shared growing up. Viktor went first, then Sebastian slowly walked through the door, looking around the room. He saw Tomas was watching him. Sebastian wrapped him in his arms.

"I thought I had lost you," Tomas said, sobbing. "I missed you so much."

"All I could think about was getting back home to you. To all of you," Sebastian said, looking up at Nadya, who was in tears as she patted Sebastian's back.

"We all missed you, brother," she said. "Our hearts were destroyed when we lost you."

"Who is that?" Tomas said, looking at Dom.

"This is Dominic, or Dom as everyone calls him. He is the leader of the Sinook," Sebastian said, holding his hand out for Dom to take and join him next to his family.

"Is he… your lover?" Tomas asked.

"Yes. We are together. One day Dom will be my husband."

The rest of the Drake clan had come into the room. They gathered around Tomas's bedside and listened to Sebastian tell his story about what had happened in the Far North. He told them of Amara, who the children had gotten to know well, and how she saved his life, then described the villages, cities, and people. He told them of the sorceress and the Alcala family, Dom's family. All listened in awe and smiled, laughed, and cried.

Sebastian spent much of his time at Tomas's side during his recovery. He felt happy to be home again and began preparing to restore his city to what it was before Barron and the Kuhar had destroyed it. He sent messengers to Torrdale and Alta Prime, making them aware of their victory and inviting his people to come home and live their lives once more.

"Have you spoken to Cyrus much?" Tomas asked Sebastian that evening as they sat alone in their room, listening to the storm roll in from the west.

"No. I am confused why he is acting like he does not know who I am. What happened to him while I was gone?"

Tomas hesitated but told Sebastian everything he knew. Nadya interrupted when she entered the bedroom and began to explain how she had helped him escape. She informed him that Cyrus had gone south to Alta Prime to join his brother, but she was unaware that he had met someone else. She stopped when she saw the hurt on Sebastian's face.

Sebastian smiled. "All is well. I am happy that I am home now. Everything is going to be better now. I promise."

He held Tomas and Nadya in his arms as they watched the storm travel into the city. He was at peace, finally.

CHAPTER 29

Last Words

It was early in the morning. Tomas was still tired, so he fell back to sleep. Sebastian took his leave and went to wander about the castle. He entered the throne room, walked up to where his Father once sat, and looked at his crown.

It was quiet as his family was still sleeping. He sat in silence with only a few candles lit on the chandelier above his head. His head was pointing looking at his onyx crown with the ruby gems glistening in the firelight.

As his family entered the throne room, he slowly lifted his head. He felt and hollow. All knelt before their king. Sebastian was, in fact, a different person than they remembered. He was much darker-hearted and severe.

"We will restore our home to its rightful glory. Under my rule, NorthBrekka will become the most powerful kingdom in all Erras. I have ordered the Sinook to start facilitating the city's construction to operate more productively than before. The castle is being reconditioned to perfect our family namesake. As fara as significant changes go, the Sinook will house in our city. We lost much of our militia; therefore, the Sinook are under my command. I expect your respect for my people," Sebastian said, addressing his brothers and sisters.

"We are happy to have you home, brother. We know with you in charge, things will be restored, and our lands can once again be our home," Nadya started. "Sebastian, we need to discuss Barron," she said softly.

"What's to discuss? Barron is a prisoner," Sebastian said simply.

Nadya stood and marched up to Sebastian quickly but stopped fast when he looked up at her with dominance in his eyes. She looked at him strangely, then backed away. "Look, what he did has had adverse effects on all of us. You should understand how delicate things are going to be."

"Do you think I haven't been affected by Barron's actions? Do you think I did not suffer? Two years, Nadya! Two years I was gone, worried, scared, angry!" Sebastian spoke loud enough that his voice echoed through the halls and scared the children. "For two long years, I did not know if I would ever get back home or if I would ever see any of you again. I was unsure of when I came home how many of you I would find dead. But you tell me I need to be delicate."

"Don't you raise your voice at me, Sebastian Tomas Drake! How do you think we felt thinking you were dead and that our lives with Barron would be our lives forever? Do not lecture me on being afraid or worried."

Sebastian looked at her with slight amusement. He knew when she spoke his full name that she was angry with him. They stared at each other until Tomas entered the room and walked forward. He walked right up to Sebastian and grabbed his hand, which made everyone gasp.

"We love you, brother. It will take time for all of us to acclimate to our normal lives. What can we do to help you?" Tomas said.

Sebastian stared at Nadya some more, then looked at his brothers and sisters, who watched him intently. He looked at Dom, who was standing in the back of the group next to Jon. He stood up and kissed Tomas on the cheek.

"I don't need you all to worry about me. Help each other heal. We all need to be here for each other. I am here for you, but I have work to do here, so please understand." Sebastian stepped forward, away from the throne, and sat with his family. He invited Dom to sit next to him.

As Dom sat, Sebastian took his hand and held it tight. "You need to be by my side. You are my lover, not a soldier. Not in the back of the room, by my side. Understand?"

Dom nodded and rested his head on Sebastian's shoulder. "I will always be by your side."

Tomas sat down next to Sebastian. Tomas was healing well, but he was skinny and frail. He was also much quieter than before. He did not speak, just sat down and took Sebastian's hand in his. Sebastian was happy to be among his family. Before, all he could think of was getting away from them, but not anymore. He was grateful to be home.

Viktor sat with his arms crossed, looking away. It was almost comical as Sebastian started laughing while watching him.

"Why are you laughing?"

"Because you are sitting there like a child who was just told he couldn't have a cake after dinner. What is your problem, brother?" Sebastian said, still laughing.

Viktor uncrossed his arms and turned to Sebastian with fury written all over his face. "Two years? It took you two whole years to come back. Why? What were you doing? Oh, I know. You were enjoying life while we were getting beaten and starved!"

He took a deep breath and reached out to put his hand on Viktor's shoulder. "I was not up there having fun and making friends. You cannot fathom how desperately I wanted to come home to all of you. When they left me there, I was bleeding to death and scared. When Amara found me and her family took me in, fed me, healed me, and housed me, I knew I would survive but could not leave yet. Yes, they made me their king. Yes, I made friends, and I fell in love, but all I ever wanted was to avenge my Father and rescue all of you. What I went through to get here—"

"You know nothing of what we have been through either! I watched him punish our brothers and sisters for speaking out of turn. I watched him beat Nadya over and over. I watched as his men tortured our baby sister and brother until they were dead. I was helpless to help Tomas as he was chained to that roof for two years with nothing but hope to see your face again, even though we thought you were dead! No one helped us, and no one came to save us. They all abandoned us. The south could have come, but they did not. They left us to die. You left us to die!"

Viktor's ranting was becoming uncontrollable. Sebastian was so angry and so upset. He did not consider the consequences before reaching out and striking Viktor hard across his face, sending him falling back. Sebastian hurried over and held his arms down.

"Everyone leave, now!" He looked at Dom, who was the first to walk away. "Go and check on the Sinook. I will join you in a moment." He turned back to Viktor. "You dare tell me that I gave up on you? I never left you! Do you remember what he did to me?" Sebastian tore his shirt off and showed Viktor the scars on his chest, then turned to reveal the scars on his back. Viktor calmed down instantly and stared at Sebastian's scarred body with pity.

Sebastian breathed heavily, his eyes burned. His hands were clenched in fists, and wisps of fire were escaping his tightly clutched hands. Viktor stared at him in wonder and worry.

"I'm sorry, brother. I forgot what he had done to you," Viktor said quietly. "Does it still hurt? Your scars, they are..."

"Hideous. They are hideous. He mutilated me. How could he do this to us? To his own family. I only wanted him to love me, but he hated me so much, and I never knew why until Father told me what I am. I am a demon, and there is nothing I can do to get rid of this power. I do not want it, Viktor. I want to be normal and live a normal life. I am a monster," Sebastian said, with tears streaming down his face.

Viktor reached up and hugged Sebastian tightly. "You are not a monster. You are a hero, a king, and our brother. I am sorry I was so harsh. Please forgive me, brother."

They sat and held each other, weeping in each other's arms. "I did what was right. I did what I was born to do and what Father expected of me. You are my family, and I would do anything for you all," Sebastian said.

Viktor calmed down, then looked at Sebastian. "What about Cyrus? I thought you..."

"Loved him? Yes. I do. I mean, I did. I don't know anymore."

Just then, Cyrus walked into sight. Sebastian nodded and stood up. "I should go and check on my men," he said as he helped Viktor to his feet, then started to walk away.

"We need to speak," Cyrus said, stopping him.

They stood remarkably close. Cyrus looked at Sebastian's bare chest and then ran his fingers across the scars, which upset Sebastian. He shoved his hand away and turned to dress. Cyrus let out a broken gasp upon noticing the wounds across his back.

"Stop staring and speak."

"The tattoo. It means you are Sinook, right? You are from the Far North."

"What is your point?"

"I am trying to understand why you seem to know me so well, but I cannot recall ever meeting you," Cyrus said, his hands shaking.

Sebastian turned away again, then Cyrus grabbed his arm and pulled him to face him.

"Don't do this," Sebastian said.

Cyrus pulled him close, and Sebastian could feel his breath on the side of his neck. It made the hair on his arms raised, and a tingling sensation filled him. He pushed away from Cyrus with a struggle.

Cyrus's eyes filled with tears. "I am supposed to kill you. You are evil, a demon. You don't belong in this world." His voice cracked as it grew louder.

"Cyrus, what are you doing? What are you hiding behind your back?"

He revealed a knife and held it toward Sebastian's throat. "You have to die. If the world is to ever be united, you cannot live in it."

Sebastian was shaking with anger. "Why are you acting like this, Cyrus? We were in love."

"How could I love you? I have never seen you in my life. Now, shut your mouth and die like an honorable man," Cyrus shouted, then swung his blade at Sebastian.

Sebastian caught his arm, then pushed him hard in the chest, causing Cyrus to stumble. Cyrus screamed, then charged at Sebastian, dagger in hand. Sebastian punched him in the jaw. He fell to the ground, then started to get up but was met with a boot to the side of the head.

"Stop, Cyrus. I don't want to hurt you."

"I have a job to do. I will not stop until you are dead."

Sebastian let Cyrus stand, then he stepped back and ignited both fists in fire, threatening Cyrus. "I don't want to do this."

"You are weak."

"Cyrus-"

"Is everything alright?"

Dom walked in and came face to face with Cyrus. "You will not harm my king."

Cyrus looked at him, confused, then shouted. "Back away!"

"Sebastian, I will protect you."

"This is between him and me, Dom."

"I will kill you both." Cyrus was seething.

"You are working yourself up, my prince?" Sacha said as he walked in and grabbed Cyrus hard by the shoulder.

Cyrus's eyes widened. "I am doing what I am meant to do, Sacha."

Sacha grabbed Cyrus by the arm and jerked him away. Cyrus struggled against him, but Sacha tightened his grip, grabbed his throat and pulled him back. "You need to rest. Come now."

Sebastian felt an uneasy pain hit him in the stomach. Something was unusual about Sacha.

"You both should leave," Dom said.

"No. They will stay."

Cyrus glared angrily at Sebastian, then was dragged away by Sacha.

"Dom, I think Cyrus is in trouble. Did you see how Sacha was grabbing on him? Something has gone terribly wrong in the south. I need to find out what it is."

Sebastian walked away quickly.

Dom walked out onto the castle grounds to consult with Jon. He saw Jon sitting on a bench, speaking to Nadya. He started walking toward them until he saw Jon beaming while Nadya gripped his arm.

"My lady, I know we have only known each other a short time, but your beauty has stolen my heart."

"You served my kingdom well and you honor me by serving my brother. He told me great things about you." Nadya blushed.

He wanted to leave them alone, but he had to interrupt.

CHAPTER 30

The Plan

Nadya looked up to see Dom walking quickly toward her and Jon.

"Jon, I need to have a word. Something is wrong."

"What's going on?" Nadya said.

Jon stood and walked over to Dom. "What is the matter?"

"Sebastian is in danger. The north is in danger. I think something bad has happened in Alta Prime. Cyrus attacked Sebastian. If he is the man I had heard stories about, I cannot imagine he would do anything like what I just witnessed."

"Is my brother alright? Cyrus would never do anything to hurt Sebastian," Nadya interrupted. "King Roman loves Sebastian like he is his son. They would not attack us. My Father and Roman were the closest of friends."

Dom took Nadya's hand. "He is fine for now. I will do whatever it takes to protect your family. Sebastian is my priority, though. Jon, I need you to put a watch over the kingdom and the castle. Do not raise any alarm. We do not need to panic. I believe something is not right in Cyrus's mind, and I think Sacha is behind it."

Dom hurried back into the castle. Jon looked stressed, but Nadya kissed him on the cheek. He smiled and knelt before her. "My lady, I will protect you and your family until the end of my days. I must work now. Stay safe until we end this madness," Jon said.

"Let me follow Cyrus and Sacha. They won't suspect anything from me."

"I cannot risk that," Jon argued, but Nadya persisted.

"I promise to be safe. I must help my family. I will not sit and wait. Not anymore. I have to fight. Besides, I need to find out what happened to Cyrus and why he has forgotten who Sebastian is. They were once in love. They were the center of this whole war, and now he acts in a sense that Sebastian never existed before he arrived here."

Jon grabbed her by the arm before she slipped away. "Princess, one day I wish to marry you. I must ask if you feel the same?"

"Yes, I hope for that as well."

Jon held Nadya's cheek, then kissed her hand. Nadya listened to him arrange his men on different assignments to guard the castle, then sending men to watch over the borders. Nadya went inside the castle to look for Sacha.

She found him in the war room, standing on the edge of the open balcony. She stood quietly, peering around through the crack in the door. She noticed Cyrus sitting on the floor in the corner, not speaking, only looking out over the city.

"What are they doing now?" Sacha said.

"I would assume they are preparing for the return of their people," Cyrus said.

"Have you forgotten why we came?"

"You said I was to kill him."

"In due time!" Sacha slammed his hands on the table. "I cannot have you running around waving your blade at him like a fool. You must get him alone, then do the job."

"Don't raise your voice to me! I will get him alone, then I will cut his head off. Do not be concerned over the ignorance of northern people."

Sacha grabbed Cyrus by the shirt and slammed him against the wall. "If you ever talk to me that way again, you will regret it. I swear that to you."

Nadya jerked away from the door and crouched down with her hands over her mouth, breathing hard.

"Don't push me, my prince. You know what happens when you anger me," Sacha said.

"I'm not trying to..." Cyrus started but was silenced. Nadya pushed herself back into the door and saw Sacha kissing Cyrus.

"Let us get this over with, so we can go home. I hate the north. It is cold and dirty, and these people are less than desirable. Although, that sister of your lover boy is quite fetching," Sacha said, laughing. "It's just a shame she has a child. I don't like children."

Nadya hurried away and into a nearby room. She could not contain her anger any longer. She sat with her back against the door until she heard Sacha walk past. She only heard one set of footsteps, so she stepped out and strolled to the war room. Cyrus was still there, leaning against the wall with tears rolling down his cheeks.

"Cyrus?" she said, walking into the room.

"You shouldn't be here," Cyrus said quickly.

"This is my home. I can be wherever I want," Nadya snapped. "Cyrus, tell me what is happening. What is Sacha planning?"

"He isn't planning anything."

"Don't lie to me. I saw him slam you into the wall. He is abusing you, isn't he? He is using you. Why did you attack Sebastian? Tell me now!" Nadya said.

Cyrus looked up at her furiously. "You wouldn't understand."

"Do you still love my brother?"

Cyrus fell silent looking annoyed yet confused.

"Well, do you still love him?" Nadya demanded.

"Why would I love him? Is everyone in NorthBrekka completely mad?"

"Then tell me what is happening, Cyrus, please."

Cyrus started mumbling in confusion, then Sacha stormed into the war room. His face was full of fury.

"Stay away from him!" Nadya screamed.

Sacha laughed. Cyrus stood and stepped between Nadya and Sacha. "This is not about her."

"Let me explain something to you, princess. Your brother is an abomination. He will die, and when he does, I will see to it that every last one of you is enslaved. You will serve my men well. You are quite beautiful," Sacha sneered.

"Sacha, leave her. Let's finish the job and go home."

"Fine." Sacha marched away and headed through the castle and down into the dungeons.

Sebastian saw Sacha take the stairway that led to the castle's underground. He quietly followed without drawing attention to himself.

Sacha stopped before a cell door. "You failed me."

"I didn't fail you. My brother has more power than I remember. Let me out, and I will finish him." Barron spat.

"No. I have Cyrus taking care of that. I had a feeling you wouldn't be able to finish the job, so I brought reinforcements."

"You brought my brother's lover. How is that working for you?"

"I fixed Cyrus. All he sees now is becoming victorious when he has Sebastian's blood on his hands. After that, I will kill him, and all will be right in the world."

"What about Tomas?"

"He is a pathetic excuse for a god. He is powerless."

"Don't be so sure."

"You could have killed him long ago, but you failed at that too."

Barron backed away and sat in a dark corner. "Are you going to release me or not?"

"Get out!" Sebastian walked out from his hiding place. "Get away from him." He looked at Sacha furiously.

"Whatever you wish, Your Majesty," Sacha said with sarcasm before leaving.

"You lying, treasonous bastard. You betrayed our Father and our family for a crown. Why?"

"Our Father died to protect you and Tomas. Once he discovered my plan, he threatened to banish me. I told him if he did, I would reveal the secret that only he and the Kuhar knew. The one I learned about that would cause the rule over the north to change hands. He would have been branded a traitor of Erras, and our family would be exiled. Therefore, I told him he had two options. To die and leave me the crown or let me kill you and Tomas. Obviously, he chose to die, so I poisoned him and Emelia."

"You killed our parents? You are demented and I will destroy you for what you did!" Sebastian asked. Barron laughed and walked into the light, coming face-to-face with Sebastian.

"Someday, you will understand that our Father wasn't the man you praised him for being."

Sara glared at Sebastian for a moment before turning her back on him. "I didn't know anything about it."

"What did Sacha do to Cyrus?"

"I know nothing about Cyrus and his empty mind," Barron said with an amused expression.

"You do not deserve the comfort of this cell. You deserve a violent and painful death!" Sebastian screamed.

"Get the hell away from us! Leave us alone!" Sara shrieked.

Sebastian was furious. He stood and stared at her angrily in the dimly lit dungeons. "Fine. Stay here and wither away until your bones litter the ground." Sebastian sat and watched them long into the night.

CHAPTER 31

Cyrus' Story

Before the war in the north, when Cyrus and Sacha made it to Alta Prime, the sun began to rise over the palace. Cyrus watched as Sacha slept their first morning home. He sat up in bed, looking out to the open curtains that revealed the warm sun and fresh sea air. Sacha's arms wrapped around his chest.

"You're awake early, my prince. You should rest. You have had a rough year," Sacha said quietly while pulling Cyrus back on his soft pillow.

Sacha lay against him with his arms wrapped around him from behind, his lips barely brushing against Cyrus's neck. Once he realized that Cyrus was becoming entranced by his touch, he reached in to kiss him on the neck. They kissed and made love until late in the morning.

"I need to go check on my brother." Cyrus said, getting out of bed.

"Your brother has maidens tending to him morning and night. I am sure he is much happier than having you in his face," Sacha said.

Cyrus smiled at Sacha while he dressed and continued to leave to visit with his brother.

"I don't believe you have moved on so quickly," King Roman said after seeing Cyrus enter his bed chambers.

"I haven't moved on. I am just trying to heal. This is not about me. How are you feeling?"

Roman groaned, then let out a sarcastic laugh. "I'm still alive if that is what you're asking, and I don't plan on dying any time soon, so don't assume you're running the kingdom already."

"I don't want to run the kingdom. I just wanted to know my brother is going to be alright," Cyrus said.

"So, what is this Sacha's story? I do not know him, but he is a captain, you say. I am curious how much you know about him," Roman said.

"Not much, but he is helping me get over Sebastian. He comforts me when I cannot stop having nightmares. That is all that matters right now."

"And you are sure Sebastian is dead? Do you have proof?" Roman asked.

"I don't have proof, but I saw what they did to him. No one would have survived that," Cyrus said sadly.

Later that afternoon, Sacha crept in the doorway in time to hear Cyrus ask the king's advisor knew if anyone had confirmation of Sebastian's death. This made Sacha angry.

Sacha stormed off and down to the market. He entered a brothel where some of his men were being serviced. When he entered, a woman was standing behind the counter, plucking through a pile of coins. She did not look up to acknowledge Sacha, just pointed to the lounge next to them.

"Pick whichever lady you want. Leave the money here."

"I'm not here for that."

The woman looked up and stared at him. Sacha dropped a gold coin on the counter. "I will only be a moment."

He stomped off down the hall and began throwing open doors. Some of the women gasped while the men in the beds yelled at him. Three entries into his search, he slung open the door to find a tan-skinned, black-haired man lying on the bed with two young women completely nude sitting on both sides of him, giggling and stroking his face and chest.

"Get out!"

The ladies looked at him nervously, then scurried to gather their gowns and hurried out of the room.

"I paid good money for those whores," the man grumbled.

"I will make it up to you," Sacha said uncaringly. "Seems that Cyrus has grown suspicious. I need it now. I need to show him that his precious Sebastian is dead."

"He isn't dead, though. It has been confirmed. I sent men back to check. They saw him in a small village only a few months ago looking very much alive."

"I don't care if he is dead or alive. I need something that shows he is dead. I need to break Cyrus's hope," Sacha said.

"I don't see how this is going to convince the king to follow us," the man said.

"They will because the line of gods, to their knowledge, are dead. There is nothing left to protect them from us. Once I can prove Sebastian's death, and His Majesty sends word that the twin has perished, the southern king will have no choice but submit to us. You heard what the witch said. The one that destroys the gods will rule over all the lands. All will submit under his power. Now give me the proof so I can work on the prince's mind some more. Once I have control over him, he will convince his brother to fall into line."

The man reached for his coat, pulled a dark brown braided hunk of hair, and placed it in Sacha's outstretched hand. "That is King Sebastian's actual hair. I cut it from his head myself."

Sacha ran his fingers over the braid and smiled. "Cyrus is such a delicate child. He will fall apart after this. I will have to be there to comfort him. It is so disgusting listening to him sob like a little girl. I am glad he is gullible and fell for me almost too easily, or else I would just have to run my sword through his throat."

"I thought you liked him," the man said while picking the dirt from under his nails.

"Once this is over, I will discard him like piss in a pot. He must not find out I spoke with you. If he recognizes you, he will inform his brother there are Kuhar in his city. Now, let us get those ladies back in here. I think I would like to have one for myself," Sacha said, smiling as he went to fetch the whores whom he had made leave.

Late in the afternoon, Sacha returned to the castle. Before finding Cyrus, he changed his clothing to ensure the brothel's perfumes were not present on his body. He pulled the braided hair from his pants pocket and stroked it again. He smiled then went to find Cyrus, who just happened to be sitting with his brother.

He knocked on the bedchamber door then slapped his cheeks to look like he was panicked. He burst through the doors, quickly breathing hard and speaking loudly.

"Your Majesty, Prince Cyrus. My men just informed me they took down a small group of Kuhar on the border only a few days ago. Before killing them, one of my men found this on one of the soldiers. He said it was cut from King Sebastian's head after they cut his throat."

Sacha held out the braid and handed it to Cyrus. Cyrus slowly reached over to take the hair. His hand was shaking hard, and tears began to fill his eyes. He ran his fingers across the braid and felt the texture of the hair.

"Is it his, my prince?" Sacha said quietly. He waited for Cyrus's reaction.

King Roman stared at his brother, who looked as if he were about to faint. "Well, is it Sebastian's?"

Cyrus nodded while he squeezed the lock of hair tight in his palm. He sobbed, "You are sure the Kuhar said they saw him die?"

Sacha nodded. "They said they watched him bleed to death, then cut the hair to give to King Barron as a gift, then they pushed his body through a hole in the ice and watched him sink to the bottom of the lake. I am so sorry."

Cyrus let out a horrible cry, then Sacha went to wrap his arms around him. Roman sat there with tears in his eyes.

"I know you hoped for better news, but now you know for sure, and you can begin to heal. I promise I will be there for you. Whatever you need," Sacha said before kissing Cyrus on the cheek and excusing himself from the room.

For the next several weeks, Sacha grew irritated, waiting for Cyrus to snap out of his depression. He would sneak off several days a week to visit the brothel, where he would spend the long afternoons with the girl of his choosing. On one hot afternoon, Sacha sat on the windowsill overlooking the bay, trying to convince Cyrus to come and enjoy some sunlight on his skin. He saw three men riding into the courtyard. It was a messenger he had been waiting on for days.

He smiled and hopped up. "My men have returned from their post in the north. Come on, let us go see what they have to say!"

Cyrus perked up a little, then climbed to his feet and followed Sacha down to meet his men. The three men walked over to Sacha quickly. One of the men was holding something tightly. He dropped it into Sacha's hand.

Cyrus looked and noticed it was a ring with sapphires set in a silver band. "That is Tomas's," Cyrus said, sounding frail. "His Father gave him that ring. He gave one to Tomas and one to Sebastian on their birthday one year. How did you get this?"

The man who was carrying it stepped forward. "It was on his finger. I found his body washed up on the shore of the river just south of NorthBrekka. He is dead, Your Grace."

Cyrus fell to his knees. Sacha grinned at his men, then cleared his smile to the look of sadness as he turned to Cyrus. "I can't believe they're gone. The line of the gods is broken. They will no longer exist in this world. Barron caused this tragedy. He has murdered half his own family. He must be stopped. Come with me."

Cyrus looked at Sacha, confused, but he followed Sacha anyway. They wandered into a run-down part of the city. The streets were littered with rotted fruits and vegetables. There were bugs everywhere, and children ran up and down the streets wearing little but dirty rags. They approached a small, narrow alley between two large buildings.

"Where are you taking me?" Cyrus said, his voice shaking. "This place is horrid."

Sacha took his hand and smiled. He led them to a doorway that was blocked by a tattered sheet. They entered the dwelling to find an older woman sitting in a chair by the fire. She was cooking something that smelled rancid in a small iron kettle.

"Madam, this is Prince Cyrus," Sacha started, but the older woman turned and looked at the young prince.

"I have heard of you. You are a witch, my brother says."

"Madam, tell our prince what you explained to me about the death of the gods."

"Ahh, yes, the young twins. You see, the twins are the last remnant of the gods who once ruled this land. The twins are the great descendants of the most powerful gods ever to exist. They were in line to rule above all. The prophecy said a man would destroy the gods, and all would fall to his feet. It said he who destroyed the dragon would rule over all the lands. Those who opposed would face devastating results," the witch said.

"Dragon? What do you mean, dragon?" Cyrus asked.

"What is the ancient word for the dragon?" she asked.

Cyrus stared for a moment, then whispered, "Drake." His eyes widened. "Do you mean, Sebastian? Sebastian is the dragon?"

The witch stared at him, looking grim.

"So, you are saying we have to follow Barron Drake?"

"That is for you to decide, Your Grace."

Cyrus started breathing heavily, then turned and hurried out of the witch's home. Sacha chased after him and caught him by the arm before he marched into the street.

"My prince, stop!" he demanded.

Cyrus swung around angrily. "I will never bow to that man! He murdered my Sebastian. He murdered Tomas, Gentry, and who knows how many more by now. He is a monster, and I will not submit to him."

Sacha looked at Cyrus with hatred, then cleared his face to resemble pity. "You heard what the witch said. You have no choice. I will not let you die. I... love you, Cyrus."

Cyrus looked at Sacha, and his mouth opened in awe.

"Did you hear me? I said I love you," Sacha said.

Cyrus's jaw shook, and he seemed to be lost for words. He shook his head and took off in a sprint toward to castle. Sacha stood in the alley, and his expression turned back to anger. He marched to the market and found his men arguing over a game of cards.

"The prince isn't convinced to follow King Barron just yet. We will move to phase two of the plan. We will have his allegiance by any means," Sacha said before stomping away.

The next evening, Roman and Cyrus sat over their dinner, discussing what Cyrus learned about Tomas and what the witch had told him.

"I told you to stay away from that witch," Roman said, irritated. "She is a crazy old woman telling ghost stories."

"Sacha told me he loves me. I don't know how to feel about that."

"Do you care for him?" Roman said.

"Of course I do," Cyrus said quietly.

Roman looked unconvinced. Cyrus continued, "She said we should follow Barron or else we will all suffer. Because he killed the gods, he is the ruler of all. Is this true?"

"I won't kneel before a false king," Roman said loudly and angrily.

The following morning, two men arrived at the castle grounds. They were unusual, with markings on their chest and arms.

"Who are you?" Sacha asked. "I am the ambassador to the king, and he is ill. I cannot permit unwanted visitors into the castle."

"We are from Icefall. We have brought word from the Far North. It is for the king's ear only."

Sacha reached out and grabbed one of the men by the neck, and Sacha's men grabbed and held the other down with their swords at his throats. "You will explain your presence to me only."

The men glared at Sacha without speaking. Sacha shook with fury. "King Sebastian sent you. You are the heathens of the north, aren't you? Your word will never reach the ear of King Roman. Your king will die by my hand, and I will rule once I destroy the gods."

"We will tell you nothing. Kill us if you must. We will die with honor."

Sacha pulled his knife and plunged it into the throat of the man he held while his men cut the head off the other.

"Get rid of the bodies," Sacha said. "I'm done playing games. It is time to make the royal family concede. Sebastian plans to march south to take down his brother's army. We will join them in battle and then, when the time is right, I will destroy him. I must convince that ignorant prince and his drunken brother to march the southern army to war. Soon, I will be the one they bow to."

"Prince Cyrus and King Roman believe Sebastian is dead. How will you explain this?"

Sacha laughed. "I have an idea. Prepare your men for battle."

Sacha marched off to the palace. He knocked loudly on a door as he tapped his foot impatiently. The door swung open to reveal Queen Lorna, looking annoyed.

"What do you want now? Have I not done enough getting you here, disguising you as a knight of my husband's army, and giving you my pathetic brother-in-law to use as your puppet?"

"It is the puppet I need your help with, Your Highness," Sacha said as he forced his way into the room and shut the door. "I need something to displace Prince Cyrus's mind. He needs to forget about Sebastian so I can use him to destroy the king of the heathens before he rises to his potential."

"You want me to erase his mind?"

"Only the parts about Sebastian. He has to forget everything about him. Then make sure he sees Sebastian as a threat. Sebastian would never expect Cyrus to try to kill him. It would be too easy. Do this, and I will promise you safe passage to Safareen."

"Give me until sunset. Now go away."

That evening, Cyrus was sitting alone at the dinner table with tears pouring down his face. Lorna walked in slowly with a small tea kettle in hand.

"Tea?" she asked as she sat down.

Sacha watched from the doorway.

"It will help relax you. You need to sleep, Cyrus. Have some tea."

Lorna poured him a cup and passed it across the table. Cyrus looked at the amber liquid with a frown. "I don't need tea."

"Just have a cup. You are in pain. Let it ease your mind."

Cyrus picked up the cup and took a sip. "I knew he was dead when I saw all those arrows in his chest, but something kept telling me deep down that I was wrong." He took another sip. "But now I know it was true all along. It hurts so bad. I loved him more than anything in the world, and now I will never see him again."

Cyrus finished the tea as he sobbed. "I wish that I could have said goodbye. I wish I could have let him know how much I loved him. He must have been in so much pain."

"He knew, Cyrus. He loved you too."

Cyrus cried some more, then stared blankly at Lorna. "What were we talking about?"

Lorna and Sacha looked at each other, smiled, then Lorna turned back to Cyrus. "King Sebastian. The heathen king of the North."

"Who?" Cyrus snarled.

"The God they call Chaos," Lorna said. "The demon god. He is king in the Far North. If his power reaches Erras, our fate will be nothing short of death. He will kill us all. No man deserves such power."

"Do you know him?"

"No, but I have heard the legends. A man wielding the power of the gods would return from the north to end the people of Erras and take rule over the lands. He must be killed before it is too late."

"You are tired, my prince. You are getting worked up. We will finish this conversation tomorrow, then we will march north, and you may destroy him however you wish. It is your duty as future King of Kings to save the people from anyone who threatens our well-being," Sacha said.

Cyrus nodded, then walked away, looking lost. Sacha waited until he could no longer see him down the hall, then sat next to Lorna.

"Excellent work."

"Remember our deal, Sacha. You know what you have to do."

"Get your son and your things and meet my men by the road leaving the city. They will escort you to Safareen. You have my word. Once you arrive, send the Safar north. If they can weaken the Sinook, then they will have no chance against the Kuhar."

"The Sinook will destroy the Safar, leaving Safareen defenseless."

"Safareen will be kept safe from war. If the Safar is successful, Sebastian's men will be weak, and it will be a slaughter in NorthBrekka. Send them, and when I am King of Kings, you will return from Safareen and rule by my side."

Lorna smiled, then kissed Sacha. They slipped away to her private chambers. Sacha undressed her. He pinned her against the wall and lifted her up. She put her fingers to his lips.

"Don't leave any marks. My husband checks."

"Please leave marks on me. I don't care if Cyrus sees them. He is completely under my control now."

CHAPTER 32

A King's Fury

Sebastian sat next to Tomas. Several weeks had passed, and things started to settle in NorthBrekka. They watched a thunderstorm roll in over the mountains. They did not speak much but watched as the townspeople began returning to their homes. Tomas rested his head on his brother's shoulder and held a smile on his face. He was happy to have his best friend by his side.

"Dom is heading home tomorrow. I do not know when he will return. I wish he would stay longer," Sebastian said.

"You're nervous," Tomas said, noticing him chewing at his fingertips. "Are you afraid he won't come back?"

"No. I think he is angry with me, with my focus on Cyrus."

"Something isn't right with Cyrus. He seems shaken. Have you spoke with him much?" Tomas asked.

"He tried to kill me."

"Why would he do such a thing?" Tomas said. Sebastian sighed deeply.

Nadya and Viktor popped their heads through the door. Nadya sat down next to Sebastian and grabbed his hand.

"Sebastian, I need to tell you something. I have been watching Sacha and Cyrus over the last few weeks. You need to know—"

Sebastian turned to look at her and interrupted, "Sacha is beating him. I can see it. I see the bruises and the cuts."

"That is not all. Cyrus truly believes he is the one that must end your life. Something has happened to him that I cannot explain, and I think Sacha is behind all of this."

Sebastian was fed up with hearing the name Sacha. He wanted him dead in the hope that he could fix Cyrus somehow. He sat quietly while his siblings talked about things happening across the North. His frustrations forced him to storm away without a word.

Sebastian hurried through the castle with fury written in stone across his face. He silently walked down the hall through the corridors, kicking every door open along the way. For the first time, Sebastian no longer looked like an adolescent boy but like a grown man, a king, a leader on a mission to defend the ones he loves against a deceitful enemy.

He did not scream out for Sacha; he did not shout threats. He checked in every corner and through every door. Once he circled back to the entrance, he looked frustrated and confused. "Where is he?" he murmured to himself.

He marched outside to see a field of soldiers of the north waiting for his return. He looked frantically across the field for Dom, but he could not spot him among the sea of armored men.

"Dom?" Sebastian said, sounding panicked. "Where is Dom?" He faced Jon looking as though his heart had just snapped in two.

Jon shook his head. "He walked away saying he was going to find you, and that is the last I have seen of him."

"Where is Cyrus? I need to speak to him."

CHAPTER 33

Unity

That night, there was a quiet ceremony in the garden by the pond. It was a dark and cold night, but that did not stop Jon and Nadya from getting married. Sebastian sat on the bench where his mother gave birth to him and Tomas. He smiled, although he felt sadness and betrayal. Not a single word from Dom. Nothing. Only distance.

They watched as Jon and Nadya proclaimed their forever love for one another. stood behind them with flowers in their hands while Viktor and Mary stood holding torches to light up the dark of the night.

As the magistrate spoke the matrimonial words, Sebastian could not stop thinking of Dom. He tried hard to stay calm, but his hands were burning hot and shaking.

"Sebastian, it is going to be alright. I can feel the fury burning through you. You must calm down."

"I am not as happy as I should be on such a perfect night. None of this should be happening. Our Father should be alive, our brother should not have betrayed us, I wouldn't be king, and I would be happy again." Sebastian stared at a torch in the distance that was flickering from the soft breeze.

"You wouldn't have met the Sinook or Dom. Think about how much they taught you."

"I wouldn't have lost Cyrus, been beaten and left with these awful scars, and wouldn't be responsible for the deaths of so many people. Everyone we love who has died has been because of me. It used to make me sad and hurt. I used to have emotions and enjoy laughter. Now all I have is a burning desire to kill anything that stands in my way. I am the dragon, Tomas. I am the one who will end us all. The prophecy was right." Sebastian looked up and realized the wedding came to a halt. Everyone was staring at him.

"You can continue magistrate," Sebastian said.

Once the magistrate finished speaking, Jon and Nadya spoke words of loyalty, trust, and love to one another, then kissed to seal the marriage bond. Sebastian stood and congratulated them as graciously as he could muster, then excused himself from the party as quickly as he could.

He hurried to the aviary to send a letter to Sedda, then another to Icefall. He knew if Dom went home, he went to his daughter, but he thought he would try Dom's parents. He just wanted to know why he left without a word. He desperately needed closure.

Sebastian went back to the garden to find Cyrus standing by the bench.

Nadya and Jon slipped away to be alone as everyone went to bed.

"You are looking for me. Are you ready to finish this?" Cyrus asked.

"We need to talk."

"I have nothing to say."

"Cyrus, I know you don't remember, but you and I were in love. Trust me. Sacha has deceived your mind. If you don't believe me, ask my brothers or sisters. They will tell you that you and I were together before. The last time we saw each other, I was dragged away from my family and you. You thought I was dead. Nadya helped you escape a year later from the tower, and you ran to Alta Prime to find safety with Roman. I don't know what happened to you after that, but you once wanted to run away with me."

"I do not remember anything about you. All I know of you is from a prophecy. You are the dragon, and you have come to burn the world to the ground. You must be stopped." Cyrus's voice was monotone.

Sebastian put his hands on Cyrus's shoulders. "I never want do any of that. I want to help the people of Erras, to make these lands prosperous, but I need you, Cyrus. I love you with all my heart."

"Sacha loves me."

"Sacha is gone. He abandoned you. Please tell me what I can do to help you."

"Why should I believe you?"

"Let me prove everything to you. If I fail, then I will let you kill me. I don't want to live without you."

"I will give you one chance." Cyrus looked calm. "How are you going to prove what you say is true?"

"Thank you. Accompany me to Alta Prime. I believe all our answers lie there."

CHAPTER 34

A Journey to Alta Prime

Everything was quiet over the next several days. Sebastian rummaged through his Father's things in a chest that sat at the foot of the bed. He pulled out pendants and ran his fingers across the metal, remembering all the times Ivan wore each piece. He found his Father's favorite coat in a wardrobe in the corner.

He pulled it on, noticing how well it fit, then he pulled it tightly against himself as if he were hugging his Father again. This nearly broke him as he fell to his knees and muttered, "I am sorry, Father, for failing you," until he heard the door swing open.

"You never failed anyone," Tomas said, sneaking through the door. "Father loved you so much. He had me write about it before he died, about how much he loved us all, but there was a particularly heartfelt passage he wrote for you."

Tomas went to get the journal out of the desk drawer. Sebastian remembered the journal he saw Tomas scribbling in when they watched their Father take his last breath. Tomas opened it to the part he mentioned and handed the book to Sebastian.

To my dear Sebastian, you are forever my greatest accomplishment in life. I see myself in your eyes every time I look at you. I have never been so proud to be a Father as when I see you rushing in from a long journey as you pretend you were not up to anything mischievous all day. I always knew better, but I beam with happiness, knowing the man you will become. I know you will face some of the most difficult challenges and losses, and you will want nothing more than to give up, but you will not. You will persevere and grow from it, which is why you will rule over all one day. The gods chose you to stand above all others because you are the strongest and bravest man ever to walk these lands. Never forget who you are and what you are. Always know I will be with you. I will forever watch over you, hold you when you fall, and lift you in the darkest times. The family will learn to grow when it is time for you to depart them, as you will soon enough. They will be fine, so do not worry. This is not your place to stop. Tomas will rule our homeland in your stead. Place the crown upon his head when the time is right and never forget: the two of you are bonded forever. Take good care of each other. You must know how much you depend on one another. Now take your place on the throne over Erras and command as the gods intended for you to. You will be a great king.

Sebastian quietly handed the book back to Tomas and stared at him, watching as tears glistened across his twin brother's dark brown eyes. Tomas smiled as he placed the book back in the desk and locked the drawer.

"I knew all along what would become of you, of me, of the family. You are leaving us for Prime, aren't you?" Tomas spoke with sadness.

Sebastian nodded. "I have to fix Cyrus. I have to fix everything. I don't know where to start, but I suspect I will find answers there."

Tomas let out a small laugh. "Imagine that! They have no idea what they're in for in the South!"

They hugged tightly and cried a little. "Tomas, I have to tell you something. I am scared."

Tomas's smile faded as he looked at his brother with pity.

Sebastian continued, "I don't know what to do. Cyrus does not even know who I am. It is destroying me. Should I try to win him back or forget him and take Dom by my side? Why am I this way, Tomas? When I thought Cyrus was married, I went after Will, and Will died because of it. Now I am doing the same with Dom. Am I that insecure? And if Cyrus and I are meant to be together, then why is the universe trying so hard to keep us apart?"

Tomas held him in his arms and rubbed against his back, feeling the scars through his shirt. "It isn't unusual to seek out a lover when you are lonely. Cyrus is your true love. Dom and Will were mere replacements for him. I know you care for them, but it is as any king does when he has needs. But they will never replace Cyrus. You need to take Cyrus and go sit on the throne of Erras as you are meant to do."

"What about you? I cannot leave you again. I only just got you back," Sebastian said.

"We will always be together. No land can keep us apart, ever. I will always find you when you need me. End this war and be happy. Find your Dom, live your life with your Cyrus, and become who you are meant to be, King of Kings. I promise that it will all make sense one day, but for now, do what is right for Sebastian and only Sebastian. Let me worry about our family and NorthBrekka. This place is no longer your burden," Tomas said.

Sebastian choked back tears as he walked over to the bedside table. He opened the drawer, pulled his Father's crown out, and held it in his hand. He ran his fingers across it and squeezed his eyes shut, remembering it resting on his Father's head all those years. He turned and walked over to Tomas and placed it on his head. He kissed his cheek, then started to walk away.

He found Cyrus already waiting in the courtyard, mounted on his horse, and holding Sebastian's horse's reins in his hand. Accompanied by soldiers of the South, they began their journey, but before they made it through the gate, Viktor came running after them, screaming for them to wait.

"Sebastian! Brother, wait!"

Sebastian turned to see Viktor looking flushed.

"These just came for you. I thought you might want to know you have messages from the Far North before you depart to Alta Prime. Brother, can I please come with you?" Viktor begged.

Sebastian smiled and considered bringing Viktor along. He thought it would be nice to have family in an unfamiliar place. He tore open the first letter that was stamped from Sedda.

My king, I am worried. You say Dominic is gone home, but he has not returned to Sedda. We have no word of him, and our sorceress cannot see him in her visions. I fear the worst. Please, if you find him, send word at once.

With love, Ketya

Sebastian swallowed hard, feeling panic rise in his stomach. He dropped the letter and ripped the second one open, which Vigoras himself sealed.

Your Majesty, please tell me you found my son by the time this letter reaches you. Dominic is loyal to you. He would never leave your side without force. I fear his life is in danger. His mother is losing hope as his light fades from her. Find our son before he is gone forever. He needs you now more than ever. War is coming fast. You must rise. Take command and save us all. Save our son. Look south, for it is where all answers lie.
-Vigoras

"Viktor, I need you to advise Tomas. I must go now. I will bring you south as soon, but now it is not that time. I love you, brother," Sebastian said hurriedly, then ran to mount his horse. He and the men of the South galloped as swiftly as they could away from NorthBrekka on to a most uncertain future.

CHAPTER 35

A City in Ruin

They trampled across the border late one afternoon as the air began to grow warmer and thicker the farther South they rode. This was the farthest south Sebastian had ever traveled. He looked to Cyrus for guidance along the way as the layout of the land changed drastically. It was no longer mountainous and rocky. The green hills gave way to vast, open prairies filled with wildflowers and small cold-water streams.

As they stopped to eat and allow the horses to drink, Sebastian turned and looked north longingly. He could see the mountains of NorthBrekka far in the distance, and he became homesick. He never wanted to be anywhere more than at home with his family in the cold, stormy winter air. Cyrus watched him from the stream as he caught fish to cook.

"All I wanted was a life of my own. Freedom. After everything that has happened, I feel like I have let them down. Now suddenly, after everything they went through, I left them without a word. Again," Sebastian said.

Cyrus came and stood next to him.

"I will miss Tomas. I hate that we have spent so much time apart, then once we are together, I am required to be apart from him once more. It breaks my heart," Sebastian said.

"It seems like you really care about your family."

"I do. I care about you as well."

"What about Dominic? If you love me, why did you choose him over me?"

"I thought I would never return home and would never see you again. Now, he has left me as well. He left without a single word. I don't know what to think."

Cyrus smiled and motioned for Sebastian to venture forward. He explained that they needed to get into the protection of the city before nightfall came. Sebastian agreed, and they continued southbound to Alta Prime.

As the sky turned from bright to a deep haze, they stood upon a hillside seeing the city's bustle that was ending for the night, but something was odd about the sight. Sebastian did not know what Prime looked like, but he knew this was not it.

Cyrus dismounted his horse and looked upon the city. The men of the southern army whispered to one another, and as Sebastian looked around, he could see that he was right in assuming the worst.

He heard about the great city being very loud and busy. There were always people rushing down the streets, trying to get their goods from one place to the next. The harbors were always filled with boats coming and going. There almost always were merchants surrounding the walls to be the first to sell to newcomers entering the city.

It was dark and quiet. There were few ships in the harbor, and the gates were locked tight. There was not anyone greeting them on the path. As they approached the city, they heard a soldier who watched from above shout to open the gates halfway for the prince.

"My name is King Sebastian Drake. I rule over all the North. I have come to Alta Prime to find my enemy. No harm needs to come to you if you can tell me what happened here?" Sebastian asked a woman crying over a small child, expecting no answer.

"He has gone mad, Your Majesty. He was angry. He came and set fire to our homes and slew our families. He kept screaming out a phrase, but we did not understand until now."

It was a young woman who spoke to King Sebastian. Her dress was torn, revealing much of her body as she tried to hold the pieces together to cover herself.

"He came here first and hurt some of the girls, including me. When he entered our establishment, he was in a fury and demanded our affection. When we denied him, he began hitting us and tearing at our clothes. Then, that is when the fires began."

Sebastian looked at her questioningly. "Who are you speaking of? And what phrase was he screaming?"

She walked closer to the king. "It was the man that stayed with him," she said, pointing at Cyrus. "The blond- haired knight. He had been visiting us for ages now, but this time, he was manic. He kept shouting that this was King Sebastian's fault."

Sebastian looked at Cyrus. Cyrus straightened his back and demanded to know where Sacha was, but the townspeople started looking at Sebastian angrily.

"This is your fault! You are the one they call Chaos. You are the one sent to destroy us all," he heard a man shout.

Sebastian turned to see a man running at him with a knife. He kicked the man hard in the jaw and rushed his horse to move quickly to the palace. Cyrus hurried after him, and the soldiers followed but were stopped by the townspeople, who were anxious to get a hand on the new king.

Sebastian saw people pouring into the streets with weapons drawn. He nudged his horse to run faster as he and Cyrus dodged arrows flying at their heads. As they approached the palace walls, they were stopped by a large crowd.

Sebastian held up his hands. "I am not here to hurt any of you. I am not here to cause you pain or distress. You are being misled!"

"King Sebastian murdered King Roman," One man shouted from the crowd. "He sent men from the North. He sent his heathens here to slay the king in his bed so that he may rule all. He is a traitor to the crown!"

"My brother is dead?" Cyrus said, looking appalled.

"I have sent no one!" Sebastian replied. "I was at war on my land. My men were at my back. I never sent a soul to come to take down the king. He was a friend!"

At that moment, the crowd fell silent as they heard clapping from above. They looked up to see Sacha standing there, smiled brightly. "Then how do you explain this?"

Sebastian's heart dropped into his stomach. It was like all the air had been sucked from his lungs. Sacha pushed a man tied up with his arms bound behind his back, legs shackled, and a gag in his mouth. It appeared he had been tortured and beaten severely.

Sebastian started shaking as he choked out one word. "Dom!"

"Yes, the young heathen captain. Your lover, if I am correct. He murdered our king Roman."

"That is a lie, Sacha. Dom was with me the whole time. Please let him go. I beg of you."

CHAPTER 36

Siege of Alta Prime

Sacha smirked at Sebastian's devastation as he fell to his knees.

Sebastian looked at Cyrus in panic, straining to catch his breath. He reached out to take Cyrus's hand and pulled him to the ground next to him. ""Please. I beg you on my life, do not hurt him. Let him go and take me in his place. Cyrus, I swear Dom did not kill your brother."

"I don't know why, but I believe you. Something strange is going on with Sacha. I have never seen him like this."

"Sacha, listen to me. You cannot condemn him for this. You know he did not do this. I swear on my Father's grave that if you do not release him, you will regret the harm you have inflicted on him and these people," Sebastian said, looking furious. His eyes burned as the thought of losing Dom was frightening, but more from the growing anger inside him.

Dom stared at Sebastian, looking hopeless. Sebastian could see it in Dom's eyes that he knew he did not have much time left. Sacha drew a deep breath and invited Sebastian and Cyrus to join him.

They hurried up the wall and stood face to face with Sacha, who held Dom by his arm. "Now that Roman is dead and his son gone missing, the crown is passed to the most powerful man in the lands. That is you. Relinquish rule over the throne to me. If you do this, I will give you your precious lover back without further harm."

"How can I trust you not to cut his throat the moment I concede to you?"

"If you don't, I will cut his throat before you, then I will come after him," Sacha said, pointing at Cyrus—"and he will suffer horrible pain before he dies slowly and agonizingly."

Dom shook his head at Sebastian. His eyes were wide, and the blue of his irises was brighter than ever. Cyrus had a tight grip on Sebastian's arm. Sebastian looked fiercely and furiously at Sacha.

"I never wanted to be King of Kings, but you are no worthy leader. If I give the throne to you, I can promise you war will come to your keep. You will regret betraying my family and harming my men."

"This is not your place to threaten me."

"It is not a threat. It is a promise!" Sebastian said as he pulled his sword from his side.

Cyrus stepped away quickly as he noticed fire escaping Sebastian's fingers. Then he saw lightning cracking from the end of Sebastian's sword.

Sacha clenched his teeth. "If you are going to play like that, I guess you won't mind if I do this." Sacha took his knife and jammed it into Dom's chest.

Sebastian screamed for Dom, and Cyrus ran forward to catch him before he fell. He pulled the knife from his chest and looked at the wound. "This isn't fatal," he said, looking at Sebastian.

"No, this was a warning," Sacha said. "I can assure you it will be fatal the next time you threaten me with your magic. Now, relinquish the throne to me, or they both die right here and now. And as for you, Cyrus. You betrayed me. You promised you would kill him the moment you had the chance, and now you stand by his side. Do you remember nothing of what you learned?"

"You killed my brother, didn't you? Sacha, you betrayed all of Erras. How can I trust what you say of Sebastian?"

Sacha signaled for his men to draw arrows on both Dom and Cyrus.

Sebastian looked around at the archers fearfully. He went to lunge at Sacha, but the crack of a whip stopped him in his tracks. He looked to see a man holding the whip, then noticed it had lashed both Dom and Cyrus in one hit. Then he cracked it again across their backs.

"Stop! Please!" Sebastian said, quivering at the sound of the whip.

Sacha smiled, remembering hearing the stories of how Sebastian had been savagely whipped. He signaled for his soldier to continue. There was a loud crack, then another, then another. Sebastian was on his knees with his face to the ground. His hands were covering his ears, and he was screaming. As he was panicking, lightning cracked from his hands and arms, and the fire had belted from his body as it shot out and caught the hay that lined the wall on fire.

He looked up at Dom and Cyrus, who were bleeding. Cyrus had a gash on his neck where the whip had sliced him open. Dom had managed to free one of his hands and held it over the cut on Cyrus's neck to stop the bleeding.

He looked at the men he loved in defeat, then stood and faced Sacha. "If I relinquish the throne to you, will you promise to let the three of us go? Let us leave these lands and flee to the North. I promise not to try anything. Just let us go alive."

Sacha smiled at Sebastian then looked over at Dom and Cyrus. "Just say the words, Your Majesty."

"Sebastian, no!" Cyrus shouted.

"Shut up! You are so pathetic. I cannot believe I gave a year of my life to you. You are a weak, ignorant child," Sacha spat.

Sebastian looked furious. "Don't you ever speak to him. You have no right. This is between you and me."

"The words, Your Majesty. I am waiting."

"Don't say it, Sebastian. He will use the throne to hurt everyone you love. Do not give up the crown!"

"I don't care about a damned crown! I care about both of you. He will not get a chance to hurt anyone once I am finished with him."

"You have no power here. Right now, I hold your people and these two pathetic excuses for men as leverage unless you speak the words."

"Sebastian..." Cyrus looked like he was begging Sebastian not to pass on the throne over Erras to Sacha.

"I, Sebastian Drake, son of Ivan Drake, heathen king of the North, the god of chaos, and the king of Kings, pass the crown and throne over all Erras to you, Sacha. I give the rights to the lands and all who inherit it to you as you are now and forever, the king of Kings."

"Now, bow to me," Sacha said as he continued to mock Sebastian.

Sebastian gave him a furious expression, then bent his knee before Sacha. He saw that Dom and Cyrus looked disappointed, but he knew it was the only way he could save them.

Sacha let out a laugh then started to walk away while signaling for his men to leave them. As they disappeared, Sebastian ran over to his lovers. He untied Dom quickly and checked on Cyrus, who had stopped bleeding. He then stood and held Dom's hands. "I thought you had left me."

"I would never leave your side. You are my reason for existence. You are the love of my life, and I could never live in this world without you. But you must tell me why you did what you did. He will never let us all leave together alive."

"I couldn't watch him murder you both," Sebastian said while wrapping his arms around Dom.

"He will betray you."

"Let him try."

They stood on the burning wall looking out to the sea of northern men watching and waiting for a command. Cyrus stared at Sebastian. He wouldn't make eye contact and kept picking at a sore on his hand.

"If you truly are here to do good, then I am sorry for everything I have done to you. I wish I could remember what was once between the two of us. It seems like it was true love. Can you help me?"

Sebastian only moved to wrap his arms around Cyrus, then kissed him on his forehead. "I will do everything in my power to help you. I love you so much. No matter what I have to do, I will be there for you no matter how long it takes. I just want us to be together again."

Cyrus faced Sebastian with tears flooding his face. "Please, we must go, or he will kill us."

He reached for Cyrus's hand. "Go north, my love. I need to end this," Sebastian said.

"We are not going anywhere without you," Dom said.

"I will not watch you die!" Sebastian shouted. "I'm going to kill him. He is going to suffer painfully for what he did! I will destroy him and his soldiers, but I will not lose the both of you. Go now! Get out of here!"

Sebastian's fury caused a gush of wind to whip around them, the ground shook, and fire escaped his closed fists. "Sacha has destroyed my family and my heart. He has taken everything from me. I will not run away!"

"If what you say about us and our past is true, then I will not leave your side!" Cyrus ranted as he pushed his way through the wind and grabbed Sebastian's hands that were still on fire. Sebastian saw that Cyrus risked his life to touch him and quickly leveled back to being human again.

The winds dissipated, and the ground stopped shaking. Sebastian kissed Cyrus. "If I lose you..."

"You will never lose me, not again," Cyrus said as he silenced him by putting his hand over his mouth.

Sebastian turned to look at Dom. "Take Cyrus and the men and go. I will handle this. Do as I command."

Dom wanted to argue but just nodded and grabbed Cyrus's arm. Sebastian turned and looked out over the city. It was nearly dark. The smoke was pouring from the buildings in the distance. "I need an army."

"You have one," a voice said as it approached him on the wall.

"Tomas," Sebastian said.

Tomas walked forward and embraced Sebastian. He then saw men of the North and the Sinook follow, and then he turned to see a massive crowd gathered below. It was all the northern armies, including those of Torrdale and NorthBrekka.

"We will destroy what is left of Sacha, this city, and the entire Kuhar clan. Sebastian, I discovered something about Sacha that I thought you must know."

Sebastian looked at Tomas oddly.

"Sebastian, Sacha is our brother."

Sebastian looked at him with anger then confusion, but Tomas continued. "I found a journal buried in the floorboards of Father's room. After Barron was born, before Nadya, Father traveled to a distant island, Khan Khar. He went to discuss an alliance with the Kuhar. While he was there, he met a woman, the Kuhar queen. They had a child together. Father refused to allow this child to come home with him. The child was raised on Khan Khar until he was sixteen, then he was sent to Alta Prime to become a soldier. He did not fit with the Kuhar, as he was pale and blond-haired. King Roman was asked by Father to keep his secret and watch over his son. After years had passed, Barron received word from Sacha after one of Father's men was captured by the Kuhar. He told Barron and Sacha about our power. Barron and Sacha made a pact to kill us so they both could sit on a throne. One in the North and one in the South. He told Barron to murder our Father while he would take down King Roman. Once you and I were dead, they would enslave all of Erras. This reign of tyranny stops tonight."

"So that is what Barron meant when he told me Father had been keeping a secret."

Tomas shook his head, looking angry. "There is one more thing I discovered. I found the reason for Father and Emelia's death. Sebastian, they were being fed lynch berries. Lynch berries are extremely deadly but kill the victim slowly over time. Do you remember how Barron insisted on preparing their meals?"

"Where did he get those from? They only grow in tropical environments." Sebastian paused for a moment, then whispered, "In Alta Prime. Sacha."

CHAPTER 37

Brothers

"Did you know about this, Cyrus?" Sebastian said in a calm, monotone voice.

"Of course not. My brother told me nothing about Sacha. He acted like he didn't know him at all when he and I first returned to Alta Prime after I escaped NorthBrekka," Cyrus said.

"King Roman wouldn't have known he was Kuhar," Tomas continued. "Father's journal states that only he and the Kuhar queen knew of Sacha's background. As far as Roman knew, Sacha was just a bastard child to our Father with no mother. Roman was sworn to secrecy."

Sebastian walked to the edge of the wall again. "Secure the city. Lead the citizens of Alta Prime to safety. Take anyone down who opposes you. I will march on to the palace. I will end Sacha myself. Now, go."

He turned to see Cyrus, who was about to retort, but he silenced him before getting a word out. "You are going with them.

Do not argue. Just do as I say. Once the city is clear, head north. I will join you when I finish this."

Cyrus still wanted to object, but Sebastian walked away and went to speak to Tomas. "You need to go too."

"I did not come all this way to leave you. Do not argue, brother. You need me to help finish this, and you know it. I am coming with you. We fight together until the end."

"Sebastian!" Cyrus shouted as he was being dragged away by Dom. "Promise me you will come home to me."

Sebastian looked at him cautiously and then opened his mouth to speak, but Cyrus interrupted him before getting a word in.

"Don't say anything else but a promise. Tell me you are coming home. I need you to come back, so I can learn why it is that I feel love for you. When I saw you in the courtyard after the war, I said I didn't know you, but I felt something in my heart. It was love. I didn't know why. All I knew was I was there to kill you, but even when I attacked you, it hurt my heart. That is why I never tried again. I need you to come home to me. I do not want to hear anything else. Please."

Sebastian felt tears forming in the corners of his eyes. "I promise. I will always come back to you. I love you both. Now, please go before it's too late."

Cyrus nodded at him and followed Dom down from the wall.

"I don't plan to escape this alive, Tomas. You should not go with me. Our family needs you more than I."

"You are not going to die tonight, brother," Tomas said. "I will not leave you. You know this."

"I cannot protect you."

"You don't have to, Sebastian. We will both be going home. Now, let us go find him and end this."

They began walking along the wall in silence as they saw people leaving their homes in the distance and the city emptying. Sebastian noticed ships sailing from the harbor and could hear fighting in the north.

They reached the palace and crept inside from a small door on the side of the castle wall. They came through a dark passage leading up to the kitchens.

They frightened cooks and handmaidens as they ran through, yelling at them to abandon the palace and seek refuge with the northern soldiers.

"This castle is enormous. How will we know where to go?" Tomas asked.

"We will turn every corner until we find him," Sebastian answered.

It did not take long for them to find Sacha sitting alone on Alta Prime's throne with a large crown on his head. As they approached, they could hear Sacha laughing maniacally.

"It's over, Sacha. Stand and fight me. Let us end this once and for all," Sebastian said.

Sacha stood up and looked at the twins, amused with their anger. He drew his sword and pointed at Sebastian's head. "I knew you couldn't resist following me. Fine, we end this now."

Sebastian went to lunge forward but was startled as Sacha ran backward and whistled loudly. Then, several Kuhar soldiers came from the chambers next to the throne. Sacha continued to back away and laughed as he left through the same chamber doors.

The Kuhar men closed around the twins with their weapons in hand. They struck forward, and the fight began. Sebastian quickly maneuvered and crashed his sword against theirs. Sebastian had three men against him and was being backed into a corner. When his back hit the wall, he kicked one soldier in the chest and stuck his sword through another soldier's face. His blade stuck as the man fell back. Sebastian grabbed his ax and threw it at the third man coming quickly after him, lodging the ax into his neck.

The man who Sebastian kicked in the chest still lying on the ground and was screaming something in the Kuhar language. Sebastian walked over as lightning cracked from his fingertips. He bent over the man and placed his hand on the man's head and let out a quick blast that took the soldier's life.

As he turned to look behind him, he saw a Kuhar soldier come running toward him. He jumped up to meet him, realizing it would be too late. Tomas jumped on the man's back and gripped his hands around the man's face. The man started screaming in pain as he fell to his knees. Sebastian saw something was emitting from Tomas's hands, but he could not tell what it was until the man started to turn stiff and blue. Tomas was freezing him alive.

Once Tomas released his grip, the man fell over with a loud thud. He was frozen from the shoulders up. The twins walked toward the chamber doors to follow Sacha. As Sebastian passed the frozen Kuhar, he stopped to crush his head with his boot.

They ran through the doorway, which led to a set of stairs that ascended to the top of the tower, where there was only one door. Sebastian swung the door open and began to hurry through but was met with a sword slicing at his head. The blade barely grazed Sebastian's face causing him to bleed as a hand grasped his hair and pull him onto the floor.

Sacha kicked him in the ribs before running over to slam the door shut before Tomas could get through. He climbed on top of Sebastian, sitting on him and bending down close to his face. As Sebastian tried to push him away, Sacha pulled his knife and stabbed it into Sebastian's shoulder. Sebastian screamed. Tomas slammed into the door, trying to break it down as he shouted for his twin.

Sacha began laughing again and pulled his knife back. He wrapped his hands around Sebastian's throat and squeezed tight. Sacha smiled as the choking sounds came from Sebastian's mouth.

"It's such a shame to waste such a beautiful man." Then he laughed louder.

He squeezed his hands tighter. As Sebastian choked, he started feeling energy coursing through his veins. A loud pop and a crack followed by a bright flash, then Sacha fell backward as he held his hands painfully. Sebastian staggered to his feet and ran over to the door to let Tomas in. Tomas checked Sebastian's wounds, but they were both distracted by whimpering coming from Sacha.

Sacha was twitching uncontrollably from the pain. The twins walked over slowly, and Tomas kicked him hard in the stomach. "That was for our parents."

Sebastian punched him hard across the face. "That was for Will."

"That was for my brothers and sisters," Tomas said as he punched Sacha in the throat then in the jaw.

"I do not know what you are speaking of," Sacha shrieked. "Barron murdered your family. I did not force him to make those choices."

Sebastian motioned for Tomas to step back. He moved to the side and kicked Sacha hard on the side of his head. "This was for corrupting my brother and turning him against us. Barron may have been a terrible brother, but he would have never done the things he did if you did not tamper with his mind. How could you? You are our brother too! You are a Drake. You belonged with us!"

"Your Father abandoned me! Your family never knew of me because your Father was ashamed that I was his son. He left me with those horrible people. They beat me for being different. I was not accepted in Khan Khar, and I was never accepted as a Drake. I was an outcast! I did what I had to in order to survive. You were never my brothers."

Sacha smiled, revealing bloody and broken teeth. "Barron was so easy to manipulate. He did everything I asked of him. I told him to murder the twin gods before they rose to power, but he could not do that properly. You do not deserve your power. You will fall under its strength because you are too weak to handle it. You will suffer once my people return and burn NorthBrekka to the ground once and for all. Your precious kingdom will be in ruin, and your Cyrus will live out his life in torture and pain once they slaughter you and your whole family!" Sacha screamed.

"What did you do to Cyrus? Tell me!"

Sacha laughed. "I erased his mind. He needed to forget every thought, every memory, and feeling he had ever felt for you. There is no reversing it. He knows nothing of you and your past together. I made sure of that."

"Why?" Sebastian said through gritted teeth.

"Because I knew if he did not know you, he would help me destroy you. It would distract your mind and destroy your heart. Then he could come in for the kill."

"Your plan backfired, Sacha. You lose. Now, you will die for your crimes against Erras. As king, I decree you unworthy of your own life."

"But, you are no longer king."

"Do you honestly think that is all it took to pass on the rule? Silly words were all that was. You know nothing of the rule of kings."

"You deserve nothing but suffering. Both of you are abominations. The world will be better off without the two of you standing over it. Do Erras a favor and kill yourselves when you bring down the palace on my head."

"You will be the only one who dies today."

Sebastian felt Tomas grip his hand and hold it tight. As Sacha screamed more, every word infuriated the twins. Their powers connected as they felt heat and cold mixing in the air. The winds became so forceful that they blew the wall to the outside away. A storm began raging as lightning crashed and hail fell from the sky.

Tomas and Sebastian stood holding each other as the walls around them were ripped away. Sacha looked up at them, blood pouring from his mouth, but he remained laughing loudly.

"I told you, this is the end for you," Sebastian said in a divine, eerie voice.

"It is the end for us, Your Majesty," Sacha corrected.

Sebastian straightened his back and stared at Tomas's blue eyes.

Tomas looked into Sebastian's. "I love you, brother."

"I love you too."

"Take my hand." Tomas reached for Sebastian.

"Are you sure about this? We do not know what will happen. We are not trained for this."

"Sebastian, he killed our family and tore us apart. Our pain is caused by his hand. We cannot let him go."

"I know, but if this goes wrong..."

"We have to end this. Take my hand."

The twins looked up at the sky, and both reached out toward the storm above them. There was a whirlwind forming above their heads, filled with energy like nothing anyone had seen before.

Along with Prime's citizens, the northern militia and Cyrus turned when they heard the loud commotion. The ground started shaking hard. All around Alta Prime, buildings began crashing down, and the winds were ripping the city to pieces. What was once a city of commerce, and a kingdom of riches was now reduced to ash. The mighty palace that's towers looked as if they touched the clouds and glistened in the sun was now a pile of stone and glass.

Cyrus stepped forward as he noticed the power forming above the palace. "Sebastian, no," he whispered. Then, the sky ignited in a fire, and a bright bolt of lightning lit the air and came down in such a force upon the twins. The castle exploded under its power. Cyrus saw the palace walls burst apart with a loud bang as fire, dust, and rocks filled the city. Then, after the dust settled, it began to snow. It never snowed in the south before this night.

CHAPTER 38

The Final Journey

It was dawn. The city was in rubble and desolation. There was nothing left but ashes, fire, and the snow that was still falling. Cyrus ran fast across the ruin where once sat a beautiful palace on the edge of the bay. He came forward, Dom by his side to the only thing still standing, the gate.

He shook terribly in fear his Sebastian was dead under all the rock. Cyrus walked across an open pathway until he came upon a damaged throne lying on its side. He knelt, reaching for something pinned under the rock. Once he pulled it away, he found the crown of the King of Kings. It was his brother, King Roman's crown.

"Brother, forgive me. I blame myself for this. I brought this upon us by bringing Sacha here. I am so sorry. I love you, brother."

He placed the crown on the throne and continued to walk through the debris. Dom was trailing behind him. In a clearing, he found a man lying on his stomach. As he approached him, he saw the familiar blond curly hair soaked in blood. Sacha was dead for sure. Cyrus stared at him for a long moment before hearing a stir behind him.

He turned fast to see Sebastian sitting on his knees, trying to catch his breath. He was bleeding from the wounds on his face and shoulder and was covered in dirt, but he was alive. Dom and Cyrus ran fast to embrace him. They sat there on their knees, not speaking, just hugging each other lovingly.

The heat of Sebastian's powers still burned inside him. As they continued to hold each other, Cyrus felt Sebastian start to shake uncontrollably. Cyrus pulled away to look at him.

Sebastian was crying dreadfully as he gasped for breath. His eyes went from Cyrus to the floor next to them. Tomas was lying there, partially covered in rocks. He was bleeding from his ears, nose, and mouth, but alive and shaking as his hand outstretched for his twin.

"I did this. It is all my fault," Sebastian managed to choke out, reaching for Tomas.

Tomas could not speak. He tried to mouth words, but blood would spatter from his throat. Sebastian struggled to push rocks away. "Help me, Cyrus. We have to get him out of here."

"It should have been me." Sebastian coughed. "Tomas, brother, I am so sorry I could not save you."

"Come on, Sebastian. You should not stay here," Dom said, pulling on Sebastian's arm.

"Do not take me away from him!"

"You have to leave. Sebastian, you must before you lose yourself and do something dreadful. Please, take my hand and walk away with me."

"I will not leave him!"

"We shall get the men to unbury him. If we do not prepare to depart, the castle will continue to fall and crush us beneath it. We must get Tomas home to a healer."

They walked away from the palace slowly. Jon and some of his men were gathered at the gate, waiting. "Tomas. He is straight through there. Be careful with him. He is horribly injured. The whole palace is ready to fall," Dom said to Jon.

Cyrus and Dom escorted Sebastian from the palace. He waved for a few of his men to assist with collecting Tomas. As they entered the marketplace, Cyrus heard a loud scream.

Sebastian shouted for Tomas and jerked free of Dom's grip, but Cyrus caught his waist and tackled him to the ground. When the palace fell, they saw Jon and the other soldiers hurrying toward them. Jon carried Tomas in his arms, placing him carefully in a wagon.

They started toward the North, homebound once more. Sebastian did not speak much of the journey. He only spoke when necessary, and it was using one or two words only. He rode alongside the wagon carrying Tomas, checking on him often. Tomas was broken, bleeding, and asleep for much of the journey.

Once they reached the realm of NorthBrekka, the townspeople came out to cheer for their king and then cry for their losses. They came upon the gates to Castle Drake. Sebastian stopped and froze in place as the others continued forward. Cyrus stopped and waited quietly next to him. Dom continued alongside Tomas. They watched as the Drake siblings came running outside. Nadya ran into Jon's arms, and Viktor came to welcome them all home happily. The others came out to see the return of their family and soldiers.

Viktor walked over to the cart that carried Tomas. He looked down, and his smile vanished. The others quickly saw as well. Nadya let out a shriek when she saw Tomas. They all began looking around curiously, then one by one, their gaze fixed on Sebastian and Cyrus, who were still mounted on their horses at the gate.

Nadya ran over to them. Sebastian climbed down to meet her. She nearly knocked him down as she embraced him. "Sebastian, are you okay? Talk to me. How did this happen? Why would the gods allow this to happen? Sebastian, please say something!" she said with panic in her voice.

Sebastian did not respond at all. When she let him go, he walked away toward the castle. Viktor grabbed him as he passed and begged for answers. The others hugged him quickly as he passed.

Cyrus stood with the others and explained everything he had witnessed, from watching Sebastian plead for his and Dom's life to how Sebastian had them clear the city while they went after Sacha. Then he continued to describe the storm he watched from the prairie, then the palace exploding with the force from the storm until he found Sacha dead and Sebastian fighting to save Tomas.

Sebastian went straight to his and Tomas's bed chambers. He lay in Tomas's bed and stared blankly at nothing; only tears escaped him that night. Cyrus checked on him often but left him alone. He only spoke to Nadya and the healers who worked tirelessly to help Tomas. His ribs, collarbone, neck, and arms were broken. He was bleeding internally, and all the medicine they had did not heal.

Sebastian demanded time alone with Tomas. When everyone left the room, he lay next to his brother as gently as possible to not disturb his rest.

"I am so sorry, Tomas. I was a fool to think I could control so much power. I am what they said I would become. I have proven that. Please, I beg you, do not leave me. I need you."

Tomas coughed out a laugh. "I told you so."

Sebastian's head shot up. "Tomas!"

"I guess you are the pretty twin now," Tomas joked. His hand shook as he reached to grab Sebastian's cheek. "We were both fools."

"What can I do to help you?"

"Just stay. Stay with me. Time will do the rest."

Over the next several weeks, Dom and Cyrus came to earn an audience with Sebastian once more. They would take long walks to talk about the world as it was now and cry over the world that once was.

One day, a man arrived in NorthBrekka. He was around Sebastian's age, blond-haired with a cocky smirk on his face. He demanded an audience with Sebastian immediately.

"Jace of Oyster Cove, you have returned to my kingdom. Why? Are you still telling people I am the villain?"

"Only speaking what I had been told, Your Majesty. Prove me wrong. If you are interested, I know of a man who can help with your powers. He may be the key to unlocking this magic inside you. This way, we will know if you are evil or if you can be good."

"If you know how to find him, bring him to me. I cannot leave my brother."

"That is not how it works. You must go to him. Your brother is in good hands. He will be healed by the time you get home. This is more important than you and Tomas. This is the only way you will not become the god the prophecy foretold. If you want to be good and save your people from yourself, you must go."

Sebastian wished it were not true, but Jace was not wrong. "I need to ask something first. I was told the Kuhar trade goods with Oyster Cove. How do I know I have your loyalty?"

Jace grinned. "They traded a small amount of explosive oil for linen for clothing and bedding, as well as cattle. Only certain men of the Kuhar were allowed access to our port. They were not the same as those men you fought that worked for your brothers. These men once served your Father long ago. I believe they were a gift from their queen. They are loyal to Erras. Not all the Kuhar are bad people."

"I am sorry if I have trouble trusting them. You must understand why."

"I do. They reside in Oyster Cove, if that makes a difference. They have lived among us since they were adolescents. I know them well."

"Alright, I trust your word. If I agree to this, I need your accompaniment. Will you join me on this adventure?"

"I would be proud to follow you."

Sebastian shook Jace's hand and told him of a date to meet him in the near future.

Months passed as Sebastian spent much of his time writing. He wrote stories of his adventures, stories of his life, and the people he loved who he lost. He wrote about his love for Cyrus and the passion they shared for one another. Tomas's wounds slowly mended, yet he was unable to walk on his own. He sat up in bed, helping Sebastian with his stories. Sebastian stopped and took Tomas's hand.

"I want you to know how much you mean to me. I would not be doing this if there was any other way. I cannot let what happened before happen again. If you had died, I don't know what I would have done."

"I will be right here, waiting for you to return to us. This is your kingdom, no matter what you say. When your ship arrives in port, I will be waiting on horseback to ride home at your side. I promise."

"I don't want to leave you."

"You must. I cannot travel, and you have to start thinking about Sebastian and what Sebastian wants for himself. You want a teacher, then find him. Learn, become the man you are meant to become, not the man some stupid prophecy claimed you to be. Do right by Cyrus. He needs you more than I. Save him. Be happy, for once, live the life you have always dreamed of. This is your chance."

Sebastian would spend the evenings around a fire with his family, telling them all about the life he had led and the future he hoped for all of them. He made plans for NorthBrekka to become the new capital city as he met with leaders from all over Erras to offer trade and protection throughout the lands. He ensured peace would last for good in Erras. Nadya became curious about his actions one day and came to speak to him in private.

"You are leaving us again, aren't you?" she said with a smirk on her face.

"Why would you assume that?"

"Because you have been working ridiculously hard lately. This is something you could have managed over a long time, but you have managed to do it all within six weeks. And, Tomas told me," she said.

"I just want to make sure everything is perfect," he replied.

"Where will you go?"

"I have to find this teacher that can help me control my power. It is the only way I can understand who I am, so I don't ever do anything like what happened in Alta Prime again," Sebastian said, looking sad. "I want to see the world. I want to know if we are the only people on it and maybe find myself again someday."

"After everything you have been through, you deserve nothing but happiness." She replied.

Before Nadya turned to leave, Sebastian caught her attention again.

"Nadya, wait. I am leaving it all to you," he said. Nadya turned and looked at him with surprise.

"I want you to take my place on the throne. You are the only one who can do what I can do. You and Jon will rule over all. I trust you with this. I am no longer fit to be king, and Tomas cannot assume the throne in his condition. I never wanted the job anyway. You know this," Sebastian stated.

"You are the best king this world has ever known," Nadya replied with tears in her eyes. "I know that you can't be tied to a silly chair, though. So, you go and find your peace. Will we ever see you again, brother?"

"I hope so," Sebastian said. "Nadya, please take care of Tomas. It breaks my heart to leave him behind. The burden weighs heavy on my mind. I need to know he will be alright again."

"You know I will care for him. Whatever I can do will be done. Tomas will be whole again. I promise. Oh, one more thing. I received word that Aspen passed away shortly after your departed Sedda. He was a good man. I am sorry."

Nadya gave him a big hug and then left the room. Sebastian frowned at the thought of losing Aspen. He sat in silence with his eyes closed, remembering their training together and all the exchanges they shared and laughed about. Then, he whispered, "Rest well, my dear friend."

He found Cyrus standing over the pond he once watched him standing over before. He smiled, remembering Cyrus asking him, *You're not going to push me in the pond, are you?*

"Cyrus, I love you. I never want to live another day without you by my side. I have completed all my affairs and set Erras into motion so everyone will live an abundant life. I decided to pass down the crown and the throne to Nadya and Jon."

Cyrus looked at him with surprise then started to speak, but Sebastian interrupted him.

"I wrote this for you." Sebastian handed Cyrus a book. "It will help you remember everything."

"The Legends of Chaos. What is it about?"

"Everything. It is about my past, how I became who I am, and about us. I hope it will help you understand why I love you so much. Read it and learn. I hope you will love me one day as I do you. But, I have a new mission I must embark upon, and I must ask, will you join me on one more adventure?"

Cyrus smiled, then went to wrap his arms around Sebastian. "I will go to the ends of the world with you."

Sebastian found Dom sitting alone on the windowsill in the twins' bedroom.

"I am not going with you," Dom said, not looking at Sebastian.

"What do you mean? I need you."

"Cyrus needs you, and you need him. Go, my love. Find your peace. I am going home to my daughter."

"Dom, please come with us. I do not want to leave you. What if I never come back?"

"You will. I know you will, and when you do, I will be waiting. I told you, you are the only one for me. I will wait forever if that's what it takes. But I made a promise to my daughter that I would come back. You must understand."

"I understand."

"I will always be with you. Just promise me that we will find each other again someday."

"I swear we will. Dom..."

"Do not let me stop you from finding yourself. This journey is important for you, and you must go. It is the only way for you to find your path." Dom took off a ring he always wore and put it in Sebastian's palm. "This is an Oscura. It is rare. There are only two of them in the world and this one belongs to you. It is critical that you do not lose it. Don't ever take it off or leave it lying around. Do you understand?"

Sebastian held the ring tight with a tear running down his cheek. "I understand."

The next morning, Sebastian called a meeting with all NorthBrekka. The people gathered as Sebastian sat on the throne with his onyx and ruby crown on his head and Tomas at his side.

"My dear friends and family. I wanted to be the first to inform you that I have decided to step down as King of Kings. I pass down the rule over Erras to Nadya and Jon. With that, Cyrus and I will be departing Erras on a ship leaving the harbor from Alta Prime in one week. I only hope for the best for all of you and wish you a happy and beautiful life. Thank you for being at my back at every turn. I will remember you all dearly in my heart for the rest of my days."

"You are leaving us again?" Viktor choked out. "Sebastian, please stay. You belong here with us. What about Tomas?"

"I do not belong anywhere, brother. I have to try to find my way. I will see all of you again someday. This is not the end for us." He cracked a concerned grin at Tomas and squeezed his hand.

"You will come home to us, and you will be a better version of yourself when you do. Go, Sebastian. You are free!" Tomas said through painful tears.

In the dungeons, Barron sat in the darkest corner of his cell. Sebastian walked down to say goodbye.

"I have instructed Nadya not to let you out. You will remain here for the rest of your days. When I return, we will speak again."

Barron looked grim. "Brother..."

"Sara, you and your son may go. I would not put the decisions Barron made on you and the boy. Nadya will decide if you may stay in the castle. Goodbye."

Sebastian started to leave, but Barron shouted. "Sebastian! You coward. Running away as usual. You nearly killed your own brother. You have to live with the monster clawing its way from inside you. Once you let it escape, the world will burn until nothing is left but you, alone in the dark, until the end of your days. You will die alone and unloved, as you deserve!"

Sebastian took a deep breath, wanting to retort, but turned and walked away, not looking back.

Sebastian, Cyrus, Dom, a small group of his militia, and the Drake siblings all mounted their horses and began their journey south. Tomas rode in a wagon led by Amara and Jon. Upon arriving in Alta Prime, the siblings saw the ruin of the once great capital city. The only thing left standing was the harbor.

There was a great ship waiting. It was beautiful, with its many sails ready to begin the king's next adventure. Sebastian went to say his goodbyes to his family. He held each of them, even Sara and her son, in a tight, loving hug. He went to Tomas last. They embraced for a long while before Cyrus followed suit and wished them all the best.

"Promise me that you will return," Tomas whispered. "Remember what Father said. You and I belong together. I do not wish to find out what he meant when he said one will lose himself without the other. The world is dangerous and unforgiving. Please be safe and come home to me, brother."

"This is not goodbye, Tomas. We will be reunited and when we do, I will never leave your side again. I swear."

"Go now. Find this teacher. You need to listen to him and not be stubborn. When you come back, you can teach me everything. Hopefully I will be walking on my own by then."

"You just focus on getting better. I will return to annoy you before you know I am even gone. Take care of yourself and find happiness in this godforsaken world."

They embraced with their foreheads resting against one another.

Sebastian pulled Dom aside. "Are you positive you won't join us?"

"You had my answer. I wish you both the happiest life. Sebastian, I will await your return." Dom held Sebastian for a long time.

Sebastian watched as Dom pulled Cyrus in for a hug.

"I hope you know I will miss him more than anything in the world, but I know he needs you and only you. Take care of him. Be madly in love and forget everything you are leaving behind," Dom said to Cyrus.

"We will come back, Dom. Sebastian loves you, and I accept that. I would never take him away from you."

"It is not safe for him in Erras. Don't bring him back until he can become the dragon he is meant to be. He will face a lot of obstacles. Promise me you will stay with him."

Cyrus looked at Dom with intensity but nodded and stepped away. Sebastian and Cyrus walked to the ship. Cyrus held the book Sebastian wrote for him.

"I will read this everyday if I have to. I want to know the truth," Cyrus said.

They boarded and took places on the side to wave one last goodbye to their friends and family as the ship was cut free and began sailing out of the bay. Jace stood next to Sebastian. He stared at Cyrus with a cocky grin, then smiled at Sebastian before turning to wave goodbye.

"So, where are we going?" Cyrus asked, looking happily at Sebastian, then resting his head on his shoulder.

"To a new adventure, in a new land. All I know is we will be together forever."

"Forever," Cyrus replied.

Tomas waved at Sebastian one last time. Sebastian stared into his eyes and thought about how hard it was to leave his twin when Tomas needed him the most. He studied his face for a moment, letting the heartbreak take hold. Still, Sebastian waved his hand in the air, which brought a strong wind about them. The crew released the sails, and they snapped into place as they caught.

"Your Majesty, we need a heading."

Sebastian turned and faced his crew. They stood eagerly awaiting his command. He took a deep breath and felt the breeze blow through his hair.

"Gentlemen, we go north!"

TO BE CONTINUED...

Rey Wicks is a creator of fantasy worlds, writing stories that are not quite like what you have read or seen before. She studied many subjects in college including, theology, psychology, history, surgical technology, and even veterinary medicine. Her favorite subjects include astronomy, medieval history, and the dark ages. Her writing career started out with music, moving onto poetry, and into fiction. Rey is inspired by Viking lore, mythology, traveling to mountainous regions of the world, and winter. Rey enjoys writing queer fantasy fiction and creating deeply whimsical realms that the reader can get lost within. When she isn't writing, she enjoys hiking to anywhere there are waterfalls and thick forests. She lives for adventure, family, and her many pets.

www.ingramcontent.com/pod-product-compliance
Lightning Source LLC
Chambersburg PA
CBHW060613300726
48975CB00005B/1547